Acclaim for

THE NIGHTMARE VIRUS

"Dark and thrilling but also full of hope, *The Nightmare Virus* is an exciting new direction for Nadine Brandes and a game-changer for faith-based storytelling."

—**Clint Hall**, author of *Steal Fire from the Gods*

"Brandes has captivated us again, this time with an all-too-relatable world caught in an incurable pandemic. *The Nightmare Virus* holds an imaginative realm of coliseum gladiators, terrifying beasts from mist, and an epic battle between light and dark. You'll be unable to sleep as you devour each page wondering if the characters will wake up from the nightmare in this inventive dystopian of the mind."

—**Bradley Caffee**, author of *The Chase Runner Series* and *Sides*

"Nadine creates stories full of adventure and depth and heart. *The Nightmare Virus* is just that, a story full of high stakes, inspiring light, truth in the darkness, and a rich, unique world to get lost in. You will find your heart caught up with Cain's as you follow his transforming journey."

—**Jenna Terese**, author of *Ignite*

"A tribute to the imagination and a feast for the soul, *The Nightmare Virus* paints an apocalyptic reality with the beauty of eternal truth. This story is a wild and vibrant ride, unique when compared to Brandes' other works, and yet told with the same familiar heart. It's the story of a young man's journey to truth but acts as a mirror for our lives today. Readers will fight alongside Cain, hope and imagine with him, despair, and finally rejoice with him in the end. It's a story filled with the beauty of what light can do in the darkest of places."

—**E. A. Hendryx**, author of *Suspended in the Stars*

"Enter a world that delves into the eternal struggle between good and evil, illuminates the strength found in truth and hope, and where faith shines even in the darkest of shadows. A world where what you create–and how you create it–has a far deeper meaning than you first realized. Brandes skillfully weaves a tale that spikes your adrenaline with nightbeasts, captures your imagination with twists and turns in a dream world that feels real, and asks questions that echo in your heart as you join Cain in search of answers. This pulse-pounding adventure will touch your heart and speak to your soul."

–**CJ Milacci**, author of the Talionis series

"Brandes delivers in this fast-paced, action-packed, high-stakes sci-fi. *The Nightmare Virus* has it all: sci-fi *and* fantasy feel–think *Ready Player One* meets *Gladiator*–high stakes, action, suspense, and heart all rolled into one dynamic story that I could not put down."

–**S.D. Grimm**, author of The Children of the Blood Moon series and *A Dragon By Any Other Name*

"With *Maze Runner* feels, Brandes drops the reader into a world where everyone is trapped in the same nightmare, and if a cure isn't found, no one will wake up. I was hooked from the beginning, with an urgency to keep reading as time ticked down with each chapter. An excellent science fiction read!"

–**Morgan L. Busse**, award-winning author of the Ravenwood Saga, Skyworld, and upcoming *Winter's Maiden*

"Vivid and haunting, *The Nightmare Virus* grabs you by the throat and hauls you mercilessly into its dark depths! With the broad, confident strokes of a master, Nadine Brandes brings to life an immersive story world that will leave you second-guessing reality and drinking caffeine to avoid sleep. This is truly one of her best novels yet. It's Nadine Brandes like never before–stronger, bolder, and chilling!"

–**Ronie Kendig**, award-winning author of The Droseran Saga

THE NIGHTMARE VIRUS

THE NIGHTMARE VIRUS

NADINE BRANDES

The Nightmare Virus

Published by Enclave Publishing, an imprint of Oasis Family Media.

Carol Stream, Illinois, USA
www.enclavepublishing.com

ISBN: 979-8-88605-130-8 (hardback)
ISBN: 979-8-88605-131-5 (printed softcover)
ISBN: 979-8-88605-133-9 (ebook)

Cover design by Emilie Haney, www.eahcreative.com
Typesetting by Jamie Foley, www.JamieFoley.com

Printed in the United States of America.

For my Creator.

From the very beginning, this one's been Yours.

And to my fellow nerds . . .

. . . we know which fandom wins in the end.

For here we have no lasting city,
but we seek the city that is to come.

HEBREWS 13:14 ESV

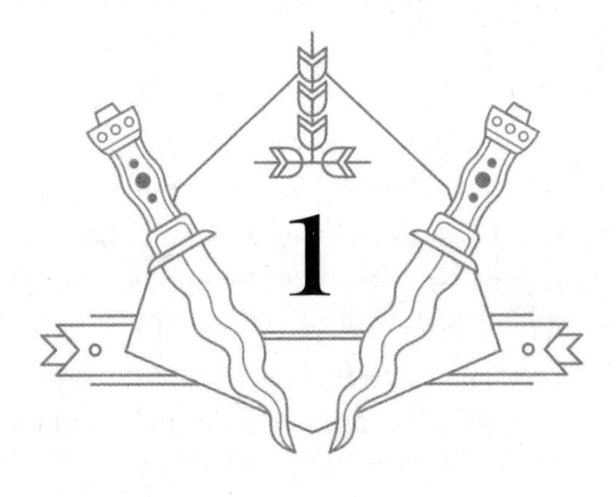

ONCE YOU CATCH THE NIGHTMARE Virus, you have 22 days until you die.

That's fact #1.

Fact #2 is that there's no cure . . . yet.

I stare at the piece of paper held up by a cracked Zelda magnet on the half fridge inside our tiny house on wheels. Equations and scribbles and questions fill the small, lined piece of paper.

Our attempts at a cure.

Nole expects me to figure them out while he sleeps, but I'm not him. My brain doesn't work the same way as his. He has a whole extra year of college under his belt. I can pull the "I'm younger and dumber" card when he wakes up to find I've made little to no progress.

He lays on the couch behind me. Dreaming, maybe.

Infected.

We call it sleep, but that's not quite right. He's had the Nightmare Virus for 19 days now and says it's like being sucked into another world of darkness and fear. He calls it The Tunnel. I don't bother to use my imagination to try to picture it because it'll come for me eventually.

It comes for everyone.

Nole and I may have shared everything else as brothers growing up, but we haven't shared the virus . . . yet.

I consult the math scribbles again–the math of the virus. If there's anything I hate more than the idea of being trapped in my own mind, it's math. Day 1 of the virus forces you to sleep in the Tunnel for 1 hour. You're awake for the next 23 hours. Day 2 of the virus, you're in The Tunnel for 2 hours. Then awake for 22. And so on and so forth until suddenly you're asleep for 22 hours and awake for only 2.

That's when you say your goodbyes.

You never wake after that. The Nightmare takes you, and you're stuck in it until your body deteriorates or starves or someone stabs you in your infected sleep.

Dark stuff. Sorry about that.

Nole shifts on the couch. I startle, looking between him and the paper on the fridge. I've calculated wrong–again. I thought he wouldn't be waking up for another hour. At least I'll have company one hour sooner than expected. But I haven't prepped any food.

I pull a packet of gum from my pocket, unwrap a stick, and pop it in my mouth. Dinner for me.

Nole rubs his eyes. I snatch a cooked potato from the fridge and plop it into a bowl with a slab of butter and a slice of cheddar cheese that has the moldy bits carved away. Dinner for Nole.

He'll be exhausted. But, knowing Nole, he'll refuse to rest. I don't blame him. His death date is set.

He groans. "Cain."

"Here." I slide the potato onto the small fold-out table jutting from the wall. "There's not enough charge to power the microwave today."

He pushes himself up. "Are you going to eat?"

"Nah." I gesture to the gum in my mouth. "I'm good."

It's easier to handle our dwindling food supply and rationing when my mouth thinks it's eating.

He doesn't bother with a fork and scoops up the potato with his hand. "Sick yet?"

"Nope."

He gives a sharp, relieved nod. "Figure it out?"

"Nope."

He eyes me before biting off a chunk of potato. "Did you even try?"

I glower. "Of course I tried." The cure. He expects me to work on it every waking hour while he's trapped in the Nightmare. He also expects me to do algebra and calculations and all the other sorts of things that got me held back in school—*plus* decipher his chicken scratch.

He holds out his hand. "Notes."

I throw him the notebook we've both been using for the cure. He flips to the most recent page, but then stops and goes back to a scrawl of a castle half set into a cliffside. "Cain . . ."

"I did that during break time," I joke.

"You don't have time for a break. If we're going to find a cure, we have to pour everything into it."

"I am." Does he think I want him to die? To stay infected? Does he think I want the Nightmare to come for me? Sometimes I just need to sketch to calm my brain enough to focus.

He traces the title over the top of the castle, written in gothic font. "Ithebego." He smiles, and we both spare a moment to acknowledge dreams before the Nightmare.

Nole is—*was*—going into his junior year in college, studying dream serums and fabrication. I'm still not used to thinking of it in past tense. Universities closed down only a month ago. Nole and I wanted to be Draftsmen—professionals who build dream worlds. We wanted to have our own dreamscape company: Cross Brothers Creations. With a last name like

Cross, I used to joke that he was the upright beam and I was the crooked one.

We didn't want to create the typical beach scenes or therapy escapes that permeated the wealthy circles. We were going to build kingdoms with swords and castles and dragons with themes from our favorite fandoms and books.

It would have changed the world.

It would have *awoken* the world.

We were going to call our own dreamscape Ithebego. It was Cain's idea to take the letters from a string of words: *In the beginning, God . . .* He liked the symbolism. *The first thing God did was create a home–a place. A story world.* I let him have his Bible moment.

I liked the name more for how it looked on paper–and the many different ways we could pronounce it. Nole may be the science brain, but I am–*was*–the vision behind the worlds. The imagination, per se.

We joined the same university–me one year behind him–and both majored in Dream Drafting and Fabrication. At the very least, we'd hoped to have more access to entering dreamscapes. I'd only ever been in one, but it was enough to affect the trajectory of my life. ImagiSerum is expensive. When it first launched, every person in the world was allowed one free entry–to get an idea of what entering and adventuring in a safe dream world while fully lucid was like.

Or to make us all addicted.

Nole and I went together. Our assigned dreamscape was a mountain top–a generic world made by a low-level Draftsman. We didn't have to worry about altitude sickness, thin air, exhaustion, danger, or even proper clothing against the elements. We paraglided off the top of the mountain. There was no fear–just exhilaration–because a person can't get physically injured in a dream. It's all in the mind.

The experience was intoxicating. Easily addicting. Which

was why people began killing for ImagiSerum when they could no longer afford it. It turned ugly fast, but not as ugly as when the ImagiSerum started killing back.

"How are you feeling?" Nole asks, flipping past my sketch of Ithebego and finding my newest equations.

"Fine." I shrug. "Surprised I'm not infected yet." With just Nole and me in this tiny space it's bound to happen eventually. Right? Does anything else matter at this point?

Nole nods and jots something down. "I think it's because you've only ever had one dose of ImagiSerum. There's not enough in your system to mutate and infect you."

His theory makes sense. When ImagiSerum was a new phenomenon, people were eager to take injections to enter dreamscapes. They lined up and drained their savings. But now we have data on the long-term effects: traces of ImagiSerum stay in your system. Mutate. Turn into a virus and trap your mind in a dark tunnel until you die.

I've entered a dreamscape only one time. Because I don't have money. I've never even had a savings account. Since Nole was a year ahead of me in school, he got to enter a dreamscape once a week as part of his curriculum . . . unknowingly poisoning his body and mind.

The scientists tried to backpedal, to find a cure. But they were the first to get infected. Their bodies entered Nightmare comas before they could make progress.

Nole is walking that same path. I don't know why I have more faith in him than them, though. It's not because he's my brother. I think it's because his motivations were never for money or self-preservation. He believed in the good of ImagiSerum and couldn't accept that it would be the end of humanity.

"Tell me what it was like this time." I poise the pencil over our notebook. "Any detail you can think of."

"Same as last time." Nole sighs. "Nothing new."

My grip on my pencil tightens. "Tell me anyway." There has to be something. Some clue. Something he's missing. If only I could enter the Nightmare too–not that I want to be infected–but I have an eye for the world. I know somehow I'll see something Nole is missing.

"Darkness that's heavy like a liquid pressing on your body. I can't see a thing. When I put my hands out, I feel ground beneath me and–"

"What does the ground feel like?"

"Sticky concrete. There are walls too."

"Also concrete?"

"Yes. Less sticky. They curve upward and around me." He finishes his potato.

I move to jot down the details but find myself sketching instead: a tunnel with goopy liquid pooled in the base. "Can you stand up in the tunnel?"

"Yeah, but it's hard."

I look up. "Because it's too small?"

He shakes his head. "Because the darkness is too heavy."

I sketch a figure, ankle-deep in goop. Hunched over with shadows hovering around his head. My heart quickens as the scene takes shape. Then I stop. Because this isn't just a scene . . . it's Nole's reality. And even with my crude drawing, the very idea of such a reality gives me chills.

Nole sets his pen down. "Cain . . . I don't know how to explain it. It's like the darkness is made of every fear I've ever had. It's almost like a tangible emotion. Suffocating me." His voice quivers. "It makes me understand Mom more."

I don't say anything. I can't say anything. When Dad cheated on Mom and left her with us, she entered a dark place of depression. I'd only ever seen her strong and stalwart prior to that. I kept waiting for her to snap out of it. All she needed to do was *decide* to be strong, but she didn't–she wouldn't.

She chose weakness, and we had to go out and try to make money so we could eat.

I was thirteen. Not a lot of options for two fatherless kids to make a buck.

Nole was more tender with Mom. He'd read to her every evening and sometimes stay with her through the night, going to work at a fast-food joint the next day with bags under his eyes.

Mom eventually pulled out of it. Took us to church. Found her strength again–*"strength in weakness,"* she'd say, which never made sense. She never returned to Mom From Before.

And I could never accept Mom of After.

Even now with her gone–taken by cancer one year later–I haven't fully forgiven her.

"You're not like Mom," I mutter. "You're stronger. You would never abandon me. You'll never let the Nightmare beat you."

"She came back to us, Cain."

"Too late." I don't want to talk about this. It's an old argument–an old wound we've discussed a number of times. It's the one thing we can never agree on. "Let's get back to work."

Nole takes out his calculator, and we scratch in silence. He tapes a few more papers on the fridge as if I'll make any more sense of those than I did the first two. I check our propane level and adjust the solar panel that gathers enough energy to charge Nole's computer and give us electricity for one lamp. We stole the panels off an abandoned house in the city after the Nightmare started claiming lives.

Our tiny house–which we named The Fire Swamp–has been ours since Mom died. We thought it'd be funny to name it House Of Unusual Size after the rodents in the fire swamp of *The Princess Bride* until we realized the acronym basically spelled HOUSE.

We sold Mom's place and, after paying off the rest of the mortgage, had just enough to get either this glorified shack-on-a-trailer or a rennovated school bus. The Fire Swamp, at least, *felt* like a home and a new start.

Nole likes to say it was God's timing, because now with the apocalypse upon us we can move around and survive as long as our truck has a full tank. I prefer thinking of it as one last gift Mom gave us to try to make up for the wreck of a life she left us with.

"I think we're about ready." Nole slaps his computer shut and waves his notebook. It's been several hours since we entered our work in silence.

"Ready?" Does he mean what I think he means?

"Ready to test our cure." He smacks the notebook with the back of his hand. "I have the amounts and list of ingredients, temperatures, and dosage all figured out. It's time for our first clinical trial."

He grins. I grin. *Finally.*

"We should be able to find everything we need in the university labs. I've got one of the keys and a bolt cutter for the rest."

"As if anyone's going to arrest us," I say drily. "The cops are infected too."

He laughs. The exhilaration of today finally being the day that we'll see if Nole's math, brain, and passion pay off fills the room. This could save us. Save him. Save the world.

"Let's go!" I throw on my jacket.

"Oh, wait." He grabs his laptop again and pulls up a video screen, then presses the red Go Live button.

"Hey, geeks. Today's the day." He angles the camera toward me. I give an awkward wave, then sidle out of the frame. Nole's viewers want an update from the brainiac they trust. Not me.

"I think I've got the formula right. We're off to test it and will keep you updated. Stay strong. Stay awake." He signs off as the comments flood in from the few who actually happen to be awake and desperate enough to watch the cure vlog of two college-age brothers.

No one else is offering the world anything.

If we can't give them fantasy worlds, we might as well offer them life in the regular world.

Nole pops up from the couch, puts the computer into his backpack and his notebook in his back pocket, then looks around the tiny house for anything else we might be forgetting.

"Okay. We're good." He takes a step toward the door and sways. "Oh man." He catches himself on the wall. "Seriously?"

"No!" I'm more annoyed than anything. "Already?" My eyes find the battery-operated clock hanging crooked above our loft ladder. Sure enough, we've used up all of Nole's awake time.

The Nightmare is here for him again.

He sighs and sits back on the couch. "Sorry, Cain. We'll have to wait for the next Awake."

"It's fine," I grumble. It's not his fault. "Besides, this is the last time you'll be sucked in. Your last Sleep. After this . . . you'll be cured."

He laughs and closes his eyes so I won't have to see the smoky gray Nightmare mist flow over his irises.

"That's right." His face gives a twitch of pain. "This is rotten timing. But I'm glad I'm with you."

I kick his foot. "Don't be a sap."

The Nightmare takes him with a smile on his face.

It's not like watching someone fall asleep. Tension tightens every muscle in his body. He lies like a board and, after several minutes, tiny beads of sweat line his forehead.

I sigh. He'll be exhausted when he wakes again–possibly too tired to do the cure trial run. Hungry too.

I do busywork, check our meager food stores. I make sure I get some rest to make up for whatever lack of energy Nole will have when he wakes. I check the small chicken coop attached to the back of the tiny house—nailed straight into the siding so we wouldn't forget it when we drove around. Three chickens, two eggs.

"Good girls." I tell them and then boil the eggs on the small gas burner, already anticipating the burst of protein. Nole will be pleased to wake up to something other than a potato.

He shouts from the couch.

I jerk around. Nole has never made a sound when he's trapped in the Nightmare. Never. I check the clock. It's still a few hours until he's supposed to wake. I cross to the couch.

"Nole?" I ask tentatively. Maybe all the time he spent working on the cure formula somehow got through to him. After all, it's a virus of the mind. Perhaps his mind is growing in strength against the infection. Maybe it's waking him up. Curing him.

His body jolts and he cries out again.

"Nole!" My voice rises. I shake his shoulder. "Nole, what's going on?"

While this development worries me, it also tells me something new is happening. Nole will wake with new information. Maybe he will finally give me intel I can use to pull my weight with this cure.

Tremors rock his body, almost sending him off the couch. I push him deeper into the cushions. "Nole!" My hopeful excitement fizzles to fear that sends roots into my chest. *"Nole!"*

A harsh yell, then he goes still. Limp.

My hands recoil of their own accord. Did I do something to make it worse? I hardly chance a whisper. "Nole?"

No movement.

No breathing.

"Wait. Wait a second." I grab his arm and shake it. It moves at my touch, heavy and flaccid. "Don't you *dare.*" I speak more to the Nightmare than Nole but pull up his eyelid all the same.

The gray Nightmare mist is gone.

So is the light of life.

Nole is . . . dead. *Dead.*

"No!" This can't be happening. "No!" I shove my brother's body. "Stop it! Stop this! You wake up. *Wake up!*"

But like when Mom was caught in depression, and just like when she lay in her cancer coffin, my protests achieve nothing.

Nole has died. Taking his cure with him.

FACT #3:

If you die in the Nightmare . . .
you die in real life.

IN THREE MINUTES MY MIND WILL take me hostage.

It's been fifteen days since Nole died, and I buried his body. I caught the virus the very next day. Ten days ago I tried mixing his cure and applying it to myself to no avail. Nole's follower count dropped dramatically as the Nightmare claimed life after life.

Hope was lost. So were his fans, his followers, his brother.

The antique, shatter-your-eardrums alarm clock ticks the menacing countdown. I trip over a discarded couch cushion on my way to the stove at the front of The Fire Swamp. I turn the burner off and move the boiling potatoes from the heat. When I wake again in fifteen hours, I'll be famished, and they'd be cooked.

My secondary alarm beeps a warning. Two minutes.

My hands tremble, and I trip back to the couch where Nole's laptop sits open with a critical battery level. Nole's notes and theories litter the screen as photos, scans, and typed details. Math. Even though I've tried his cure and it didn't work, I'm sure there's something I'm missing. Maybe I added things up wrong. Maybe I read a note wrong. The only reason his cure wouldn't work is because of me. I'm the weak point, and I will not let him die in vain.

My heart roundhouse kicks my ribs at the very prospect of being able to free myself–and everyone else–from this death countdown.

A third alarm clock goes off, but I don't bother to snooze it. I'll have to finish my attempts when I'm awake again. I shove aside the textbooks on dementia and dreamscape side effects I nabbed from the university lab, save the computer files, and shut down the laptop to preserve its battery. It'll be charged once I wake–the curse of my infection is that I'm always sleeping during the daytime. I'm awake at night. My last sunset was two days ago. I miss the light of the sun, but at least it will charge The Fire Swamp while I sleep.

"I can fight this." Like the other fourteen times I said this, my words hold no power. My determination, my health, my smarts . . . change nothing. The virus came for me despite Nole's theory of my not having enough serum in my blood to mutate. It came for me the day after his death–not even giving me time to grieve.

Thirty seconds.

I spit out my gum so I don't choke in my sleep, then double bolt the door, drop the shutters on the windows, and avoid the reflection. I hate watching myself break like a whimpering child. Nole always sat on the couch and sank into the Nightmare with resignation. It either affects me differently or I'm just weak. It makes my knees buckle, my body tremble, my mind panic.

Maybe I am like Mom.

"I . . . *can* fight . . . this." My words dissipate into mental mist as I sink unwillingly to the hard floor. "I . . . can . . ." Every word is like spitting out bricks. I turn my focus elsewhere–to keeping my eyes open. "I will . . . *not* sleep." It comes out as a croak.

I don't want to go.

Fifteen seconds.

I launch to my feet. "I will not sleep!" Every blink brings the weight of a dumbbell to my eyelids. *Don't blink.*

I stand alone in The Fire Swamp, eyes wide open, fists clenched against my temples. Sweat rolls down my temples. Fog rolls in.

It's not real.

The fog swirls around me, clouding my vision and taking over my mind. This is the fifteenth time the virus has claimed me, and it shreds my courage as swiftly as the first time. I stumble away from it, careening into a corner.

I blink and barely manage to squint my eyes open again. Anger rushes in at the injustice of this infection. It grows like black veins, clawing its way into my irises, taking over my sight.

My knees buckle again and I slide to the floor, balancing on the balls of my feet, my sweaty back pressing against the wood-paneled wall. The chill does nothing to wake me. My strength flees and my eyes droop. Close.

The alarm rings, startling the atmosphere with its shrill scream, yet fading into nothingness . . . disappearing.

I bury my face into my folded arms as the Nightmare consumes me.

THE NIGHTMARE

THE DARKNESS CLINGS TO MY BODY like tree sap.

I'm in the Nightmare now.

No light relieves the strain of my eyes. Blackness is everywhere, thick and dragging my head down, pressing upon me like invisible anvils.

Like always, I'm tempted to lie here, cheek against the sticky concrete ground. But like always, I force myself to my hands and knees against the emotional suffocation. I force a deep breath, but tar coats my throat. I grope against the walls and inch my way upward, locking my knees against the weight until I'm finally, finally standing.

Trembling, but standing.

Nole was right. The Nightmare is nothing more than a sticky, black tunnel of soul darkness. The first several times I entered, I tried to find or see the things I just knew Nole must have missed. Nothing. Nothing to see. Nothing to feel except slimy, curved concrete walls.

I don't know what got him in this Tunnel—what killed him—but I'm not going to wait around and find out. I refuse to cower to this disease and let it take me.

Just like the other fourteen times I've been in this Tunnel, my first few steps are hesitant. Forced. The darkness wants me to cower. It wants to win. I growl at it. That's something new that I've embraced: emotions are higher and stronger when I'm in here–and memory of life in the Real World dims and weakens until I can hardly remember details.

My anger is on the surface constantly.

In the Tunnel I see no reason to rein it in.

My pace picks up. The ground curves upward too suddenly, and I fall to one knee. My palm slides up the curved wall, through an unseen coating, giving me a small semblance of orientation in this Tunnel of night.

Panic chokes me as a memory stirs of a different place–a need.

Light. I need light. Sunlight. Candlelight. Lamplight. *Anything.*

The more I think about light, the quicker my lungs heave. The thicker the tar in my throat becomes. Desperation turns into a live animal writhing inside me.

I'm losing it.

A voice–my voice?–whispers from far away in my mind. *Breathe.* I don't want to. I *can't.* The voice can't understand the impossibility of its demand.

Breathe.

I force an inhale. Exhale. And with that motion, a different reminder leaks in. I've been here before, in this Tunnel. And every time I've woken up again–returned to life. Today will be no different. I won't let it.

The weight of shadows pulls at me, trying to drag me to my knees, but I dig inside myself–deeper than the emotional daggers can reach. *I won't quit. I won't stop.* I swallow some of the tar. Let it kill me eventually, but not until I find light.

I move.

I stumble.

I run.

My hands slide along the walls, guiding me. As though realizing they can't beat me, the shadows relent. My feet propel me forward until my equilibrium spirals, and I fall. The shadows pull at my ankles, my clothing, my hair, trying to keep me down. But I lurch upward again, breathing hard.

I close my eyes, and some semblance of sanity returns. I grasp for it with the tendrils of my mind. Then I start forward again at a controlled jog. I steady my breathing and command logic to come forth. It obeys, but slowly.

Virus . . . virus . . . virus . . .

Ah, there it is. This place is not reality. It is the Nightmare Virus. To my knowledge, this is the fastest I've regained my senses while in the Nightmare. My logic and memory are beating the shadows. Is this . . . progress?

It has to be.

"My name is Cain. This is my fifteenth time in the nightmare." I continue forward, letting the sound of my own voice calm me even though its echo tells me how long and endless and unknown this Tunnel is. "My brother is Nole."

The details of memory stop there. I know other things–broad things–but can't remember what was happening in the Real World before I fell asleep.

I open my eyes as I jog, and blink. Ahead is a very distant glow.

This . . . is new.

I increase my pace, feeding off the thrill of alertness. The first glimmer of hope. From what I recall, no news reporter ever mentioned something other than the black Tunnels of the Nightmare. Did Nole ever see this glow?

No, he would have told me.

Keep going, I command myself. I'll reach that light no matter what, no matter how much despair sets in. If there's one thing I've learned at the end of the world, it's that hope is stronger than despair.

Hours pass.

I fall back to a walk. More hours pass. I don't stop.

Without a watch or the sun, I can't tell how much time is consumed by the shadows. Certainly a day has passed, maybe even two. Time works differently in the Nightmare. It lasts longer. I can't quite remember the exact calculations. Five Nightmare hours to every one? Something like that.

More math.

Life Above is still fuzzy, foreign. The Nightmare fog is too thick, fighting against me to keep my thoughts contained.

The next time I look up, the light glows the size of a quarter. Maybe if I don't focus on it . . .

I race time. Burst through barriers of seconds, minutes, hours. Shapes appear in the light. Movement? Sweat clings to my skin and drips down my head, sticking my hair to my face. Then, as though passing through a portal, I trip over a lip at the mouth of the concrete and fall to my hands and knees in the light.

Gravel digs into my skin. I press my palms firmly against the small rocks, letting them pierce my nerves. The invisible claws and voices and shackles that nipped at my heels in the Tunnel are gone. Subdued. Outrun.

These pricks against my skin, the divots in my palms, are something other than darkness. Finally.

Relief. Sore, sweaty relief. I heave in deep breaths.

A shout interrupts my solace—a *human* shout. I spin toward the Tunnel, ready for whatever might emerge after me. Whatever might pursue me.

Nothing comes, but the voice calls out again.

"I've got this one!"

I bolt to my feet, fists at the ready—though I'm still shaking free of the blindness. My vision clears and meets a pattern of dark bars against a gray misty light. A cage. I've left the black concrete tunnel only to enter a new Tunnel of thick wood poles that curve into sharpened points above my head.

Like the rib cage of a Leviathan.

Crude ropes hold the poles too tight for anything thicker than an arm to fit through. But this cage is not in darkness. I'm . . . outside. Kind of. The sky above is a black gray without stars, moon, or sun but with plenty of low-hanging clouds. I can't pinpoint where the dim gray light comes from.

The air is much like what I'd encounter walking the streets of New York at night–moving, carrying various scents and stenches. Am I still in the Nightmare or have I woken up?

A padlocked door at the end of the rib-cage prison keeps me trapped. Behind me is the entrance to the Tunnel. Still in the Nightmare then. But . . . what is this place? The relief I felt moments ago flashes into defense.

I shake one of the bars. "Hey!"

"Ooh, we've got an Anger," the voice says. I turn, trying to find it.

"Finally," someone else says. "I'm so sick of Fears. They're dull."

"And predictable," the first voice chimes.

"Don't know how they get out of the Tunnel at all."

I search for the source of the voices, but my gaze catches on three other tunnels like mine, their mouths forming a semicircle around a gravel clearing. The tunnels disappear into an earthen wall with dead grass along the brow–almost like possessed hobbit holes. In front of each tunnel sits a cage like mine, and each holds two to three other people, though they all sit in their prisons with their heads tucked into their arms, while I have my fists up by my face.

A campfire crackles not far away with a few sawn logs for seats, though the fire doesn't give off the warm glow I tend to associate with flame. A pot rests in the coals to the side.

Four people sit around the fire, sipping from dented metal cups.

This . . . this is a *world*. There are people here. Clouds and fires and smells. This Nightmare isn't a mutation like Nole and I thought.

I'm in a dreamscape.

4

A BODY STEPS UP TO BLOCK MY VIEW of the other tunnels and the campfire. A male, blond and pale with hardly a muscle visible in his gangly limbs, he keeps his distance. He is writing something on a clipboard or perhaps a tech pad of some sort.

I'm still reeling: I'm in a *dreamscape*. Meaning this place was *designed*. It's not a mutation or a virus. It's intentional. Even the Tunnel. I try to reconcile the revelation, but as quickly as it came so does a fuzz in my mind that mutes any clarity of thought.

I can't seem to think outside of this cage. This moment. It's like my thoughts as well as my body are confined. I strain for my Real World knowledge and survey the man in front of me, scanning for fantasy hair or unnatural bone structure. Anything to clue me in to what sort of blueprint was used for his design.

He wears more weapons on his body than an armory display, most of which look ancient. A short sword hangs at his side and a dagger is tucked in his belt along with a strap holding spiked spheres that look like a cross between grenades and medieval mace heads. No guns.

"I'm not an enemy," he says to me, sounding almost bored.

"Let me out," I growl, my emotions bringing me back to my present predicament.

"If I do, you'll be killed." He has yet to look up at me.

Is that a threat? "I'm not afraid of you."

"Not by me. That cage is for your own safety."

Right. A Nightmare human covered in weapons locked me in a cage for my protection. He finishes his scribbles, and I now see it's no tech pad but an old piece of parchment, nailed to a thin slab of wood.

He waves to his fellows. Only then do I realize the Vetters have hauled a cage cart into view and have loaded six of the captives into it. They direct the cart to the third cage.

"Where are you taking them?" I ask as the next three climb into the cart like mindless sheep

"Somewhere safe."

I shake the bars, and the wood snickers with amused creaks. "Give me specifics!"

"Ooh, a *curious* Anger. You're an interesting mix. It brings a nice balance, actually. The last Anger who got out of the Tunnels throttled two of my fellow Vetters before we could cage him."

The idea of throttling this guy sounds rather appealing. But my desire for understanding is greater–it always has been. Someone used to call it my greatest strength. My memories strain. Who? Who do I know? Who said that? I shut my eyes, irritated by the lack of clarity.

No one . . .

No. That's not right.

No . . . le.

Nole. Nole said it. My brother. He said my curiosity led to resourcefulness. Mom said it would get me killed. Now Nole is dead, and I'm caged by a Nightmare stranger.

Mom was always right.

Focus. My memories of Nole and Mom dry up like

waterdrops on hot asphalt. This guy's a dream avatar. Trying to logic with him isn't going to get me anywhere. His responses are programmed. If I want to keep surviving, I'll follow his directions until I can wake up again and sort through all of this with a mind that's not saturated in heightened emotions.

The man sighs. "Look, I was caged, too, once, okay? Right where you are–same Tunnel actually. Except I was a Fear–that emotion got the best of me for a long time. In here your emotions are going to be stronger. Deadly. Better get a hold of yourself. It's going to be a rough ride to the coliseum."

Coliseum? The only encounter I've had with one was seeing the original Colosseum on a screen in *Gladiator*. I roll my eyes.

"Thanks for the warnings." I know better than to trust anything out of his mouth.

"The name's James. And I'm no avatar." He gives me an annoyed look. "Skepticism is written all over your face. You might as well know, I'm infected . . . like you."

I back away from the bars. "A real person?" Not a creation of the Nightmare?

"I'm as real as they come. Born in Chicago. Will probably die there too. My infection finalized about a week ago." Finalized. Ended. No more time awake.

He's talking about another life–another life I'm a part of but can't seem to grasp for more than a few seconds.

"It'll get easier to remember your old life," he says. "Easier to forget it too. It's up to you." He's here in the Nightmare until his physical body deteriorates. But how can he be in here if we didn't fall asleep in the same dream batch? How can he be in Chicago and me in New York, yet we're both here in the same dreamscape?

A headache throbs behind my temples from the strain of clinging and clawing to the little details I can remember from real life.

That's impossible, isn't it? No one has even created a

dreamscape stable enough to support more than 100 visitors. But this Nightmare . . . it's infecting the entire *world*.

"Let's go." The cart rolls up to my cage and lines up its door to mine. James unlocks it and it swings inward.

I don't move.

"Don't make me force you." James lifts a long rod from the bench seat of the cage cart. "I poke first with a stick. After that, it's a gladius."

I eye the weapon on his belt. Gladius. Defiance wants to plant my feet firmly on the ground and make him unsheathe his half sword. See what he'll do if I don't budge. But curiosity is king in my mind. I want to unravel this puzzle, and the only way to learn more is to cooperate.

So I move–purposeful and powerful–before the stick or sword tip can use their voices. The other nine people–the Fears–scoot aside to make room for me in the cart. It's a tight squeeze. No one makes eye contact. All seemed subdued. Nervous. Scared. Are they real too? They don't act like avatars. If James is telling the truth, they are infected like me, and they managed to escape the Tunnel.

"Look at that, you're already starting to tame." James slams the door. "I half expected you to kill these ones."

The others in the cart cage whimper and scoot farther away from me, then farther away from each other. The cart sways from their movements, its wooden wheels creaking.

"I'm not going to kill you," I mutter. I may be battling enhanced waves of tension and fog brain, but I haven't lost my humanity.

I sprawl on the cart base. It's nothing more than a cage, secured to a flatbed wagon, and I still have a full view of our surroundings. One other Vetter yokes a horse to the front of the cart. I'm not sure if it's the dim lighting or the horse's actual color, but its coat is coal black. Not shiny like a sleek stallion but stained and matted and so dark that I can hardly follow its movements through the shadows. Its head hangs low, and it hardly reacts to human touch. I think it'd be perfectly content dying where it stood.

What have they done to this creature?

And what does that mean for me?

The four Vetters gather around their firepit for a sip of whatever is in the pot on the coals. I catch a whiff of coffee. My mouth waters. Then one of them holds out a bag. Each man slips a hand in and withdraws a fist enclosing something small. At the same time, they all open their palms and reveal a rock.

James holds a red one. The rest hold black. He curses and tosses the rock back into the bag. "Save me some coffee."

The other three grunt but look grim. James strides our way.

"What's your name?" One of the men next to me asks in a low voice, daring to lift his head an inch. He doesn't cower as much as the others.

It's such a normal question I almost don't answer. "Cain. Cain, uh . . . Cross." I say my full name solely with the intent to remind myself I actually know it.

"Religious parents, huh?" he asks, not unkindly. What is this, small talk?

"Mom and brother."

"Was your brother's name Abel?" His attempt at a joke falls flat.

"Might as well have been," I respond tersely.

"I'm Erik." He reaches out an unsteady hand. "We've got to keep some level of humanity in this place, eh?"

The tension in my chest eases a bit. "I guess." I give his hand a shake.

Something sparks, like an empty lighter. The brief light is unusually bright in the thick darkness and disappears so fast I can't locate where the flash came from. Our hands? Behind Erik? Something else?

James is stock still, halfway between the fire and our cage cart. "Did you guys see that?" Fear thickens his voice.

"See what?" one of his buddies hollers, looking up from the fire.

"That flash."

Erik pulls his hand back inside his coat, but not before I catch his trembling. Something has spooked him too. Should I be afraid? What did I miss?

"I didn't see anything." One Vetter goes back to his mug of coffee, but his eyes drift to the gladius near his feet.

"I think we need an entourage for this one," James comments.

"No way, man. I already filled my quota for today. The Spores haven't attacked for a couple weeks."

"Meaning they're overdue," James grumbles.

"Isn't this your last delivery today, James? You're good after this. Get a week off, enjoy the Games."

James stomps to a lone scraggly tree a few yards from their fire, where a ring of keys hangs on a nail. He tucks them into his belt. "The Emperor should give us nightbeasts for this." Sweat clings to his hairline.

What sort of place is this that a little light would cause so much fear? I log away the new words–*Spores* and *nightbeasts*. I've never heard those terms in a dream parlor. At least I don't think I have. I give Erik a side-eye, but he's tucked himself into the cart corner and doesn't seem any more in the know than I am.

James grabs the rope hanging from a crude bridle on the horse's nose and gives a cluck. "Come on, you."

Off we go, down a rickety dirt road, rutted by wheel paths. The Tunnels shrink away behind us, and no matter what lies ahead, I'm glad to leave them behind. While I'm thankful for the dim gray light, there's a distinct lack of illumination. It's like when the sun sets and there's just enough light to find your front door, but not enough to keep the fringes of spooked nerves from tickling your mind.

If I were adding this shade to a sketch on my tablet, it'd be

#7A7A7A. It's nerdy that I know that. But I can't help it when I see the mist. No sun. No evidence of where this dim gray glow originates.

A 7A sky.

We descend a hill toward a sea of fog. It rests like a blanket, and James hesitates for only a moment at the edge.

"Figures." He then enters, withdrawing his sword with his free hand.

It's unsettling seeing James on guard. Maybe this cage isn't to keep me in but to keep something out. If James fears this place, the message is clear: I may be out of the Tunnel, but this Nightmare is far from safe.

And after Nole's death, I now know that anything that happens in this place can be fatal–to both my mind and my physical body in the Real World.

Is that how Nole died? Did he make it out of the Tunnel and get killed by a Vetter? Another Anger? Something from the Nightmare?

The cart lurches, and I grab a bar to keep from slamming against the side. Then we break through the underbelly of the mist. It now hovers above us, threatening to drop and suffocate. It doesn't look or act like a cloud, neither does it act like fog. Everything below it is darker. What gray glow exists in the half-night 7A sky barely penetrates the mist.

Yellow lights speckle the space before us, some mere pinpricks. Homes? Candles? Fireflies? Others blink. Eyes watching us, bodies hidden by shadow. None of the lights are warm.

James quickens his pace. It takes several tugs to get the horse to follow suit.

"How . . ." A man in the cage farthest from me licks his lips. "How long until we arrive?"

The sound of his voice feels all wrong in the eerie dim. An interruption of the sacred demand for fear. He shouldn't have spoken. The tension coiling through James's back and shoulders affirms it.

Something snaps from the darkness to our left–not a twig. More like the jaw of a creature readying for a meal. James's head jerks toward the sound, then he smacks the horse on the rump. It surges forward in a trot. I and the other cage occupants topple onto our heads and elbows and backs. Bumps send us flying into each other.

Another snap. A growl.

James gives a shout. We approach a city of sorts. Is he calling for help? Calling out a warning? Not a single body appears. We pass dwellings with arched doorways and pillared corners, sweeping curved steps and clay-tiled roofs. All encased in shadows and webs.

All empty.

I hoist myself up onto an elbow and try, through the bumping and jostling to catch a glimpse of our pursuer. There's nothing to see besides the dead-looking houses and a cobbled street flying away behind us. We round a bend and our cart bangs a corner.

The horse yanks us around another, then onto a broad street twice the width of the one prior. James doesn't bother to direct the animal. It knows the way. The lines of abandoned homes melt into the shadows while the street stretches forward in a long descent, growing wider and wider, eventually ending at . . .

The coliseum.

There really is one, but it's not like the dusty broken one in history books. This one is quadruple the size, curved walls stretching skyscraper high toward a dark, stormy sky. Girth so broad I have to turn my head to see where it bends out of sight. Evenly spaced flags line to top edge, but what draws my gaze and keeps it is something else entirely.

The coliseum is on fire.

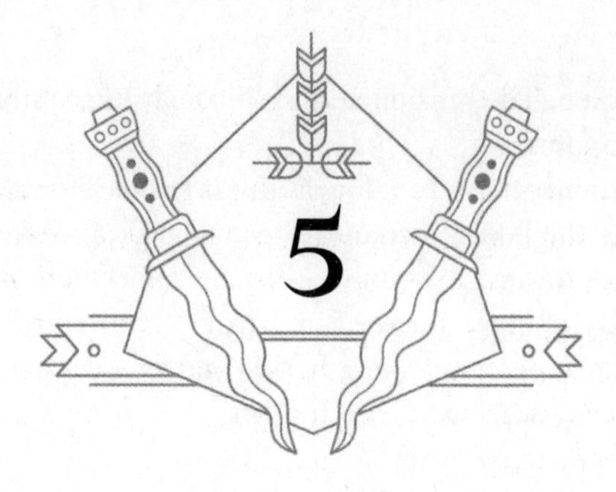

FLAMES CONSUME THE STONES AT THE base of the coliseum and fill the archways with angry glowing eyes. Double iron gates bar the way through a mammoth arched entryway like the closed mouth of a forge. Three marble statues, stretching half the height of the coliseum itself, form a semi-circle around the entryway and stand unmoved and unbothered by the flames licking their feet–Shadrach, Meshach, and What's-His-Name unharmed in a fiery furnace.

This thing is huge. It's not merely a fighting arena inside the city–it *is* the city. And it's about to collapse.

James and the horse keep lumbering toward it.

"Stop this thing!" I yell at him.

He doesn't seem to hear. Closer and closer we get. The crackles of fire grow louder than the clamor of the horse cart, and heat hits my skin.

James fumbles with the keys at his belt. At this rate it seems like he's going to let us careen right into the deadly flames. Then a giant beam of wood lands in the road in front of us. Human forms, cloaked and hooded, stand on each side of what could be a railroad tie. Each wields a single sword.

"Spores!" James shouts, as if that means anything to us. He pulls up short, flailing his little gladius. He seems resigned, like he expected this type of roadblock by these mysterious people. Spores.

I don't have time to get a good look because even though James has stopped running, the horse has not. It leaps over the fiery beam with a whinny of terror.

The wagon does not.

Wheels catch stone. We go airborne. A suspended moment of horror. A mere breath before impact. I throw my arms up to shield my head. The cage shatters in a smash of spikes and slivers. I tumble, bone on stone, down the road. I brace for the impact of the cart, still picturing it flying through the air. After enough breaths and the cacophony of crashes and screams, I dare to look up.

The cart lies several feet away–on top of a different body. One of the caged. My muscles and bones groan against my command to lift myself up. Sharp pain shoots up my back, neck, and left arm. It hurts, but not enough to imply anything broken.

I rush to the cart at the same time Erik does. Together we lift it off the other man. Blood covers the downed man's head, and his chest doesn't move. I'm the last person able to perform any sort of CPR. I'm pretty sure he's dead. My mind processes the fact the same way it might the death of a video game character, which concerns me.

I don't want to lose my humanity in this Nightmare, but did it follow me into the virus to begin with?

"Sorry, mate," I say quietly to the dead man.

Erik shakes his head. "This is messed up."

The other captives scatter. A few bodies lay within the flames of the coliseum. Unmoving. Burning up. A cry comes from behind us. One of the cloaked Spores leaps at James with a mighty yell. James throws out his little sword and deflects a blow. Only now do I realize that no one is actually holding those Spore swords. The weapons float and fight of their own accord.

One cloaked and hooded attacker surveys the wreckage while his sword keeps James busy. Then I see the other three Spores running straight for me and Erik. I head toward the smashed cart and pick up a length of wood that's far too long and heavy for me to wield against a sword, but with the right swing it could knock a man out. I twist to meet the attack.

Two Spores go for Erik, who holds one of the spoked cart wheels as a shield. A disembodied sword gets trapped in the spokes and tossed aside. The other comes for me.

A cloaked, broad-shouldered man a head taller than me whirls to meet me with his sword. I catch bursts of a sickly smell–like hot tar and manure. This dude needs a shower.

Stench's sword swipes over my head and sinks into my wood bat. At least it has poor aim. I grope for the hilt, but it burns my fingers like an electric stovetop on high heat. I recoil and instead yank my wood bat free.

I swing for Stench's head. He ducks and loses his balance. We are so close to the coliseum, which at first seemed like a second prison but now seems to be a place of refuge. Except for the fact that it's burning down.

The doors are still closed. Between me and the door, James lies in a heap on the cobblestones. I assume his keys were for the coliseum gate, though it's so huge I can't imagine it being unlocked with a single key. It's more of a crank-and-chains type of gate. Also . . . still on fire. It may melt soon.

A smaller cloaked Spore steps up to James–a female, maybe? Her floating sword zooms in front of her and presents its hilt. She grips the pommel in both fists and plunges the blade downward into James's skull.

He doesn't even twitch. Doesn't scream. That's how quick his death is.

Rage boils my blood, though I have no loyalty to James. He

was nothing more than my captor. But he was a human. These Spores, however, don't seem to be. Nothing with a beating heart would treat another person this way.

A clatter snaps my attention back to the two Spores attacking Erik. I spot a fifth Spore back in the shadows, watching the attack. The shortest and smallest of the Spores and, if I'm not mistaken, a child.

Erik's cart wheel falls to the ground. That's all the opening they need. I expect one to run him through, but instead both Spores lunge and grab Erik's arms. He tries to shake them off. Another latches on to him, and he yells for help.

I rush toward them, but Stench regains his feet and jumps into my path. I barrel into him and land a fisted blow to the side of his head. He cries out and crumples to the ground.

"Stay there," I growl.

The other two Spores now have Erik by the ankles and drag him across the cobblestones toward the shadowed houses and the child Spore. Erik claws at the ground, groping for purchase.

"Hey!" My bellow shakes the heavens louder than thunder. *"Hey!"*

They look up.

I stalk toward them, fists curling. I've been in enough street fights to hold my own. Maybe not against swords, but that's the beauty of fury–it blinds the senses and makes one feel invincible. The idea of pain even sounds appealing. As long as I can get one solid strike in on these monsters.

But they don't stick around for a fight. They take one look at me and flee, dragging Erik with them. I give chase, but Stench's sword yanks itself free from the wood and blocks my way. I duck and roll as it nearly takes off my head.

A black shadow swoops across the sky. The Spores glance up. The child-size one screams, "Go!" It's the first sound I've heard from any of them, and it affirms my suspicion: it's a kid. Girl by the sounds of it.

Another woman—taller than the one who killed James—hurries to James's body. She starts to pull him by his sandal strap. Cannibals. They must be cannibals. Why else would they want James's body. And Erik?

A spear strikes her in the chest, pinning her to the cobbled ground and freeing James's corpse. No, not a spear. Something jagged and crackling with static. Black when it should be blinding white.

A lightning bolt.

Her cloak falls back, revealing a simple woman's face, frozen in shock. I'm not sure what I expected, but she looks eerily normal. Human. The shadowed lightning bolt dissipates.

"No!" Stench finds his feet and stumbles toward her. His sword flies away from me toward its master.

Erik still grapples with the other two Spores, who hesitate.

Stench waves at them from over the speared woman's body. "She's dead. Just go!"

Another swooping shadow. Another bolt of black lightning. A disembodied sword slices the bolt from the sky before sheathing itself at Stench's belt. I look up, whether to embrace the lightning spear coming for me or to catch a glimpse of this mysterious defender who can fly, I'm not sure.

But it isn't a person soaring through the air. It's a beast with enormous wings that don't belong in a sky. Nor should it be the size of a B-2 Bomber, but it is. Blacker than night, catching air currents as though in a sea skimming the clouds.

A stingray.

Long tail whipping after its mighty swoops, it glides past me, mere yards above the rooftops, and that's when I see a form on its back, balanced in a wide stance with a crackling black lightning shard strapped to its back like a quiver, holding reins in the left hand and a thick coil of rope in the right. The figure guides the stingray in a low, stomach-dropping dive and hurls the rope in a giant loop. It lassos the smallest Spore around her neck and shoulder, then tightens with a pinch and jerks her into the air. She screams.

Another Spore female also screams and stumbles after her. "Olivia!"

But the child is hoisted skyward too fast, dangling like a carrot on a string. The stingray, the hero, and the Spore child disappear over the flaming walls of the coliseum.

Stench abandons his dead comrade and sprints after the others. He drags the screaming female Spore back into the shadows, and then they're gone.

Erik is gone. James is dead. I stand—the last survivor—on a foreign battlefield of burning stone.

Hands grab my shoulders. I pivot to fight, but a tall stranger shoves me toward the coliseum. He wears a thick leather breastplate with a red cape, secured at his throat. The first word that comes to mind when I see him is *centurion*, though I've no idea if that title is accurate. He holds James's key ring.

"Get inside. Get safe. More are coming."

The enormous gate is now open. I didn't hear or see it move during the attack. Get inside? Get safe?

"It's on fire." Is he blind?

"I know." The centurion turns and walks into the fire as though it doesn't exist. Like soldiers in salute, the flames part for him and hold their position, creating a small path straight into the coliseum.

Depleted as I am from the crash and the battle, I argue no further. If there's one thing I know about this place . . . it's that I'm new here. And if someone's offering me sanctuary, I'd better take it.

I run after him. The flames don't part for me. In fact, they lean forward, trying to get a taste of my flesh. They singe my arms and crackle the sweat off my skin, but after a brief flare of heat, I'm through the open gates.

I stumble to a halt inside, standing in the open maw of an entryway, the fire at my back. The gates start to close at a mere nod from the Roman centurion, creaking with chains and bolts like I expected. He stops and waits for me to catch up. To commit. To fully enter this new and dangerous game.

And I, like an indentured gladiator, enter of my own free will. Whatever awaits me in here has to be better than what I'm leaving behind.

THE COLISEUM GATES SLAM CLOSED behind me.

There is no blazing fire inside. No sounds of crackling or scorched stones. The interior is strong and stable. I don't have the energy to make sense of it all, so I suspend my disbelief and accept the oddity. The best I can gather, the fire is some sort of defense mechanism–not actually a mishap.

With the doors shut, an odd–almost echoing–silence descends. It feels out of place after the battle and deaths. Three other survivors–two men and a woman from the Tunnels–stand inside the gates. I try not to imagine the families of the dead, trapped above in the Real World, clinging to the unmoving bodies of their loved ones . . . never to know what happened to them.

Like I had to.

I force my focus forward. The coliseum is straight out of a time machine. With a fantasy twist. Tall, arched hallways made of gargantuan slices of stone mark the pathways toward its heart. No electricity, but plenty of torches with the scent of smoke and burning oil.

The Roman centurion claps heavy irons around our necks before I have a chance to resist. Each iron is connected by a short chain to the captive in front. The metal pushes down on my shoulders, pinching my clavicle. I try to shrug it into a better position, but he gives a tug, and we have no other choice than to move.

To march.

We are led through a long tunnel, up some stairs, and over a barred walkway that passes above a wide street. People occupy the street below, all in togas of various muted shades or tunics and sandals. Some look up as we pass overhead. A few point and cheer.

It's not a happy cheer, it's more . . . hungry.

We enter a new tunnel and descend again. There is no turn, no alleyway, no alternative but to follow.

I run my fingers along the walls. My skin picks up dust mites, runs over small pockets and dents of stone. The intricacies in this dreamscape are delivered at a level of expertise I never encountered in my years of studying dream design. Can this still be a mutation? The Nightmare? Everything seems too intentional. Too detailed. And definitely too Roman.

"This way." Our centurion says, stopping outside a closed wooden door with a lock on the outside. Finally, he faces us with one hand on the hilt of his sword and the other hand still holding the chain to our leashes. "My name is Crixus. If you want to survive here, you'll do what I say."

Crixus. That can't be his real name. It fits the theme too well. He's accepted this place and it's become part of him, which seems to be exactly what he's after. All muscles, broad stature, and leather-strap sandals that wind up his calves. He looks as though he's stepped off a production of *Gladiator,* still in costume, and forgot to drop the act.

"You're noxiors now," he says. "Our word for gladiators."

My companions practically melt to the ground at the word. Crixus's announcement doesn't faze me. I'm not surprised. What did these other people think we were chained up for?

"The coliseum isn't a prison. You're here for your own protection. And I'm here to help you."

I snort, and his gaze slides to me without a twitch of change in his expression. No annoyance. No sneering. His neutrality speaks its own language.

"You just called us gladiators," I say. "We're not idiots. We know what gladiators do. That's not my idea of 'protection.'"

"You're here only until you earn your citizenship. You do that by proving you can survive the Arena." He unlocks the door. "You'll get more answers tomorrow. For now, sleep. Even here in Tenebra, it's necessary to rebuild your strength."

Sleep? What does he think we're doing right now? And how does that work, sleeping inside a nightmare? Dream within a dream sort of thing? Can sleep in the Nightmare really rejuvenate me?

My three nervous companions pass tentatively through the doorway. He removes the shackle around their necks as they go, leaving the weight to pull against mine. I stand my ground, though I know there's no leaving this place until my Sleep runs its course. I'd rather gather intel from Spartacus here than face the Spores weaponless again.

"Tenebra?" I ask.

"The name of our world." Crixus allows a soldier of sorts to guide the other three captives past the door to wherever the preschool nap mats are. "The Nightmare."

He's trying to make it sound like something more livable than it is. I won't adopt that language. This place killed my brother.

"I want an explanation."

To his credit, he doesn't shut me down but merely waits.

"This place is a dreamscape, isn't it? Not an infection."

"Or possibly both," he says with a shrug. "Dreamscape gone wrong." He steps forward to take the shackle off my neck. He smells strongly of blood, body odor, and some cloying undertone I can't place–nor do I want to.

That stench is my future, I expect.

The chains drop to the ground. There's no point in fighting him or trying to escape. I chose to enter this place knowing full well what it likely held.

"But you're a real person, right?" I press, focusing on a dreamscape gone rogue rather than the shadows of dozens of sleeping bodies on the other side of the threshold. "You have a body in the Real World?"

"Yes." It's interesting how many notes of emotion can latch on to a single word. Crixus doesn't sound happy about his real body. Does he wish it would disappear and he could simply exist here in the Nightmare?

"So how are we both in the same dreamscape? This shouldn't be possible." I grope for details that usually come easily to me. Why is this world confusing me so much? What are the rules I know? Something about the dream serum and having to take it at the same time.

Crixus nods toward the holding place. But I'm not done. I take in the bodies. Sleeping. Snoring. I don't enter, but gesture toward the room.

"Is everyone here a real person?"

"There are no avatars," Crixus says.

"Not even the Spores?" Those creatures who attacked us are real people? With disembodied swords?

"Not even them."

"This shouldn't be possible!" I exclaim. Programming a dreamscape for multiple entrants is complicated. Too many entrants and the whole thing would collapse. How can this place exist–staying stable under the occupancy of possibly thousands of people forced here against their own will?

"This is your future," Crixus says. "Best get used to the

idea." His hand drops to the hilt of his sword–the same type James, the now-dead Vetter, wore. A gladius. "Get some rest."

"I'm leaving this place." I head into the dark room without breaking eye contact. "And it won't be through that front gate."

"There's no leaving, Cain. You're infected. No matter how many Sleeps you have left, you'll be back, and you'll wake up right here, on your dirty, unwashed cot. And I'll be waiting for you." He twitches a smile.

I'm not cowed. I'll show him. He may have turned himself into some cosplay centurion and found a shiny sword, but I'm not giving up on the Real World yet. I won't surrender.

He slams the door. A lock clicks.

I settle onto the first empty cot my feet hit. He was right. It's dirty and unwashed, and it smells like ten other sweaty men. Or maybe that's the room in general, which seems to be snoring from its very stones.

I won't let this Nightmare beat me, no matter how intricate it is. I will figure out how it works . . .

And then I'll tear it down.

FOR THE FIRST TIME, I RESURFACE from the Nightmare with relaxed breathing instead of tight muscles. I'm back in The Fire Swamp. The Real World. Home.

My body rests in . . . awe? Determination? I can't pinpoint the new feeling, but I know why it's there . . .

The virus. There's an entire world inside it.

Now that I'm awake, my thoughts are free of the muddled chains of Nightmare. I can think clearly and pull up all the knowledge and lessons I've lived and learned.

News reports have only ever spoken about the endless Tunnel of Death. They never knew about the world beyond the Tunnel. What did Crixus call the dreamscape? Tenebra? Surely someone would have woken back up and said something.

I open my laptop and search the term. All that comes up is that it's related to the Latin word *tenebrae* which means "darkness." Seems appropriate. But no news clips, no blog posts, not even a Tweet about this world in the Nightmare.

But people are there. Erik. James. Crixus. Maybe they don't wake up anymore. So then what have they done with their bodies?

That's the darkest part of the virus. Once you've managed to survive the first 22 days of being infected, you're trapped in the virus forever—never to wake—leaving your body at the mercy of whoever's with you.

Nole and I had each other. I was going to take care of his comatose body for as long as I could. Keep him alive. We were going to either find the cure or "borrow" a LifeSuPod—a Life-Support Pod—until we figured it out.

But now I have no one. Once I'm trapped in the virus, I'll have at best a few days before my body starves to death. And yet, I'm not afraid, though I probably should be. Call it ignorance or blind hope, but I think I found the missing part to our cure.

All this time Nole and I were trying to figure out how to eradicate the mutation that took over everyone's mind. But we don't need to counteract the virus, we need to *rewrite* it. It's nothing more than a dark, twisted dreamscape.

Dreamscapes don't create themselves. Someone made this place. It was programmed.

Which means it can be hacked.

I lurch for my notebook and pen. Laptop would be faster, but I can't waste the charge. Best to write it out and then upload a photo of my notes. I pull a candle out of the box of dollar-store candles we stocked up on before things got so serious. I light it, then peek out the window. Night. Not even a whisper of dusk.

I don't know what I expected. It's already past nine. But since my Sleeps come at 6:00 a.m. I'll never see the sun again. I haven't seen it the past couple wake times—not fully. But it's still a hard fact to swallow.

I pull out my time card and mark my new status, filling in one more hour bubble to indicate the progression of the virus. Only seven more Sleeps.

I stuff the paper back into my pocket as if I can crinkle up the knowledge along with it. Then I take a fresh stick of gum. I'm running low—just a few sticks left. The bright orange sends a sharp zing to my tongue. It's my favorite brand because it tastes like more than a mouthful of sugar. It has depth.

Nole used to make fun of me. *"You like your gum like you like your dreamscapes. Layered and overcomplicated."*

I let my memory of him fuel me. As I write my thoughts, my brain speeds after the ripple effects of what this Nightmare dreamscape could mean, how we could change it. I mean, how *I* could change it. The Draftsman in me wakes up, passion and studies multiplying in my memory. Instead of always feeling one step behind Nole and his science skills, I finally feel like I could be the person to do this.

The person to bring the world a cure.

I force myself not to rush, despite the clicking secondhand from our battery-operated analog clock growing louder and louder. I think through every ripple effect, every potential outcome. When I need a break, I spend it sketching the coliseum on fire.

It takes hours to finish my notes and reconcile them with Nole's equations. When I finally think I have something to work with, I pull up Nole's neglected video channel. The last time I updated it was after Nole's death. His followers deserved to know.

Now there's a glimmer of hope, and I can't keep that from them. From those who are still alive, that is.

I do a quick Live video, sharing how I've had a breakthrough for the cure.

"I'm still working on it. I have Nole's notes and share his blood. It's not the end yet." I almost mention that there's an exit to the Tunnel, but at the last minute I keep that information to myself. The world outside of the Tunnel almost killed me and resulted in my being trapped in the coliseum for gladiator servitude. From this perspective, the Tunnel almost seems safer.

Is that how Nole died? He escaped the Tunnel and the Spores got him? Burned to death from the coliseum flames? Died in the gladiator Arena I've yet to see?

I've hardly finished filming the Live when comments roll in and several people click the "thumbs up."

>>I needed this today. Even if it goes nowhere, I needed the glimmer of hope.

>>I'm willing to try anything at this point. Even if it poisons me.

I glance at the clock. 5:00 a.m. Already I'm a mere hour from reentering the Nightmare. Did I really spend all my Awake time working on this already? It feels like I only just woke up.

I move faster, stuffing a cold hard-boiled egg into my mouth. I toss some feed into the chicken coop and gather one more egg. Then I spend the final 30 minutes looking at my notes. Double-checking and pushing my focus to deeper levels than any professor ever achieved.

If I'm going to rewrite the Nightmare dreamscape, I need ImagiSerum. Fresh, unused, unprogrammed ImagiSerum to mix with Nole's cure. To write my own dreamscape that counteracts the Nightmare.

I don't need to create a new world. I merely have to create the end of one. The serum needs to tell the brain, *The dreamscape is over, time to wake up.* Just like when people sit at the ImagiLife parlor and their 60 minutes are over.

The dreamscape kicks them out.

At first I consider finding an ImagiLife parlor to see what stock might be left in the back, but all that stock will have been pre-programmed. No, the best place to get unadulterated ImagiSerum is the university.

I still have Nole's keys.

Time to break the law.

8

"I DON'T CARE IF YOU DIE, AS LONG AS you die with style," Crixus says from the front of the mess hall.

I've only barely entered the broad, doorless entryway to find him addressing all the sleepy-eyed noxiors at what I assume must be breakfast. This Roman version of a mess hall is as large as a public-school lunchroom but with low ceilings and rough, wooden tables instead of the typical foldable particleboard ones.

I slip onto an open bench nearest the door.

"Wrong table, mister." A woman in the middle of the bench nudges me with her elbow. She seems to be in her late twenties, maybe early thirties and has a splash of freckles across her cheeks. In another life she'd seem welcoming, but the unyielding set to her grim face matches the battle-worn leather gladiator clothing on her tense body.

Wrong table? Surely she's kidding. What is this, high school? And she's head cheerleader? Except older.

"New recruits sit up front," she says simply.

Up front. At Crixus's feet. I see the noxiors from my last Sleep—the Fears—quivering on their benches, hardly touching their food.

"I'm good here."

"Not for long." She nods to three beefy guys who lumber

toward us, each holding his own bowl of breakfast. They stop at our table.

Two sit, but the largest glares at me and says one thundering word. "Move."

I don't want to pick a fight. Really, I don't. It'd be foolish. But something about this cliché bully who is no older than me causes my temper to flare.

"This seat's taken." I mean for the sentence to come out casual or even kind of cocky, but instead it's a growl.

"Ooh, another Anger," the woman says, and she almost sounds happy. "It's about time. Just sit, Rolf. We're not here long anyway."

"But, Helene . . ."

"Sit." She gives the command in what I can only describe as a mom tone, leaving no room for argument.

But I don't want some lady to defend me. I want to fight. Crixus is going to train us, so it might as well start here. I start to rise, but to my surprise Rolf sits across from me, and the woman, Helene, slides her own bowl of breakfast my way.

"Eat. It'll settle your emotions."

Eat? What a joke. This is a dreamscape. What good will food do? I eye the bowl of stick-to-your-bones oatmeal anyway. As confused as I am about my body's relationship with the Nightmare, I *am* hungry. I take a bite, and it actually feels filling when it hits my stomach. Energy returns. It may not be real food, but my brain processes it like real food with the same mental benefits.

So I eat.

It has about as much flavor as the leather on Crixus's sandals. Now that I look around, everyone is wearing sandals. Leather. Roman regalia. They're too busy embracing this bizarre world to realize it's killing them. Killing us.

I'm the only one still in jeans and a T-shirt. I'd like to stay that way. Crixus isn't going to get me in any Halloween garb. I'm not going to feed his fandom.

For now, I'm in the Nightmare to study it. I entered several hours ago in the middle of the night, trapped in that room of snoring people until some soldier let me out. I spent that time working on keeping my emotions from swelling.

Nothing irritates me more than wasted time.

My emotions may still be on the edge and heightened–a side effect that never existed in original dreamscapes–but I try to keep them contained so I can learn more about this world I'm going to override. The only problem is the fog rolling into my memories, blocking details and clarity the same way disturbed silt obscures the vision of a scuba diver.

And I should probably try not to die.

"The Arena is where you earn your place in our world," Crixus says.

He doesn't seem to care if we live or die, and that's a problem for me, especially when I have so much riding on my survival. I can't let myself die–not even if it's in style.

"If you want to live here and start a life, you need to prove you can survive." Crixus flips his gladius, then expertly slides it into his belt. Roman fandom or not, he's Level 99.

I'm Level 1. Okay, with my Draftsman knowledge maybe I'm Level 2.

"So it's a vetting system but with slavery," another noxior says. He has short, curly black hair and hasn't touched his oatmeal. "Who made you Caesar?"

"The Emperor. And if you make it to the top, Skyler, you can meet him." Crixus folds his hands behind him like a centurion at ease. "You'll train every day and you'll compete every day. The battles will progress in intensity and opponents until you've earned your citizenship."

"Compete?" a shaky noxior asks. "Battle? What are we fighting for?"

"Fight for yourself, first and foremost."

"We don't have time for this!" I tighten my grip around my wooden spoon as my anger spikes like fuel on a spark. The utensil cracks beneath my knuckles. "While you play your gladiator games, some of us are trying to survive in the Real World. We need to learn about this Hell, not turn it into some role-playing fantasy."

"This is how you learn about it." Crixus eyes my spoon, almost bored. "Your first fight is tonight. Since you're new to Tenebra, you'll be opening acts in the Games. The real noxiors will fight later . . . when people actually care about watching."

Across from me, Rolf snickers. Helene merely rises and leaves the mess hall. Her three cronies follow.

Doesn't Crixus see what a waste of time this is?

"I'm not going to be some puppet of entertainment."

"Then we'll kill you." The statement drops like a kettlebell on concrete. "And if you die in Tenebra, your body dies in the Old World too." He raises an eyebrow at me. "Or did you not realize that?"

"I know it." From the paling faces of the noxiors around me, they *didn't* know this fact. Lucky them. I've seen it with Nole and here in the Nightmare with James. I will not go down the same way. I have too much to do when I'm awake. "So we either fight in your Games and die—or you'll kill us."

"Or, if you stop being a cocky meathead, you learn to fight, to survive, and you earn your citizenship."

I throw my empty clay bowl at his face.

Crixus cuts through it with his gladius before I see him draw the weapon. The severed pieces of the bowl smash against the wall behind him, but he doesn't blink. In fact, he turns his attention to the other noxiors.

"Weapons through that door." He points behind us with his free hand, then to the archway at his left. "Training after meals through that hallway."

I hate to admit it, but I kind of like him.

And I don't mind learning to fight and survive in this place. I'd be a fool to think I won't be here for the long haul and not take advantages when they're handed to me.

Crixus points to me. "You, come with me." He leaves through the archway.

The anger coiling in my chest makes me want to stay behind in defiance and run after him to throttle him, despite knowing I'd lose that fight. Some echo of logic manages to speak up from the shadows of my mind. Crixus is the only way to get a weapon in my hand and answers about this dreamscape. And I'm not used to such wild emotions. I need to defeat those before I can hope to defeat anything else in this place. I take several deep breaths, then shove away from the table and stomp after him.

I find him in the weapons room.

"We don't get a lot of Angers," he says. "Maybe one or two a month. Helene was our last. But Angers tend to do better in the Games. The Fears are boring to watch and even worse with their weapons."

"Lucky me," I drawl.

"You need to tamper your anger, otherwise it will keep building until it consumes you."

"What's wrong with being consumed by it?" That sounds powerful. I could take Crixus down and get out of this place. The very consideration builds the emotion even higher. I *want* to feed it.

"I'll kill you before you get that far." He doesn't look up as he says this.

"Go ahead and try." This Tenebra that Crixus worships took Nole's life. Anyone who accepts it as their new world is an enemy.

Crixus tosses me a short knife with a smoking black blade. "I was an Anger when I first got here. I kept it under control through fighting–not because hitting and defeating people released it, but because it exhausted my body, so I was too tired to feed the anger."

"What body?" I grumble. "You're a figment of your own imagination."

"Then explain how I get full when I eat, hungry when I don't, and die if I'm stabbed."

An opening. "Can *you* explain it?"

He eyes me. For a moment I think he might answer my question, but then he says, "Opening fight starts in three minutes. Keep heading down that hallway, through the two gates, and you'll be in the Arena."

"I don't get to train first?"

"For you, this *is* training."

Even through the haze of building anger I know my limits. "I'm not going to kill people."

"Someday you will. Someday you'll have to. It's inevitable if you want to get out of the Arena." He examines a hefty, knotted net hanging on the wall before straightening a javelin beside it. "Right now you're nothing more than a tadpole in the pond of noxior fighting. You won't be killing or even fighting other noxiors today. It'll be nothing more than a couple nightbeasts."

"Like the flying stingray yesterday?"

"You're thinking way too big for your first fight."

I start piecing it together. If this were a video game, the stingray might be an entry level boss. I'll mainly be fighting NPC enemies. I can handle that. It's like what I'd hoped to create as a Draftsman–an adventure world with enemies that allowed dreamers to fight and go on adventures without true danger to themselves.

I toss the smoking knife from hand to hand. "What's with the smoke?"

"A mistblade will kill only nightbeasts—creatures created in Tenebra."

"Created? By who? Do you know the Draftsman who made this place?" The words feel like sludge on my tongue, almost like speaking a different language, and for a moment I'm unsure if I even used the right term. Draftsman is a word, right? It means something. I know it means something.

"Just focus on the fight, Cain."

I gesture to the blades along the wall that don't smoke. "And those? They're not smoking. What are they for?"

"You seem smart. Figure it out."

Real blades for real people. "Got it."

I brush past him with my mistblade and jog up the wide hallway toward the enormous half-moon barred gates at the end. Two men stand beside them and with a single glance open them to let me through into a holding place between two barred areas. Like a large elevator with gates on both sides instead of doors. Through the opposite gate stretches a swath of lit sand.

Sun.

It's enough to make me want to run into the awaiting battle. But the longer I look at it, the less sunlike it seems. Not quite golden enough.

I press my face against the bars and squint at the sky. No sun, but spirals of yellow flame line the top of the Arena walls behind the last row of spectators. That's the source of light.

"Does the sun ever rise here?" I ask one of the soldiers.

He merely looks at me. Probably not allowed to speak to noxiors.

"What's with all the fire?" I've gathered by now it isn't destroying the coliseum. No one inside acts as though their city is burning down.

Still, he doesn't answer. I turn back to what I can see of the Arena. It's grander than a football stadium. Almost double in circumference. It would take a lot of effort simply to cross the sand to the other side, let alone chase some opponent until I could catch and defeat them.

If this world can trick my body into thinking it's eating calories, maybe I can learn to trick my body into being stronger than it is Above.

The stands are filled to the brim. The crowd lets out a loud cheer, and I scan the sand to see what they're cheering for, but there's nothing there. Then the noise dies down, and a voice echoes from a projection. No speakers, no microphone. The crowd goes dead silent.

I press against the bars, trying to see the source of the voice, but can see only a few heads above the sand turned the same direction, toward a spot on the Arena wall outside of my view.

"Welcome to another day of Games, citizens!" It's a man's voice. Young. He leaves a pause for cheering, but none comes. To my surprise he laughs. "Shall I get right to it then?"

Now there's a cheer, but it's short lived. They're waiting for something. He's here to say something important. "I'm pleased to say we have rescued *three* children from the Spores! One, sadly, had already been infected, but the other two were saved in time. I'll be sharing the first surname now and the second at the end of the Games."

The crowd explodes–some cheering, but also desperate chattering. Two forms walk to the center of the Arena. A small boy, escorted by a Roman soldier. Someone from the crowd screams. But a mass of voices hushes them.

Silence.

The announcing voice speaks again. "You know how this works. If the name I call is yours, and you know this child, come out to the sand and claim him with his name." A pause, then a shout from the speaker. "Surname *Whitlock*!"

The crowd cheers again, though there's a tinge of

disappointment in it. Two people are trying to bulldoze their way past other spectators. Those around them laugh and give them a clap on the back. They disappear from sight for a few minutes, but then reappear on the sand, sprinting toward the child. A young mother and father.

The boy lurches toward them, but the Roman soldier's hand holds him back.

The mother screams again and again, "Tory! Tory! His name is Tory!"

The crowd laughs again. A white handkerchief flutters to the sand from wherever the announcer stands out of sight. The mother picks it up and holds it like a lifeline. Everyone cheers. The mother, father, and child embrace.

Of all the things I expected to see in the Nightmare, this was not it. A reunion that puts a lump in my throat. A family brought back together on the same sand on which I'm about to fight for my life.

A war wages inside me as I watch them leave. A desire to rejoice with them, but also an envy that they are free and united and whole while I am about to become entertainment for these same people who seem to cherish family so much.

How can they be so moved by a child finding his family and yet tolerate battles to the death?

Perhaps I'm supposed to see this scene and think, *That could be my future.* But it won't be. I don't have family anymore. I have only myself and I am trying to survive for the good of everyone still willing to fight for life in the Real World.

Anger wins. I turn toward the others in this holding space to see if they share any of the same fury at such a spectacle. The other noxiors don't even seem to have paid attention. They bow beneath the weight of their puny mistblades and the pressure of fear. Trembling. Thin and hollow-eyed. Pathetic. For some reason that makes me more angry.

Angry that they could allow this Nightmare to cow them so much.

Angry that I'm being controlled by Crixus and his system that takes advantage of those of us infected with the Nightmare Virus.

Angry that the only place I get to experience a pathetic display of false sunlight is while fighting for my life as an entertainment pawn.

Angry that I'm stuck in this holding place while my fury builds. Builds. Builds.

Fine. They want a fight? I'll give them a fight.

I tighten my fingers around the strange knife. If they don't open the second gate soon, I might lash out at the guards.

"Let us out," I grind out to the man on the other side of the gate. The man with the key.

"Soon, man."

I walk up to the gate and jab my knife through the space, even though it's a supposedly harmless mistblade. "Now."

He rolls his eyes. "Always eager. Always dead. Whatever. Burn a bit longer on the sand, then." He fits the key in, and I feel the click of the lock in my chest, granting permission to unleash.

I am first through the gates.

First on the Arena sand.

First to hear the roar of a crowd from above, like thunder from a storm of bloodlust.

There's no burst of sunlight. The shadows are wrong, they flicker too much, and the warmth comes and goes. It's a good try, but it's not enough. This is a world of darkness.

I take in my audience, hating them instantly. Tiny pinpricks of heads and clothing stretch in rising rings above me. They cheer, but not for any of us. They cheer for the sport. My predicament exists because of them.

I roar back.

Some of them laugh. Their cheers increase. I assess the light-gray wall rising from the sand. On an impulse I bolt toward it. Leap. Plant my feet, one, two–my hands scrape the stone, and I slide back to the sand.

The crowd howls at my attempt to breach the barrier and throttle them. They see me as an animal. I *act* like an animal. What am I doing, trying to climb a wall to fight people?

Am I that out of control?

A clash of inner voices hits me. One voice saying, *This isn't you.* And another voice saying, *This is the real you.* A tiny echo of Crixus telling me to *tamp down the anger* tries to wiggle into my mind.

Before I can muddle through any of it, a clang comes from the opposite side of the Arena. Enormous wood doors fall flat, like dropped drawbridges, and a beast bursts forth, but not the type I've seen in films. No tigers on chains or half-starved lions.

Instead an enormous black bull charges onto the sand with four horns on its head. Rather than flesh and blood, it seems to be made of smoke and shadow, lacking the true intricacies of color.

The bull snorts and paws the ground, then scans the Arena, aware and bloodthirsty. It spots a clump of three noxiors cowering against the curve of the coliseum wall–two girls hugging each other and crying. A man with a puny mistspear tries to squeeze behind them as though to disappear. A fourth noxior clings to the gates from which we entered, begging the guard on the other side to let him back through.

Are they going to sit there and die so easily? Is there no fight in them?

The bull charges the three.

They scream, and the man splits off from the girls. The bull thunders across the Arena after him. The man turns and fumbles with his spear. He gives a weak throw, but it bounces broadside off the bull's right flank, then skids in the sand beyond.

The bull gores him.

The crowd lets out a collective groan, laced with amusement. The man's body thumps to the ground, blood marking the spot of his death.

He's dead. Just like that. His real body Above is likely being shaken by the people with him who are still awake. Who still love and care about him. Crixus said this would hardly be a fight–it's mere entertainment.

My ears ring. Some entertainment. The onlookers take pleasure in this, mere minutes after cheering on the reunion of a mother, father, and son.

When watching movies about gladiators, it never quite struck me how disgusting it is that another human could laugh at the death of others. It felt so far removed from real life, settled in a dirty, twisted past. Impossible in present day.

I suppose we've been so desensitized by fiction and film that seeing it in real life feels unreal. Detached. A show instead of a slaughter.

The bull wheels around and heads for the two girls. They scream and squeeze each other tighter. They look like sisters.

A spectator climbs over the wall and drops to the sand, shouting and waving his arms. The bull redirects toward the man, and I barely make out the shriek of one of the girls over the crowd.

"Daddy! No!"

"Hey!" I throw my mistblade. It pings off the bull's shoulder, leaving no mark but getting the creature's attention. The creature rounds on me and huffs as though to say, *Finally, a fight.*

The dad runs to the girls and uses himself as a shield. They cling to him desperately as though they've not seen each other in months.

I tear my gaze from the odd reunion, unsure what to make of it.

The bull paws the sand.

I stand my ground. "Come and get me, you beast." I have no weapon now other than my building anger. I abandon Crixus's advice. He didn't send me into this Arena to tame the anger. He sent me here to die. All he gave me was a puny dagger.

He doesn't expect me to come back.

I charge the bull and drop what little restraint I have left. Anger pours into my veins like water from a burst dam. Seconds before we collide, I leap into the air, over the bull's four-horned head, and land on the other side in a somersault. I regain my feet and spin before the bull realizes he missed.

I'm . . . not exactly sure how I did that.

As the bull regains traction, I catch my breath. Every inhale fuels my anger, my determination. It presses against the underside of my sternum like an inner weapon. It blinds thought. Banishes logic. It takes over my mind, promising power by emotion alone.

The bull rounds on me.

I plant my feet. Lean forward for impact.

The bull charges. Thunder cracks. Fury builds. Then my chest splits open.

Smoke bursts out of my body and propels me into the sky. I hover in the air for a moment. Giant black wings of mist unfurl from my back. The shadows that pour from my chest turn into a spear in my left hand.

I dive toward the ground as the bull reaches where I'd been standing moments earlier. With a shout I plunge the spear through the top of the bull's skull and into the sand beneath. It splinters on impact.

The bull collapses.

I straighten, and the smoke wings disappear. The bull

wiggles for a few disturbing seconds before succumbing to death, pinned to the sand like a bug to foam.

The pressure of emotion vanishes. I gasp for breath and survey the scene before me with fresh eyes.

The bull, dead.

The spear, broken.

The crowd, silent.

Time pauses. Then four men in armor enter the Arena with their own spears made of wood and metal that look very ready and able to stick me through. They surround me, but I have no interest in fighting them. I've emptied myself of my conviction and energy.

Whatever just happened has scared them.

Scared me.

The other noxiors cower against the inner wall of the Arena. A soldier holds the dad and two daughters at sword point.

Crixus saunters across the Arena and stops near the circle of foot soldiers. He crosses his arms and regards me.

"Well, well, well. You've been keeping secrets." He smirks, but it doesn't hide the wariness behind his eyes. "Tirones," he says to the soldiers. "Bind him. We're taking him to the Emperor."

The spell over the crowd breaks at these words. As the soldiers–tirones–lead me away, bound by chains, the people are back to cheering again. They holler in a way that makes them sound far hungrier than when I first walked in.

I'M TAKEN TO A CELL "TO COOL OFF." I don't need to cool off. My emotions are drained from doing . . . whatever I did. I made wings. Flew? And then killed an enormous Nightmare bull.

How?

Something tells me this shouldn't be possible–some knowledge from my life in the Real World. But I can't pull up details. This Nightmare brain fog is starting to grate on me. I close my eyes, and I think I sleep at some point. Time passes, but there's no way to determine how much.

When Crixus comes for me, it's to take me to the Emperor.

Does this make me a citizen now? It'd be nice to graduate out of their sick games. "Are you going to explain?" I ask.

Crixus opens my door with a creak of rusty hinges–how have they had time to rust? The Nightmare hasn't been around that long. Whoever created these cells added the rust for effect. No detail left behind.

"Save your questions for the Emperor." Crixus smells even more of blood, sweat, and something foul. Maybe they don't have showers in this place. How are my olfactory senses even working? Isn't this all in my imagination?

"Will the Emperor answer them?"

"I guess you'll find out." Crixus leads me through the

training grounds to a double-gated door guarded by four soldiers, tirones.

There is no escaping the noxior indentureship. One can only be released from it. I like to hope that's what's about to happen to me. The tirones nod to Crixus as he passes, then lock the door behind us.

We exit from an alleyway into a wide road illuminated by the false sunlight that is really fire on the top of the coliseum walls. The road runs along the coliseum's circumference inside the wall. Crixus hauls me aside as two chariots, each drawn by four horses, speed by. Racing through the streets? They could kill someone.

"Four horses to one chariot," I say. "Overkill, don't you think?"

"It's called a *quadriga*." Crixus resumes our walk.

I give him a side-eye thinking he must be joking. "It's called *Ben-Hur*." He really has embraced this whole Roman Nightmare world. "I don't know if your knowledge of ancient Roman terms is concerning or just nerdy."

He stays in character. No smile. No response. One hand keeps its grip on my forearm, and the other holds the hilt of his gladius. It's not like I'm going to run. I want answers, and so far, it sounds like he's taking me to them.

Homes and apartments are built into the thick walls of the coliseum, strings of laundry crisscrossing the sky above our heads. Market stalls exist underneath the dwelling spaces at street level. "Who all lives in here?"

"Citizens."

"All citizens?" I ask. "What about the houses outside of the coliseum?" We passed several on our way here.

"Abandoned. Some people refuse to enter the coliseum. They're not interested in learning to survive and earn their right to live here. Non-citizens."

"So you kill them?" I ask, disgusted.

"Tenebra kills them." Tenebra. This world. "Citizens don't leave the coliseum unless it's absolutely imperative. If a citizen leaves the coliseum without permission, they lose their citizenship."

"How can someone leave while it's on fire?"

"The fire won't burn a citizen."

That explains why Crixus could part the flames for me and why they still scorched my skin. "And yet if a citizen leaves without permission, you kill them?"

Crixus shakes his head. "You keep thinking we want everyone to die. That citizen would merely return to noxior status and have to earn their citizenship again. Earn our trust again." He gives me a hard look, not breaking his stride. "You saw what was out there."

I think of the hooded and cloaked people who dragged Erik away as he clawed at the road. Who killed James the Vetter. Who caused our cart to crash and crush a man. "The Spores."

"You learn quickly."

"What does it matter? We're all dying in the Real World anyway."

"Not all."

I snort. "What does *that* mean?" Nole and I studied this Nightmare. We watched people use up their final 22 days and then get trapped in the Nightmare coma, withering away in a matter of days.

"How long have you been infected, Cain?" Crixus dodges my question.

Now that I'm not consumed by angry energy, I'm able to think about other things, though thinking about life in the Real World seems hazily distant. Like an old stew of memories neglected and then vaguely stirred. I try to pull up a timeline of my real life but can't seem to settle on exact numbers.

I instinctively pat my pocket for my time card, but it's not there. Obviously. My clothes followed me in here, but not the items in my pockets. Go figure. No sticks of gum either. And here I thought this place couldn't get worse.

"I believe this is my fourteenth . . . maybe fifteenth . . . time in the Nightmare."

Crixus shakes his head. "Unbelievable."

"Now I get to ask a question. Am I in trouble with the Emperor or about to be rewarded?"

I've been hauled away for a night in jail a handful of times–mostly for getting caught with Nole when he did something illegal like breaking into research labs or stealing books from important libraries. It felt a bit like this. Except this time I don't know how I broke the rules of this twisted universe. It's hard to apologize to the Emperor if I don't understand my crime.

"Save that question for the Emperor," Crixus says for the second time.

"So he's in charge of this place?"

"In a way."

I'm in the Nightmare that killed my brother. Anyone labeled "in charge" is likely untrustworthy. But the man in charge is also the one with knowledge. How much does this Emperor know about this dreamscape? "He's got to be the Draftsman."

"Why do you say that?"

"He's the Emperor. The villain is always the guy in power." He must have *some* control. Some leg up on everyone else in this cursed place.

"He's Emperor because he escaped the Tunnel faster than anyone else. Well, until now."

"Until now?"

"Until *you*."

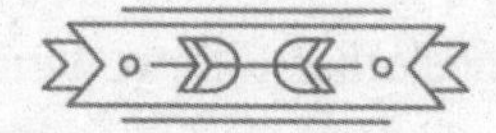

The Emperor's citadel is encased in fire. By now I shouldn't be surprised. Flames encircle a tower that stretches far above the rest of the coliseum lighting up the turrets and spires with swirls and tongues of heat, but they don't crackle. They don't burn. I'm getting major Moses-and-the-burning-bush vibes the longer I'm in this place.

The citadel gives light, but it's not the type that makes you turn your face upward to soak it in. It's a harsh, hot thing that makes me want to turn my back on it. The more time I spend here the more I crave true light.

"Do you ever get a sunrise in this place?"

He gestures to the citadel. "This is our sun. It dims at evening and brightens in the morning."

That's a no then. There's no sun, no moon, no stars. Never will be.

"The Emperor built this citadel to give us light so we're no longer lost."

How can someone build from fire? "So he's the Draftsman."

"No, he created it after he was trapped here like us."

That's not how ImagiSerum works. At least, I don't think so. What I'd give to have my full mental clarity back.

We approach the citadel to silence. Crixus parts the flames like he did in the coliseum gateway, and I walk through the entry into a courtyard. Shadows contradict the glow of the fire. Moving. Almost alive and with substance. Is that a shadow–or a creature? As I turn my full attention to the movement, any shadow I thought I saw melts into the ground before I can make out specifics.

The inside of the citadel is made of stone. No fire burns inside. I expect rustic stone, archer windows, and spiral stairs into dark corridors, but the interior of the citadel is a mix of modern and ancient Rome. Stone spiral steps move as escalators, and we step on them so quickly I have no chance to glance at the mechanism. Light comes from scattered small window squares in the wall, letting in the fire glow from outside. The escalator pauses at each landing that leads to a new corridor but then ascends again after a few moments. It feels otherworldly.

We reach the top, a broad open landing with a floor-to-carved-ceiling window, completely open with no glass or lattice. If I wasn't paying attention, I could walk right out of it and plummet to my death.

Crixus stops halfway to the enormous window, faces the stone wall to his right, and knocks. The escalator continues to slide into the floor and disappear.

Crixus knocks on the wall again, and this time it melts away. Strings of gold slither from the cracks in the ceiling and spread along the wall until it forms an elaborate peaked frame to double doors, which open of their own accord.

"Go on in," Crixus says.

"You're not coming?"

He shakes his head.

I shrug and walk through the doors. I likely have an hour or two left inside this place, so if things get weird or dark–well, darker than that doomed Tunnel I'd been trapped in–at least I'll wake up soon.

"Come in! Come in!" The voice that beckons is casual and young. I've heard it before. In the Arena, calling out the last name of the boy who reunited with his parents.

I enter the foreign space and make it only a few steps before pulling up short. The hexagonal room has walls made mostly of floor-to-ceiling windows, open and also without glass. But what throws me most is that the room is split into what seems like two worlds.

On my left are sofas that look as though they've housed a

thousand naps on their cushions. A coffee table with scattered cans of soda. Steam rises from a box of fresh pepperoni pizza.

The right half of the room couldn't be more different. Thick-trunked redwoods rise through holes in the ceiling. Scattered pine-needle flooring with moss-covered stumps surrounds a low crackling campfire. Fishing poles, woodcutting axes, and old-fashioned metal lunchboxes rest in a pile beside a fallen log. Hot dogs roast over the flames.

My mouth waters.

The only thing off about these two scenes is their coloring. Dim, like a photo that needs some hardcore editing to ramp up its exposure and brightness.

"I didn't know if you'd be more the man-cave type or caveman type, so I set up both."

It takes me a while to locate the source of the voice. A young man–not much older than me steps forward from the center of the miniature worlds. He's pale like he hasn't seen the sun in . . . ever. Dark hair combed but mussed at the same time. He wears a white draped tunic, pinned atop his shoulder, and strapped sandals. A laurel crowns his head.

Hail, Caesar, blah, blah, blah. Is *this* their Emperor?

He studies me with a tilt of his head. "I'm sensing man cave."

I look at the forest and a pang of longing hits my chest. Last I spent time in nature–tangible, touchable nature that wasn't on the other side of a screen–was when Nole took me camping as a kid. Before I learned about the shadows of life.

"Definitely man cave. You look like the forest is about to devour you." The trees melt down into the floor, the campfire turns to smoke, then ash, then dirt, and the ratty carpet from the lounge side of the room spreads across the forest floor, shoving the pine needles out a window. Beanbag chairs spring up with a popcorn cart and a big-screen TV.

The forest is gone.

"And yet you're not afraid of it. That's good." He surveys me with a smile, revealing a diamond incisor. "Wary, but not afraid. Skeptical, but not dismissive. Angry . . . but not wild. You're quite in defiance of this Nightmare world, aren't you?"

I try to set aside the questions sending my inner Draftsman spinning. "What do you mean?"

Of course I'm defying it. Who would accept it when it's claiming all our lives? I'm going to defeat this thing one step at a time. And hopefully get free of it forever. For Nole's sake. For my own.

"In the Nightmare, emotions are heightened. Sudden and strong, like when our physical bodies used to dream. There's very little balance to them here, which takes a lot more self-control than it used to in the Old World." He waves a hand as though to brush away that topic altogether.

"Anyway, I wanted to create a space you'd be comfortable in. Maybe I should have started with asking your name."

I stare at the expanded man cave, trying to reconcile what I saw him do with what I understand about ImagiSerum.

"What do you mean *create*? Are you the Draftsman?" How can he make a forest? I feel as though I've observed something out of a video game, except right in front of me. Real. Or is it? The level of detail used here would take an expert Draftsman a week to design and program.

"Like what you did in the Arena. Now that you're out of the Tunnel, you'll hopefully be making a lot more out of the Nightmare." He plops on a couch and holds the box of pizza my way. "Pepperoni okay? Please don't tell me you eat the kind with pineapple on it."

My stomach growls. Is that in the Nightmare or from the Real World? "Pepperoni's good." I sit and take a slice. Pizza. I've been living off potatoes for almost a month. I can hardly remember the taste of tomato sauce, bread, or any sort of meat.

I take a bite and my eyes widen. Real or not, I plan to eat

half the box. If what the Emperor says is true, maybe I'll be able to make my own pizza someday. Out of nothing.

That sounds way better than another spear or set of wings.

"I'm Cain Cross." I swallow. "And you're . . . the Emperor?" It feels weird using the lofty title, like we're play-acting.

He folds a slice of pizza in half to eat like a taco. "The name's Luc. Some call me the Emperor because I create so much, but aside from that I let the people rule themselves."

"No last name, Luc? Ifer, maybe?"

He laughs. "There's that skepticism. Good! Good." His calm and humor set me at ease despite my wariness. "And no. Luc Jupiter. Luc after lucid dreaming–a former passion-study of mine."

"So it's not your real name, then?"

"Is Cain Cross yours?" he asks.

Maybe I should have given a false name. That hadn't even crossed my mind, but now it explains why Crixus sounds so Roman.

"You get one chance to restart your life, Cain. I took mine. Don't miss yours."

Another person who's embraced this eerie world. I stop poking him with offensive questions and shift into intel mode.

"How can you create what you do?" I glance at the opposite side of the room to the forest, now replaced by shag carpet. Shame. Whatever happened to me in the Arena was all smoke and shadows. Misty wings that propelled me into the air, a smoky spear that impaled the bull. Nothing like a richly detailed living forest.

Luc shrugs and finishes off his slice. "I was the first one here."

I wait. He can't leave it at that.

He looks at me and chuckles. "I like you, Cain. I was the first person to escape those Tunnels. This world was quite different from the one you see now. Empty. Void. Dark and overrun by shadows. I had to learn quickly or die. I got out of the Tunnel on my nineteenth Sleep. After that, this became my new home."

He leans back into the cushions of the sofa, twining his fingers behind his head. "That's why you're so amazing, Cain. You've been infected only, what, fifteen days? And you made it out of that Tunnel. That's the fastest anyone's ever managed."

"It can't be that rare." Even if it is, so what? "I just kept moving. What's the fastest after me?"

"Me." Luc isn't grinning now. "Anyone else who's made it out of the Tunnel only did so with one visit–on rare occasions two visits–to the Old World left."

Nole was on his second-to-last visit. He might have been so close to making it out. Did he make it out? Will I ever know?

I don't miss how Luc talks about real life. The Old World–like he has no desire to return or find a cure. Then again, if he is trapped in here . . . that means his real body is in a permanent coma somewhere.

My next questions is, well, rude. "So how are you still alive?"

If I'm learning anything from the Nightmare Virus, it's that we're all painfully aware of how short our time is. There isn't enough time left to worry about offending someone. If Luc is offended, well, we're both going to die soon anyway.

"My physical body is in a LifeSuPod. My dad had connections."

My mouth goes dry. Luc has a LifeSuPod? Those cost hundreds of thousands of dollars *before* the Nightmare Virus took over. Now . . . anyone would be lucky to get one for a crisp million.

So he's rich. He's one of the elite who was handed a LifeSuPod by his dad. "What about everyone else living here?"

"Some also have LifeSuPods. Most don't. Everyone's lives

have been shortened, Cain. But that doesn't mean they have to be lived less."

"Easy to say when your rich daddy puts you in a LifeSuPod for five or ten years."

So the people who are surviving this virus are the ones with deep pockets. The ones who caused the problem in the first place. Those who had the bucks to create ImagiSerum, test it, and offer it to the world, and now we're reaping the consequences while they cheer from the Arena stands at our deaths.

"LifeSuPods aren't just for the rich. They're also for the loyal."

I raise an eyebrow. "Meaning . . . ?"

"Those who are faithful to Tenebra and"–he tilts his head in mock humility–"to their Emperor, have the chance at a LifeSuPod. It could be in *your* future, Cain."

"By becoming your servant?" This conversation is getting weird fast. "You only just met me."

"You have power here in Tenebra. Not only that, but you still have access to the Old World. I'm not asking you to become my servant. I'm giving you an opportunity to serve this New World in a way that would benefit everyone."

His offer reminds me of something I heard from traders on the Shadow Web where Nole and I used to buy ImagiSerum to practice our own Drafting. Enticing, a touch manipulative, and maybe even desperate. Luc has all the power he needs here, so why does he want me?

I'm not about to indenture myself to the guy in charge, even if he does reunite children with their parents.

Luc holds up his hands. "I'm not your enemy, okay? Let's get that settled. There's a whole different culture in Tenebra, and you don't know what that is yet. There's not a high survival rate. Those of us who have our senses about us band together.

We help each other survive. It's a brotherhood, not some back-door power play."

"Survive?" A shadow of sarcastic anger swells. "By putting me in a gladiator arena? You call that surviving?"

"It's better than putting you on the streets to be devoured by the first nightbeast you encounter. Or worse."

I think of the Spores. They would have killed me had the Stingray Rider not shown up. It takes me one look at Luc to connect that the guy on the stingray was him. He saved us.

"You train for a marathon. You go through boot camp for the marines. Here in Tenebra, you have to compete to earn the right to live. There's limited housing, and one weak citizen can be the demise of a thousand. It's the only way we make it. There are enemies in Tenebra, constantly trying to take our lives. Consume us. Turn us into mist and death."

His explanation doesn't settle much for me. "You make the Arena into entertainment. People relish spilled blood and combat. It's sick. Did you ever think about what sort of citizens are filling up this place?"

"Every single one of them competed in the Arena, Cain. They fought and survived through level after level after level until they earned their freedom. Those people in the stands aren't there just for entertainment. They want to see you survive. They want to welcome you–and the other victors–into this world. No one wants anyone to die."

My wariness settles. Somewhat. Whatever his motives, he claims he can help me get a LifeSuPod. I'd be a fool to throw away such an opportunity.

Luc claps his hands together once, and the food trash vanishes. "Think on it, okay? This is a lot to take in, but your time is ticking. For tonight, stay here in the atrium."

The scene grows fuzzy. Is this Luc's doing or am I that tired?

"Where will I be when I come back?" If I come back. "Will I remember any of this?"

"I'm hopeful you'll remember it all. And you'll wake up wherever you call home. If you don't have a home yet, it'll be where you last fell asleep." His terms are backward—referencing the Nightmare as waking up and the Old World as being asleep.

I need to watch out for this guy. I'm not about to trust him so quickly. Or even slowly.

"See you in a few days, Cain. Well, for you, it'll be a few hours."

The world blinks off like someone snuffed out the moon.

IT'S CURE TIME.

I practically leap off the couch as the scene with Luc fades from my vision—but not my memory. I relish the clarity in my mind now that I'm awake again. It's not like when I used to wake up from a vivid dream where it trickled away like sand in a sieve. Every conversation and event is crisp in my mind, like I lived it here in the Real World.

The only things that grow more muted by the minute are my emotions. And I'm definitely okay with that.

There's a lot of new information to sift through—Luc's offer of a LifeSuPod and the fact that I created wings inside a dreamscape. Now that I'm awake again, the many rules drilled into my head at university come flooding back. Creating wings and a spear should have been impossible. One of the cardinal rules is that only the Draftsman can create items in the dream. It's more than just a rule: it's impossible to do otherwise.

Dreamscapes are programs. For a visitor to create something in the dream would be the equivalent of someone hacking a website by scribbling in the dirt with a stick.

So how did I do that?

The infection must connect me to the dreamscape somehow. But there's no Wi-Fi where I am. I haven't shared ImagiSerum with anyone. Can everyone in this Nightmare do something like that? Clearly not, otherwise they wouldn't have been so shocked when I did it. More than shocked: frightened.

But Luc can do it. I assumed he's the Draftsman, but now that I've done the same thing, I don't know what to think. I can't wrap my brain around it.

My concave stomach growls a demand for food. Luc's pizza clearly doesn't carry over. The memory of it on my tongue, however, does. I throw a cooked potato from the fridge into a bowl with a meager slice from my last cube of butter, then update my time card to reflect exactly how many days I've been infected and how many I have left.

Infected: 16

Remaining Sleeps: 6

I tear my gaze away from the paper as panic blooms in my chest, then I flip open my notebook and speed-scribble everything I can remember from this last entrance into the virus: the fight with the bull and how the swell of my emotions seemed to turn into weapons. I'm not usually quick to anger—at least I didn't think I was. I know what anger can do here in the Real World. It's even more dangerous in the Nightmare. There, it felt impossible to control.

Good thing it was a bull in that Arena and not a person.

If I reenter the Nightmare, will I awaken in Luc's man-cave tower? I'm supposed to go back in eight hours. I'm curious—even anticipating a return. But no matter my new discoveries, the Nightmare Virus is still killing people. Killing me. Taking away my life and stealing my choices.

I can't give it an inch in my mind. I must keep fighting—always fighting.

I bite away a quarter of my potato and finish entering my log. I add any remaining notes on how I plan to program the ImagiSerum. The dream code brings me back to memories of classes, back when we all still had dreams for a future. It reignites my passion of being a Draftsman for fictional worlds, video games, all our favorite adventures. I'm still not ready to accept that that future is dead.

I pop in my gum from the last time I was awake. A fresh piece would be nice, but I have four sticks left and seven Awakes. Got to ration.

Now it's time to go to the university and finally test this cure theory. It's as though I've assembled the innards of a jigsaw puzzle and finally located the pieces that make up the border.

The Fire Swamp is parked in the empty lot of Somnus University. I hope the ImagiSerum is still in the labs. It's not hard to break into the science building.

At the beginning of this virus, people had banded together, trying to find a way to save one another. They shared necessary goods, checked in with their neighbors. But as the Nightmare spread, the panic buying began, which eventually turned into panic stealing once the stores ran out of products and business doors shut. Now people mug only for money and the hope for individual life-support machines.

LifeSuPods.

When I thought the Nightmare was nothing more than the dark Tunnel, I never understood why people wanted LifeSuPods to keep them trapped in there forever. But some people fear death so much they'd rather live under torture.

Now that I know there's a whole world beyond the Tunnel, it makes a little more sense. Though I still don't understand how the Nightmare can kill someone from the inside out. Is it a seizure? A stroke? A message telling the brain it's over?

I step outside and jog across the darkened campus, appreciating the little moonlight I have, simply because it's light. Moreso than the gray glow and fire in the Nightmare.

I reach the science lab and circle to where the back door is covered by several trees and some overgrown bushes. I insert my key into the padlock on the lab door. A week before his death Nole had cut the original and replaced it with a padlock of our own. Not only does it keep up appearances of security, but it also makes it look like I belong here.

Once in the lab, I pull my own personal supplies from my lunchbox-size cooler and place them on a long, empty metal table. I then visit the consecutive lab doors until I find the one with the coolers and cabinets that hold the serum. There are only six tiny jars of ImagiSerum.

I use a dead computer monitor to break the glass on the cabinet, then lift one jar from its little bed of foam. A sudden image of my hand slipping and the vial smashing on the vinyl lab floor makes my fingers tighten. No mistakes. This is my only shot.

I return to my own lab area and boot up the ImagiLife programming device, jerry-rigged to The Fire Swamp's generator. It should power the thing for at least a couple hours.

I follow Nole's notes like I would a recipe until I get to my own alterations. I carefully pour two vials of unprogrammed ImagiSerum into the device. Then comes the fun.

I imagine novelists or game designers or screenwriters feel this way when they stare at a blank page with nothing but the story in their head. Visuals of a whole world known only to them.

Except this time I'm not programming a world. I'm programming an alert to the brain to wake up—to leave the dreamscape. My fingers fly. I've done it a hundred times in my mind and a dozen times in real life. This is one thing I was born understanding.

I program the serum and then send the command for it to eject from the device. I place an empty beaker in the spot to catch it like one would a cup of coffee from a Keurig. A preparation clock shows a twelve-minute wait. I spend that time reading and re-reading and checking my math.

The serum dribbles out, looking the same as it did going

in. My breathing quickens, and I stare at it for a long moment before I dare to start mixing. I stretch every neuron in my brain and take copious notes on every single action and adjustment I make.

I need Nole. I need his brain. He'd do this faster. He'd do this right.

But he'd also tell me to shut up and get the job done.

I let myself imagine what might happen if this works. I'll have a solution. Everyone else gave up on a cure months ago. Scientists worked tirelessly on an antidote until they realized 90 percent of the world was infected. Then no one was left to work on it.

Once they gave up, what was left of the government spent trillions of dollars outfitting every pop-up hospital they could with LifeSuPods. For the elite, of course.

But Nole never lost hope, even once he was infected. That gave me the courage to hold on too. If this cure works, we'll be the kids who rescued humanity. Nole would not die forgotten.

I also really want to live.

A night-shattering clang startles me so severely I almost drop the beaker. My head turns toward the sound, pulse slamming in my skull like the beat of a kick drum.

My alarm clock. It vibrates so hard against the metal table that it inches toward the edge. I catch it before it falls. I check its face. Once. Twice. There is no way eight hours have passed! I haven't slept and I've eaten only one potato.

My blinks turn to sandpaper, assuring me that eight hours have, indeed, flown by. The Nightmare is coming for me again.

"Wait, wait." I scrambled for my phone. It has 10 percent battery. "I'm not ready." I plug it into The Fire Swamp generator.

My alarm ticks toward the second warning–the five-minute countdown. I open Nole's video channel and start a

Live recording. Only as I stare at myself on the screen do I realize how hard I'm breathing.

"Okay, Cain Cross here. It's September, uh, fourth, and I've been infected with the virus for sixteen days. It is supposed to strike at 6:00 a.m., except . . ." I hold up the clear beaker. My hand shakes. "I have what I hope is a cure."

I want to give credit to Nole. I want to say something deep. But my alarm goes off again. I silence it. "Five minutes."

I leave the recording going and grab the concoction, then consult the notebook one last time. I don't want to overdose. Nole said different amounts are needed for different stages of the virus.

I place a tiny dosage cup on a scale and fill it with the amount that should be appropriate for a person sixteen-days infected.

My heart drums a *rat-a-tat* of anticipation.

"Here we go." I down the mixture with a splash against my throat. One swallow.

It tastes stale and strange, leaving a metallic aftertaste on my tongue. Entrance into a dreamscape is typically done intravenously, but Nole insisted on concocting an oral cure. Either that or a cure through eye drops, but he couldn't fit the proper dosage into eye drops. He said oral dosage would be easier for average people to administer.

I place the now empty beaker back on the table, then I glance at the clock. 5:59 a.m.

"One minute to go."

The seconds close in. I hold my breath. I probably should have drunk the serum sooner, but this is going to work. Not because of my smarts, but because of Nole's.

Thirty seconds.

I see the mist. "Man." I press a hand against the table. "Sorry guys," I say to the livestream. "I see the mist." The

Nightmare vapor that always precedes entrapment. "I'll try again when I wake up next."

Though I can't fathom what I need to change in the formula. *Thanks a lot, God.* The two people who trusted Him the most are both dead. I shouldn't have expected any help from Him in the first place, but I thought maybe He'd take pity on me after everything He took away.

Ten seconds.

Nole's followers are all going to watch me crumble into a pathetic heap. I don't want to be seen in that vulnerable state. I'm about to turn off the live stream, except the mist lags, like a pale morning fog instead of a black ocean of cloud.

I rub my eyes against the pull of sleep, feel it calling to me. But as the fog reaches me, I stare it down. I don't waiver. The cure is in me. Nole knew what he was doing.

I shift my thinking and send up a desperate prayer–habit, I suppose.

The cloud fingers recoil. A flash of black crosses my vision and then . . . then my alarm turns off. And 6:00 clicks to 6:01.

I am still awake.

The cure. It worked.

"No way," I breathe. I feel my face. Blink my eyes. Check the numbers on my alarm clock again. "Wha . . . ?" I reach for the notebook. Gaze at the beaker. As though staring at objects will help me process what just happened.

The comments on the live stream explode.

My head pounds with a sharp headache, but it's almost laughable compared to the freedom I feel.

I whoop. "We did it!"

I turn back to the live stream. Most of the comments are asking how they can get the serum. Telling me how long they have left before they're trapped.

"Hold on, hold on everyone. I need to check on my

stock. I need to find more–" I glance at the three remaining ImagiSerum vials.

"Give me some time." I turn off the stream and shut off my phone, preserving the generator's energy as much as possible.

I go still, staring at my workspace in awe. We did it. We actually did it. Then, as if someone hits a splash cymbal, I burst into action. Spastic movement without much direction because, aside from imagining praise and success and a receding virus, I'd never thought about the logistics.

How do I get more serum? More of any of the ingredients? I have almost no money. How can I make more antidote and distribute it to others? There is no postage system anymore. And lives are relying on me.

There's still so little I know about it, like how long it lasts or if it'll work on people already trapped or if I need to take it every day for the rest of my life, and if so, do I need to increase the dosage every day . . .

"It doesn't matter," I say to the empty lab room. I'll figure it out. There's no time to wait. I have something that fights the virus, and that is more than nothing. People are at the end of their virus lives. There are thousands out there who may have only days–hours–left before they're trapped in the virus forever.

I can't be like the health experts who have yet to find an antidote. Who say they can't release anything until their concoctions undergo clinical trials and testing. No one has that kind of time.

I flip open my laptop again. The first thing I do is send an email to the higher ups in public health. Then, on a whim, I copy the email and send it to as many important people–leaders, doctors, senators, pastors, news reporters, politicians–whose emails I can find. I say I found a cure and I used it on myself successfully. I tell them we need to get it into production somehow for the masses. I include the live-stream link. When I rewatch it, I see the telltale black veins creeping into the whites of my eyes at exactly 6:00 a.m. and then receding.

It really worked.

I leave the university science lab and head back to The Fire Swamp to recharge the generator with the solar panels. I need food. I also need sleep, but I'm not about to risk shutting my eyes. What if that triggers the Nightmare and overrides the cure?

Two potatoes later, my phone and laptop are plugged in, sucking up what remains of the solar energy. I tend the chickens and notice the brightening of the sky. It's overcast with dark storm clouds, and I can almost taste the sun on the other side of the gray canopy. Miles away I think I spot a bit of blue sky.

This storm will pass, and then my solar panels will get their charge.

Then I'll see the sun.

My heartbeat quickens at the idea of sunlight. Such a simple, overrated thing. Yet I'll see it again. And again. And again. Because I'm cured. I almost laugh at the storm overhead.

I barricade myself in The Fire Swamp, pull out my notebook, and dive into dreaded math calculating how much of each substance and ingredient I'll need to make 100 cures. I check my email every five minutes. No responses from anyone.

I let the battery charge a little more, navigating dead and closed and broken websites until I find information on how and where to get more product.

My heart is racing. I still can't believe this.

I'm here.

I'm cured.

I've saved the world.

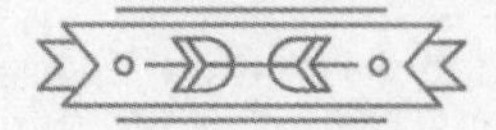

I bolt awake ten hours later. The coils of my notebook are pressed into the side of my face. I fell asleep?

I scramble for my computer. So much time wasted. How could I let that happen? Ten whole hours lost. Then again, I didn't enter the Nightmare. I *slept*. Like in regular life. Victory feels heavy and rich.

My computer is only partially charged. I glance out the window. The storm has gone, but so has the sun. All that blinks at me from the sky are stars and a half-risen moon.

Tomorrow. I'll see the sun tomorrow.

I have no new emails. Not one response in all those hours of waiting. I hadn't expected every leader to take me seriously and beg for more information, but I thought I'd hear at least something, even if they are interested only for themselves.

I can't wait for their help or provisions. I have to take matters into my own hands. I need more ImagiSerum, and there's only one place to get it.

I press a couple keys and go where Nole and I promised each other we'd never go again.

The Shadow Market.

CONNECTING WITH SOMEONE IN THE Shadow Market was surprisingly easy. Easier than getting an email response from a reputable leader in the health-care industry. I found a guy selling undiluted ImagiSerum and plenty of it.

For a price.

I don't have enough in my bank account for even one jug. I don't tell the guy why I want the stuff or how much. Hopefully he hasn't seen my videos on Nole's channel. I was foolish to post all of that live online. It puts a target on my now-very-well-known face. If this black-market dude finds out the serum is for a cure, he might jack up the prices. Then again, maybe he's desperate enough to sell it all to me because who else is going to buy it in a dying world?

The only way for me to get the money is to pre-sell. Luckily for me, the guy lives in New York, hardly an hour from me. At least, that's where the pickup location would be. He's not dumb enough to tell me where he lives, and I'm not about to ask.

He says he can deliver the goods upon payment.

The amount of money he wants would put him in a good place to bargain for a LifeSuPod. Even with the banks closed and electricity shutting off in another city every day. But I don't ask questions.

Instead, I make promises.

I'll have the money in an hour.

I put together an online landing page with payment details and then upload a new brief video with instructions to Nole's channel. Its activity level is dependent on the time of day, due to spotty internet and people sleeping their lives away, but the moment the new video goes live, the viewer count is triple what it normally is.

People have told their friends.

The community isn't dead. Not yet. If anything, it brought us more together during the Awake periods. People shared fears, diagnoses, conspiracy theories, memes, and now I'm sharing a cure.

A very expensive cure.

I charge them only for the ingredients plus one single dollar profit so I can pay for food–if I can find anyone to sell me food.

What else am I going to spend my money on? one commenter says.

Payment comes through a minute later. Nole used to tell me that if the apocalypse happened, money would be obsolete. We'd have to trade in butter and cigarettes and things. I think our country grew so reliant on valuing virtual dollars that it was too hard to break the habit.

Another payment comes in.

Then another. Then 10. Then 20.

I get tag alerts from the few social media accounts I have: *I trust this guy. Worth a shot. Here's hoping he found true help.*

It snowballs from there.

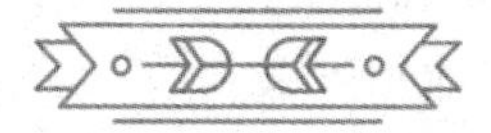

One good thing that came from the virus is efficiency. Since people's lives are counting down, they don't hesitate to take action during the handful of hours they have before their next Sleep.

As soon as payments roll in, I purchase the serums. The Shadow Market dealer delivers it to a set of lockers in an abandoned train station within the hour. There's a moment of tense exchange when I send him some money and wait for him to give me the locker codes. But we both follow through and then trade in bigger numbers.

Only a few hours pass before I'm back in the lab concocting again.

Hundreds of orders have rolled in with the information I asked for–body weight and current time-card status. I have enough serum for all of them. As careful as I was programming the ImagiSerum for myself, I'm even more careful knowing this is being programmed for other people. I can't afford a single mistake.

I complete over two hundred orders and take a break to let the generator recharge, as well as deliver the orders. For the first time in weeks, I'm not worrying about how much time I have. I'm not rushing, though I'm tempted to.

There are no more Nightmare Sleeps for me. The sense of freedom and hope is so strong it banishes the desire for sleep or food or anything other than spreading the good news.

Was this how the twelve disciples felt? Having the answer? Hope? And being able to tell the world?

I snort at the thought. It's something Nole would say, which is probably why it enters my mind. The only thing missing from this picture of victory is his presence. But this is for him. He always saw it as his "Great Commission" once the Nightmare started spreading.

I can't say I get much inspiration from the disciples. Robin Hood, however . . .

Delivery is tricky to figure out. I don't want to use the train lockers like my Shadow Market guy did because 200 people converging at the same train lockers could result in violence. Like people fighting over lockers or killing someone else for an extra dose of the cure.

Instead I do something far more illegal.

I choose a handful of neighborhoods nearby and assign each order an address. Then I slip a cure into the respective mailboxes. It's a federal crime to put anything in someone else's mailbox, but I don't even know if there are any cops left. I include a note in the email cautioning people to please check the mailbox during the day if possible. And be safe.

Now I sound like Mom.

That's the best I can do to ensure everyone's safety.

What's hardest is ignoring messages from people who don't live near me. All I can do is hope they find a way to travel to New York. There's no other way for me to get the serum to them. Snail mail has been down for I don't know how many months.

Orders keep pouring in. I finally pause the form with a backorder apology, otherwise I risk not having enough ingredients.

Messages, posts, and comments spread over social media.

> I got my cure serum! Three hours until I use it! – @w.sherrodfashion

> I can't believe the timing! My sister has one day left until she's trapped in the 24-hour

nightmare cycle. I had given up hope until this point. – @2014ninja

On my way to pick up my cure! Please, God, let this be legit. I used the last of my money on this. – @shortbreadredhead

What a crook! Can't believe how much this guy is charging for his snake oil and ppl are actually buying it! Fools. – @spacebeast147

This last comment irks me. I know I shouldn't reply, but I do anyway.

I'm not making any profit. The cost is for materials only.

He answers with a rude GIF.

I don't have time for this. As though agreeing with me, my alarm clock rings a 15-minute warning. Time to take my own dose. I don't even know if I need to take it, but I'm not willing to risk it and end up back in the Nightmare.

The exchange with Spacebeast147 eats at me. It sends a wiggling worm of doubt into my mind. So many people are resting their hope, their savings, and their *lives* on this formula. I remind myself this is like clinical trials. I showed people exactly what happened to me. They know I'm not Nole. They know I'm not a doctor. They know I'm doing the best I can.

But I wish I could find the confidence I felt last night when I first tested the cure.

Too late. I've committed. I've promised them something and taken their money. There is no going back.

I swallow my dosage–a little more than yesterday's to make sure it combats the extra hour–then I return to fulfilling orders. I hope people are taking precautions as they pick them up. All it takes is one mugger lurking in one of the neighborhoods, waiting in the shadows to steal their lifeline.

But the people who have survived this long must have some amount of street smarts.

I pull an empty glass vat over to me to start another batch. This should be enough to fulfill the rest of the current orders, and then I'll ask the Shadow Market guy if he has more serum. If so, I can reopen the form. People have already said they're traveling across the country to get the cure. That's almost more dangerous than spending time in the Nightmare.

My hand shakes as I pour. I'm too tired. I need food again. I really shouldn't be mixing these while I'm on such low energy. That creates a higher risk of making a mistake.

When I finish this batch I can sleep.

Just push through. I take a deep breath and try again. My measurements have to be perfect. The shaking continues. My vision blurs.

I release an irritated sigh and set the serum down to rub my eyes. That's when I see the black billows of fog rolling in. My gaze snaps to my silenced alarm clock: 6:00 a.m.

It isn't exhaustion taking over.

It's the Nightmare.

I'M LYING ON A COUCH. LUMPY AND firm and . . . foreign.

I sit up and see I am next to a short table beside the couch with some brass bowls and an empty pizza box. Then a face. Pale skin. Dark hair. Serious. Too serious.

The fog of disorientation muddies my thoughts as I try to reconcile this scene with the lab where I was making the cure. But the more I try to think about the lab or the cure, the more it fades away into the back of my mind.

Unreachable. Vague. Hidden in gray.

Memories from the Nightmare take the forefront. The man sitting before me is the Emperor of this terrible reality. He sits on the edge of the table, next to the pizza box. His name catches up to me, followed by details of our one and only conversation.

"Luc."

I am, without a doubt, in the Nightmare. It's like my body and mind aren't even fighting. Crushing disappointment hits first. Failure, though I'm still trying to scoop up the running sand of my thoughts. Of what just happened.

"Where were you?" Luc hardly moves a muscle. His lips are tight. White. His eyes seem sunken, like he's skipped sleep.

I press my palms against my temples. "In the Real World."

What is the term he likes to use? Past World? "Where else would I be?"

"You were in the Old World too long."

Old World. That's what he calls it–like he's left it behind. Like it's expired and we've graduated to World 2.0.

I drop my head in my hands and rack my brain, desperate to remember the reason I feel such emptiness right now.

A glint of black metal catches my eye through the gaps in my fingers. Barrel. Trigger. Luc's fingertips brush metal that's far too shiny and modern to fit this Roman universe.

A handgun.

I lift my head, on alert. For some reason, my heart won't slow. Any clarity of thought is drowned out by a growing hum of irritation. Who is this teen Emperor to question me? To corner me? To threaten me?

"I . . ." What can I tell him? That something happened in the Real World that has left me wrung out and confused? Something having to do with a cure . . . I think. Frustration bites at me. Why can I remember some details but not the important ones?

Luc's hand is wrapped around the handgun, unsteady.

"Where were you?"

"I thought I found a cure." The confession tumbles out–words disconnected from my brain. They invite a slug to the emotions. Shame and failure flash in my mind.

A cure. *The* cure. Failed.

I acted too fast, handed the public hope with a false promise.

The wintry seriousness thaws from Luc's face a little, replaced by a frown.

"A cure?"

"For the virus. Nole–my brother–had been working on one before he died." I fight to remember. "I thought I figured it out. I skipped a Sleep. But now . . . now I'm back." Why? Why didn't it work?

"There is no cure for the Nightmare. Trust me on that." Luc leans back on both hands and when I look down at the table again, the gun is gone. Did he stow it away or make it disappear into the mysterious Nightmare air?

Luc looks more worn and ragged than when I first met him. Is that because I skipped a Sleep? Was he *that* concerned? I don't buy it. Something's going on, and even though the gun is gone I stay alert. Emotions are weird in here. That's what Crixus said. Or was it Luc? If emotions are higher, faster, more sudden and crippling in the Nightmare, maybe Luc is struggling with his.

"Sorry for the rude awakening. Literally." Luc's tone turns conversational. The shift in his demeanor is more concerning than the former rigid coolness. "I thought you might be a Spore."

I'm still not over the fact that he was ready to shoot me for missing a single Sleep, and I tense at the accusation.

"Those people who attacked our cart? You thought I was one of *them*?" I spread my hands out. "I don't even have a magic sword."

"There's more to them than their swords."

"Like what?" There's a lot I still don't know about this world and the people in it. They're much harsher here than they are in the world my physical body currently inhabits. Is this my future? To transform into a hardened version of myself?

"When Spores escape the Tunnel, they're able to enter and exit Tenebra at will. They're not trapped here like the infected are." He sucks in a hissing breath through his teeth, diamond incisor catching the light.

"What? They can wake up in the Real World whenever they want?"

"So it seems." Luc's countenance darkens. "The only others able to do that are children. So the Spores kidnap our children to use them. Since the origin of the Nightmare, we've been trying to rescue the kids from the Spores. But they are vicious to a level no human with a soul should be."

I think of the child Spore Luc lassoed from his stingray. Was that a kidnapped kid? Was that a rescue?

"You might think we, the citizens of Tenebra, are rough and unyielding, but we have to be if we're going to survive against the Spores. And if we're going to get our kids back."

If the Spores can leave the Nightmare whenever they want, why do they attack people coming out of the Tunnels? Why kidnap children? Why not just live their own lives in the Real World?

"They must have a cure," I conclude. How else could they come and go? My mind startles. They must be the Draftsmen. Somehow they created this world, and now they're using both worlds to serve them and whatever they desire.

It makes sense the more I think about it. A dreamscape of this magnitude could not have been formed and programmed by just one person. It must be a group of elite Draftsmen who formed it and now control it.

"How many Spores are there?" I saw four plus the child, but if there are enough to kidnap numerous children coming in and out of this place, they must have a hidden force.

"Too many. We kill them every chance we get."

"At least they can be killed." I stop myself short. These are real people we're talking about. "Are they given a trial or something?"

"Their crimes are judgment enough. We see what they're doing–*you* saw it. If we don't kill them, they'll kill us first."

"You came on the stingray."

He nods.

"You saved us."

"I do what I can."

"If these Spores have that much control over the Nightmare,

they could be the creators of this whole thing. Have you ever questioned one?"

"Never get a chance. We have to be careful not to get too close." He looks at my feet. "If they touch you, they can twist your mind so you serve them. They plant Nightmare lies right into your subconscious. You might even become one of them—I've seen it before. Or they might kill your mind. They do it all the time. And if you die in Tenebra, you die in the Old World too."

"Oh, I know." That's the one thing I do know about the Nightmare. The one thing that I can't unknow or unsee.

Luc eyes me. "Your brother?"

"Nole."

"How did he die?"

"I was in the Real World, and he was in the Nightmare. Second-to-last Sleep. For all I know, he never made it out of the Tunnel."

"I doubt that." Luc rises and walks to a wood-and-marble cabinet along the wall. "If you're related, I'd expect him to get out of that Tunnel earlier than the others."

I shake my head. "He would have told me."

Luc opens a long thin drawer and pulls out a thick binder and places it on the table in front of me.

"I have records." He sits back down.

The book rests closed with the weight of a thousand anvils. My throat turns dry. "Records?"

"If Nole made it out of the Tunnels and died here in the Nightmare, these records will tell us how." His hand rests atop the notebook, the last barrier between me and answers. "Do you want to know?"

There's no question. "Yes."

He flips the book open. I want to tear it from his hands, flip the pages faster, read it myself.

"Nole Cross," I say then spell it to make sure he finds the right name and that there are no mix-ups.

He stops on a page, runs his finger down its columns. I can hardly breathe. Then Luc looks up at me and simultaneously flips the book to face me. I pull it toward me.

I find my name first:

Cain Cross: Noxior, alive

Beneath it is Nole's name–a beacon of black ink against a white backdrop.

Nole Cross: Deceased [A. N. 250]. SPORED.

"They got to him," Luc says quietly.

I picture a ring of Spore people in their cloaks, their floating swords circling Nole. Stabbing him through the skull the same way they did to James. Him fighting them off with whatever he could find: fists, sticks, dust thrown in their eyes.

But in the end, Nole was overcome. Overwhelmed.

Murdered.

Not by the virus, but by dreamers within the virus. Real people for whom Nole was trying to find a cure.

Luc is talking, but he might as well be underwater for all the good it does. Nothing breaks through the spiral of my thoughts. I thought I'd find relief to learn Nole hadn't died in the Tunnel, but this is worse.

He probably escaped the Tunnel in that final Sleep, maybe even anticipated waking up and telling me everything he'd discovered. He never got that chance.

I crush my fingers together, tensing against my emotions. Hatred becomes an anthem in my blood. Something clatters at my feet, and I startle.

A wicked dagger with a wavy blade rests at my boots. Half of it is shining steel, the other half is dark and misty. A dual blade. I glance at Luc. Did he toss it there?

Luc lifts his hands. "That wasn't me." He indicates my clenched fists. "You made that."

I look at the dagger. Simple handle, but a serpentine blade, wavy and double-edged. Luc picks it up, examining it.

"A kris dagger. This is fine work for only your second time creating from nightmist."

"I don't even know what nightmist is," I growl, but it's not hard to put two and two together.

"Take a moment to cool down." Luc presses the hilt of the dagger into my hands and walks past me to the door. One of his knees buckles, but he keeps his feet.

"I'll be a few minutes." He opens the door but turns toward me and flicks his hand. I feel nothing, but when I look down a leather belt with a masterful sheath rests at my side against my jeans–a clash of modern and Roman. The belt is black and smoky, like most things I've noticed in the Nightmare, but there are also shades of dark brown leather.

"That'll hold you over until you can make your own." He leaves.

I stare at my new weapon, sliding a thumbnail along the blade. A thin shaving of nail falls to the ground. Deadly sharp. I made this? Out of nightmist? I shake my head. How am I creating while inside the dreamscape?

I hardly know anything about this world, only that nothing seems to shake Luc. He has all the answers–including how Nole died.

Spores. Poisoned people wandering about and poisoning others. They can exit and enter the Nightmare at will. They must have some sort of cure and some deeper understanding of this place. Even if they're murderers, I want answers. From Luc and from the Spores.

More than that. I want justice.

For Nole.

If Luc hates the Spores, that makes us allies. But he's inviting me into his space not merely as a welcome. He wants something. No one in power invests in others out of the goodness of their heart. He has his own motives, yet why should that stop me from pursuing mine?

Luc returns to find me sitting on the floor-level couch, kris dagger now sheathed. Crixus is with him. He walks over and takes up a post a mere yard from me with one hand on the hilt of his gladius.

I push myself to my feet, not liking how vulnerable the low Roman sofa makes me. Crixus takes a step closer.

"Ignore him," Luc says to me. "He's here as my protector."

"Against me?" My annoyance is growing.

"Of course." Luc gestures to my dagger. "You're untrained, Cain. I can't take chances."

I glower. I like to think I wouldn't attack another person–particularly the Emperor–without meaning to, but he has a point. I'm unpredictable because of this Nightmare. I want to be able to control myself–to control my "power," as Luc called it.

"You seem calmer," Luc says.

"I am." I try to say it without a growl. The emotions have not disappeared–they've calcified into a lurking threat beneath my rib cage–like a caged animal pacing and waiting for its day of freedom. Until that day, I have plenty of food to give it.

He wants Crixus here as his bodyguard? I can deal with that. "Tell me what you want from me."

"Are you sure you're ready to hear it?"

I appreciate that he doesn't deny wanting something.

"Whether or not I agree to your requests, we'll see."

"Fair enough." Luc reclines on his Roman sofa and bowls of fruit and a platter of sliced meat form on the table between us. I don't help myself to either. Neither does Luc, but the atmosphere turns serious. Ready for whatever topic is about to be served.

"I need a man on the outside–in the Old World." He takes

a deep breath and tucks away any potential emotional display. "My father's dying."

He meets my gaze, his own hardened. But I glimpse fear there as he continues. "He's in a LifeSuPod in the Old World. He's been trapped in the Tunnel since the beginning of the Nightmare, and I'm doing everything I can to find him and get him out. But the Spores have discovered that he's my father. While you were in the Old World testing your cure and skipping a Sleep, they tracked down his body and cut power to the LifeSuPod. And to the entire building he's in."

Crixus shifts his weight. I steal a glance at him only to catch a frown directed at Luc. This news about Luc's father seems to surprise him. That tells me Luc is fairly private, even with his own bodyguard. And yet he's confiding in me. Interesting.

Luc doesn't seem to notice Crixus's reaction. "I've been trying to find someone–*anyone*–who still has Awake time in the Old World to move his Pod to a secure location." His eyes lift to mine. "I'm hoping that can be you. The children we house here aren't capable enough to do such a task."

Children? That derails my train of thought for a moment. "You house children here?"

"The children who have no parents in Tenebra. We rescue them from the Spores, but no one claims them." He shrugs. "They need a home somewhere."

But he told me kids can enter and exit the Nightmare at will, just like the Spores. Is that because they're like Spores in some way? I want to ask more questions, but I also don't want Luc to think I'm ignoring his main point.

"Okay, so your dad is trapped in a dead LifeSuPod." I give him no verbal assurance. Not even a blink of sympathy, though my heart remembers my own desperation to save Nole. "What's in it for me? Travel in the Real World is deadly. Not only that, but in many cases it's impossible. Blocked roads, empty gas tanks, muggers. And, now that you bring it up, the

Spores who killed my brother and want you dead might be guarding your dad's building. Where is he even located?"

"Upstate New York."

I quirk an eyebrow. "That's several hours from me." At least, I think it is. Am I remembering right? Before the virus, a couple hours of driving would be nothing. But with only one tank of gas and pulling The Fire Swamp over broken and blocked freeways, well . . . I'd be risking my life.

"What's in it for me?" I ask again.

"I'll give you your own LifeSuPod."

I still. A LifeSuPod? Free of charge? Suddenly upstate New York doesn't sound so far away. I eye him. "Does it actually work?"

Luc laughs. "Of course. I'm not that twisted."

"All you need me to do is get your dad to a place with charging power?"

"A very specific and safe place."

"And where is that?"

"The address is with my father in the LifeSuPod. Once you save him, you'll know where to take him."

My eyes narrow. So Luc's dad planned for this? "If he had a safe location, why didn't he place his LifeSuPod there in the first place?"

"It was a backup. The location he's in right now was supposed to be safe too."

"Why would you give me a LifeSuPod? They cost millions."

"Millions of dollars mean nothing in Tenebra. Life is currency here. And if I'm able to give that to others who are willing to join my team, to show loyalty and commitment to building a new life in this new world, then there's nothing greater."

It sounds too good. What's to stop him from cheating me? He dropped the loyalty card, but surely he must know I have no loyalty to him just like he has none toward me.

What if I save his father and then he kills me or something? Besides, who is this guy who happens to have all this knowledge of LifeSuPods in the Old World? He's hardly older than me.

Luc leans forward and rests his elbows on his knees. He takes a deep breath, opens his mouth to say something, then stops. After a moment's deliberation, he decides to speak, and by now my ears are that much more attentive. Whatever he's about to say, he's torn about saying it. Which means I want to hear it.

"Listen, Cain." His voice is low. Even Crixus shifts his weight to lean a little closer. "I'm not ashamed of what I'm about to tell you, but if it gets to the wrong ears, it can cause chaos. You've seen what chaos does to people in this place."

Yes, I've seen. They cheer for death.

"My father . . . he's the Draftsman. Hex Galilei is his name. He created Tenebra."

My thoughts reel, but my body remains stone cold. Luc's dad made this Nightmare? It's not the Spores, then. He's the cause of the virus. He infected the world and killed millions.

"Murderer," I spit out before I catch myself.

Luc nods somberly. "Yes. He is. But the virus wasn't the plan."

I rise to my feet. "That's no excuse! How can you ask me to save the man who has ripped life away from us all?"

"Because . . ." Luc's voice hasn't changed in tone or decibel. He's every bit as serious and somber with each word. "My father has the cure."

THERE'S A CURE. A REAL CURE.

Not created by me, not by Nole, but it exists. And it's in the dying brain of the man who created the virus. How fitting. How ironic. Of *course* he'd be the one to have the cure. And I'd be the one asked to save his life.

"Your dad–Galilei–is the one to blame for Nole's death. Not the Spores." A swell of fury fills me, but Luc remains calm. Accepting of my anger.

"He's responsible for this dreamscape we're trapped in," he acknowledges. "But the people here have their own free will. Spores choose to kill. Thousands of other people have managed to survive in here. My father is guilty of creating the setting, but not the actions of its inhabitants."

I know he's right, but that doesn't slow my heart rate or breathing. My hands itch to throw something, crush something . . . or someone. I glance at Crixus, and he gives me a hard look. He takes a long deep inhale, and I find myself doing the same, expelling some of the overwhelming emotion.

I turn back to Luc. I don't want to save his old man. I don't want to help. But if it will bring the cure to the masses, I have to.

"Even if I did rescue your dad's LifeSuPod, he's still

unconscious. He's stuck in this Nightmare the same as we are. How would we get any information from him?"

"He's in the Tunnel. I'm working on getting him out. But he has to stay alive, first."

I force myself to consider the details of the offer: I'd get my own LifeSuPod, and we'd access the cure. Not a bad exchange . . . if Dear Old Dad truly will hand over the information we need.

"My truck bed can fit only one LifeSuPod. There wouldn't be room for an empty one of my own."

"The location you'll take my father's LifeSuPod to has an empty one plugged in, charged, and stocked with all the medical and caloric necessities to preserve your body for two Old World years. All you'd have to do is get in it."

That's ten years here in Tenebra. He's not merely offering me a way to stay alive, he's offering me a new life.

"Why will I need a LifeSuPod if your father has the cure?"

"Just in case we can't administer it in time. You know what I mean–your Awake time is dwindling. My father's body not only needs to be saved, but we need to get him out of the Tunnel too. That's the only way to communicate with him."

It's interesting to look at this young man–this Emperor–and think of him having such care for his father despite his father trapping all of us, all of humanity in this death dream.

But then I picture Mom. Even at her worst, when she let depression win and emotionally abandoned Nole and me, I would have done the same for her. I'd want to save her. Because of hope–hope for life, hope for second chances.

Can I deny Luc that?

"Why not try to restore power to the high-rise?" Crixus asks in a low voice from the corner.

Luc swivels. "Crixus! I almost forgot you were there." He laughs, but it's weak. "That's not a bad question." He turns back toward me. "How are you with electricity?"

"About as good as I am with math."

Luc laughs again. "No luck then. Besides, what's to stop the Spores from cutting the power again?"

"They'd likely not expect it–"

Luc holds up a hand. Crixus resumes a submissive stance. I appreciate his willingness to consider alternatives. A Plan B is always a good idea.

"So what do you say, Cain?" Luc has a carefree tilt to his head, but there is a shadowed sheen of desperation hovering behind his eyes. "I know this is all new to you. I don't expect you to trust me or help me. I'm merely appealing to your humanity."

"And I'm trying to stay alive."

"A LifeSuPod will help with that." He smiles.

I get that his dad is dying. That's unfortunate. But this is about more than that–the cure. My life. I hardly know Luc, and I certainly don't trust him. Surely there are other factors that haven't crossed my mind yet, but my thoughts are too foggy–too infected–to think through any of them clearly.

I need clarity of mind, and the only place I have that is in the Real World. "Give me one more Awake to decide."

"Very well." Luc nods to Crixus. "Give him some extra training, would you? And get him in proper noxior attire."

I frown. "You're sending me back to the Arena?"

"It's essential, Cain. The battle with the wings, spear, and bull slaughter was a great sign. The dagger an even better one. But like I said, you're untrained and therefore *need* training. Even I can't hand you citizenship until you earn it. You're still a noxior."

"I could die in there!" One wrong move and I get gored by a bull horn. Done. Dead. No LifeSuPod. No cure. No saving Luc's dad.

Crixus slides his gladius from its scabbard with barely a *shing.*

"You're willing to risk that?" I press. "I thought I was your only chance to save your old man."

"I'm willing to risk it." This statement is so firm and confident that a pulse of anger propels me forward but thin sharp metal meets my throat. Crixus.

"You're proving my point right now," Luc says.

So if I don't help him, he'll force me to keep fighting. "You're blackmailing me into agreeing to save your father."

"No. I am staying true to the laws of Tenebra as any responsible Emperor would. I want you to fight, and I want you to *win*. To grow so you can have a real life here." His eyes are hard now.

"I don't need a life here if I'm the one rescuing your dad and he gives us the cure!"

A knock on the door interrupts us. Luc crosses and opens it. A woman stands hand in hand with a small boy of about six or seven. She hands Luc a scroll. He smiles at the boy, then opens the scroll.

"Hello, Eddie. Are you ready to find your mom and dad?"

Eddie's little chin quivers, and the woman passes his hand over to Luc's.

I'm not done with him yet. "You're the Emperor. Aren't you supposed to take care of your citizens?"

"You're not a citizen, Cain." He tucks Eddie's name scroll into his belt and stands in the doorway with the boy. "None of the noxiors are until they achieve freedom from the Arena. If I recall correctly, that happens with your first kill."

"I killed the bull."

He gives a wry smile. "I'm not talking about nightbeasts."

People. I have to kill a person–probably another noxior. That isn't going to happen, but I'm not about to tell him that. His dad is as good as dead.

"If you don't earn your way out of the Arena and into our

society, no one will accept you. In all honesty, they'll probably kill you. No one will trust you. Least of all me."

"Some New World this is."

"Frankly, Cain, if you can't survive the Arena with your unique nightmist power, I'm not sure I'd want you in Tenebra anyway. I protect my own, Cain. I fight for my own. You're not my own. Yet."

I pick up my kris dagger, flip it once and catch it by the hilt. Then I walk out on the Emperor of Tenebra and his centurion lackey. The little boy cowers behind Luc as I stalk back toward my prison within a prison.

Crixus catches up within a few seconds. I don't bother to look at him or talk to him. Fine, I'll go back into their sickening Arena. I'll learn the tricks and fight. But not at the cost of my humanity.

"I refuse to kill a noxior," I spit to Crixus.

He's silent for a long time as we exit the citadel. The only sound is his Roman sandals slapping against the dusty Roman road as we walk toward the barred training area. He unlocks the gate and holds it open for me.

"That doesn't mean the other noxiors will refuse to kill *you*."

"YOU'RE AN ANGER. YOU TRAIN ALONE."

And that's how I find myself locked in a training arena, wearing noxior garb with nothing and no one around but weapons.

For the third day in a row.

It's a decent space with sand beneath my feet, a vaulted wood-beam ceiling, and all kinds of weapons along the only solid wall. Metal bars make up the other three walls, so I can see into the other training areas.

The weapons don't entice me. Gladii, spears, swords, chains–nothing modern that I might actually be good with. A few dummies are spaced around the room, one filled with straw, another with sand. But this so-called training is pointless. Crixus doesn't even come in to instruct me.

I'm left with a few punching bags. Sure, I can whack at them, but what does that do? They don't whack back.

A clang from across the room draws my attention. Helene walks in–the woman from the "popular crowd" breakfast table. A soldier, a tiro, closes the gated door behind her.

"Careful," I drawl. "I'm an Anger. I could attack you with my rage."

She grins. "Ditto."

I actually smile, that's how desperate I am for any sort

of interaction. If Luc's plan is to bore me into a decision, it's working.

"Did Crixus send you?"

"I sent me." She walks to the wall of weapons. "I want to train."

"With a newbie like me?"

"You need to train too. Otherwise you won't survive another fight."

"I think Crixus is hoping that's exactly what will happen."

She tosses me a mistblade javelin. "Maybe it still will." She grabs a weighted net for herself and a mistblade trident. "Now. Come at me."

I let the javelin fall to the ground. "No, thanks. Crixus is right–I'm not in control of my emotions yet. I don't know what a fight might do to me." Maybe my anger will spike and I'll injure her. Or create some nightmist weapon again.

"These are mistblades. They can't hurt me, and I can't hurt you. I need to get some energy out, so work with me, okay?" Her voice grows more tense while she talks, and I consider the fact that she's an Anger too. Maybe she really does just need to shed some energy.

I pick up the javelin. Her shoulders relax a bit. Okay, then.

She rushes me and thrusts the trident. I dodge and knock it away with the staff of the javelin, more out of defense than skill. She whips the weighted net, and it tangles in my weapon. Just like that, I'm disarmed.

"Dead," she declares with a fake stab toward my chest.

We go at it again, and it's a nearly identical scuffle. I block, dodge, she disarms me. But this time when she jabs with the trident I duck and roll, sweep her legs out from under her, and yank my kris dagger to her throat.

"Dead," I say with a grin.

Her eyes go wide, and she leans away with a true flicker of fear. I frown but then note the cause: my knife. It's a double blade–mist and metal. I reel backward. If I'd accidentally struck her, I could have killed her. When did I even draw the weapon? It happened so fast, so instinctively, I can't explain it.

"Sorry." I offer a hand to help her up, but she gets to her feet on her own. "I suppose that's why I'm locked in here alone."

"Seems to me you don't have to train after all," she says, a bit out of breath.

"Besting you was luck. Nothing more." I don't care if we spar again. I only want her to know I wasn't actually trying to hurt her. "Are you close to getting your citizenship?"

"A fight or two away." She sounds grim.

"You're really going to kill someone?"

She hoists the trident over her shoulder and doesn't meet my eyes. "If it comes down to it, I guess so."

"Living in this place really means that much to you?" I'm sick of this complete willingness to murder.

She walks to the gate, and the tiro opens it for her.

"I have a daughter out there," she tells me. "Four years old. She's lost in the Nightmare. So, yes . . . she means that much to me. If I have to kill to find her, I will."

We're both pawns in this new world. Playing Luc's game.

She leaves, and a few minutes later Crixus takes her place.

"You're done for now. Get some food."

I stalk past him toward the mess hall. I don't know why I'm annoyed. The trapped feeling? The forced fighting? The fact that Helene has to murder another person in order to find her lost four-year-old daughter?

Sure, we're trapped in this "New World," but who created this structure? Who decided this was how people earned citizenship or a right to live?

I see Helene down the hall, entering the holding place between training and an Arena fight. My feet carry me there instead of toward lunch. Helene talks to the tiro. She's going into another fight, and for some reason I want to make sure she comes out of it alive.

Several other noxiors wait in the holding space. Their demeanors are completely different from what I witnessed before my first fight. These people hold weapons and stand straight and determined.

One young girl—maybe twelve years old?—stands apart from the other noxiors. Her bronze hair is braided and tied in knots at the base of her neck. Her gaze is firm and forward—toward the Arena—and a shield is on her arm.

Why is a kid here? Is she some sort of tiro in training? One of the orphans Luc mentioned?

The chants of the crowd come through the ceiling, and the gatekeeper inserts his key into the padlock to let me in.

"No." Crixus steps up beside me. The gatekeeper pauses, then slips the key back into his pocket. "This isn't your level," Crixus tells me. "You're still training, Cain."

"Train? You mean poke at a mannequin in isolation?" We're all infected, doesn't he *get* that? Every five minutes wasted here in the Nightmare is a minute of life lost in the Real World. I'm not allowed to leave the Arena until I'm a citizen. And since my own cure didn't work, I'll definitely be spending more time here in the Nightmare.

There are places to explore, things to learn, intel to gather about this dreamscape. If Spores and children can wake up from the Nightmare at will, there's got to be *some* escape. Which means I need to compete. Impress the crowd. Get them to award me my citizenship as soon as possible.

They went wild when I killed the nightbeast bull. If I can keep doing things like that and prove my prowess and skill, why couldn't I get my citizenship without killing another noxior?

The crowd quiets as Luc's voice echoes over the Arena, following a similar script as last time. The boy, Eddie, enters the center of the Arena.

"The fights get more difficult as they progress," Crixus warns in my ear, though it doesn't sound like he's trying to deter me, more like he's disappointed. "You could go far with the right training."

"Then tell me how to make more things from nightmist," I hiss. "How did I get the wings? How did I make the spear?" If I can create weapons from nothing–which is apparently a big deal–then I can fly through these fights, or even fly out of the Arena to explore.

"It comes down to controlling your emotions. You're nowhere near being able to do that yet."

"I created the spear and wings, didn't I?" I don't tell him about the kris dagger at my hip. Let him believe Luc gave it to me. He doesn't need to know I made it.

"A lucky accident that came from your wildness. You need to deny your anger. Tame it."

"That doesn't seem to be Luc's view."

The crowd cheers, and a mother runs across the sand to embrace Eddie.

"There are different ways to teach," Crixus continues, unmoved by the reunion of mother and child. Calloused. Even the victories in this place feel like defeats.

"I have my job for a reason. Every single citizen of Tenebra exists because I kept them alive. We put you through the Arena fights so you learn to control your heightened emotions in a secure environment."

"Secure environment? You're making us battle nightbeasts." Their terminology still feels strange on my tongue.

"Secure environment for us, the citizens. It keeps us safe until you're safe enough to live around." Crixus turns and speaks to the tiro with the key. A dismissal.

My irritation spikes and immediately feels beyond my control, which only serves to incense me further. My emotions are proving him right. Why can't I control them? What does he mean "deny them"? I've never been such a victim to my emotions.

"Just get me in a fight," I grind out.

Crixus must sense the building of my anger because he looks me up and down. I think he's giving it real consideration. "No."

He disappears down the hall.

I'm breathing hard, and I try to hold back the burst of frustration. For a few seconds, at least. My mind creates visions of hurtling after Crixus, shoving him against the wall. Some semblance of sanity remains long enough to turn my body around so I slam a fist into the Arena gate instead.

The gatekeeper jumps away. Helene raises her eyebrows and folds her hands, as though curious what I'll do next. One noxior nudges his buddy and snickers, pointing. They're not afraid, they're ready for a fight.

The little girl, however, backs into the shadows, pulling her shield tight to her chest. A long red scab, as if from a burn, curls up her neck.

"Let me in," I growl.

"Sorry, noxior." The gatekeeper plants his hands on his belt. "Not your fight today."

"Let me in!" Smoke bursts from my body. It dissipates only to reveal a wicked black chain rope around the gatekeeper's neck. His eyes bulge–more in shock than strangulation.

I stagger back, and the chain rope melts into thin air.

The other noxiors go silent. No nudging and laughing now. The gatekeeper catches his breath, then without a word, steps forward and unlocks the gate.

"Best get you killed sooner rather than later," he mutters.

"We'll see," I say, but for the first time I wonder if Crixus is right. Am I a danger to all these other people? A danger to myself? Maybe I do need training. But if only they knew why I'm so impatient: I'm trying to save people in the *Real* World.

The silence of waiting for the upcoming fight almost

makes the snowball effect of my thoughts worse. There are no distractions to slow them or stop them. Like the opening of a floodgate, my emotions multiply. Frustration at how oblivious these Tenebra people are. Anger that Luc will keep me in the Arena unless I agree to work for him. Fury about how the Spores killed Nole. Why didn't they drag him away like they did Erik? Why kill Nole without reason?

My thoughts screech to a halt.

Wait. They had reason. The cure.

That must be why the Spores murdered Nole. They knew he was trying to undo the Nightmare. Since they can enter the Real World, they probably saw our video blog, knew Nole's face, and slaughtered him. They want to keep people trapped in this place, dying on both sides. Then they'll have the power.

The helpless, hopeless, and desperate messages I received from people buying my attempt at the cure is not my fault. Their despair is the fault of the Spores.

The Arena gates unlock. The other noxiors step out onto the sand, but I sprint.

I spare one moment to wonder about the blast of heat that should be from the sun except there is no sun. All an illusion contained only to the Arena. I don't know why that is the final straw.

I hate this place. I miss the sun while no one else seems to.

A wall of weapons welcomes me to the left. I veer that direction and yank a smoking javelin from the armory. The noxiors behind me all grab mistblades as well. At least that means we're fighting a nightbeast and not people.

I wait for the doors on the opposite side of the Arena to fall open and release our opponent.

They don't. The other noxiors in the Arena are at the ready, albeit a bit shaky. But they don't cower like the noxiors from my first fight.

Then I see the girl with the braids at the weapons wall.

She glances over her shoulder at the rest of us, then grabs a gladius. A regular shining gladius. Not a mistblade.

Does she not know the difference?

The gladius seems too heavy for her, and she shifts it awkwardly in her hand. She's not some tiro in training. They put her here to fight. This *kid*.

It has to be a mistake. Luc said the citizens of Tenebra *rescue* kids. Spores kidnap them. So what is this girl doing in the Arena? Shouldn't she be reuniting with her family? Even if she's an orphan, she should be serving snacks to the audience or something.

The crowd doesn't seem to notice. Or maybe they don't care. Luc is in the Emperor box, speaking with someone, his attention off the sand. I'm about to yell his name, but then the sand beneath our feet swells like a shaken blanket.

The crowd salivates as one. We're the third act of entertainment for the day–the first two were warm-up fights, meaning the crowd is thirsty for blood. I picture Maximus Meridius and have half a mind to get all the noxiors to work together.

The crowd cheers and stomps their feet, eggs us on.

"It's Icarus!" A woman screams in thrilled frenzy.

I look around wildly to see what they see that I don't. What's an Icarus? That's a name, right? Isn't that the Roman dude who flew too close to the sun? Are we fighting some flying creature? I search the skies, and something smacks me in the face. I duck, but not in time. Its softness surprises me.

Something else flies my way. Then I realize the crowd is throwing things at me. I dodge one more item before I make out what they are. *Flowers.* A few gold coins clink off my head.

"Icarus!" someone else whoops.

They're calling *me* Icarus. Because of my wings and slaughtering the bull. I'm just some popular show character to them. Disgusting.

I roar at them like an animal, then crush a rose beneath my heel. They cheer louder. The little girl with braids pockets some of my coins. Have at 'em, kid.

The sand undulates more, and I tune out my true enemy—the murderous crowd. A beast bursts forth like a Leviathan from the depths of the sand sea.

A giant snake. Something that fits much better in a Harry Potter movie than in front of my eyes. Its irises are red slits, and when it hisses, two sets of fangs extend, dripping venom. Halfway down, its body splits into two tails. Its head sways side to side, searching the sand for its first victim.

The little girl fumbles her gladius but picks it up again with a squeak. The crowd laughs. Moments ago they cheered for Eddie as he reunited with his mom, and now they're laughing at a small girl about to be eaten.

She holds her ground, gripping the gladius tighter. Does she realize it's not a mistblade? It won't hurt the creature at all.

Another small squeak causes the serpent's head to swivel until its Sauron-like gaze catches on her. It's found its first victim.

The snake lunges.

I throw the javelin, and it glances off the creature's scales but knocks its head off target. Its fangs sink into the sand a few feet away from the girl.

She screams. The snake rears back for a second strike.

I race toward the girl and tackle her, and we tumble to the sand. I flip onto my back, but a yell and a launched trident pull the snake's attention around.

Helene. She gives me a sharp nod, then coaxes the snake away. The beast doesn't want a fight. It wants food. And I'm being too difficult.

A prick of pain pierces my bicep. The girl holds her gladius up with a small glint of blood on the tip as she tries to gain her feet. Did she cut me? After I just saved her?

She swipes again. I knock her hand aside.

"Hey! Quit it!"

The weight of her weapon pulls her back down into the sand. She stabs at my feet. I plant a foot on her wrist, pinning it to the sand and rendering the gladius useless. She screams, and the snake swivels around to find the sound.

It must know Helene isn't going to be easy prey.

I don't have time for this nonsense. I withdraw my kris dagger. I could club her in the head with its hilt, even knock her unconscious. But then she might get eaten.

Her eyes go wide at the sight of the blade, and she whimpers.

"This is not for you." Hopefully that'll get her to stop fighting me. "Just stay down, okay?"

An animalistic shriek comes from above. I brace for a strike from the snake, but the beast is across the Arena eating another noxior. *Eating* him.

I gag and look away as it swallows the man whole. More shrieks sound—both from the audience and from the sky. I look upward and see broad red-gold wings, vivid against the muted fire pillars. For a moment I think it's another stingray like from my first night in Tenebra, but then it flaps, and I see a spray of feathers. A long streaming tail like a beta fish. It glistens against the gray sky as a splash of color in a dull gray world of war.

A phoenix.

I brace myself for a new fight, but no shadow or mist rises from the creature. Somehow this phoenix is different from the nightbeasts I've seen so far. Not only because of its color.

The phoenix swoops lower, and the snake raises its head at the cry.

A young woman rides the back of the phoenix as though it's a steed. A hooded cloak streams away from her shoulders, revealing sand-blond hair and the ferocious face of a girl about my age. She has a sword at her hip. A sword that, I know, has a mind of its own. A whiff of manure and hot tar reaches my nose.

A Spore.

Several people in the crowd scream as she swoops over them. Some abandon their seats, arms over their heads, and sprint for the exit. A few throw things at her. The little girl next to me claws at my foot with her free hand, tearing off some skin exposed from my useless Roman sandals. I relent but kick her weapon away.

The Spore swoops my direction. She and her kind killed Nole. Her gaze is locked on me and it's narrow and furious. This Spore is here for me.

She knows I've picked up Nole's work and that I found a cure in the Real World. It's strange. What she doesn't realize is that it didn't stick. I'm back in the Arena, aren't I? That doesn't seem to matter to her.

The Spore girl leaps off the phoenix and lands on her feet in the sand, daggers in each hand. They don't smoke with nightmist, which means only one thing: she's here for flesh. Blood. Human.

Me.

I flip my kris dagger as the fury builds in my chest. I let it. I urge it. I abandon Crixus's advice to control and deny it. Luc is Emperor, and he said the emotions are what create. So I let them. I picture the fury pouring into my veins like viscous power building me up for an attack.

I charge, leaving the little girl on her back in the sand.

The Spore's eyes widen. I plow into her. The crowd hollers encouragement, regrouping into their seats.

"Icaruuuuus!" someone shrieks above the rest.

She tumbles and does a backward roll to regain her feet. I'm already attacking with a thrust. A swipe. I've never fought like this before in real life or in my training cell, but it's like my memories of films and books have made their way into my muscles and veins. The attacks come naturally, as if instead of creating smoke wings or a spear, my nightmist is creating talents and physical skills.

I don't question any of it.

Spore Girl dodges. The crowd roars, a frenzy of bloodlust stronger than ever before. She is everyone's enemy. She's trying to take me down with an audience. To prove her power?

I charge her again, and this time she turns to run but trips over the carcass of the giant snake. I didn't realize it was dead. Then I see Helene at its head, her trident sticking out of its skull.

I leap over the snake's body and land on top of the Spore woman, pinning her wrists with my hands, digging my knee into her chest.

The little girl flees with a terrified cry.

The phoenix lands in the center of the Arena. The other noxiors jab at it with their weapons, and the little girl joins their throng.

Beneath me, the Spore writhes, then releases her two daggers and claws at my hands. Her green eyes are filled with hate. Her Spore stench fills my nose. Her chest strains against my weight.

I hold her there for a moment, breathing hard while she suffocates. I picture her rage-filled eyes being the last thing Nole saw before he died.

"Don't like being so helpless?" I grind out. "This is how my brother felt before you killed him." The words shatter any remaining restraint in my body.

I yank my kris dagger from the sand and plunge it straight into her heart.

Once.

Twice.

She screams but it gets cut off with a groan.

I startle. My blinding fury flows out of me like a deluge.

The phoenix releases a piercing cry, then leaps from the sand with one great flap, sending the other noxiors tumbling back. As it gains height, it swoops and grabs the little girl in its talons like a sky hunter would a mouse.

"No. *No!*" the little girl screams, reaching her free arm toward me. Tirones from the edge of the Arena shoot arrows at the phoenix. It falters and drops the girl. She lands in a heap in the sand.

The bird swoops away, disappearing into the dark sky.

The Spore girl beneath me coughs. Again. I scramble off her convulsing body, horror numbing my limbs.

She's covered in blood. I'm covered in her blood. The hatred in her eyes fades as she looks at me, then turns into something far more wrenching: fear. Despair.

Suddenly I want to scoop her up. Hold her like I held Nole in the end. Tell her it will be okay–that death won't take her.

The crowd roars its approval. Stamps its feet. Chants.

"Icarus! Icarus! Icarus!"

Her body shudders. I drop to one knee. Any light in her eyes fades. Then she goes still. Dead. My kris dagger sticking out of her chest.

15

I LIE ON A SLICK WET FLOOR. Blood. I bolt upright and crawl out of the wetness. Blood everywhere. I cry out. Then my eyes focus. It's not blood. It's sweat. I'm on the floor of the Somnus University lab.

I'm awake.

Emotions zip in and out of my veins, sending my heart pounding and my breath gasping. The heightened Nightmare emotions fade to a dull pulse, like old dreams used to.

The scene I just lived through does no such thing. My actions scream at me, pointing an accusing finger. Reminding me of the kris knife in my hand, the Spore girl pinned to the sandy floor of the Arena. My arm striking her.

Striking as though it was the only thing that mattered.

In the Nightmare, it was. It consumed my mind and my impulses, yet in the Real World, I can't explain it. But I know one thing:

I'm a murderer.

I murdered a girl in the Nightmare. Not by accident either. I craved it. I picture her body on a couch under the care and watch of a loved one, twitching like Nole's did. Her breath disappears. Her green eyes never open.

Her skin turns cold.

Her mom or sister or boyfriend won't know what happened

to her. They'll be left to wonder what could have possibly gotten to her in the Nightmare to stop her heart from beating.

I crawl to the nearest trash bin and am sick. How could I lose myself in the Nightmare so deeply? That's not who I am. At least, it's not who I *was*. But it's who I am now. A murderer.

The clock reads 12:02. Midnight.

Something about that doesn't seem right. I spit several times into the bin, then wipe my sleeve across my mouth, trying to recall what happened before I entered the Nightmare. It all comes back with another sickening wave. The cure. It failed me.

Not only that, but when it seemed to work yesterday–was it only yesterday?–it hadn't delayed the virus but merely skipped a single day. I look at the clock again. I returned to the Nightmare for eighteen hours instead of what should have been seventeen.

But it didn't work at all the second day. Why not? I'd done nothing different. Luc said the virus couldn't be cured. Not without his father, Hex Galilei. Galilei holds the answers . . . for both of us. For all of us. Maybe that's why Luc hates the Spores so much–he's jealous that they can wake up at will.

But if that's true, why didn't the girl I killed simply wake up before I stabbed her? Why didn't she save herself?

I pull up my email. There are 96 new messages from clients. The first 5 are enough to tell me what I need to know. The cure hasn't worked on them–not even the first time. From what I read, I'm the only person who had positive results. Many of the messages are from people who are afraid they took the dose incorrectly.

I don't know what to tell them.

My social medias show the same responses. Several people call me out as a fraud and crook. Others demand their money back. Some ask where I've gone–I sold the serum and then disappeared.

I slam the laptop shut and press my fist to my eyes.

What have I become? A failed-cure-peddling monster who murders people inside the Nightmare. I feel like I'm watching someone else—viewing a movie screen and not my own life.

Messages keep coming as the approaching morning gains speed. All I can do is sit and read them. I read every single one, hoping beyond hope for a positive response. Just one single success apart from mine.

The closest I get is a woman whose entry into the Nightmare was delayed by an hour.

One hour.

That's proof that *something* inside my serum fights the virus, but I have no idea where to start in figuring out what that is. And I have little heart to try. I can't return anyone's money, it's spent. Gone. I have nothing to give them except the snake oil I concocted.

So I do the only thing I can: I fulfill the last of my orders to cries of outrage and emails with death threats. In a detached, zombie-like state, I finish mixing the serum. I package it and deliver it to the designated mailboxes.

I welcome the email threats. I deserve to be killed for what I've done here and in the Nightmare, even though no one knows what I did in the Nightmare. No one needs to know.

My thoughts screech to a halt. Someone might know. Someone could have been in the Arena audience and now recognize me out here in the Real World. Unless everyone inside Tenebra has run out of time or unless they're all in LifeSuPods.

Crixus hinted as much: that everyone else in Tenebra had run out of Sleeps, earned their citizenships, and accepted their new lives.

But still . . . nervous energy wiggles in the back of my mind.

I pull The Fire Swamp up to the final house and deliver the last package to the mailbox. Then I move a couple streets down and park in the dark. Sunrise nears. I won't be awake to see it, but I long for it.

The night is gone, and I'm starving. It's only an hour until 6:00 a.m. My Sleep time. How did it come up again so soon? At this point, it would almost be a relief to leave the Real World.

And yet I fear returning to the Nightmare. I fear what I'll do when I'm back in there. Will I kill someone else? Will those deafening emotions take over again? Will I be placed under arrest and sentenced for my crime?

I've never felt so out of control.

I fill my lone pot with potatoes and water and set them to boiling, hardly paying attention to my actions. I collapse back onto the couch. I'll need to move the house–haul it to a new city, a new state. A new . . . somewhere. I don't need the university lab anymore. In fact, I don't want to be anywhere near it.

I close my eyes and try to stop thinking, to shut out the voices, including my own. I focus on the hiss of the propane feeding the flame beneath my pot. The soothing roll of water boiling. The subtle *tick, tick, tick* of my alarm clock. It's been silenced since yesterday, but I don't move to turn it on. The Nightmare will come. My serum and my will are useless against it.

I feel it before I see it–the chill and the darkness stealing over my body. Lapping at my emotions like a stray mutt on the streets. It feeds off my helplessness, off my defeat. And it draws me toward it like a captor would coax its prey.

I don't want to go back. I don't want to kill. I don't want to face what I've become inside that place.

As the black veins crawl across my vision, I notice with a sick lurch that I've left the potatoes on the hot burner. They've been boiling for too long and a plume of gray smoke rises from the pot. The water has evaporated. The potatoes are burning. The pot is burning.

A spark of flame. I struggle off the couch and crawl toward the stovetop. The Nightmare joins the race, pulling at my ankles . . . my mind.

My muscles turn to jelly, and I strain to lift a hand. The burner is right there. So close.

The Nightmare gives a violent jerk on my mind.

My hand falls limp, inches away from the stove.

I go down in flames.

16

THERE'S STILL BLOOD ON MY HANDS. That's the first thing I notice when I wake in Tenebra. The next thing is that I'm still in the Arena, since that's where I "fell asleep" or woke up or whatever I'm supposed to call it.

It's empty. No battles taking place. No snake. No noxiors. No crowd calling me Icarus.

No dead girl.

What happens to the Tenebra version of our bodies when we die? I wasn't here long enough to see. Did someone bury the girl? Did she disintegrate or vanish like when we return to the Real World? I picture Luc and the others burning her body on a funeral pyre. Or maybe that's only for someone they want to honor.

I don't want to know what they do to the corpse of an enemy. Nail it to a cross? No, they put Jesus on the cross when he was alive, not dead.

I push myself to my feet and look around. My emotions seem even more out of control. I suddenly have a greater appreciation for my mom when she had a struggle day. I used to think she simply chose not to try on those days. I wish I could take back some of the words I said to her.

I'm also glad she's not alive to see this virus take the life of one son and the soul of the other.

Sweat trickles down my temple, though the sky is no brighter than the other times I've entered Tenebra. In fact, the pillars of fire on either side of the Arena are practically at a simmer. So then why am I so hot? Something tickles the back of my mind—some piece of crucial information I need to remember. I can't quite grasp it.

"Best come inside, Icarus." Crixus stands on the other side of the Arena, holding the gates open. He doesn't look pleased to see me.

I cross the Arena. "Where's the girl's body?"

He shakes his head. "Don't do that. Don't make the Spore human. She infiltrated the Arena and tried to kill you. She tried to gain more power, but you stopped her." There's no conviction behind his words. He knows as well as I do that I abandoned every piece of his advice and murdered after I swore to his face that I wouldn't.

"She looked human," I mutter, wiping more sweat from my brow. "Even though she smelled like a Spore." I can still smell the strange mix of manure and hot tar, though it's dimmer—like a memory and not an actual scent.

But isn't everything in this place a memory? Or at least in my mind? Even scents?

"Spore dust is deadly." Crixus looks me up and down. "I'm surprised you didn't get infected. You're lucky, you know. You survived. The Emperor says you saved us."

Lucky. Survivor. Savior. I want the words to make me feel better, but my gut and soul know that even though the girl was an enemy, that doesn't excuse what I did. It wasn't even in self-defense. She'd relinquished her daggers.

"So what now?" The question ends in a harsh cough. I frown and shake my head.

"You're a free man. A citizen. You can start a life in Tenebra."

I cough again. Harder. The tickle in the back of my throat turns into a burning in the deep part of my throat.

"Yippee. So the graduation test really *is* to kill someone."

"Not always. But it doesn't matter now. It was more than enough for you to be granted your citizenship." He holds out a sealed scroll. His hand trembles for a mere moment. Is he afraid of me?

One glance at his face says no. He's definitely not afraid. He doesn't seem to have ever felt fear. But that tremble . . . something's up. I keep watching the scroll, trying to catch another tremor.

"It's your temporary citizenship," he says, misreading my hesitance. "The final one needs the Emperor's seal, and that's when you'll choose your conscription."

"Conscription?" No one mentioned that before. "Luc has an army?" I still don't take the scroll, as if touching it will imply my acceptance of the rules of all things Tenebra.

"That's one of the options. It's a mere three-month conscription of your choice. You'll see the options inside the scroll."

I'm not about to serve in some Roman army for three months. I don't even care for the citizenship. I can't seem to care about anything right now. I cough again.

Crixus steps forward and tucks the scroll into the side of my belt. "You okay?"

"Are you?" I snap. Opening my mouth makes me cough more. Sweat pours from my brow and gets in my eyes. What is going on? My next breath is labored.

Then it comes back.

There's fire in the Real World. Near me. Threatening my physical body.

"I'm trapped," I say hoarsely. No. Wait. I'm *burning to death*. I need to wake up. I grab Crixus's arm. "Take me to Luc."

"The Emperor? But–"

"Now!"

Crixus seems to piece together the urgency of the situation and hustles me from the Arena. "We'll go the back way."

I can hardly breathe past the running and certainly don't

pay attention to the route we take, but it's far shorter than the first time he took me to Luc. It involves keys and closed doors. I stumble. Crixus drags me by the leather straps of my noxior garb across my chest, and I'm not sure I'd be able to move without his help, though it seems to tax him.

Up the escalator.

Through the disappearing door.

I land on my hands and knees in the room that used to be a man cave but is now a Roman atrium with a pool in the floor, a hole in the ceiling, and short lounge couches along the wall. Two young girls are in the room, tidying and cleaning.

"Luc!" I holler, managing one painful, deep breath. I want to slip into the pool in the floor–douse the heat in my bones and lungs. But even now in my agony I know it's all a dreamscape. It will do nothing to help me.

"He'll be here any minute," Crixus says anxiously. He flourishes a hand at the girls, and they scuttle from the room. "Keep holding on."

"I'm burning to death!" I rasp in panic. "On the other side. I entered the Nightmare in flames. You have to wake me up."

"That's impossible."

"If the Spores can do it . . . there must be . . . a way." I heave scratchy inhales between words. Already, I can tell I'll be too late. My voice drops.

"I deserve this . . . after what . . . I've done."

For a moment Crixus stands there, statuesque with a stony expression. Perhaps remorse is foreign to him. After all, he sees people die nearly every day. He's practically their executioner. But then he settles to one knee beside me.

"There's always redemption, noxior."

I shake my head. "Not . . . for me."

A thunderous swoop of wings precedes a body falling through the hole in the ceiling and landing in the pool with a splash. Luc wears a black tunic that looks like it was made of woven shadow.

He sees me and crosses the pool in three strokes. Climbing up the edge of the pool seems to take extra effort. His arm slips once, twice. Crixus comes to the edge and helps Luc out of the water.

"Cain's burning on the other side," he informs Luc.

"Help me," I croak. "I'll join you, Luc. I'll save your father. Just . . . save me."

Luc sits on the edge of the pool, breathing hard from the exertion of climbing out of the water. But a look passes between us. He knows I'm not making an empty promise—if he saves me, I will be his to command.

"Crixus, go to the lararium. There's a sealed box on the center pillar. Bring it back to me."

"It's too far—"

"Go!"

Crixus bolts from the room. I fall to my knees, sucking in a breath but finding my lungs won't cooperate. Roaring fills my ears. Wet fills my lungs.

"Hold on, Cain," Luc says quietly.

To what? Life? What little hope I have in Luc being able to save me dissipates.

"I . . ."

"Hold on," Luc repeats. "No matter what, don't lose consciousness. If you do . . . all is lost." I hear desperation in his voice. But it's not for me, it's for Galilei. For the cure. I'm our world's only hope.

I try to hold on. I really do. My vision flashes, and my arms buckle, drawing another hacking cough from my chest.

"Crixus!" Luc bellows toward the doorway.

My arms give out, and I collapse fully to the cool ground. Whatever Luc sent Crixus after, he's not going to get back in time.

"Just fight it, Cain," Luc begs, looking more like a young helpless boy than ever before.

"I . . ." My vision turns black. "I . . . can't."

The world spins out of reach and ends.

THERE'S A GIRL ASLEEP IN MY TINY house. I barely make her out through the dark shadows of a sun that set hours ago.

The girl is on my couch with a fire extinguisher in one hand and a damp cloth in the other. An oversize hoodie engulfs her head, cinched tight around her face. What would be the exposed part of her face is tucked under her arm and facing the cushioned back of the sofa.

I woke minutes ago, face up on the kitchen floor–almost in the same place I'd fallen trying to turn off the burner. The windows are open, and it's raining outside. My breaths come in raspy wheezes, and my throat feels filled with cotton. My brain wants to assemble the puzzle pieces of what happened, but I'm forced to take a moment and focus on breathing.

I woke up . . . that's a positive sign. But how? Luc's secret box?

A note rests on my table in front of the girl, soaked through with the foamy mess of what must have been the fire extinguisher's contents.

> Sorry about your little house. It was either this or let you burn to death. Also, I had to restart your heart so if

you're sore, I'm sorry about that too. It took only a few chest compressions, so I didn't have to kiss you or anything. Please don't be a creeper and kill me while I'm asleep. You don't have to let me stay here, but if you dump my body, please do so in a safe location.

Stranna

This girl saved me. She fought a fire and restarted my heart. Who is she? And why save a stranger?

I briefly pat her hoodie pocket for her Infection Time Card, careful not to move any other part of her. It seems invasive. I don't want her to wake and think I've done anything to her. But her pockets seem empty. No card to show how many Sleeps she has left.

I take in her resting form. What was she doing here in an abandoned neighborhood? She just happened to see my burning tiny house and decided to save me?

I don't buy it. Then again, she's left herself completely at my disposal.

Maybe she's like me and there's a draw in her to stay near the university: clinging to the hope of learning again someday. My fellow Draftsman students and I all had such big dreams when we entered college. Is that how every college student is? We think we're going to change the world until we actually start living in it and realize that if it had been possible to change the world, someone would have done it a long time ago.

Forget that–I can't even change myself, can't even control myself in a dreamscape.

I spot a backpack on the couch next to Stranna. The top zipper is open, and for some reason I know it'll hold the answer. It's like my subconscious has suspicions that my active mind refuses to acknowledge.

I move aside rolled articles of clothing and a few water bottles, crinkling some snack bags. Even though I'm famished, I don't pull them out. I don't want to see what food she has and tempt myself. But then I encounter a plastic grocery bag filled with a variety of soft things and clinking glass bottles. I open the mouth and peer inside.

My cure serum.

My heart drops in my chest, and I recoil as though scalded. She's one of my customers. That's why she was in the neighborhood. She was picking up her cure from the designated mailbox.

This girl can't afford more than a bag of chips and drained her bank account to buy my failed cure. And here she is, trapped in the Nightmare right in front of my eyes. On my couch. Experiencing the failed cure for herself. Writing me a note not to kill her or dump her body in a river.

Is that why she saved me? Because she recognized me as the cure maker? Does she think she'll get a free cure or that I'll be able to fix the problems?

She didn't say anything in her note about who I am. But if she literally restarted my heart, how could she not recognize me?

I flop onto the other side of the couch. "What a day." My voice doesn't sound like it belongs to me. "Murder someone at night, burn to death in the morning, rescued in the evening."

I shouldn't make light of it, but I have to, otherwise I'll go insane. Well, more insane than I already am. The two lives are starting to blur together. When in Tenebra I hardly remember life in the Real World. And here in the Real World I recall everything from the Nightmare with creepy clarity. They're at war with each other. I need to stop trying to separate the two. They are both my life, and if I don't let them work together, I'll end up wasting both.

I've been given a second chance in both worlds.

Luc wants me to save his father. Since my cure failed, it looks like I'll need a LifeSuPod after all. And with this girl, Stranna, having rescued me while I ruined her life . . . I feel obligated to take her body with me and care for it the best I can. Maybe I can bargain for a second LifeSuPod.

Better than that, I can save Luc's father, get the cure, and free humanity–Stranna included. Her note implies she doesn't have a place to go. For now, The Fire Swamp is her new home as far as I'm concerned.

After killing the Spore woman, I have no reason not to work for Luc. He is the most powerful man in Tenebra with a tempting offer and the only key to salvation I can see. And I seem to be the only one who can help him. If I succeed in saving Galilei, we can distribute the cure together.

If I fail and I'm trapped in Tenebra forever, maybe I can set up a new life for myself. The citizens of Tenebra idolize me. I'm a celebrity in that world. If I can get myself to swallow my guilt and self-disgust, maybe I can have a decent life.

Besides, the Spores killed Nole. If I join forces with Luc and his knowledge maybe we can find more answers about the Spores and, subsequently, how they control the Nightmare. We could end them. Free the kids.

I run a hand down my face. My hand comes away covered in thick soot. I wipe it off on my pants, then push myself off the couch. I need to clean up and make myself busy to get some relief from my thoughts.

I take in the mess of The Fire Swamp. The stove looks like someone hurled ABE powder all over it and the meager kitchen. Black potatoes sit in a half-melted pot. The ceiling above the stove is blackened. Part of the wall is charred rafters, stripped of insulation and paneling. Ash rests over everything else.

Fire Swamp, indeed. Nole would get a kick out of how it's living up to its name.

Structurally, The Fire Swamp seems salvageable. Maybe movable. Even livable. This girl, Stranna, saved me. Whether or not she had ulterior motives, I can't deny that she saved my life.

Not Luc. Not me. This girl–a stranger. Maybe it really comes down to simple humanity: she saw me dying and chose to save me. Somehow I sense that if she faced a Spore in the Nightmare she wouldn't have killed them.

Burn blisters cover both her hands and some exposed hair curls up in singed strands.

Good people still exist in this sick and dying world.

I won't let that go to waste.

I gingerly make my way to my bathroom, brushing against the soot around the left side of the door frame. The first thing I do is run the tap and chug water, even though I typically save that water for emergencies. It temporarily soothes my throat but doesn't eliminate the cough. That will take time.

I wipe soot from the mirror. It mostly smears but gives me a wide enough clean streak to see my face. For a startled second, I think someone else is in the squished bathroom. I don't look like myself–a coating of ash adds a hardened tone to my eyes.

There's no way Stranna recognized me as the guy on Nole's video channel.

I turn to the shelving above the toilet where I keep toiletries and first aid. The box that held my standard first aid kit has melted into a blob of plastic. I crack it open in pieces only to find burned or disintegrated gauze pads and a burst tube of antibiotic ointment. I locate a single cough drop in the narrow cabinet above the sink, the wrapper is covered in dust and the bottom part of the drop melted to the paper. I peel it away and tuck it into my cheek.

There's nothing to help with Stranna's or my blisters.

I change my shirt and use the inside of my burned one to wipe the soot off my face. My stomach churns, so I head back into the kitchen area. I eat a raw potato and try to tell myself it's just dirt-covered celery. Because obviously that's better. I read in a book once that someone can live solely off potatoes. That doesn't make it taste better, but my stomach appreciates it all the same.

Then I film my last live video to Nole's channel.

"Sorry I disappeared." I give them a scan of the burned part of The Fire Swamp. "Almost died, but I suppose I deserve that after what's happened with the serum." I shake my head. "I'm sorry. I know it's not enough but I'm really sorry. I tested it on myself, and it worked . . . once. I didn't want to wait. I wanted you all to have a chance at life. It was only after I sold and delivered it to you all that it didn't work for me the second time. I don't know why it failed. I-I'm so sorry."

Sure you are. A commenter says.

Give us our money back.

There's no grace to be found in the chat. No understanding. I can't blame them.

I close the computer and whisper, "I'm sorry," one last time. Then I get to work.

I chuck anything ruined out the window and into the street. I check on the chickens in the back–the majority of the fire was toward the front of The Fire Swamp, so they and their coop are fine, except they're very hungry. I should clean their pen, but my time is getting shorter, so I dump the last of their feed inside and grab the two eggs to cook if I get the stove working again. I'm lucky the whole thing didn't explode.

I'd leave an egg for Stranna, but I don't know if or when she'll wake again.

The blankets in the loft are still usable, even though they smell like smoke. I fold a couple and tuck them on the floor by the couch in case Stranna rolls off at some point. I hope she doesn't mind going on a little trip. If I knew where her home was, I'd drive her there.

I check The Fire Swamp multiple times to make sure it's

not going to crumble from the burned timber, but it holds. I hop into my rickety truck and start the engine. It takes a couple rumbles to get going. The neighborhood shrinks in my extended side-view mirror along with the tops of the distant university buildings, taking the many hopes and dreams Nole and I shared with it.

I drive to the storage-container lot on the other side of town. After enough walking and exploring, I've learned which route to take so I won't get The Fire Swamp stuck. I could have made this drive without The Fire Swamp, but I don't want to risk leaving Stranna behind in a parking lot where anyone could loot it. She'd gotten in, after all, so anyone else could too. And they would not be as likely to pass over a vulnerable girl as they would a vulnerable guy. I have a chance to help, keep her safe.

It's not enough to atone for the other things I've done, but it's a start.

I arrive at the storage unit. It's a cloudy night, so the alleyways between units seem particularly dark. Nole and I rented this after we sold Mom's house. When we moved into The Fire Swamp, we put her belongings in storage, having no idea the virus would take over mere months later–one of the best timing accidents we'd had. We paid only two month's rent before the owner got infected. He forgot to charge us. Another month later, he died.

We kept the key.

Some people turned their storage units into places to live until the virus trapped them. Because of that, I'm on alert whenever I visit. They could jump me. Especially now that my face is blasted all over the internet, jabbering about a cure.

I'm such a dummy. I thought being public–being vulnerable in live videos–would build trust and take people on the journey with me. I thought it would gain respect for Nole's work and show people I was picking up his torch.

Instead it's put me in more danger and tainted his entire memory.

I should have left the soot on my face.

I hop out of the truck into shadows. Always shadows. Always night. I miss the sun. Tenebra may have "daytime," but it can't replicate nature. It is limited by man's imagination, which is a far cry from the creativity of God. No matter how bitter or resistant I am toward Him, I still know He gets the credit.

I haul open the storage door to the sight of a dozen five-gallon gas cans. Two are empty from the last time I came here. I empty four straight into the tank of my truck and then load the remaining six into the bed. Then I collect the last of my food supply.

It's not much. A few boxes of pasta that make my mouth water just looking at them. A bag of potatoes that have gone to seed. Some canned beans and a jar of peanut butter come along too–the self-control I had to enact to keep myself from eating these a long time ago is a thing of the past. I unscrew the peanut butter and take a huge scoop out with my fingers. I allow myself ten whole seconds to savor it, then I haul the contents into the cab of the pickup and bid the storage unit goodbye, along with what's left of Mom's furniture and belongings.

I'm tempted to leave the door open or the key somewhere for someone to access if they need to, but I might need to come back someday. So I lock the door and pocket the key.

By now, some of the clouds have moved on, and the moon seems to shine on me like a spotlight.

I climb into the cab of the truck, start the engine, and press down the clutch. A prickle runs down my spine, and I look up.

A man stands in the narrow space between storage units, illuminated by moonlight.

He blocks my way out, a rifle aimed at my head.

18

"GET OUT OF THE TRUCK," THE MAN with the rifle shouts. "I want the real cure. The one you swallowed."

So it begins. He thinks I sold him a vial of olive oil while I kept the real cure for myself. Does he even spare a moment to wonder what I'd gain from that? Absolutely nothing.

"Get out of my way," I respond with as much gusto as I can. Unfortunately smoke inhalation has turned my voice into a wheeze. I'm not sure he even hears me.

He takes aim with the rifle. "Have it your way."

I duck beneath the dash, but he doesn't fire. Instead the truck shakes. I peek out the back window to see another man tossing my last six gas cans out of the bed of the truck.

"Hey!" I pop open my glove compartment and pull out Nole's handgun. It's a revolver with six bullets and six chambers. Why Nole ever thought this was cool is beyond me, but at least I know how to use the thing.

I aim through the window but can't make myself shoot. This isn't a dreamscape. I can't blame my actions on heightened emotions. I don't want to kill. Again. Especially when it's someone who paid me their life savings for a failed cure.

The man throws a fourth gas can over the edge, still oblivious to the fact I have a weapon. I drop the barrel and shoot low. The glass shatters, and the man falls over the edge of the truck bed with a cry. I aimed for his leg, but there's no telling if that's what I hit. The rifleman shoots, and the windshield explodes in a shower of glass. I pop up and aim with my revolver, but he's nowhere in sight. I glance out each window and catch movement in my side mirror.

The man yanks at the door of The Fire Swamp.

Stranna.

I shoot a wild bullet his way in the hopes of deterring him. He ducks, but then pulls on the door again. Even though I locked it, the frame is weakened by the fire. It won't take much more–

The door tears out of the wall so suddenly the man loses his footing. I shove the truck into gear. It jumps forward as I let off the clutch too fast, but it works in my favor because the man isn't quite able to mount the wheel well to enter The Fire Swamp.

We crawl forward, and I shift into second gear. The exhaust belches a burst of black smoke, but she gets her wheels under her, and we pick up speed. I take the corner around a line of storage containers too sharply, and one scrapes along the side of The Fire Swamp until it catches on the door gap and tears off a piece of siding.

I don't stop.

The rifle goes off again, and something slams into the side of the truck.

I don't stop.

He yells profanities and shoots again, running after me with an awkward gait.

I don't stop.

I lumber over the curb, drive through one of the barrier gates, and make it to third gear once I'm on the road. I finally reach a speed that can't be overtaken on foot. I drive with my eyes level with the steering wheel in case another bullet comes from behind. When I glance at the clock, my heart jolts stronger than a rough shift to fourth gear.

5:53 a.m.

Seven minutes until the Nightmare comes for me. I drive as fast as I can to put some distance between me and the storage units. The guy and his pal got some gas cans out of their attack. Hopefully that will mollify them.

I get onto the freeway, dodging the few stalled cars abandoned in lanes or on the side of the road. There aren't that many, but there are enough to make me nervous. Anyone could be living in those cars. Or dying in them.

A look at the clock. Three minutes.

I take an exit onto an overpass that bends high into the sky over the other freeways and keep to the center lane as much as I can so it's harder for anyone on the ground to spot me. With two minutes left, I stop the truck there and leap out. For a moment I think of putting the remaining two gas cans somewhere safer—like the cab or even the living room—but if someone wants to steal them or mug me, they'll have nineteen hours to figure out a way to do it. No lock or key will stop that.

I lumber into The Fire Swamp to check on Stranna. She's on the floor now, cushioned by the blankets I placed there, face smashed into the base of the couch. I ought to put her back on the couch, but I opt for a quick letter instead. I want her to wake knowing she's safe.

You're safe with me. If you're still in the Nightmare Tunnels keep moving forward. There's light at the end. You can escape the Tunnels into a dreamscape. Once you get out of

the Tunnels, ask to see Crixus, and
then ask for Cain. Or Icarus.

I upend the couch and cram it into the doorframe until it's jammed so good it'll be a feat to get out, let alone in. That'll have to work for now, but at least it's a barrier against the elements and the curious.

Nightmare mist creeps in and I barely manage to crawl up the ladder into the loft. As I collapse on the mattress, my last thought is that I didn't get to eat my pasta.

"FATE SEEMS TO FAVOR YOU, CAIN." Luc toasts me with an earthen cup of something liquid.

I'm getting faster at mentally adapting to Tenebra when I wake. The Real World fades almost instantly. I don't know if that comforts or frightens me. I'm more bothered by the fact that I thought of this place as Tenebra instead of the Nightmare and of myself as waking up instead of falling asleep.

"Last I witnessed, I'd stopped your heart," he says.

"*You* stopped it? How?" I push myself to a sitting position.

Luc rests on several cushions. Every time I see him, he's smaller, paler, weaker. He gestures to a locked box in front of him. "I have a theory on how to send someone back to the Old World. I tested it on you." He grins. "You were burning to death, right?"

Definitely. But somehow I survived. And not because of Luc. Because of someone else. Someone in the Real World. Why can't I remember?

"How nice to have someone to test it on," I say drily.

"You were dying anyway." He shrugs. "Now I can make some tweaks to it." He sips, seeming amused. He doesn't ask how I survived, probably because he knows I can't quite recall or put it into words.

"What happened after my heart stopped?"

"I waited for your form to fade. It usually takes some time, but you didn't fade. After a few minutes your heart started back up. You must have a strong will."

Even with the mental fog, I know it had nothing to do with my will. "So, my body laid here until I woke up just now?"

"No. You were unconscious. Once a person goes unconscious in either world, there's little anyone can do from either side. The mind has shut off–it can't awaken in the Old World or in Tenebra until it's ready. Your body remained here until you woke in the Old World. Then it disappeared. That's how I knew you survived."

The more I learn about this place, the more I realize I don't know. Luc seems to have studied all the rules and has all the answers. I suppose since he's been here almost from the beginning of the virus, he's had plenty of time to learn. A tinge of respect grows in me for what he's had to overcome to survive. I wonder what he's had to fight.

What he's likely had to kill.

Which brings me back to what happened the last time I was in the Arena. The girl–the Spore. I killed her, and Crixus handed me my citizenship to Tenebra.

Citizenship through murder. What does that say about the other citizens of this place?

Luc continues to sip his drink, watching me. He doesn't seem quite as confident as before. I can feel the pressure of a question hanging between us, held back by his force of will.

I speak first. "I'm still going to help your father."

He seems to relax and sounds more young man than Emperor. "Really?"

"Tell me what I need to know." He thinks I'm doing him a favor. But I'm doing it for me.

I murdered a Spore girl. I've doomed hundreds of people in the Real World with my cure. I've become a villain there. But in here, I still have a chance. I want to do something right.

Helping Luc save his father against the attack of the Spores seems a good place to start.

Finding a working cure will undo all I've destroyed.

But at this point, I'm no better than Hex Galilei. And I'm determined not to die that way.

A knock sounds on the door. At Luc's acknowledgment, Crixus steps in, bringing the usual stench of sweat and blood with him. Luc's nose wrinkles.

"Do you ever bathe, Crixus?"

At least it's not just me.

Crixus just grins. "I have Cain's final citizenship papers." He holds a scroll tied with a strip of cloth. I forgot the ones he gave me earlier were temporary. Like a driver's permit.

Now I get the license.

"Very good." Luc takes the scroll over to an ancient desk against the wall and unfurls it. He lights a candle and drops some wax onto the bottom corner of the scroll, then presses his ring into it.

Now it's stamped with the Emperor's approval.

He gives it back to Crixus.

"Thanks," I mutter. "So now I can walk through the coliseum fire?"

"As long as this scroll is in your belt, yes," Crixus says as he holds it up.

"And as long as you have permission to leave," Luc adds, ensuring I remember who's really in power here.

"There's also Tenebra clothing for you in the taberna." At my raised eyebrow, he elaborates. "The clothing stall in the Macella Quarter." Crixus holds out the scroll. "Just show the shopkeeper your papers. They should be your size."

"I don't want to dress like some Roman actor," I say. "My noxior costume is ridiculous enough."

"And I don't like to pay taxes, but that's part of life."

Taxes? Those things followed us into Tenebra? I take the scroll, tucking it into my pocket.

Luc pulls a leather portfolio from a cabinet and tosses it on the table. Then he sinks onto the couch as though his recent actions taxed him. Again, he seems weaker. It makes me think of Mom. And that's when I connect it.

His body above must be sick. That happens, even to people in LifeSuPods. They catch colds or the flu or have an asthma attack, and it still gets to them here in Tenebra.

He gestures to the portfolio. "Study these." Inside are ancient, crinkled, stained papers, but when I spread them out, the contents are quite modern. Floor plans, security details, and road maps of New York. Why bother having the facade of old parchment?

"My father's in a high-rise here." He taps at a space on the map. It's not too far from Somnus University, actually. "Where are you and your truck located, Cain?"

"I'm on the road." I think that's right. Or am I still at the university?

He leafs through the papers and tosses another one in front of me—a map of my city. He points to a spot on the edge of it.

"If you can make it to this warehouse, there should be fuel inside. As long as it hasn't been compromised."

I stare at the map, but my brain doesn't comprehend much. Something tells me this should be familiar, but it's like trying to recall details of something that only played in the background.

"Focus, Cain!"

"I'm trying," I growl.

University. Warehouse. High-rise. I try to set the routes and locations to memory. He's offering me a fuel-up, but how do I know if his sources are safe? The best way to conserve gas is to ditch The Fire Swamp altogether, but it's the last bit of home I have left with Mom and Nole gone.

I grab the papers and move to put them in my pocket before I realize I won't be able to take them with me.

Luc walks me through potential routes. "Once you get to my father's LifeSuPod, you'll find the new address inside my father's suit-breast pocket, tucked inside his handkerchief."

"Your dad's wearing a suit in a LifeSuPod?"

Luc waves a hand. "Why not sleep in style?"

Okay, whatever. Weird.

"The new location shouldn't be more than a quarter hour from the high-rise, so plan accordingly."

In other words I need to find Galilei immediately so I have enough time to complete this job. "And that secret address is where I'll find my LifeSuPod?"

"Precisely." He eyes me shrewdly. "Don't think you can double-cross me, Cain."

"I won't." What does he think I'm going to do? Leave Galilei to die and claim the LifeSuPod for myself? That'd leave us all without any hope.

"Sir." Crixus steps forward.

Luc shifts his eyes over to Crixus. "What?"

"I see a lot of potential for failure. Cain could get robbed, he might run out of gas, the warehouse may not have fuel . . . shouldn't there be a backup plan? I still wonder if fixing the power to the high-rise is a better option."

"You're repeating yourself, Crixus." Luc levels his centurion with a glare. "What was my response the first time?"

"I thought perhaps you'd reconsider."

Luc waves his hand again. "Go train the new noxiors."

"Sir." Crixus bows in submission and leaves the room. Poor guy, only trying to help.

"What do you think, Cain? Want to try to restore power to the high-rise?"

"It's a good idea, less complicated. But I don't have that skill set. That would have been my brother, Nole. And I couldn't guarantee that any power grid patchwork would hold. The Spores could just cut it again."

"Precisely." Luc gestures back to the parchments. "This new location is safe only because it's unknown. Out in the middle of nowhere. Off-grid. Solar and wind powered."

I raise an eyebrow. "And you're trusting me with the details?"

"*Trust* is an interesting word when desperation is involved." He locks the parchments back into the cabinet. "But you'll keep its location to yourself because that's where your physical self is going to be as well. Whoever you tell would become someone who would know where and how to kill you."

"Clear enough." We sit across from each other in silence for several minutes. We aren't friends and we certainly aren't going to be. This feels more like a dangerous business partnership where we both know exactly what we have to lose and what we have to gain. Once I complete this job for Luc and am either cured or in my own LifeSuPod, our interactions will be over.

I need to start building a life for myself in the Nightmare. In Tenebra. At least until I can track down another Spore and figure out how they control the Nightmare and the how and why of their ability to reenter the Real World. Until then, I might as well start using Luc's terms and playing his game.

"So what do I do while I'm in Tenebra? Buy some land? Build a house?" Already I miss my truck and tiny house. Whatever I build here will likely be carefully controlled since the dreamscape is only so big. I doubt they'll let me build anything on wheels.

"You don't build. Not with your talent."

"Talent?"

"With nightmist . . . you create." He gestures to my kris dagger.

"So far I've made wings that disappear after a few seconds,

a half-constructed spear, a dagger, and a chain rope. You think nightmist can make a *house*?"

Luc spreads his arms. "How do you think this coliseum was built?"

I look at the stone and only now realize what my mind has been neglecting. Nothing in Tenebra is actually tangible except in our minds. The foundation had been laid by the Draftsman who created the original virus, yet Luc figured out the loopholes of this ever-growing and ever-spreading virus. Nightmist and nightbeasts are all new. All created by the mind.

If he was able to figure out how to create when he's not the Draftsman, then I can too. "If this coliseum was made by someone's mind, what happens if that person dies?" If I build my own house, will it disappear if I get killed?

"It depends on their roots." Luc lifts his boot, and thick roots retract from the floor of the room into his boot like snakes. "The more you ground yourself in Tenebra, the more permanent your creations are."

I'm tempted to lift my own foot to see if I have any roots, but I'm not sure I want to know. I don't want tentacles attaching my body to this place.

Luc sets his foot back down, and though I don't see the roots grow into the floor, I hear the hiss and crackle of their movement.

"But you're not going to start with a house, Cain. First you need to create defenses. You may have left the Arena after killing a Spore, but those were acts of heightened emotion. You need to be able to create and defend yourself in calmer moments too. Like right now."

"How do I learn that?" Crixus only ever handed me a spear, unlocked the Arena gate, and told me to deny my anger.

"Simple." Luc lifts his hands, and the room dissolves around us. "I'm going to train you."

A SABER-TOOTHED TIGER PACES IN front of me.

Luc's version of training me is to put me in another arena—his own created one that's smaller and located in his atrium atop a coliseum tower.

Instead of fighting other noxiors or Spores, I'm up against his creations.

"He won't attack until I tell him," Luc says, standing across from me.

"How comforting." I don't really feel like fighting, especially not after the last battle. But I'm going to have to learn eventually.

I spare a moment to consider Crixus's tips on creating, tips that conflict with Luc's methods. I've never seen Crixus create anything, yet Luc does so with ease and never seems to lose emotional control.

I chose my instructor by his example.

Luc's tiger arose from a swirl of sand. It isn't a pet that will come and go or be chained up. It's at the whim of Luc's nightmist control. He just as easily could have created ten tigers, or one giant tiger twenty feet high. Is he the one who creates the nightbeasts that enter the Arena? The snake that devoured the noxior? The bull I killed?

The tiger growls.

"He's hungry," Luc remarks. "Just because I created him doesn't mean I can fully control him. Just like you can create a child, but they have their own will and personality. You can only hope they obey you."

"Have a lot of children, do you?" I keep my eyes on the tiger. Luc is the same age as me. I suppose he could have kids, but it's not like he's lived long enough to raise any.

He smirks. "What do you want to create?"

"Ideally, a stick of gum."

Luc snickers. "Focus."

"On what? You haven't done anything other than pitted me against a tiger." My irritation grows. Maybe it really *is* because of the lack of chewing gum.

"You're getting angry."

"Do you blame me?" I say tersely.

"Channel that anger into a word. Anger makes you want to do something. Destroy. Hit. Strike. Your choice here is to make something that will allow you to do those things."

Pressure builds in my fists when he mentions hitting. I've punched plenty of walls before and learned a painful lesson with a wrapped hand, bleeding knuckles, a furious brother.

Nole hated displays of anger. He always talked about self-control. I was never any good at it. I tried to be, to make him proud. Whenever he lost his temper, he immediately apologized afterward. I tended to stomp away and stew in my bitterness.

"Humble human nature tells you to fight the anger," Luc is saying.

I want him to stop talking, but I don't know if that's just irritation.

"Suppression is unnatural. Your body feels anger for a reason, so you need to give it a target. Instead of choosing a target that already exists, make one."

I try to direct the waves swelling in my mind. He says I'm feeling anger for a reason, but that reason is that emotions in Tenebra are heightened. It's this place. It's Tenebra's fault.

Saliva slips down the fangs of the tiger and drips on the floor.

"Hurry, Cain," Luc says in soft warning.

What does he mean *make* a target? A creature? A thing? Like the dagger?

The tiger growls.

I growl back, and some of the tension in my chest releases. My nerves tingle. I focus on the tiger and think about what I'd do to defend myself, then to release this buildup of energy. My first thought is to shoot the creature if it charges, but then I imagine fighting it. Tackling it the way another tiger might. A stronger, larger, fiercer tiger in a showdown I might see in a documentary.

Another growl. But this one comes from beside me.

A second saber-toothed tiger–larger than Luc's–flickers with extra tendrils of nightmist curling off its back. Did I create this?

My breathing slows. My anger and emotion settle into something calm. Cool. Detached. I glance at Luc.

He shakes his head with a half smile.

"You truly are amazing, Cain." He says it the way a professor might. Impressed with my skill but still acknowledging that I'm not as skilled as he is.

I'm okay with that. I'm used to that. I'm not used to being the smart student. Yet here in Tenebra, I'm Icarus. I'm the guy who created wings on his first visit to the Arena. I'm the guy who killed a Spore and befriended the Emperor.

And now I just created a tiger. This is not like a spear or a dagger. Up here the battle of emotion has been far easier than when I'm in the Arena.

"How do I get rid of it?" I put plenty of distance between

me and the nightbeasts, now that the two tigers eye each other instead of me.

"Ah, that's the trouble. You don't." Luc gives a clucking sound to his tiger, and it lunges.

With one swipe of razor claws, it slices open the throat of my tiger. Mine falls to the ground dead, liquid shadow blood pulsing from its neck. Then Luc throws a dagger into the skull of his own tiger. It flumps to the ground. A stream of shadow blood comes from its temple.

I stare at the spot where my tiger lays. Killed before its first real fight. Before its first meal. Something feels rotten about the death of the nightbeast even though my mind formed it. It wasn't real . . . right? Yet somehow I feel dishonorable.

No more than when I killed that girl.

I need to stop thinking about her. I need to stop letting that haunt me. According to Tenebran citizens I did a good thing. I was avenging Nole. Instead of a murderer I'm a Tenebran soldier–or tiro, or whatever–defending his people.

But they aren't my people.

This isn't my home.

And Nole would be ashamed of me.

I killed her because the Nightmare infected my emotions and took control of me. But even as I allow this thought in, I know I could have stopped myself. I could have stayed my hand and let her live. But I gave in. I gave in and I paid for it. Though no one else saw me this way, I will always know myself as a murderer.

Murder comes from the heart before it comes from the hands.

"Very good." Luc sinks into a chair. He seems unnerved. "I expected an object–a cage, maybe. Or a whip. Not a living, breathing, nightbeast. How are you so advanced already, Cain?"

Nothing feels advanced to me. I still feel lost in this world, struggling to understand how its nightmist magic works.

"I wanted to be a Draftsman."

He nods. "You would have been an excellent one. But now you get to do even more than a Draftsman could–instead of creating one world and pressing Play, you get to create as you go. The more you create, the easier it will get. And then you can get more complex. Your nightbeast was still a bit wavery. Commit to its creation. Don't hold back your emotions."

"My anger, you mean."

"The faster you're able to channel it into a creation, the less hold it will have on you." He tosses me a small leather pouch. It plops halfway between us, victim of a weak throw. I cross the space and pick it up. The pouch clinks upon my grabbing it. Coins?

"Go treat yourself to something. A new sword, a nice meal . . ."

"A nice meal," I say flatly. "It's not like it affects my real body."

"But your mind processes taste, hunger, satiation. And because food and drink are very much a part of this world, they will affect your Nightmare form the same as if you were in the Old World."

I'm not ready to celebrate or revel. I still want answers. I need to find the Spores. But I don't expect them to let me waltz in and ask a few questions. Not after I killed one of their own and not if they know I'm helping Luc.

I leave Luc's training and venture into the coliseum proper. I take it in a bit more now that I'm not burning to death or overwhelmed with the New World. It still amazes me that this coliseum has an Arena, yet it's also a city. I gaze at the broad street that forms its circumference, protected by the high walls with locked gates and bars for windows, opened to the sky.

The road is made of cobblestones. Homes are built into

the thick walls on each side. They seem to be for the wealthier citizens of Tenebra. The homes we passed on the outside of the coliseum were all abandoned–part of the original dreamscape design, but not safe enough for anyone to dwell in. Is that where the Spores live?

I see very few children. Those I do see band together and play outside the front of a home in small groups of two or three. The adults without children seem weighed down.

No wonder the citizens attend the Arena every day. It's the only way to know if their child has been rescued. How many of their kids have the Spores kidnapped? And what are they doing with them?

I find myself scanning the streets for brown hair, which is ridiculous because every other person has brown hair. I can't pinpoint why, but I think it has something to do with the Real World. My thoughts are muddled. I hate this part of Tenebra. Some things come to mind clearly, and others remain behind a misty veil.

I'm looking for a girl, but somehow I don't know what she really looks like. Why a girl? Why do I care?

I wander down the street labeled *forum* and am surprised to find shops carved in between homes and into the thick stone wall. No doors, just arches with little decoration aside from different paint colors–brick red, dusty brown, and other ancient-seeming colors. A few have cloth awnings and curtains tied to the side that would do little to deter a thief. I suppose they don't need to worry about poor weather or bugs. Unless the Spores make them.

My thoughts screech to a halt. If the Spores have enough control over Tenebra to enter and exit at will, wouldn't they also have control over the creation? Luc considers them enemies. The girl attacked me in the Arena. But if the Spores are so powerful, why don't they attack with nightmist? Make it darker. Send mammoth dragons. Why didn't the Spore girl in the Arena try to kill me with a bow and arrow or giant lion? Why come into the Arena herself?

It doesn't make sense.

I have too many questions and hardly enough answers. And as much as Luc wants me to stay in the coliseum, make a life for myself, stay alive so I can save Galilei, I have my own life to live while I'm in here. I'm a citizen now. And I'm not confident enough in Plan A–saving Luc's father.

So I'm making sure there's a Plan B and Plan C.

Luc can't stop me. He's not really going to strip me of my citizenship if I exit without a hall pass from him. I didn't enter another world simply to be controlled and tamed by its Emperor, no matter how much we can help each other.

I wander down the Macella Quarter–the market quarter as Crixus explained–looking for the exit gate. I'll walk the whole circumference of this place if I have to. The more my feet walk the stone slab streets and my eyes take in rough wood tied together to form stalls and canvas blowing in a wind gust, the easier it is to see this place as real.

The citizens seem to have embraced the ancient Roman attitude. They dress the part, know the words like *macella* and *taberna*, and sell goods to add to the world. Plush cushions for lounging on at a meal, leather goods like sandals, bracers, and belts. Nothing is colorful though. It all kind of blends in with the muted tone of this place.

A few stalls sell uncut cloth with some pre-sewn tunics, which reminds me of my Romanesque clothes waiting for me. My noxior clothing attracts plenty of stares and a few whispers of *Icarus*.

It's hard to imagine people giving up their way of life in the Real World, but as I look at the tunics, I realize they likely can't make much else in this Nightmare without the use of a sewing machine.

Hex Galilei must not have been fond of electricity since he

sent us all back into ancient times. But at least we don't have to eat ancient food. The food stalls smell and look incredible, and people swarm them with their coin purses. Do they not realize that this food doesn't benefit them? No calories, no energy . . . just useless flavor that is nothing more than a trick to the brain.

Yet they pay for it. They eat it.

Isn't that every dieter's dream? Eat whatever you want with no consequences? It's not like people in the Real World used to eat solely out of necessity–it was more of a culture and an addiction than anything else.

I pass a booth with weapons, some smoking with nightmist and others with shining metal. There are several kris daggers–though they're not double bladed with metal and nightmist–labeled "Icarus's Spore Dagger."

Wait, *my* dagger? They've already made duplicates of what I used to kill the Spore girl?

As I stare, someone actually buys one. Another person points at me and whispers. I don't like being watched, so I detour to the taberna stall and pick up my Roman clothes. I snort as I look them over and almost hand them back to the stall tender. Impractical sandals with leather straps that tie around my ankles and partway up my calves. There's a sleeveless, knee-length tunic with a belt and then a long draping robe to wear over it if I really want to look stupid.

I pull on the tunic and tuck the noxior garb into a satchel that slings across my shoulder in case I want to fill it with other imaginary items.

Once I look the part, I breathe easier at the lack of stares. I pass a physician's stall, where several people sit outside on benches, cradling a wounded limb or propping up a cut foot. Interesting. We can be injured in the Nightmare but also healed? How does that translate to our physical bodies?

A small stall tucked back in the shadows pulls me up short.

Counseling. I roll my eyes. People really would do anything to make a buck here. What sort of counseling can help anyone trapped in Tenebra? We all know we're going to die once our physical bodies run out of food.

Perhaps I stand staring too long because a woman steps quietly from the tent. "Want to come in for a rest?" She wears a long plain dress that brushes against the dirt, belted at the waist with a thick piece of cloth. Her hair is platinum white, shaved on one side and swept behind her ear on the other.

The air from inside the tent smells heavily of incense and something a little more foul. "I can sit on the ground just as well for free." I'm not about to waste my time with some person who preys on people's heightened despair emotions.

"We don't charge you to sit and have a breather."

"And I don't believe you're only offering me a breather."

She shrugs and pours water from a pitcher into a cup, then holds it out to me.

"What's the use?" I ask. "It's not like it'll actually quench my thirst."

"It will lessen the thirst you feel while you're here in the Nightmare."

She's the first person I've talked to who doesn't immediately call this place Tenebra. I take the cup and down the liquid, enjoying the sensation of quenching my thirst, even if it is a lie.

Only then do I realize how quiet the Macella has become—one of those odd moments where you feel like everyone has just heard your conversation. I turn to see if there's a cause. Though nothing seems off, a few people begin murmuring, and everyone's eyes seem to be searching.

Then a brief whiff of hot tar reaches my nose. I've smelled it twice before. In the cart from the Tunnel and in the Arena.

A Spore is here.

The people know it. Almost everyone has stilled. Almost. Two forms move, inch by inch. One is covered head to toe in a thick brown robe. A female, judging by her height and build. She grips the hand of a small girl with braided hair wearing noxior attire.

The little girl I saved from the snake.

Her head is ducked, and she follows close to the hooded figure. As they get closer, the smell gets stronger.

A Spore is trying to kidnap this child . . . right under our noses.

"There!" someone yells, pointing.

The hooded woman breaks into a sprint, dragging the girl behind her. The crowd acts as one with a burst of fury. One lady from a pastry stall throws a braided cord with a weight on the end. It tangles around the Spore's feet, and she falls. She's back up in a moment and gives a shrill whistle, yanking her hood farther down.

A bird's echoing cry pierces the air. Does every Spore have a giant pet phoenix?

It swoops over the coliseum wall and into the Macella. Several people scream and duck, but the phoenix glides right past them and grabs the little girl in one claw and the Spore woman in another. As it flaps to gain height, a vendor grabs onto the Spore's ankle and rips her out of the phoenix's grip.

She crumbles to the dirt, and it's like throwing raw meat into the den of a starved lion. Vendors and shoppers alike converge on her, kicking and screaming and stomping. One wields a club. Another a dagger.

They're going to kill her.

Even though I was guilty of that myself in the Arena, I can't watch it happen again. So I turn away. But that feels wrong. The phoenix keeps flying, taking the iittle girl with it.

No one can save her now. She's phoenix food.

I look back over my shoulder at the mob. Black smoke curls off shoulders and weapons of the attacking citizens, creating a cloud around the commotion. As new as I am to Tenebra, I still recognize the emotions being given free rein to create–and destroy. It's almost like the Macella was waiting for an excuse to unleash its fury.

Someone swings a club. The Spore on the ground screams.

My body jerks toward her of its own accord.

"Hey!"

No one heeds me. At the very least, the Spore should be taken to Crixus or someone for proper justice. Or questioned. It gives me chills to think people are allowed to enact justice based on the volatility of their emotions.

I shove through the edge of the crowd, peering through the growing nightmist. The figure crouches on the ground, covering her head. A man moves to swing his club again, but I grab his arm, my own wave of anger surging.

This is all the opening the Spore needs. She shoots upright and throws off her cloak. Lightning explodes from her body, shattering the nightmist as though it were made of thin glass. People scream, though I can't see how the light could hurt them in any way. It didn't affect me except for a blinding effect.

"Kill her!"

She runs three steps. Someone yanks her by the hair. She tumbles backward. I leap forward and catch her. She twists her body in my arms, ready to fight me off, and I finally see her face.

It's the same Spore girl from the Arena.

The girl I killed.

Except now she's alive. Whole.

And ready to claw my eyes out.

21

I KILLED HER. I STABBED HER TWICE and watched her blood leak out of her body. Watched her skin pale. Watched her eyes go vacant. Heard the cheers from the crowd and received the pat on the back from Luc.

Yet here she is. Alive. *How?*

I need to know.

The people pull her away from me and claw at her clothes, hair, skin. She tries to bolt. She doesn't seem to have another lightning burst to help.

"Wait!" I shove my way after her. I haul a man back by his tunic and shoulder a woman with a whip. "Move aside!" I holler.

No one listens.

The masses are too thick. I can't get through. "We need her alive! The Emperor needs her alive!"

Not even a pause in their assault. So much for respect for the Emperor—or even their little Icarus hero.

I roar and release my own emotions mentally, transporting myself back into Luc's atrium. The saber-toothed tiger forms with a swirl of nightmist, as large as a horse and more solid than my first attempt.

Without thinking, I jump onto its back. As though reading

my mind, it lunges into the crowd and tosses aside a vendor with a shove of its head. Someone notices it and screams.

The tiger snaps at her.

We bound into the center and step on a person or two to get there. Oops. I reach down and haul the Spore girl onto the tiger by the back of her tunic. She flops over his back, unsteady on her stomach but I don't slow. One of her hands grips my tunic, perhaps accepting that she's going to get caught by *someone*.

The tiger clears the crowd with a great bound, then shoots out of the Macella Quarter. It's all I can do to hold on. The Spore girl's nails dig through the material into my skin. She squirms, and I urge the tiger on in case the Spore decides to leap off its back.

I have too many questions to let her get away, but I have no idea where to go, having explored only a small portion of the coliseum. The tiger takes no directing, even when I want him to go one way over another. He is on his own path, darting down a set of stairs, into a tunnel inside the wall, out again and into an alleyway, past apartments that stretch to the sky in the stone walls.

The tiger finally stops in a shadowed alcove beneath an arch, where a small fountain bubbles. It laps at the liquid. No one is around.

The girl tumbles to the ground. I slide from the tiger's back and meet a sword tip pointed between my eyes. She's not holding it, but it seems connected to her mind–her fury. Just like the tiger is connected to mine.

I put my hands up in defense.

She takes me in, scanning from toe to head. When her eyes land on my face, she blinks.

"You?"

I get straight to the point despite the weapon poised at eye level.

"How are you alive?"

Her mouth quirks. "How are you not stabbing me again right now?"

"You have me at sword point this time." And I'm not stabbing her because I'm not consumed with anger. Does that mean the Spore fumes are rubbing off on me? Can that happen so quickly after one shared ride astride a tiger? I still smell the burning tar, but it's not as strong.

The tiger finishes its drink and then eyes us. Its gaze lands on the girl and her magical sword. It rumbles a low growl in its throat. I pet it behind the ears, and the growl turns into a purr.

I take a discreet step backward, both for her sake and mine. "We have to start somewhere."

"All right." The sword lowers and goes point-down but doesn't return to its scabbard. "Thank you for getting me out of the Macella in one piece."

If she were truly thankful, wouldn't she answer my question? "You're welcome." She seems to be favoring one leg. A beating like that would take down anyone. Maybe if I show her I care, she'll loosen up. "You okay?"

"I suppose we'll see." Her casualness shows that she's hardly bothered by the fact that she's facing the guy who killed her in front of a cheering audience.

"Why are you taking people's children?"

She levels her eyes at me. "Seriously?"

"That's why everyone attacked you," I say, though now I'm less confident.

"They tried to kill me because I'm a Spore." She huffs. "And you really are ignorant for how famous you've become."

Facing her like a regular person makes it much harder to imagine she and her kind are mass killers and kidnappers, but I can't let up. Not yet.

"How are you alive?"

"If you think I'm going to hand you answers that easily, think again." She brushes off her tunic then starts to leave.

"Hey, I just saved your life!" I jog after her. The saber-toothed tiger waits by the fountain, licking its giant paw.

She rounds on me. "A little reminder. You *murdered* me. So excuse me for not thanking you for not doing it a second time."

"You were coming right at me in the Arena. I killed you in self-defense!" Only as the words come out of my mouth do I realize how odd they are. I'm talking to a girl who died by my hand. Talking to her about her death–trying to find out about her resurrection.

"Don't fool yourself. You killed me because you were a green noxior, drunk on anger. I wasn't coming for you. I entered that Arena for my sister."

The little girl with the braid. The girl her phoenix kidnapped is her sister? It had nothing to do with me or Nole.

"But you died."

She looks hesitant, then winces at the memory.

"Yes. That hurt very much, you know."

"Sorry." I can't let her go without getting answers. She's done what Nole could not and acts as though it's no big deal.

"I know who you are, Cain."

I pull up short. Cain. Not Icarus. She used my real name. It sparks thoughts, visions of my other life but, as usual, they're blurred and unfocused. I strain to recall them. I know bits and pieces–the big points. The cure. Nole.

Her eyes turn to storm clouds. "You're the man peddling a fake cure to those who are dying. You're handing them false hope and taking their money without a care in the world. I'm not about to tell you anything."

Yes. Yes, that's what I'm doing. I can remember my goal behind those things even though the specific memories of success or failure are muted.

"At least I'm trying to help people. You're surviving this

Nightmare and keeping the *how* to yourself. Your kind killed my brother because of the cure. Don't act like you actually care about anyone in the Real World."

She laughs. "The nightmist has truly turned your brain–or maybe this is simply what you're like. I don't even know who your brother *is*. We don't kill. Not if we can help it."

I roll my eyes. "Right. You're all little saints. I saw what you did to Erik and James and the other people in the Tunnel cart–"

"That wasn't–"

"And if you're so against killing then why did you enter the Arena with daggers?"

"To save my sister, whom you were *attacking*."

The nerve of this girl–but then I recall the fight. I'd used my kris dagger to threaten the girl with the braids so she'd stop resisting me. That was when the phoenix and this Spore girl showed up.

Was that really her whole reason for entering the Arena? It can't be. These people are child traffickers. She could be telling me anything to get away with kidnapping that girl.

"Why was your sister in the Arena anyway?"

"Because she was of no use to your Emperor. He's the one who kidnapped her."

"What do you mean?" Then I remember my first night in Tenebra, when Luc rode his stingray and lassoed the braid girl right out from the midst of the Spores. "How was he to know she was your sister? He was trying to save her. He *saves* kids." I've seen it. Tory. Eddie.

"No, he uses them while they can go in and out of the Nightmare. But once they age out and get trapped here in Tenebra, they are subject to the Tenebran law."

"Which is?"

"Survive the Arena to get your citizenship. Surely you know at least that much. After all, I was your ticket to those clothes you're wearing." She walks off.

"Would you just stop?" I start after her, but then my feet quit working. They stick to the ground like I've stepped in wet cement. "What in the . . . ?" I yank enough to see roots going from the sole of my sandal into the dusty stone.

I try again to follow her, but the roots won't let me. I can't even take my sandals off. Luc didn't say anything about the roots restricting me. I let out a frustrated yell and reach for her.

Her sword bursts from her side and presses against my forehead again. I stop straining. The girl eyes the roots, and then looks at her sword. She seems annoyed.

"Really?"

Is she talking to me or the sword? "Can you call off your pet crowbar please?"

"No can do." She lets out a long sigh. "You're at a crossroad, Cain. I don't like you. And while I don't really want to do this, it's going to feel kind of good. For me, anyway." She takes the hilt of the sword in her hand, touching it for the first time.

I lean back, but my roots keep me in place. "What are you . . ."

She advances, her eyes shuttering. Detaching. Not quite looking at me.

Dread fills me. "Wait." I picture James. Erik. Nole.

She takes a deep breath, then rears back with the sword. I throw my arms up as a guard, but she's faster.

She thrusts the blade straight through my skull.

MY VISION AND BRAIN EXPLODE IN white pain. The world spins. I'm blind. I'm dead.

Wham.

Two worlds collide in my mind: Tenebra and New York. I live through both, in synchronization, and they spin past my eyes and memory like an old VHS on fast forward. Threads tie the two lives together. Everything is clear. Nothing is veiled in smoke or mist.

The emotions that come with that integration almost cripple me–Nole's death, the cure failing, stabbing the Spore, the desperation to live, selling my soul to the dark world of Tenebra, the guilt of being resuscitated by Stranna in the Real World and being stabbed by the Spore girl in the Nightmare . . .

I wrench myself out of the drowning flood of thought.

My vision flickers, eyes flutter.

I'm awake. Stone arches above me. I'm still in Tenebra. There's no sword in my skull and no Spore Girl. But something's different.

I sit up gingerly, a headache pulsing behind my eyes. But there's no more fog. I think of life in the Real World, in The Fire Swamp, and it's clear. A regular memory not dimmed or dulled by confusion. I can see both my lives with clarity.

Did the Spore girl do that with her sword?

I touch my forehead, still feeling the piercing heat of pain, but my fingers encounter no blood, wound, or even a scratch. I thought she was taking her revenge, but her weird sword seems to have sliced through the barrier between these two realities. It feels like a good thing, but that can't be right. Why would she do that?

Luc said the Spores mess with the mind. Twist truths. Deceive people into believing Spores are the good guys.

They got me. I've been Spored.

Yet I still believe she's an enemy. So maybe her Spore infection didn't fully work. Or maybe it's going to take time to chip away at my will. Either way, I push myself to my feet with care and look around. No one is here except my tiger. There were no witnesses to her attack on me. Not much time seems to have passed, though the Spore girl is gone.

I tuck away this new clarity. I can't tell Luc about this. He'll think I've been infected. But whatever she did to me, I can fight it. I *am* fighting it. I'm still me. But somehow I feel compromised.

What did she sneak into my head?

It was one thing to be suspicious of Tenebra and the Emperor, but it's a whole other thing to be suspicious of my own mind.

23

THE GAS TANKS ARE GONE FROM THE BED of my truck. The tank siphoned down to less than a quarter full.

Someone looted us while I slept.

Thankfully they left The Fire Swamp alone. Maybe it's the scorch marks on the outside, or maybe they didn't want to risk encountering someone who might wake from the Nightmare. No matter the reason, I'm thankful to be alive with at least a half-hour's worth of fuel.

It's nighttime, like always. I absentmindedly update my time card so it reads:

Infected: 22

Remaining Sleeps: 1

I don't know why I do this. It serves only to remind me of how little control I have over my own fate.

Stranna is where I left her. Unmoved. My letter is untouched. It's been 24 hours since I found her in The Fire Swamp, and if she hasn't moved in all that time, that means only one thing.

She's trapped in the Nightmare.

Her time awake is spent. She is now at the mercy of . . . me. It's up to me to keep her body fed, watered, and taken care of. Perhaps that's why she saved me from the fire: in the hope that

I'd be a decent soul who would keep her from dying now that she's stuck in Tenebra.

Why am I always thinking someone has an ulterior motive?

Perhaps because they do.

I sigh. I failed Nole. I failed myself.

I won't fail this girl. I may not have a LifeSuPod, but I have an extra bed and enough food to see us through for a few more days. At the very least I can keep her alive that long.

I assess the gas situation again. Whoever robbed me did it fast, not even sticking around to empty the whole tank—a small win. But it's not enough to get me to the high-rise. I go to tend the chickens, but they're gone, eggs and all. My gut twists. I don't blame the thieves, it's hard to say no to fresh meat. But those hens served me and Nole very faithfully in the worst housing conditions. I hope they're given swift deaths.

Back in the truck cab, I consult the map shoved in the glove box. I mark all of Luc's locations while they're still fresh in my mind. I have no choice now. I have to head to his secret fuel stash. I don't like it. He didn't guarantee there will be gas there, and I'll be on empty by the time I arrive.

It's an all-or-nothing trip.

I shift into gear and we head out. I stop a handful of times near abandoned vehicles to see if I can siphon any gas, but they've all been picked clean by other travelers. And there is no telling who is living inside those abandoned cars with guns at the ready.

I direct us back onto the freeway, letting my mind return to Tenebra and the Spore girl. She'd come back to life somehow—defying everything I know about the Nightmare. Proving that there's a cure beyond Galilei's knowledge. The Nightmare isn't the end.

So why wouldn't she answer me?

I understand her desire to run—I had, after all, stabbed her to death. But that was only because she'd been coming for me, or so I'd thought. I think about her claim that she and her ilk hadn't killed Nole. Supposedly they don't care about killing me either. I want to disbelieve her, but if she wanted me dead, she could have killed me there under the archway when I was vulnerable from her sword in my skull. Spill my blood, get my tiger to eat me.

Instead, she walked away and acted as though *I* was the darkness.

It takes 20 minutes to reach the part of town where Luc's fuel stash is supposed to be, and my meter blinks empty. I pass a few scattered lights. Not a good sign. If people live here they're already watching me. That means the fuel is probably guarded. Or gone.

I'm not feeling up for another battle. I'm lucky I wasn't blasted to smithereens by the rifleman at the storage unit. I reload my revolver. Six whole shots. I park the truck and The Fire Swamp along an empty street–easily accessible if I need to make a break for it.

Luc sent me here. I have to trust that he set things up so I could get gas without dying.

I've hardly taken a step when a child's voice says, "Icarus?"

I freeze for a moment, then relax as a little girl with bobbed brown hair steps out of the shadows. A boy is at her side, an inch or so taller and far more stern than his age should allow, but neither child looks older than 8.

"Hi," I say gently so as not to startle them. "Yes, I'm Icarus. Or you can call me Cain."

"The Emperor said you'd come!" the girl says. "We've been keeping your gas safe." She looks behind me like I might have a backpack or something. "I'm really hungry, but I've been patient!"

"We've all been patient," a firm voice behind me states, followed by the cock of a gun.

I slowly lift my hands, my revolver tucked tight in my belt.

"I'm not here to hurt anybody." I dare a glance over my shoulder. A man, late forties, holds a rifle at the ready, but he doesn't look like the type who'd shoot. Casual tennis shoes, jeans, and a T-shirt that says *Dad Beast* on it with some dumbbells beneath it.

I cautiously turn. "I'm with Luc. The Emperor."

"I knew it!" A girl of around twelve pops out from around the corner. "You're finally here!"

"Get back inside, Becca."

"But, Daddy–"

"Inside."

She steps back into the shadows, but her silhouette remains visible. She doesn't go back inside, which likely means I'm safe. This guy is protecting his daughter, not trying to rob me.

"I'm here for a few cans of fuel," I say. "That's it."

He gestures to the gun in my belt. "Drop it and you can come inside."

"We can both leave our weapons out here," I counter. Doesn't he know that no one drops their weapons during an apocalypse?

"Leave it in your belt then, or I will shoot."

I follow him to a thick, dented metal door. The two little kids trail after me, but the man stops. "Not you two. Stay out here."

"But you said–"

"I *said* stay out here." They don't argue, almost like they've had a similar exchange with him before.

I hazard a guess. "They're not yours?"

"They're lackeys of the supposed Nightmare Emperor."

"Lackeys?" I swallow a laugh. "They're children."

"I don't care. They're not allowed near me or my family. They're only here to make sure you find this place and get what you need. They told me enough. I can take over from here."

He makes it sound like he's doing all of us a favor, but I can read between the lines. This guy is still trapped in the Tunnel, and he learned from these kids that there's hidden fuel. He set up his own camp.

Now he's in charge.

His daughter Becca skips inside ahead of us. It's odd seeing something so cheery as skipping when her father threatened my life moments ago.

The man walks across the great expanse of a cold concrete space. The opposite side of the room holds the first semblance of warmth. Some lit candles, piles of blankets, a little bookshelf, and four cots–one of which holds a sleeping woman and another acting as a seat for a young man.

To the right, in the corner, rest several gas cans. I catch a whiff of their contents.

"Help us with these, Zaff."

The man on the cot stands and tosses a cigarette on the ground, stamps out the ember, then stashes the stub in his pocket. "You sure about this, Clark?"

"When will you start smoking that poison outside like I asked?" Clark gripes.

"Sorry." Zaff gives an apologetic glance to Becca.

Clark heads over to the gas cans and picks up one in each hand. Zaff does the same. I follow suit. I don't ask how many I'm allowed, but six full cans is more than I expected. They help me carry them to The Fire Swamp, but not out of courtesy. I see their gazes scouting, assessing what I have. What might benefit them. I stay on guard.

They load the gas into the back of the pickup while I empty my two directly into the tank.

"Now get us food," Zaff demands, eyeing the door of The Fire Swamp.

"Are you going to share with those two kids?" I ask. I don't have much food, but I'm not about to hand it over to them if they're going to starve out the children.

"They're not ours," he restates sullenly.

At least he's honest. They're going to hoard it for themselves.

"Of course we'll share," Clark says with an exasperated sigh. I'm not sure if that's the dad in him or if he's merely trying to mollify me. Clark lowers his voice and comes closer to me. "We've gotta have food, man. The kids told us their Emperor said that would be the exchange."

"Luc never said anything of the sort to me." I place a friendly hand on his shoulder, knowing the route of honesty right now is the most dangerous to take. But I can't bring myself to lie to them.

"I don't have much, but I'll give you what I can." I grab the can of beans and a single box of pasta from the cab. After a moment's hesitation, I also grab the peanut butter. That's all that's in there, and I'm not about to open the makeshift door to The Fire Swamp.

Clark takes the beans, peanut butter, and the pasta box but looks disgusted. "That's it?"

"I'm sorry." There's a can of chicken broth in The Fire Swamp, but Stranna needs it. And I can't risk entering and exposing her to them.

The door to the warehouse opens, and Becca comes out, holding the hand of the woman who had previously been sleeping. Her hair is mussed, and she blinks wearily, waking from what seem to be hours–perhaps even days–in the Tunnel. She is bent over while she walks, her stomach so hollowed out she looks about to fold in half.

"See, Mom? He's got a whole house with him. I bet there's plenty inside."

The mom lifts her eyes. The moment they land on me, she staggers into her husband. "Clark. Clark! That's him."

"Who?" Clark looks at me.

Her bottom lip trembles. "The one . . . who made the . . . the cure." She lifts a tremulous finger. "You've killed us all."

Becca gasps and pulls her mom back toward the door.

"This is that guy?" Clark asks, incredulous.

Zaff grabs Clark's rifle and aims it at me. "We spent our LifeSuPod savings on that cure! We used the last of our own gasoline to pick up the vials."

I back toward the cab, slipping my revolver free. "I don't want a fight."

"Of course you don't!" Zaff yells. "You want to take our money, our gas, our food and split, leaving us to die!"

"Becca, get your mom inside," Clark says in a dark voice.

"Don't kill him!" Becca sobs. "Please! Don't kill anybody else!" It is the mom who tugs *her* through the door.

This isn't good. "I was up-front about everything." They need to know that I'm no charlatan. I truly believed in the cure. "It was new. I used it on myself, and it worked that one time. I took a risk in the hope of saving lives."

"Of robbing us." Zaff cracks his knuckles against the trigger of the rifle. "Serving false hope and profiting from it."

"I didn't profit. I charged only what it cost me to make–"

Boom. A bullet slugs me in the shoulder.

The gunshot echoes against the metal buildings around us. I'm on the ground. Disoriented. Burning pain. Bleeding.

"Check the house." Zaff reloads the rifle.

Clark kicks in the couch from The Fire Swamp door.

"Wait," I groan, my vision and mind spinning with shock and growing pain. I push myself up with one arm.

Boom. Fire explodes from my cheek. At least that one only grazed me. I raise my revolver, but Zaff kicks it out of my hand.

"There's food!" Clark calls from inside. "And a girl."

Zaff brightens. "I like both of those things."

Clark tosses two boxes of pasta out into the dirt and the can of broth. Then he emerges with Stranna over his shoulder. Her hair tumbles over her head like a shadowed river.

Zaff grabs a handful of it and lifts her head. "She's a cute thing too."

Rage explodes within me. "Leave her alone!" I kick out and catch Zaff in the knee. It buckles, and he falls to the ground, yanking Stranna partially off Clark's shoulder.

I see her face for the first time, and it's enough to paralyze me. Because I know her. I saw her mere hours ago in the Nightmare.

Stranna is the Spore girl.

The Spore girl I killed, who then came back to life and rode on the back of a saber-toothed tiger with me and stabbed me between the eyes. She's right here. It's the same girl who saved me from the fire.

Zaff slams the butt of the rifle into my ribs, and I jerk inward, curling against the pain. He turns back to Stranna. I don't know what he's about to do next. All I know is I'll die to keep him from doing it.

I roll to all fours, brace myself, then launch myself through the air. I tackle Zaff and get one hand around the barrel of his gun. He's a big man. He boxes me in the side of the head, and my vision goes black.

I strike out blindly, hit something. It hits back. I want to yell at Stranna to run but she's asleep. She's trapped in the Nightmare.

Zaff shoves me, and I roll to the ground, limp and fading. I use what little voice I have left to appeal to the one person who might have some humanity left inside them.

"Clark, let her go," I croak. "Please. You can have everything else."

"Take the girl inside," Zaff says. Clark looks between the two of us.

Please, I mouth.

He turns his back to me and walks to the warehouse. Becca bursts out, screaming, "Daddy! Daddy no! Uncle Zaff! Wait!"

Zaff pauses for a moment. "Clark?"

Clark stops his retreat. "Yeah?"

Zaff levels the rifle against my forehead. "Plug Becca's ears." There's a far off *flump.*

I close my eyes tight and wait for the impact–wait for the end.

A gun hammer cocks.

I flinch at the *thud* of metal on skull. I open my eyes and manage to scoot away as Zaff collapses face-first into the dirt. Clark stands behind him, the butt of my pistol in his hand.

He knocked out Zaff.

Stranna lays in the dirt a few yards from me. Becca bends over her. I struggle to my knees. "Thank . . . thank you. I–"

"I don't want your thanks," Clark growls.

Then he steps over and slams the butt of the pistol into my temple.

I WAKE TO SNIFFING. SOMETHING WET is at my ear. I twitch, and a creature lopes away from me, startled. I breathe in dust before I blink in my surroundings. Before comprehension comes my brain whispers: *something's wrong.*

I sit up with a groan, but my left arm buckles beneath me. My shoulder is in agony, and I can't seem to breathe. A headache stronger than the fires of Mount Doom slams behind my skull.

Low moonlight. The heavy silence of night. I manage to get my bearings. Dirt. Desert? All around me. There's desert in Tenebra?

Then I spot a dark form next to me. Stranna lies huddled on her side. The exposed part of her face is scraped and crusted with blood streaks.

I'm not in the Nightmare. I'm still in the Real World. Still awake. Tire tracks surround us. I'd recognize them anywhere: The Fire Swamp. It's stolen. Gone. There is one set of footprints—tennis shoes.

Clark.

He opted not to kill me or Stranna. His daughter got through to him. I can't say I'm thankful he dumped us in the desert. That's merely choosing a slower death for us. But it's a second chance. He took my offer that he could have everything else literally.

I squint at the sky, and my sluggish pounding head struggles to piece it all together. We're maybe an hour away from dawn. The Nightmare will come for me.

After that, I'll have one more Awake.

Just one.

I don't see how I can save Luc's father now. I've been stripped of anything of value. No truck. No phone. No revolver. Not even my belt. Just my T-shirt and jeans. I stick my hands in my pockets and am surprised to encounter a crinkle of paper.

My time card, my folded map, and my pack of gum. Two sticks left.

Small blessing.

I pop a stick in my mouth and close my eyes at the burst of flavor. It distracts my body from the pain for a moment. But the chewing reignites the burn on my face from Zaff's bullet. I need to get it together and figure out what to do next.

A spread of brown taints the dust beneath Stranna. I don't know why it catches my eye, why it sends my heart galloping. But then I realize.

It's blood.

Dried blood.

"No!" I scramble over to her. My shot arm collapses beneath me. I turn Stranna over and find the source. It's from her calf. A gunshot. There's another one in her back. She's not bleeding anymore–it's clotted. Why would Clark shoot her? She's been asleep in Tenebra this whole time. It makes no sense . . . until I think about the location of the wounds.

It looks like someone shot at her while she was being carried.

While Clark was carrying her.

Zaff. He must have regained consciousness when Clark was loading our bodies. Zaff shot at her–or maybe at Clark–and then Clark left us both for dead.

My anger surges. If I were in Tenebra it would explode into . . . something. A nightbeast to carry us to safety.

But there is no safety. Stranna is limp, and this isn't the Nightmare. If she dies here in the desert, it really *is* my doing. And she'll stay dead. I know that much.

Clark wouldn't have wasted gas to drive us very far, so we can't be more than a few miles from the warehouse. I pull out the map and unfold it, angling it to get a little light from the moon. I don't see any desert. This is New York. There's never been desert here. I lower the map and survey the hills and dirt. There's something unnatural about them—not made from nature.

Click: we're in a landfill, not a desert.

I stand and follow the tire tracks, one weary, aching step at a time, until I crest one of the hills. The tire tracks travel away from the landfill and down to meet an abandoned highway. I look at the map and scan the area around the warehouse. There are a couple highways that could be the one in front of me. I need to get closer to see a number. And a mile marker.

Two stalled cars sit in the expanse of what I can see in either direction. I think I see silhouettes of buildings stretching into the sky what looks like five miles or so away, but I can't be sure without proper light. I'm not sure I can carry Stranna that far in the state we're both in. Even if I could, what good would it do? We'd reenter the city with nothing.

For now, the cars are my targets. If I can get us in one of those and knock out the windows—or better yet, roll them down—we could be protected from the sun during my next Sleep without getting heat stroke. And I could figure out what to do from there.

I can't wait for someone to drive along. I don't count on a car having gas in it or a key to start it. I could try my hand at hot-wiring, but without gas that wouldn't matter.

I head back to Stranna. Her breathing is labored, and she looks pale, but I tell myself it's the lighting.

"God, help her." I pick her up with effort and sling her over my good shoulder. My knees threaten to collapse, mostly from hunger and loss of blood. Once I get us out of the landfill, I set my gaze on the green Suburban.

I owe this to Stranna.

I've never been the rescuing-knight type, but Stranna is giving me plenty of opportunity. Then again, I'm also the one who tossed her into the jaws of the dragon so there's that. If I fail now, Stranna won't resurrect. Not from this. This is real life.

For the first time I wish we were in Tenebra instead.

She groans, and I try to soften my shoulder beneath her, but I can't adjust her body or I'll drop her. I'm not sure I could pick her up again.

I stumble the last few yards across the flat dusty ground and finally reach the Suburban. I set Stranna down, then try the doors. They're all locked, so I smash one of the back passenger windows with a rock.

A burst of rancid heat comes out. I recoil and almost retch. A brief glance shows me the source.

A body. Some person captured by the Nightmare who died in their back seat.

I'm not about to clear out the cab and have us shelter in here. I check the gas tank. Bone dry. Likely the reason it's here.

I cover my nose and mouth and do a brief quick search of the Suburban. I find a half-drunk bottle of water and tuck it into my back pocket. Then I pick up Stranna again and start the longer trudge to the other vehicle–a small green Jeep–praying it isn't occupied by anything dead *or* alive.

The windows are already smashed, and the gas flap hangs open. Not occupied, but not good for anything beyond shelter.

I lay Stranna in the back and then give myself a long moment to catch my breath.

How has it come to this?

Luc, that's how. Luc promised those warehouse kids food, and the kids were taken advantage of by a needy family. I never should have gone there. I should have risked finding the high-rise with the gas I already had. I never should have sold that serum.

Never should have . . . never should have . . . never should have . . .

So many regrets. When will my life turn itself around and start making good for a change? Have I lost sight of that? I'm spending all my time in Tenebra training and surviving and helping Luc so I can get a LifeSuPod in order to . . . keep living and training and surviving. I'm living so much of my life trying to keep myself alive in order to live life.

An endless cycle.

There must be more.

I adjust Stranna along the Jeep's back seats and bunch my shirt under the bullet wound at her back. Then I use a seat belt as a pressure bandage of sorts around her calf. It's clotted quite a bit already, but all that movement from me carrying her has made both injuries bleed again.

No food. Hardly any water. No form of communication. I still have a half hour to . . .

What? Wait? Wait to enter Tenebra where I will hopefully enlist help from Luc? But what can he do? Send a group of eight-year-olds to save us?

This is bad.

I get back out and start walking. I venture over the next hill until I find another car—some beat-up old Volvo. Doors open, unoccupied. No gas. Aside from that, there are no other cars in sight.

Time's almost up. It won't do me or Stranna any good if I collapse on the road to burn up like a stranded worm.

I take note of our nearest mile marker and the highway number, then return to the Jeep and consult my map. We're farther away from the high-rise now. Of course we are.

I give Stranna a dribble of water. She manages to swallow it without choking, but also without waking. That's a good sign. I take a swig and then give her the rest in small doses.

I'm certain my time awake is almost over, so I use it the best way I can: brainstorming. My usual resourcefulness is stumped. I can't carry Stranna out of this, there is no working car to steal, we have no one to contact for help on this side, and we have only Luc and his servant-children in the Nightmare . . .

Wait. What about the Spores?

Stranna is a Spore. Her people can supposedly wake up when they want to. But if that's the case, why hasn't Stranna woken up? It's time I got answers. The Spores have them. The only question is will they give them to me?

I think they will. Because I have Stranna's body as leverage.

Nightmare mist gathers at the edge of my vision. Finally. For the first time, I welcome it.

25

"HOW COULD YOU BE SO CARELESS?" A spray of nightmist glass flies from Luc's hands at his outburst. He directs it away from me, but I take a step back all the same.

He falls against the wall, breathing hard. One hand gropes for the edge of a marble bench before he sits there.

I'm still out of breath after running up the stairs into Luc's atrium. Each inhale fights against the pain it brings in my bruised ribs and shot shoulder. I'd ask if he's okay, but I'm too irritated by his accusation.

"This was done by *your* kids who were guarding the gas! I was trusting you by going there in the first place."

It's strange to recall with such clarity everything that happened in the Real World. There's no disconnect, no struggle to pull up memories. Instead I woke up here in Tenebra as though it was a mere blink from one world to the other.

This is because Stranna stabbed me with her weird Spore sword.

"You should know I can't control people from here," Luc snaps. "Never ever blindly trust."

"I didn't trust them blindly. I trusted *you*. I was as careful as I could be." Except for having a recognizable face. It's all because of my stupidity with that cure attempt. How can trying to do good end up so badly? Could no one see that I was trying? Could no one see my motives, at least, were good? Sure, I failed but . . . where is the grace? I'm suffering from my failure too.

I should have worn a bandana or something to mask my face.

"Who else do you have in the Real World who can help me?"

"No one!" Luc's voice grows in ire. "You were my only man awake. If I had another one more reliable than you, I'd have *him* helping my father. All I have are useless kids who can't drive or lift anything heavier than a backpack."

"So I'm stranded at the landfill to die?"

He smirks. "Shall I send a kid there and tell them the highway information and mile marker?"

"You're being the childish one."

"My father is stranded in the high-rise. He's *dying*. Starving to death. Atrophying." Luc starts pacing, but his breaths come fast and thin. His entire frame trembles, and after only a few back-and-forths, he sinks onto a cushioned stool.

"What about you?" I ask quietly. "You aren't well."

"I know that," he retorts. "I just want to see Dad again. Before one of us is gone for good."

Even though I'm the one in imminent danger, I find myself doing damage control. There will be no benefit to letting Luc's despair take over. If he's given up on me, I won't get that LifeSuPod.

"You and I want the same thing." I keep my voice as calm as I can manage, even though I picture Stranna bleeding out in an overheated Jeep at this very moment. "We want Galilei alive. We need to find a way to make that happen . . . no matter what."

"I have no one." That seems to be all Luc can say. "This can't be the end." Small nightbeast creatures slip out of his hands and drop to the ground. Little snakes, snails, a mouse, a tiny badger that snuffs and snorts when it hits the floor. Luc doesn't seem aware of them. I've never seen him out of control like this.

I know what it's like to care about someone–to dread their dying and to miss them–but most of the world has had to face losing a loved one. Surely Luc has considered that maybe we won't be able to save his father in time.

Luc is young. As young as me. Maybe he's never lost anyone before. And I know from Mom's long, drawn-out end that the fear of loss can often be greater than the pain of it actually happening.

I can fix this. And I've already primed the pump.

"I have an idea," I venture. Luc seems desperate enough that he might consider it.

He stops and looks at me with the first glimmer of hope. "What? What is it?"

"Ask the Spores for help."

His hope vanishes, replaced by a glower. "They are *causing* this problem. They cut the power to the high-rise in the first place. They're trying to kill my father."

"But they don't know that I'm trying to save him." I need to find Stranna. She has no idea what predicament her body is in. Here in Tenebra, I'm her enemy. But after I rescued her from the Macella Quarter I think she'll listen to me. Her people will help me if it means helping her. That is, if she's not dead already.

"I can try to find them," I say. "Ask for help. Put on a face and get them to trust me."

"Why would they trust you? You killed one of them."

"Because I saved one of them in the Macella." I eye Luc's hands while I say this, waiting for him to create a gun to kill me as a traitor, but he sits there giving me his full attention.

"Explain."

"I had questions. About Nole. It was the only way I saw to ask them." I didn't tell him the questions were because the Spore girl came back to life. "The Spore didn't give me many answers, but I think maybe she'd give me more if I pretended to be on their side."

"That was foolish, Cain." He looks me up and down. "You could be Spored for all I know. To get that close to a Spore again is a death sentence."

"No more than the death sentence I'm already living. And I'm not Spored." I hope. "Do I smell like tar to you?" I don't wait for an answer–maybe because I fear it. "I'm trying to save Galilei and save myself. If I fail, we don't get a cure, I don't get the LifeSuPod, and I'll die. If the Spores distrust me, they kill me. Same end. But the Spores are the only ones outside of the kids who can go between Tenebra and the Real World at will. You said so yourself."

He is quiet a moment, but then relents. "Fine. But I want you to find their base. Both here and in the Old World. Find out where they stay and live. We need to cut off *their* power after all this is done."

I turn to leave, hoping he reads my silence as assent.

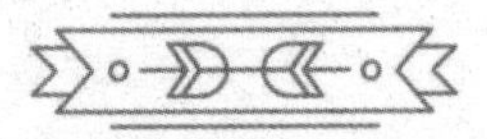

My saber-toothed tiger is dead.

It took me twice the time it should have to make it back to the fountain where I last saw Stranna in Tenebra. I came here for my tiger, assuming he'd be pacing and waiting for me. Hoping he would be. I'd been working on a backup plan in case the tiger had run off while I was in the Real World.

I didn't expect to find his carcass with a nightmist spear through his skull.

I stroke his enormous muzzle and give him a little scratch behind the ears. "You're a good tiger," I whisper, feeling oddly sentimental about seeing him dead a second time. He's still warm, almost like he's merely sleeping.

Which means this was a recent killing.

I snatch my hand away. The tiger stayed in this spot for hours, waiting for me to return. Then someone came and killed it. It could have been anyone, but the timing and the spear imply it was an intentional strike against me.

Maybe Stranna. That would mean she's nearby. But it's been so long since we spoke here. I can't picture her sticking around or killing the beast after it saved her, even if she sees me as an enemy. She saves strangers from burning tiny houses.

I manage a pained step. Now I have nothing to ride. My emotions are too muted beneath my pain for me to create the tiger again. I'm not even sure how that would work since it's dead. Would I create the same one or would it be like a sibling?

Nightmist is confusing.

I pull myself together and look around. "Stranna?" I whisper. Luc said Spores can enter the Real World at will, so she needs to wake up, to get up there and save us. Contact her people.

A shadow moves. "Oh thank good–"

Crixus steps forward. I swallow my words. He looks around, frowning.

"Who were you talking to?"

I casually avoid his question. "What are you doing here? Does Luc need something?"

He's assessing my dead tiger but doesn't seem surprised. Did *he* kill it? I don't know why that makes me so angry. He doesn't have a right to kill my nightbeasts.

"I'm here because you created a deadly saber-toothed tiger in the middle of the Macella and then ran away with a Spore. I'm sure you can see why I'm suspicious."

"I've already talked about it with Luc. If you want to know

the details, take it up with him." I turn my back on him. "I'm busy."

"Leave the Spores be, Cain. You're endangering everyone. You've killed one and earned your citizenship. Now go live your life."

"What life?" I growl. "I don't have a LifeSuPod. I'm on borrowed time." Crixus has never seemed worried about his own existence, which tells me his physical body is tucked in its own LifeSuPod somewhere. He wouldn't be Luc's right-hand man otherwise.

I turn back around. "How do I get out of the city?"

"The gate," Crixus responds unhelpfully.

I stride away as best I can with my injuries. The pain has lessened–possibly because being awake in Tenebra distances my mind so much from my physical body. Or maybe the pain is lessening because I'm dying. How deadly is a shoulder wound like mine?

I think I leave Crixus behind, but then I hear footsteps following.

"Leave me alone."

"Are you injured, Cain?" This is the first note of true concern I hear.

"What's it to you?"

"You're a citizen of my city."

"*Your* city?" I jab. "Are you the Emperor now?" I don't know why I'm so irritated. It's this blasted Nightmare world heightening every negative emotion. It makes me angry, which the Nightmare will exploit.

Crixus doesn't bite. I don't give him any information about my injuries. He stays right behind me as I slowly walk. My shoulder hurts the most and breathing is labored, but I gain energy with every step.

There should be several gates spread around the exterior wall of the coliseum. I suppose all of them are fair game for the citizens, but then I see crisscross chains across the face of the first one. No handle in sight. There's a crank on the wall, but before I can give it a try, Crixus speaks up.

"You'll be killed in minutes if you go out there."

I round on him. "Have you been assigned to watch me or something?" It can't be coincidence that he's always popping up wherever I am. And now he's following me. Trying to deter me. I get it. Luc wants to find the base of the Spores. But he asked *me* to do that. If he's sent Crixus to follow me, that means Luc doesn't trust me.

"You're injured, Cain. And you're a new citizen, not able or ready to fight for survival out there. Even seasoned citizens don't go out."

"I thought the whole point of the Arena was to teach me to survive in Tenebra."

"That was the hope. You've taken an unconventional path."

"Meaning I got out because I murdered someone, not necessarily because I learned anything."

"You said it, not me. But you're valuable to the Emperor. I can't let you throw your life away with your recklessness."

"I'm dying already!" I kick the door crank, but it doesn't move. "We all are!" My ribs scream. "Now open this gate."

"You may have done us a great *service,* killing that Spore, but I don't think that makes you any safer to our society. Your emotions are still beyond your control, and who's to say they won't lead you to killing a citizen next?"

If I had it my way, I wouldn't kill another person, Spore or citizen, ever. "The Emperor is training me." I have to believe it's possible to become safe. Controlled.

"To be frank, that was *my* job."

Ah, so it comes down to ego. Luc walked on Crixus's turf by training me, and Crixus doesn't like it. "I think I prefer the Emperor's teaching methods to your practice of handing me a spear and shoving me in an arena."

"You were safe."

"Safe like the noxior who was eaten by the giant snake?" He opens his mouth to reply, but my irritation–or is it desperation?–grows, and as much as Crixus annoys me, I don't want to prove him right by losing control and attacking him.

I pound against the door and chains. It's not going to accomplish much, but it feels good. Then I see the enormous ancient padlock tucked behind the crank and chains. I turn to Crixus, breathing hard, and my voice comes out in an utterly different tone. Serious. Pleading.

"Let me out, Crixus."

He stands there, arms crossed, unchanged. There's nothing more I can do at this point except hope he bends. I'm a citizen–I have this *right.*

"Say please." I think he means it as one final jab, but it comes out flat.

I'm tempted to say please with my fist.

"Please," I spit out.

He pulls a key from a cord around his neck that was tucked beneath his tunic. He opens the lock. This time when I turn the crank it needs only a nudge before gaining momentum, and the doors swing open with unearthly shrieks.

Billows of fire greet me.

I hesitate. Behind me, Crixus chuckles.

"I just walk through them?" What about being a citizen has suddenly made me immune to these flames? I feel no different.

"As long as you have your citizenship scroll with you."

I pat my belt. The scroll is tucked tight. Okay then. One hesitant step and the flames dart away from my sandaled foot. I take another step. The fire seems hungry but reluctantly slinks backward. A strange sensation of power fills me. My strides turn confident. The flames part.

And then I'm out.

Out of the coliseum and into the wild, deadly night.

This is a different location from where I entered after the Spore battle. No broad cobbled road here. A dusty path winds into a section of abandoned houses, like an invitation to step from dusk into full night. A haunting promise of deep shadows. Otherworldly. It brings me back to when I first arrived at the coliseum with barely the blood left in my veins.

"Get out before they get in." Crixus doesn't bother to clarify who *they* are.

I take the final step, and he hauls the doors closed. I thought he'd come with me. Luc's lackey and all that. Or it's just a stroke of good luck.

I turn and face the darkness like I would a nightbeast in the Arena. I enter it at a jog. The jolt against my shoulder keeps me alert. I could be going in the complete wrong direction, but I have to move.

Once I'm several yards from the coliseum, I call out, quietly against the threat of the shadows, "Stranna!"

The Spores don't live in the coliseum. Stranna arrived at the Arena on a giant phoenix, which tells me she probably flew a distance. I try to remember which direction she originally came from, but there's no sun or mountains to navigate by.

I unsheathe my kris dagger. I need something–anything–to help me find her. I rack my brain for any piece of information she might have given me during our brief conversation. Anything Luc might have said when he first told me about the Spores.

Nothing.

"How do I find her?" I speak the words to the sky, as if they'll float up through this dark misty ceiling of Nightmare, into the Real World, and up to the heavens. As if God would hear. He never heard me before when I asked him to drag Mom out of her depression and wake her up.

But is that true?

It's almost like hearing Nole in my head–challenging

my bitterness. I mean, if you want to get technical, Mom eventually got out of it, with the help of Nole's reading to her and the small family church she found. But by then it was too late. For me, anyway. Her indifference and darkness had already cracked my heart beyond repair. We never really had a relationship after that.

Nole would say that's my fault.

"Shut up and help me find her!" I shout, not sure if I'm talking about Mom or Stranna.

Soft footsteps break the silence behind me. Close.

"For night's sake, Crixus!" I whirl, dagger in hand. The footsteps stop, and I see the source. It's not Crixus. It's a hunting dog. Floppy ears, long nose, spry and strong legs. Its colors are a mixture of blacks and dark grays, but immediately I know he's mine. I made him. He's a little transparent and missing a tail, but he wags his bottom as if he has one anyway.

"Can you take me to her?" I ask.

He pants. I'm about to slide my kris dagger back into its sheath when I see the dried blood on it from the last and only time I used it. Stranna's blood. My stomach turns, but I'm thankful I was careless and didn't clean my weapon.

I hold it out to the dog. Eager to please, he sniffs the weapon thoroughly, leaving a smear of snot on the silver. Then he sets off, smelling the air and following a scent only he can detect.

I've seen this work in movies, but I didn't expect it to really work here. Or maybe it isn't working and he's detecting a Nightmare hotdog stand or something. Then again, maybe he's acting the way I want him to act because he isn't a real dog at all. He's a nightbeast, and when I created him, I was thinking desperately about finding Stranna.

But it's the only hope I have.

I follow the padding of his paws on the path, keeping track of our trail so I can find my way back to the coliseum later. Hours have already passed here in Tenebra. I have many, many more to endure before I wake up again to see what damage has been done from Stranna's and my wounds, from the sun, and maybe even from raiders who find us in the abandoned car. I can only pray we're both alive when I wake. I don't want to be responsible for Stranna's true death.

Well, maybe I won't *pray.*

Maybe I will.

I still don't know how I feel about that whole thing.

The hound dog weaves into the mist. I decide to call him Larry. He looks like a Larry.

Squat houses with clay, half-circle shingles emerge from the mist like silent ships in a sea of stone. I pass by them, eyes constantly scanning, kris dagger drawn in case Larry needs another sniff. My emotions lap at the surface, tempting anger. Tempting fear. I'm careful not to push them too far down. If I need to create something in a pinch, I want the emotions accessible. I'm half tempted to form that saber-toothed tiger again–if I could guarantee it would walk by my side and not eat me.

I don't bother with supplies like food, though I'm sure it's possible to create them. I won't starve, no matter how far I travel to the edge of the Nightmare.

Every dreamscape has edges. I know it in theory from my classes. But Nole knew even more. What I'd give to have him at my side. He'd see so much beyond what I can. His mind analyzed at a level college professors envied.

I make it through a few sections of homes but see no one. Not even light in windows. I hear plenty. Every particularly dark shadow I pass greets me with a crackling sound or even a growl, like some small beast hides in its depths.

The longer I walk, the more I find myself searching for light–any light. A candle or a star or anything. It's a gray midnight journey, and I feel it like a weight. I'd originally thought the light in the coliseum to be dim and unsatisfying, but compared to this darkness, it is as bright as a firework burst.

I follow Larry for hours, as he weaves and walks left and right, through an alley, back the way we came, forward, and all manner of directions. If I'd walked a straight shot, it likely would have taken less than an hour to get to where we are.

Maybe he can't find Stranna because she's dead already.

I groan. "God. Please, no."

The hound dog stops abruptly and raises his snout, ears lifting. Alert. Something's there. I stop, too, and listen. I think I catch footsteps, but then there's silence. Larry doesn't give chase, doesn't howl. Wouldn't he bay or something if we'd arrived where Stranna was?

We stand like this for a minute, then he sniffs again and turns right, nose to the stones. Then right again. He whines. We're going in circles. He's lost either the scent or the trail.

But we have to be close. I risk calling out gently. "Stranna?"

Now that we're standing still, the gloom becomes palpable. A low hiss, like a burst steam pipe, fills the silence. I turn toward it, but another hiss joins from a different direction. Larry whines. In less than a minute, there are so many hisses it's impossible to tell which direction they come from.

I scan the streets but see only shadows and darkness. Then the shadows move, slither across the stone toward my feet.

The hissing grows louder.

They aren't shadows. It's nightmist. Nightbeasts.

Snakes.

Hundreds of snakes cover the ground, a moving writhing carpet from every angle. I grip my kris dagger. Larry snaps at a cobra. I try channeling what emotions remain in me into a second weapon—maybe an Indiana Jones whip or something—but then the cobra lunges toward Larry. I lose my focus but not my instincts. I slice off its head before the strike.

The other snakes slide over the carcass of their dead companion.

Larry dances backward, barking and snapping. A rattler latches onto his shoulder. I kick at three snakes coming toward my feet, one of which is a python as thick as my bicep. If ever I hated the useless show of Roman sandals, it's now.

I swipe and kick and try to channel my emotions into another nightmist creation, but I can't pause long enough. Can't focus.

More snakes latch on to Larry. I yell, as though that can scare them off. Larry growls and spins, chasing them with his teeth, but no matter where we run or how we fight, the snakes multiply in our path.

One bites my calf, and fire spreads up my leg. I rip the snake off. Another slides around my ankle shaking a rattling tail. Snakes fully cover Larry's body by this point, and he's gone from fighting to whimpering.

"Get off him!" I shout, kicking at the snakes, but four of them have already bitten me and hold on, fangs in place. I sprint away from the madness, but they're everywhere. Filling the streets, dropping from the air, climbing the walls. Can regular snakes slither up walls?

I glance back. Larry is a lump of writhing snake bodies. Unmoving. The snakes feast. I send him a mental promise to create him again with a full tail and solid body as recompense for his death.

The other snakes give chase, gaining on me. Grabbing my feet, calves, sandals. I kick at them, but fangs pierce my ankle bone and muscles. I hack with the kris dagger. This can't be how I go. The snakes didn't get Indy, and they won't get me.

Then one twists around my neck and tightens with a hearty squeeze. My air is cut off immediately. I stab at it with the dagger, careful not to slice my own skin. It doesn't relent.

These aren't like real snakes. They'll squeeze and bite until they die. They don't care about self-preservation because they're made of fear and darkness.

Something passes over me like an inverted shadow–lighter

than my surroundings. I glance up wildly, half expecting to see a chopper with a spotlight.

A tiny spark starts in the sky and drops through the air. The snakes pause. The light lands among them.

A single lit match. Or something close to it. Like a grain of fire.

The snakes scatter, but the fire catches–on what, I don't know. It spreads like a beast itself, consuming the snakes. I cringe and hold my ground, allowing the heat of the fire to kill the snakes on my body. It's hot–burning, even–but not eating my flesh the way it eats up the snakes.

Is this the same type of fire from the coliseum?

When the hissing finally stops and the slithering comes to an end, I'm left standing amid the carcasses of a thousand blackened serpents. I can't bring myself to look at Larry's dead body.

A gust of wind blows from a side alley. Then footsteps. Then . . . she's here. Right in front of me.

Stranna.

"Sorry about your dog." She looks at me the same way one might look at a shower drain clogged with hair. "Now we're even. Okay?" She spins away.

I lurch after her and grab her arm. "Stranna!" I don't care that she's annoyed or that she probably wishes the snakes had eaten me.

She's still alive.

She tenses at my touch. I release her, hoping I haven't grabbed her too hard.

When she turns, her face carries only fear. Wide eyes and pale skin. Quick pulse.

"How . . . how do you know my name?"

"You have to wake up. Now!"

"What?" She backs away, but that movement alone reveals her weakness. Her hand finds the corner of a home, and she leans half her body against it to stay upright. She must sense that her physical body is injured.

"Wake up! Get back to the Real World. Contact your people for help." I grab her forearms. "You're not safe. You've been shot twice, and we're overheating in a car, completely stranded."

She tries to pull away but instead gives a pained gasp.

"What are you talking about?"

I release her, afraid to strain her mind or body. Can't she sense the urgency?

"I'm the guy you saved from the fire. The burning tiny house. That's me."

"What?" she breathes. "No. I saw your face . . ."

"Covered in soot."

"No." She looks to the heavens. "You wouldn't be that cruel. I saved the guy who killed me? The cure guy who robbed me?"

"Forget that!" I slash the air with a hand. "Are you even hearing me? We're lost. We're bleeding. We're probably dying. I've done everything I can to get here and to find you."

"I found *you*."

"Who cares!" This is maddening. "Can you wake up and get help or not?"

"It's not that simple!"

The fight goes out of me. "You and the other Spores can enter and exit the Nightmare at will." I say it more as a hope than a belief.

"Not at will," she says. "There has to be a cause."

"The Emperor said–"

"The Emperor doesn't know anything about us."

I deflate. All these victories to conclude with this?

"So you can't wake up?"

She shakes her head. "Not the way you seem to think I can." She looks around the alley. "We're still alive for now."

"But for how long?"

She lifts a shoulder. "I guess until you return to the Old World and figure out how to save us. How many more Awakes do you have?"

"Only one. The next will be my last." How can she be so calm through this? This isn't like her dying in Tenebra and magically resurrecting. This is her body I'm talking about. The real one. The one that stays dead once it's killed.

She swallows hard. "I hear you, Cain. But I really can't do anything. I just have to hope . . . and have faith, I guess."

"Faith? Are you serious? What's that going to accomplish?"

Her tone turns cold. "It's helped me in plenty of other ways and in times far worse than what you're describing."

"Great. Fine. Have faith that someone will coincidentally wander past our abandoned vehicle and take it upon themselves to save us." I want to stomp away, but it took so much to find her. She's just like Mom. She doesn't even *want* to save herself. Is it because it's easier to be ignorant and distanced here in Tenebra rather than suffering in the Real World?

We stand at an impasse, neither knowing what to say next. What is there?

Stranna's too busy having faith like some brainwashed megachurch attendee. She shuffles her feet, and I try to imagine what it might be like for her–to learn that she saved the guy who killed her in the Nightmare and then he got her in an even worse situation. And now her body is at his mercy. She's trapped here like I am, and all I did was give her information that will eat at her mind.

Of course she'd cling to faith and hope that everything will be okay. What else does she have? Isn't that the natural last resort? When people are desperate, they turn to God–like I did when searching for her. But then we pull ourselves out of our weakness and realize we can do it ourselves.

Nole used to say turning to God wasn't weakness. That being weak is where the true strength came from. Yeah, well, he and Mom are dead, so . . .

I search for something to say, my eyes jumping from one snake carcass to the next without truly focusing. The wind has gone out of my sails, the panic out of my bones, and a half-hearted acceptance takes its place. I gesture to the snakes.

"These nightbeasts were . . . something else. I think I would rather battle a thousand real snakes."

"Mmm."

"You defeated them with what . . . a match?" The small talk grates on me.

"Something like that." She folds her arms, but her voice is thin. Weak. She doesn't have her magic sword with her this time. Does that mean she has some other secret Spore weapon tucked away?

"How are you alive, Stranna? Do you have some sort of cure?" But if she had the cure, why was she buying mine in the Real World?

"I'm not sure you're ready to hear it."

"Try me."

She glances at my feet. "You're growing roots here. That's the difference." She lifts her own feet, and there's no sign of root or twig. "You're allowing yourself to become part of this world. I have accepted that I'm not of this world. This is not my home and never will be."

"That's ridiculous! I'm committed to the Real World. Tenebra isn't my world either." I've resisted every Sleep, every new term, every Tenebran law. She knows nothing.

"The Real World isn't my home either."

"You're speaking in circles. The Emperor says you and the other Spores practically run this place."

"Everyone needs someone to blame."

"So you deny it?" I ask.

"Of course I do! Would you have been able to kill me if I were in control of this place? Or its creator? Take a moment and think about what a creator might do here. They'd be in charge. They'd be the king, and they'd be able to create anything they wanted." She raises an eyebrow. "Sound familiar?"

It isn't the first time I've wondered if Luc has some sort of power over the Nightmare, but his dad is the Draftsman who's still trapped in the Tunnels. Luc earned his role as Emperor on his own merit.

"Someone in control of the Nightmare would be beyond death here. And *you* resurrected."

"You're hopeless."

"You never gave me an answer." I try to catch her eye, but she expertly fixates on anything but me.

"I gave you all the answer I can."

"Your people attacked me and the other tunnel escapees on our way to the coliseum. Why?"

"To keep you from becoming noxior slaves."

I roll my eyes. "So we could live happily ever after in this ghost town?"

She huffs. "I don't expect you to understand. At least we're giving people a choice."

"Oh, so that's what you did to Erik? You gave him a choice as your friends dragged him into the darkness by his ankles? Then what did you do to him?"

"The most we could. We encouraged him to keep running toward the light."

That's the first thing that sort of makes sense. Running toward the light is how I escaped the Tunnel. Luc can't even get his own father out, so it must be up to the person themselves. It's a choice to escape.

I'm growing soft toward her–buying her excuses and explanations, as cryptic as they are. But Luc has records. The Spores killed Nole, and I can't let that go.

"Well, goodbye." She turns.

"Wait!" I can't accept defeat like this. This journey has been useless so far. "Where are you going?"

"Home."

"There's nothing you can do to save your body?" Our bodies.

She hesitates and that tells me enough. "There might be a way." Her eyes slide to me. "But it's a slim one."

"What is it?"

"Tell me the coordinates of our location."

I open my mouth to do so, jumping at the chance to hope, but catch myself. After a moment's thought, I say instead, "Can I come with you?"

"Where?"

"To wherever you live in Tenebra. Your base, or whatever."

She snorts. "So you can report our 'base' to the Emperor? You'd put us all at risk! You've already put us at risk by coming after me."

"Let me come with you. I can't keep creating a hound dog from nightmist to find you." I try to sound lighthearted, not desperate.

She lets out an exasperated sigh. "You should stop creating from nightmist altogether."

"Says the girl who flies on the back of a phoenix."

"It's not a nightbeast." She walks away, limping and using the wall as a support. I follow her.

"Your body is with mine. Only I can tell you what's happening in the Real World. You really want to leave me behind?"

"We'll set up a communication system."

"What, letter delivery by owl?"

She looks at me in surprise, then shakes her head. "Nerd."

"I won't tell you the coordinates unless you take me with you."

"I guess our bodies will die then." She rounds the corner of a house and climbs atop an old barrel to reach the edge of the roof. It seems to take all her effort.

She grips the edge with her fingers and moves to haul herself up, but one arm slips. She tries again, but her body works about as well as a damp piece of paper. I form a step with my hands and give her a shove that would tear my shoulder open if this were my real body. It propels her atop the roof.

She doesn't offer me a thank-you. Or a hand up.

In fact, she walks out of sight. I hurry to haul myself up behind her, even though my lungs are on fire and the stretch pulls my muscles with a bungee cord of pain.

On top of the roof, her phoenix rests with its head tucked under its wing. It's enormous–the biggest nightbeast I've seen. But instead of being dull-toned and shadowy like every creature Luc or I make, its feathers are a shiny gold and brown with rich red accents that are stark against this dim night.

Stunning.

"Stranna."

Her shoulders tense.

"I'm trying to save your life. If I'd wanted to kill you or betray you, I would have done it already. Come on . . . have faith." It's a low blow, manipulative, but it works: just like it used to work on Nole and Mom. I feel guilty that they did have faith in me, yet I am still the prodigal they always dreaded.

I don't want to be a prodigal. I want to believe like Nole did, have faith like Stranna does, but not in the weak way I always tend to see. Why does it seem like "to have faith" means to abandon all strength and gumption? Turn into a doormat or let people punch you without retaliating.

Stranna sighs, then unties a cloth from around her wrist. It's dirty and stained, but she holds it out to me.

I take it. "What's this?" Some sort of token to let the hound sniff the next time I need to find her?

"Blindfold." At our voices, the phoenix's head pops up. It stretches its wings and nearly knocks me off the roof.

I take the blindfold, not daring to say anything more and risk her changing her mind. I'm about to tie it around my eyes, but a nagging at the back of my mind stops me. I take her arm as carefully as I can. This time, she doesn't yank away.

I have to ask. One last time. "Did the Spores kill my brother?"

"We don't even know who your brother is." She eases her

arm from my grasp. "My guess is that he died in the Tunnel." Her voice is gentle. "I'm so sorry, Cain." She takes the blindfold from me and ties it around my eyes.

A lump forms in my throat, surprising me. It's been so long since I've felt any sort of gentleness. Gentle touch. It has nothing to do with it being Stranna. But it makes me think of Mom and all the things I've lost.

"Thank you." For telling me. For tying the blindfold. For taking me with her.

Her exhale touches my cheek, and her hand finds mine, leading me to the great phoenix. "The Spores don't tend to kill people, Cain. I hope you can believe me."

"That's not what Luc says. And it's not what I saw during the attack on the Tunnel cart."

"Oh, and is the Emperor in the habit of leaving things alive?"

I think of my tiger. Sure he killed it, but he spends every Arena Game reuniting children with their families. He's not the evil overlord she seems to think he is.

"My brother's name was Nole Cross. Luc had a ledger with the cause of death next to each deceased citizen's name. It said he was Spored."

"I didn't realize your brother was a citizen."

I stop. Nole wasn't a citizen. He would have told me about the coliseum. Only now do I wonder why and how Luc had Nole's name in that ledger. No one in Tenebra took down my name when I first exited the Tunnels.

If Luc can make a forest or living room from nothing, couldn't he have done the same with the leger?

Stranna climbs onto the phoenix in front of me. It rises unsteadily, and I grip her around the middle. I barely make out her next words over the increase of flapping before we take off.

"Spores don't kill. We *die*."

26

THE AIR IS COLD AS WE FLY. IT'S THE first time I notice the temperature in Tenebra. And it seems odd since my physical body is likely overheating in the Real World. Or maybe burning with fever. Is that why I'm cold? Is it even daytime up there? I wouldn't know–I can never keep track of time here in Tenebra.

I think that's how Luc wants it.

Though why I'm now thinking he can control this place is a testament to how deep I've let Stranna's words take hold. I need to keep my wits–don't be swayed by Luc. Or Stranna. Draw my own conclusions.

Is this another side effect of being Spored?

We don't fly for very long, but Stranna directs the phoenix left and right, circles and dives to ensure I'm thoroughly confused. The phoenix doesn't seem to like it. I feel the creature strain against her direction, and her body strains back.

Then her body loses its tension for a moment. She slides a little to the left. I grip her waist in a sudden panic that she's about to fall off. My touch seems to wake her up. She straightens, and shoves my hands off her.

But then she slips once more, and I grab her again. "Stranna! Land!"

"I know what I'm doing," she argues, but in a weak,

desperate voice. I manage to haul her back so she is secure against my chest. She squirms away. I grip the phoenix with my legs and the blindfold sends my equilibrium spinning. I release Stranna with one hand and tear off the cloth.

Wind hits my eyes, and they immediately water. I spy the phoenix harness in Stranna's hands and take it in my own, careful not to pull one way or another. She doesn't protest. I don't have to do much–the phoenix seems to know its route. It falls into a dive, and I yell, trying to grip both Stranna and the bird. Just before the ground the phoenix slows, then flaps wildly moments before landing. I topple off its back and land on hard ground.

Goodbye pride, hello Spore base.

Stranna's body seems to slip in slow motion from the shoulders of the phoenix. She clings to the harness at the last moment and lands on her knees.

I try to help her sit up, but she shrugs me off.

"Sorry, I don't know what happened."

"Your physical body is in distress," I tell her. "That's what's happening."

Her gaze lands on me and she frowns. "Where's your blindfold?"

Really? That's her first thought. "Can you stand?"

"Of course I can." Is she so prideful she can't admit she nearly fell off the phoenix? She takes it slow, pausing between movements. Then gets her feet. "Close your eyes then."

"Are you serious?"

She mutters something and pulls another wrap of cloth from around her ankle. "Rags aren't easy to come by here. Don't lose this one." She cinches it around my eyes so tight it sends an instant headache to my temple.

I want to say something snarky like, *"You're welcome for saving you again,"* but truthfully, I'm mainly relieved she's functioning enough to guide me. The sooner we get help to our abandoned Jeep the better. I think she gets the urgency now.

Her hand takes mine. "This way." She tugs me one direction, and I stumble after her. She drops my hand and grips my sleeve instead. It sends all the message I need. A small pang hits me in the chest, and I almost laugh at myself for wanting her hand in mine. For a moment, the brief intimacy felt like it could be forgiveness. I know she bought my cure, and I know it didn't work for her. She saved me in The Fire Swamp. In return I risked everything–my tiny house, my food, my life–to keep her safe from the idiots at the storage unit and the warehouse.

Hand in hand implies trust. I want to be trusted.

But I'm not sure I'm trustworthy.

Maybe it's because I miss Nole. Or maybe it's because life is lonely in the Real World. And in Tenebra. But a part of me cares about Stranna, and I want her safe. Which means she should stay away from me, and I should stay away from her.

Is this the Spore infection talking? Making me care more about her life than mine? I still want a LifeSuPod. Luc's current terms are to tell him about the Spore base, plus save Galilei, whom the Spores ambushed.

I'm their enemy.

"Watch your head." Stranna's voice is gentle, and she leads slower. I duck, but not far enough because my scalp clips what feels like a rough stone frame. Sound changes, and our footsteps turn loud and lonely as they scrape uneven ground.

We take a few turns, and even though Stranna holds only my sleeve, I've unintentionally reached out with my other hand to grip her wrist for a more secure lead.

I hear the strike of a match, then smell burning oil.

"Okay."

She unties the blindfold.

I'm met with darkness. I blink several times, and a small oil lamp comes into focus, held in Stranna's unsteady hand. An old clay one you might see in a museum. All around me are tunnels, carved-out alcoves in stone, shadows . . .

"Catacombs," Stranna fills in. "Not what you thought, I imagine."

My distaste must show on my face. I don't know what I expected. She defeated nightbeasts with a single match. She has a magic sword. Her phoenix shines with color instead of shadow.

"I guess I expected . . . light." Maybe it's my hunger for the sun that's speaking, but for some reason I thought the Spores would have it. Something more than the 7A sky over the coliseum or the pressing darkness of the abandoned world outside.

Instead . . . they live in catacombs.

Tombs.

It's worse than the coliseum. Here, there's not even sky.

"Light?" Stranna almost laughs. "That's long dead."

For the first time I question her knowledge. Prior to now I was accepting her words–accepting that she's been here longer than I have, knows more than I do. But now I see something else that taints her words. Bitterness, or maybe fear.

"You can't kill light," I retort. All this time I thought the Spores had some secret hideaway filled with control and life and secret creation powers beyond even Luc.

Stranna turns her back on me and lifts the oil lamp high enough to illuminate the path. "Well then, since you're so sure, I'll leave it up to you to find it."

"You have it!" I gesture to her, though she's not looking at me. "You exploded lightning in the Macella Quarter! What do you mean it's dead? You and your kind caused panic and mobs in the coliseum because of a single spark." I recall my first hours out of the Tunnel. When I saw a brief spark after clasping Erik's hand.

It scared James. Then the Spores stabbed him and dragged Erik away. Erik must have been Spore-infected and not known it.

Stranna stops but doesn't turn. The oil lamp in her hand trembles more fiercely, and she transfers it to her other hand. "You . . . you can see those lights?" she asks, raising her head.

"It's hard to miss light in the darkness of this Nightmare." Only now do I realize how inaccurate the term Spore is. Spore makes me think of green toxic gas. Not lightning. Is Stranna implying that some people can't see it?

"But that doesn't make sense." She turns and reaches down and tugs at my foot. Instinctively I lift it, and the roots from my sole stretch from the ground, trying to pull my sandal away from her hands.

"How can you have roots here and still see the light?"

Then as if catching herself, she releases my foot and straightens. "It doesn't matter. Follow me. Unless you're scared of the dark."

I pushed a button or something. She jabbed at my desire for light, but I don't let it bother me. The Nightmare roots and Spore lights are equally confusing to me. I set aside my curiosity and remind myself why we're here: to save our physical bodies.

And Stranna said she might have a way.

We wander through the catacombs, and no matter my counting, I lose track of the direction we take. I'll never be able to find this place again, let alone get out of here without getting lost.

Along the crude stone walls are hollow cutouts—places for dead bodies. All are empty.

"No corpses in here?" I venture.

"The catacombs have been here since we arrived. There are no bodies to fill the tombs. If you die in the Nightmare, your form disappears because it's really only your consciousness. There's nothing left to bury."

So then why do the catacombs exist? "I guess that keeps things neater."

"And sadder." Her voice is heavy. "It's hard to say a proper goodbye or find closure when people you love fade from your arms like that."

For a brief, twisted moment I'm thankful I got to hold Nole after he died. I got to bury him.

"I'm sorry," I say, though I don't know who she's lost or even if she's referencing something personal.

We reach another stretch of tombs, but this time they're not empty. As the oil lamp passes them I see their contents. Pillows. Blankets. A pitcher of water in one with a stack of stained towels.

Then there's a body.

A child's body.

I recoil so fast I bump against the opposite wall. Stranna follows my horrified gaze, then gives me an eye roll.

"Get a grip, Cain."

"I thought you said bodies disappeared once they died here!" What sort of sick people are the Spores to horde the corpse of a child?

"We're still learning the rules." She reaches out and ruffles the child's hair.

He pops up from his spot in the tomb, and I press against the wall even more. For one wild moment I think maybe she's resurrected him. Or he's a nightbeast or something.

Stranna bursts out laughing while the boy rubs bleary eyes. "He was *sleeping*, Cain. Good grief!"

"Oh." I relax, though my heart still thunders. I'm such an idiot. Of course. Pillows. Blankets. Kid.

But this is the first child I've seen with the Spores. I scan his body through the shadows as best I can. No shackles. Nothing sinister. Nothing more than a boy without his family. Are his parents in the coliseum, attending the daily Arena fights and hoping he'll be the next name called?

"Hey, Stranna," the boy says, though he eyes me with suspicion. "Who's he?"

"A guest for now."

Without a word the boy climbs from his tomb bed and follows us. I notice a little paring knife in his hand, one that might be used at dinner rather than as a weapon. "He's not going to take any of us, right?"

"Not if I can help it." I hear the smile in Stranna's voice.

So the Spores have convinced the kids that *we* are the enemy. That Tenebran citizens are the ones trying to kidnap kids. Does this boy realize his parents are probably waiting for him? Longing for him to be found and reunited with them?

I want to ask Stranna about it, but even I know that's crossing a line of discussion she won't allow.

We pass more children. Some sleeping in their little tomb alcoves, which disturbs me no matter how many times I tell myself they're stone-carved bunkbeds. Then I see a head of braids. The girl props her chin on her hands as we approach.

"Stranna!"

Stranna gives her a kiss on the forehead as she passes.

The girl glares at me. "What's *he* doing here?"

"Long story."

It's the girl from the Arena, the one the phoenix carried away. Stranna's sister.

"Glad to see the phoenix didn't eat you," I say.

"Can't say the same for you." Feisty little thing: a similarity between sisters, I suppose. "Besides, it wasn't going to eat me. It was trying to rescue me."

"Olivia," Stranna warns, but I want to hear the story.

"How'd you end up a noxior anyway?"

"Got roped by the Emperor and his stingray." So she was

the Spore child who got lassoed when I first arrived. Luc thought he was rescuing her.

The farther along we go, the more chatter and giggles and bickering I hear. Every now and then there's a carved-out space, lit with oil lamps, where kids play games or wrestle. One is even reading a book, but I don't catch the title.

There are books in this world?

The boy who's following us must determine that I'm not a threat anymore and ditches us to play a game of marbles with two other kids. Marbles. It's like we've stepped back in time. No video games, no theme parks, no Legos.

Two kids try playing some sort of ball game, but the only ball they have is a crudely knitted cloth sphere filled with what sounds like beans or rocks. It aches to watch them. I remember when Dad first left and Mom was trying to foot the bills, find us a new place to live, and garden so we wouldn't survive solely off boxed pasta. As a teenager I see now how much she sacrificed and strove for us, but the main things I remember from that time are how Nole and I would have given anything for a skateboard, baseball and bat, basketball, or anything beyond the big pile of nothing we had. Stick swords and tree climbing took us only so far.

Perhaps that's why we have such vivid imaginations.

Eventually we turned to books, spending the majority of our days in the public library while Mom worked. Narnia and Hobbiton and Hogwarts and all such places sent us adventuring and living stories so epic that once ImagiSerum took over the world we knew we had to create fantasy worlds for ourselves.

Still . . . I'll always have that little longing for a soccer ball or basketball that's all mine.

The *thud* of rubber on stone breaks my reverie. *Thud . . . thud, thud.* Something bumps my foot. I look down. A basketball, black and still smoking.

Half the kids stop their playing and stare at me and the new sound.

While it may not *look* like a regular basketball, when I pick it up the weight is right. It's filled with air, and when I toss it into their group it bounces with so much energy the kids scream as one.

It's like they've never seen a basketball before, even though they lived in the Real World only a few months ago. Well . . . months ago in Real World time. In Tenebra time, it's been much longer.

They fight over it for a moment, but the excitement brings an extra level of patience as the quickest boy secures it first. He dribbles clumsily, then bounces it to another kid. They form a circle within seconds, and it doesn't matter what game they're playing or if it makes sense or has rules.

They squeal and clap and laugh. Tiny sparks of light blink amid their play–like blanket static. Too sudden to identify the source. The bag of rocks lies abandoned in a corner. I grin so wide I almost forget where I am.

Stranna stares at me. If she doesn't like that I handed them a nightmist creation, too bad. I'm not about to take it away.

She looks like she wants to say something, but then clamps her lips shut and walks away from the scene. I follow. She turns two more corners, and things grow quieter, despite the sounds from the children behind us. She holds a finger to her lips. Only then do I hear dim voices. Stranna lets out a low hissing sound with three short bursts. The voices go quiet.

"Wait here," she says to me, then continues through an arched doorway.

I'm not really the obedient type. After she's been gone for a few seconds, I inch toward the arch and peer through into a broader space that looks like the closest thing to a home I've seen in Tenebra. Beds with actual frames and mattresses that are not in the Roman style. They look like they were taken out of a modern house in the Real World. There are at least six beds littered with a myriad of belongings. Clothes hang over the metal footboard of one with a mussed flower comforter. Another has a blue-plaid bedspread with no less than six pillows propped along the head. Tied packs, boots, and cloaks are all shoved partway under the bed or propped against the legs.

Only one bed is occupied, and that's where the voices come from. Stranna whispers urgently to three other people who currently block my view of the person on the bed. All I can see are feet, bare and covered in blood.

The room smells of flowers that have sat in a vase too long–I know that scent because Mom always wanted flowers in her room, but I was too lazy to change them out once they wilted. Not a bad smell, not a good one. Is that Spore fumes or death scents from the body on the bed?

Their whispers grow incensed, and they don't sound happy. Stranna gestures toward the archway opening and looks my way before I can duck out of view. Another Spore spots me and glowers.

"I'm here to help," I say and they all hush me. I move to enter, wanting to get to the bedside of the injured person even though there's nothing I can do.

Stranna strides over. "I told you to *wait*."

"Sorry." But I'm not.

"You've seen what you demanded to see. Now tell me the location of our bodies."

I'm still staring past her at the bed. One of the bloodied feet twitches. A tortured groan rises from the bed, followed by soothing shushes from the people around. Stranna looks pale.

"Can I help?" I ask in a choked voice.

"You can tell me our location." She looks over her shoulder at the small group. "Now."

"It's a landfill." I tell her the mile marker and highway.

"Thank you." She relays the information to the other three, then grabs my arm to haul me back out, but her knees buckle.

"Stranna!" I cry and catch her before she hits the ground.

One of the other Spores rushes over. It's Erik. The guy from the Tunnel cart who got dragged away. I falter back, still holding Stranna.

Erik looks like them, cloak, toga, and all. Sword at his side. They got to him. They got to his mind, and now he's trapped in their wiles.

"I can take her," he says without a single acknowledgment of what we went through.

Stranna manages to find her feet but takes a while to catch her breath. "I'm fine."

"You're alive," I marvel to Erik.

"Alive and well." He actually smiles.

"What did they do to you?"

"Saved me from a lot, it sounds like." He takes in my Roman garb. "You okay?"

"I'm fine," I snap. "I wish I could say the same for James."

"He's with us too," Erik says. "Well, another group." He closes his mouth like he's afraid to say too much.

Another group exists. James is with them. Somehow I'm not surprised. I hadn't let myself think too deeply about it, but James was stabbed with a Spore sword. So was I. I know from experience it doesn't kill.

"Well, what about the other people who got crushed beneath the cart when these Spores attacked us?"

Erik stands in front of me acting all rescued and happy in this new life hiding underground and kidnapping children, like he and I didn't witness death together, didn't fight together, didn't fear for our lives as the Spores wreaked havoc.

"Their deaths weren't intended," he replies.

"Well then, you and your Spores need to think of a different way to stop a Tunnel cart." I don't know why I'm so angry. It feels like months ago, but seeing Erik not seeming to care for those who were killed in the attack eats at me.

"Adelphoi," he says.

"What?"

"We call ourselves *Adelphoi*. Not *Spores*."

I roll my eyes. "Just another Roman word to keep track of in this place."

"It's Greek."

Stranna places a hand on his arm. "Let it go, Erik."

The anger has begun to pulse beneath my skin, and I know what's happened the last few times it escalated out of my control.

Stranna turns to me. "I think you should go now."

"Go?"

She doesn't say it again. Instead, she makes her way back toward her comrades, eyes on the bed of the wounded Spore. Adelphoi. Whatever.

Erik gives me an apologetic glance, then follows her. Another Spore trembles and buries their face in Stranna's shoulder. I'm an invader here. I don't belong.

I backtrack into one of the catacombs, though I don't know how to get out. Stranna knows I'll get lost, but she told me to go. I stalk down a tunnel, not really caring where it leads. I don't get far before footsteps catch up to me. It's the oldest of the kids, the one who got to the basketball first. The one who followed us when we first arrived.

"You're trying to get back to the coliseum, right?"

"I guess." I don't really feel like going back. I can't stay here, though. I'm not welcome.

More than ever I feel homeless.

"Thanks for the basketball," the boy says. "Follow me." He doesn't blindfold me. Doesn't ask for secrecy. He just leads me through the maze toward the exit of the catacombs.

Neither of us says anything for a while, but then I see the opportunity for answers.

"Thanks for leading me out. I'm Cain."

"Yeah, I know."

"What's your name?"

"Everett." He ducks under a broken bit of arch. Who designed these catacombs to be in such disrepair? Any decent Draftsman would want the dreamscape to sustain itself. Once places start falling apart the rest of the dreamscape unravels too. But Tenebra seems outside of all the rules I learned at university.

"How did you get here, Everett? To the catacombs?" I try to ask the question delicately so I'm not accusing him of being kidnapped. If the Spores are so good at poisoning and tricking the mind, then Everett likely sees them as allies.

"I woke up in Tenebra like anyone else after I got infected, but I wasn't with Mom and Dad. They told me they woke up in a dark Tunnel, but I woke up in a wheat field. There were other kids there too."

"Any nightbeasts?"

"Yeah, but they couldn't enter the field. Angry dogs and things without faces. It seemed like the more scared we got the more there were. So we stayed in the field and didn't get near the edges, but the longer we waited the more kids came, and we started running out of room."

From what Everett says, it sounds like kids have their own entry point in the Nightmare. They didn't have to escape a Tunnel, but they were still trapped in a field somewhere.

"No adults woke up in the field?"

"Nope. We didn't see any grown-ups until Stranna and the others came to harvest."

Harvest kids? Or harvest grain?

"What did the Spores do?"

He looks at me quizzically. "Spores?"

"Uh, Adelphoi. Stranna and the others." His ignorance

of terms tells me he's never been to the coliseum—at least not for long.

"You call them *Spores*?"

"What do you call them?" I want to make sure I'm saying that Greek word *Adelphoi* correctly.

"Friends." He seems bothered by this turn of conversation. I'm not sure what to say. They're not my friends, though I wouldn't mind that with Stranna.

"They don't stink, you know," he adds.

"What?"

"Olivia, Stranna's sister, told me what citizens say about them. That they stink and that they kidnapped me. It's not true."

"You're young."

He stops in the open doorway that leads outside. "You think I'm stupid."

I should have bit my tongue. "Of course not. But where are your parents? What happened to them? They could be out there"—I gesture outside—"waiting and looking for you."

"They're dead."

"Oh."

"A lot of our parents died in the Tunnels, but Stranna and Jeremy fought the nightbeasts and got us out from the wheat field. They gave us a home until the Emperor and his tirones attacked us. Every time he attacks, they protect us, and they make us a new home later."

"How many times has he attacked?"

"Four."

"But he doesn't kill anyone, right?"

"Sometimes his soldiers kill the older ones. Like me. Sometimes they turn us into noxiors like they did to Olivia. They take the littlest ones away, and we never see them again."

Because Luc reunites them with their families. I've seen

it. But that doesn't explain why he'd let his tirones kill the older kids.

"Olivia came back. So I hope that means we'll be able to rescue more. I'm finally old enough to fight." He puffs out his chest, and something inside me dies. This kid fights? "Erik and Jeremy have been teaching me."

"Why do the Emperor's men want to kill you?"

"I can't wake up anymore." We exit the catacombs, and the gray gloom seems brighter compared to the dark tunnels. Everett points. "The phoenix's nest is up that hill."

"Thanks."

"Okay, well, bye." He disappears back into the catacombs before I can ask any more questions. Not that I need more answers. There is plenty to ponder right now. Luc's tirones rescue only the young kids who can wake and sleep at will. I saw Olivia in the Arena. I knew she'd been turned into a noxior, yet I never asked Luc why.

Everett didn't sound deceived or brainwashed. He sounded like he was telling his tiny life story the same way he might talk about spending a day at the park. He was childlike. Open.

I reach the phoenix, and she raises her head at the sound of my feet. I put up my hands and talk softly.

"I was told you could take me back." She narrows an eye at me, and for a moment I wonder if she'll peck me. But then she spreads her wings and gives a little shake, like she's preparing for flight.

I cautiously climb on her back. It takes a moment to yank my feet from the ground as the roots from my soles hold tight to the stony surface. The phoenix squirms, and I wonder—can she feel the roots?

She leaps into the air with rough flaps, and it's all I can do to hold on to the harness. She circles a bit to gain height, and now that I'm not blindfolded or holding a wounded Stranna on her back, I take in my surroundings.

The catacombs aren't very impressive from above. They look like nothing more than a derelict ruin of an unfinished amphitheater. The tunnels and maze are below the earth. I scan the terrain beyond the catacombs. It's hard to see far in the darkness, but a glimmer at eye height catches my attention.

A star.

Light.

The phoenix swoops toward the coliseum, away from the blinking star. I gently tug the harness, and to my surprise, she obeys and turns. We head toward the glimmer. The sky is a dark gray–not quite dark enough to be midnight, but not light enough to be dawn. I lean low on the phoenix, and she drops closer to the ground.

In a matter of seconds, we glide a distance that would take me a quarter of an hour to walk. I scan the space ahead for the star, but now the golden gleam comes from the ground. We near, and I see it's a wheat field. The stalks of wheat are fully grown and ready for plucking. More than that, they seem illuminated–not by sunlight but by themselves. It's light and welcoming. This must be the field Everett was talking about.

The phoenix circles over it, but as she glides around the farthest side something clips her wing and smashes my leg. We hit a wall with a jolt. A window? The phoenix is thrown from the sky, and we spin.

A few flaps and she manages to slow her momentum just enough to pull off a rough landing.

For the second time today I tumble from her back. Instead of landing on stone, I'm cushioned by wheat stalks. I jump to my feet and look around. I don't see the wall we hit, but my throbbing leg tells me it wasn't my imagination. The phoenix picks at her feathers and favors one wing, but it doesn't look broken.

Thank goodness. Stranna would kill me.

I catch my breath and take in my location. Now that

I'm in the bright wheat, it feels almost like I'm standing in daylight. Somehow it *is* sunlight—contained within the stalks themselves. Glowing around me and warming my face like a perfect summer day. I close my eyes and soak it in. Emotion pricks at my throat and my eyes.

I miss the sun.

I miss light.

I don't get it in the Real World anymore because of the timing of my Sleeps, and my bones have begun to ache for it. I open my eyes again and breathe out, long and slow. This is where I want to live. If I have to put my body in a LifeSuPod and build some Nightmare house to dwell in, this is where I want it to be—in this field.

I pluck a head of wheat and rub it in my hands until the small thin shells fall from the grains. Then I chew them. I've never done this before, but somehow I understand it. The grain is sweet and chewy and brings a comfort wholly separate from sustenance. I do it again.

A growl breaks the peaceful moment.

I look quickly to the phoenix, but it didn't come from her. The growl is at one edge of the field. It takes a moment for my eyes to adjust to the darkness, but then I see the form of some creature on all fours. A mangy pit bull bares his teeth at me. I shove the fistful of wheat kernels into my pocket and fumble for my kris dagger. But the dog stays at the edge of the wheat field.

More sounds—a bark, a grunt, nails on hard dirt. All manner of nightbeasts gather at the border of the wheat field, eyes on me. Hungry. Angry.

I inch toward the phoenix, hoping not to startle them. Maybe we can take off before they attack.

But some *are* trying to attack. One massive wolf lunges, then recoils the second it touches a stalk of wheat. They can't come into the field. They can't come into the light. Everett had said as much.

My body relaxes a touch. They can't get to me. The phoenix and I are safe.

But nightbeasts line only three sides of the field. The edge behind us is clear. Could I really walk safely out of the field on that side? What keeps the nightbeasts from attacking there?

I take some steps toward the clear edge of the field. The nightbeasts gather in more dense packs at the corners, and I hear the same *thud, thud, thud* from when the phoenix hit the mysterious wall.

Like the creatures are bumping up against plexiglass.

"Oh." A grin crawls over my face. I approach the clear line of the field until the toe of my sandal meets the resistance of an invisible wall. I press my hand against it as I would a windowpane.

I've found it.

I've found the edge of the Nightmare.

I PUSH AGAINST THE INVISIBLE boundary, my Draftsman logic spinning as usual. Typical boundaries in dreamscapes are built to fit the dream—a castle wall or mountain range that encircles the design. Something impassable or unscalable. Cheap dreamscapes have chain-link fences. If someone were to pass the fence and somehow cross the boundary of the dream they'd wake up. Simple as that.

But this one is see-through. On the other side are random ruins of Roman structures, like buildings discarded by the Draftsman. It's a scene projected to make Tenebra seem endless, but it's not. There's an end. There's always an end. And if I can somehow figure out how to get through this boundary, I might wake. For good.

Could this be the cure to the Nightmare? Simply cross the barrier and be free of this place?

Something moves in the ruins on the other side.

I trip backward as the form grows larger, as it runs toward me. A nightbeast? But then I make out the figure. It's human. A child. A little girl with pigtails, a pale-yellow ruffle shirt with red cherries on it, and jeans with a torn knee. Her eyes are wide and her running stops. She stands mere yards from me . . . but she's on *that* side.

How is this possible?

I'm getting tired of asking that question.

Despite my confusion, I manage to raise my hand in a small wave.

She resumes a tentative advance. Her fixed gaze tells me she sees me as clearly as I see her. She can likely see the sunny wheat field as well. Can she feel its warmth at all?

I get the sense I've seen her before.

She walks closer, and I gesture to the barrier, though it's invisible.

"Careful!" I don't want her to get a bloody nose.

But she doesn't stop.

Instead, she walks right through the clear wall–a small seam of light cracking it open for a moment. She squeezes through, hardly paying it any mind. I gape. She stands before me and breathes deeply, the same way I did when I first landed in the field.

"I'm Heidi."

"Cain," I say numbly. What am I seeing here? None of this aligns. I'm starting to think that my Draftsman college program was one of the worst in the world. Everything I learned and studied and all the rules that were drilled into my head don't seem to apply to this place.

She holds up four fingers. "I'm four and a half. I'm going to be five in November. When I'm five I get bubble gum."

"Oh. Uh . . . that's cool." November is a couple months away. Will she even live that long?

"Is that your chicken?" Heidi asks, nervously glancing at the phoenix.

I smile. "She's a phoenix, and she's nice. In fact, I rode on her back to get here."

"Wow," she breathes. "Did you come to get me?"

"Um . . ."

"Mom said there's usually a Tunnel, and then someone gets you and takes you to a new home."

"I don't know where your parents are, but I know someone who can help you find them."

"Okay." She takes my hand. Her simple trust gets to me somehow.

The yapping of the nightbeasts increases as they spot the little girl, even though the wheat stalks almost block her from view. She moves closer to my side.

"When are we going to leave?" she asks in a whisper.

"Right now." I pick her up and settle her on my hip as best I can despite being sore and injured in my real body. I limp toward the phoenix, and the creature readies herself for mounting, like she knows the seriousness of the moment.

Heidi reaches out and pets the phoenix's head. "Hi, bawk-bawk." I suppress a laugh and situate her on the phoenix's back, her legs in front of the wing joints. "How long until I see Mom?"

"I don't know," I admit, climbing on behind her. "It could be a while. Hold on tight now." I give the phoenix a cluck like I heard Stranna do. The bird launches into the sky with rough, powerful flaps. Heidi screams, but I grip her tightly. I'm not about to let her fall.

The nightbeasts howl–robbed of their meal.

"Where . . . where are we going?" Heidi gulps.

"I'm taking you somewhere you'll be taken care of." I hope. "Somewhere safe."

Once we gain enough height, I direct the phoenix away from the mysterious wheat field of light . . . and head back to the catacombs.

28

I SPEND HALF MY TIME IN THE catacombs hollering for Stranna. Or Everett. I don't go too far in because the last thing I want is to lead Heidi into an underground tomb maze and get us lost.

Everett is the one who finds us.

"You're back," he says matter-of-factly and then notices Heidi.

"I found her in the wheat field."

He brightens. "It's been a while since we've had a new friend."

Heidi relaxes at the word *friend*. Everett beckons for her to follow, and she does. So do I, even though I should turn and head back to the coliseum. Part of me says I should have headed there with Heidi in the first place.

But it didn't feel right.

The tunnels smell distantly like cinnamon rolls. Do they have some sort of kitchen somewhere? Imaginary food or not, I'd totally go for cinnamon rolls right now.

We reach the part of the catacombs I now recognize. Beds and pillows and squeals clutter the corridor. The bounce of the basketball still echoes. I grin to myself.

"Here, you can sleep next to me." Everett takes a spare pillow and a pink blanket from a little alcove filled with extras, then stuffs them into a tiny tomb a few inches above ground level.

"Pink is my favorite color," Heidi declares, reaching out to tug the blanket to her chest and hug it like it's been hers since birth.

Girls.

Everett wrinkles his nose but doesn't say anything.

Boys.

Stranna steps into the corridor. "You're back." The way she says this is very different from Everett's greeting. A little bit like someone saying, "The termites are back," after their house has just been fumigated.

"Are you going to help me find Mom?" Heidi asks Stranna as she presses up against my side once more.

Stranna's gaze drops, and her face softens so suddenly she becomes a different person. She squats.

"Hi! You're new! How'd you get here?"

"He said I'd be safe here," Heidi says in the smallest of voices and now hides fully behind my leg.

Stranna's eyebrows shoot up. "He did, huh?" She looks at me with a furrowed brow. I don't blame her for being confused.

"Just find her parents, okay?" I say gruffly. "Sounds like they escaped the Tunnels and are in the coliseum somewhere." I turn to leave.

"Cain." She grasps my arm, and I stop. "She will be safe here. Okay?"

"Thanks." I'm grateful she doesn't bring up the obvious fact that I chose the Spores over the Emperor. She's made it clear I'm not welcome with her group.

"You guys were closer," I say. "She didn't like flying on the phoenix anyway." Why am I trying to defend myself?

"The phoenix was really fun!" Heidi says happily, blowing my facade. "Daddy told me I'm brave because I like being in the sky. Sometimes I'm a hot air balloon!" She fills her cheeks with air and rises up on her toes.

Everett laughs. "Hey, do you want to play basketball?"

"Okay." Heidi heads down the tunnel, leaving me with Stranna.

"How are you feeling?" I ask Stranna immediately, as if I didn't see her mere hours ago. One hour in the Nightmare is about twelve minutes in real life. Not much can have changed for her in that time.

"Weak. Warm." She shrugs.

"Did you . . . Did they . . . ?" Is it too soon to ask if she managed to enlist help from her fellow Spores? I already know she won't explain it to me.

"They're doing what they can." Her tone is somber, and I wonder what that sort of request cost her–cost them. "Honestly, I'm not sure what to think about you, Cain. One moment you're–"

A *yip!* comes from down the tunnel, and Stranna stops abruptly. The sound is from behind us toward the entrance.

She freezes for one moment, and I freeze too. Another *yip!* and then a muffled grunt. Human. Male. A clatter of metal.

Stranna's eyes snap to mine.

"What have you done?" She doesn't spare a moment for the drop of my jaw at her accusation. She bolts up the corridor, away from the noise.

I follow, but the sounds get louder and as my confusion fades, I piece together the clamor. Metal rustles against leather, the same sounds I heard in the Arena and training areas. The yips are from some sort of nightbeast, similar to the ones surrounding the wheat field.

Someone–rather, multiple someones–has breached the catacombs. And they're after the Spores. They're after the kids.

I find Stranna swiftly ushering the children into different alcoves. Erik and the other Spores emerge from their room at the noise. I glimpse James the Vetter for a brief moment. He *is* alive. And despite the current state of panic, he seems energized and focused. Not bitter and trembling–like when I first met him.

Stranna tries to keep the kids quiet, but they're protesting as the basketball is left behind. Straining against her.

I scoop up a little girl in one hand and shove the basketball into Everett's arms.

"Follow Stranna, and take this with you."

"There!" A shout comes from behind.

I glance over my shoulder. A clump of tirones surges through the tunnel with sickly skin-and-bone dogs on leashes straining against their chains to get to us.

The kids scream. Stranna screams.

The tirones release the dogs.

The children bolt up the tunnel while Erik and another Spore move their way toward the tirones, wielding mistblades, to meet the dogs. James cuts one down. Erik stabs another, then holds up his hands toward the tirones. His magical sword stays in its sheath.

"We are not your enemie–"

A tiro thrusts a gladius through Erik's heart.

I watch stunned as he crumples to the ground. A child wails from an alcove next to me. Heidi. She witnessed the whole thing. And I told her she'd be safe here.

Something within me snaps.

"Stop!" I bellow, dropping down next to Erik, but he's already gone. Pale and lifeless. Stranna's past words echo in my head: *"We don't kill, Cain. We die."*

"That's him!" One tiro points to me. "Icarus!"

Several of them rush me and grip me from all angles, dragging me away from the group. The others swarm up the corridor after the kids.

Tiny little spark sounds sprinkle the air, like a dozen people trying to start lighters at the same time. As the tirones catch up, kids start disappearing left and right. Some squeeze their eyes tight and then simply snuff out like an extinguished flame, and tirones grope at air.

They're waking up. Going back to the Real World.

A tiro grabs Everett, and he shouts, yanking against the man. Everett squeezes his eyes shut tight, but nothing happens. He tries again, then looks around in panic.

"Stranna! I can't do it! I can't do it anymore!"

Stranna leaps at the tiro, drawing her sword, but it falls from her hands at the briefest deflection. She collapses against him like a damp towel, giving a valiant fight but having no strength or energy because of the weakness of her physical body.

Four men carry me up the corridor away from the attack, one on each limb. My injured shoulder shoots blinding pain through me. My own weak body can't resist.

Stranna crawls away from the tiro attacking her, shooing the remaining children around the corner. The tiro lifts his sword and hurtles after her.

"No!" A bend in the path blocks the fight from my view.

So much for saving Stranna. So much for getting Heidi to a safe place. So much for starting a new life. Somehow this is all my fault.

But why aren't the tirones killing me? I look like a traitor to the Emperor. And maybe I am—I've been found with the Spores, delivering a child to them instead of to Luc. I strain against their holds as my emotions build. Smoke curls from my body. I egg the emotions on.

C'mon. C'mon, saber-toothed tiger!

"Look out!" one tiro says. "Knock him out before he creates something!"

One of them drops my arm, and my left shoulder thuds to the ground. I scrabble for someone's ankle or weapon, but a sword hilt finds my temple first.

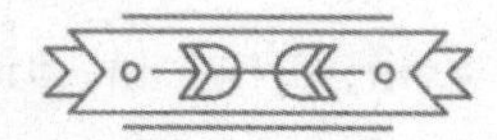

I'm still in the Nightmare when I wake. It feels like ages ago that I was in the landfill with Stranna's unconscious body. When am I going to return to the Real World? Everything is still clear in my mind since Stranna stabbed me, and I do the math easily.

It's because my wake times are so short in the Real World. Next time I wake up, I'll have only two hours left awake. That's the last leg before permanent Sleep. I've been in Tenebra for a couple days since falling asleep in the Jeep. I'm probably close to waking up, but there's no way to tell how close.

I'm in a dark cell made of close-set blades instead of bars. They alternate between silver metal blade and mistblades. I expect that's to guard against any sort of creature I might create from nightmist. But they don't need to worry about that. I'm empty. Even when the tirones hauled me out of the catacombs and my emotions throbbed inside my mind, the nightmist felt far away.

Why?

Is it the weakness from my physical wounds or is it from all the time I spent with the Spores?

"Cain." Emperor Luc is at my cell door. It's his voice, but he's not the same Emperor I met when I first arrived in Tenebra. He sits in a chair on the other side of the bars—a crude wooden chair with carved wheels half the size of wagon spokes. Almost like a wheelchair. He's thin and bent and paler than a corpse.

Crixus stands behind him in the shadows, but not enough to be invisible.

I'm on my feet, facing them in moments. I don't give an apology because I'm not sorry. No explanation because I have none.

"Luc, what did you do?"

Luc's eyebrows rise as though the answer should be obvious. "I rescued you, Cain."

I almost slam a hand against one of the bars before I remember that they're blades that would slice deep into my palm. "Rescued? We talked about it beforehand! I was there to see if the Spores could save my body!"

"And to find their base," he reminds me.

"Yes! And to bring that information back to you!" Which, I admit to myself now, I wasn't going to do. "There was no plan involving you attacking the catacombs with me in them."

Luc waves a bored hand. "And yet, here you are. Unharmed."

"In a cell," I spit. "Should I even ask what you did with the kids?" Did they get Heidi? Everett? Equally important, I want to know about Stranna and the other Spores, but I still possess some awareness that such a question would be foolish to ask right now.

"I rescued them, Cain. That's what we do." His voice is weak and papery. Each sentence seems to send him out of breath.

He's deteriorating quickly. I'm hit with a pang as I realize he's using what are probably his final weeks in Tenebra trying to save the kids and reunite them with their families. Maybe Luc and the Spores do have the same goal and just don't realize they're on the same side.

"Where are they?" I imagine little Heidi in a cell like mine and feel sick.

"Somewhere safe where the Spores can't get them. We're in the process of collecting their information in the hopes of reuniting them with their parents."

His story has stayed the same since I met him, but my faith in it has dwindled. I can't pinpoint why. Maybe it's because he had me followed. How else would they have found the catacombs? Did they see me at the golden wheat field when I found Heidi? I don't know why, but I hope not. That place brought me joy, and I want to keep thinking of it as my own—as a refuge of sorts that I can go to someday if I need to. It promises safety, even if it doesn't make sense.

"We got my father," Luc says. It takes me a moment to realize what he means. "We got him out of the Tunnel."

Galilei. The cure. "So he's still alive." Then why doesn't Luc look happy?

"I fear we're too late," he states.

"No, we're not. I still have one Sleep left. If the Spores follow through with what they said, then I can get the cure information from Galilei, take it to the Real World—"

"Not too late for him, Cain. Too late for *you*."

I try not to let my confusion show. The statement hangs in the air, waiting for me to piece things together. Luc is the only route to a LifeSuPod—to life. I need to salvage this.

"I'm not quitting on this job, Luc."

He shakes his head. "You're infected. I can see in your eyes that you don't trust me. You're not on my side."

I almost laugh. "We've never trusted each other! We only used each other. And it's worked so far. You're trying to save your father, and I'm trying to save myself." And the rest of the world. "Let's finish the job."

For the first time I wonder if Luc doesn't *want* us to get the cure from his father. After all, what life would Luc be going back to? A body with Stage IV cancer? Tuberculosis?

"You stink, Cain."

I glare at him. "Sorry, I haven't showered enough for you."

He laughs, but it turns into a wheeze, and his arms tremble as they grip the sides of the chair until the cough passes. "What I mean is that you stink like a Spore."

I actually sniff the air. "I don't smell anything different."

"You wouldn't. Because it's coming from you."

"Are you implying I'm a Spore sympathizer now?" Anger bubbles inside my chest. "I risked my neck to find their base so I could save my own life in order to save your father's. And now I'm being punished for it? You gave the okay. You sent me out there."

He sighs. "Look, I'm not against you. Otherwise I'd have had my tirones kill you. Instead, I sent them there to rescue you, Cain."

The scene clicks together in my mind. The tirones looking through the attacking Spores. Spotting me. Calling me *Icarus*. Dragging me out, but not killing me.

"We were trying to get you out before you got Spored."

"I'm not Spored," I insist.

"Tell me then, what did the catacombs smell like?"

"Dust. Dirt. Stone. What do you expect?"

"How about . . . cinnamon?"

I freeze. He sees the response in my body language, but I don't care. My mind spins. He's right. The Spores got to me. Their tunnels *did* smell like cinnamon when I brought Heidi in. Cinnamon rolls. I thought they were baking when really they had infected me.

I've been standing here defensive. Distrusting. Doubting every word from Luc's mouth. But logic kicks back in. He said the Spores could weasel their way into my mind and change my very thoughts. I lift up my foot to inspect the roots that have been there the past several times I've entered the Nightmare. They're weak and brittle and small.

"I'm trying to help you, Cain. But I need to know the extent of the damage. *You* need to know."

"What do I do?" I breathe, a hand inching up toward my head as if I can scrape out this Spore infection. "They didn't even say anything. But somehow I started thinking they were good."

Then I picture the kids playing with the basketball. The

little beds tucked into catacomb tombs. I think of Stranna reuniting with her sister Olivia and the camaraderie between her and the other Spores.

I think of the golden field surrounded by nightbeasts and how I knew—really *knew*—Heidi would be safer with the Spores than in the coliseum.

Luc says I'm infected, he says they wormed their way into my mind. But the thoughts and convictions of my heart feel far clearer than any others. I don't want to be deceived, but if this is deception . . . it feels so much more free and clean than Luc's truth.

Maybe I'm willing to be deceived.

It's the first time I feel a little bit of life in this place. I certainly can't tell Luc that. That I'm okay with being infected. He needs to think I'm still on his side. After I get Galilei and my LifeSuPod, then I can be branded a traitor. For now, though, we need each other to accomplish what he desires. And we both know it.

I expel a long breath. "I can get past this, Luc. Just give me a chance. One more try. When I wake up, I'll either still be trapped in that landfill or the Spores will have rescued my body, and I'll be able to help your father."

"Okay," he says. "But you need to remain in the cell for now."

I flare at this, but the reasoning makes sense. "Fair enough."

"Don't let me down, Cain. I know you're trying to do the right thing, but remember that I have Spores in cells just like this and an Arena filled with nightbeasts. If you're on my side, you won't care who or what I send to the Arena. If you're not on my side, well, consider their lives incentive to follow through with your promise to save my father."

He sees through me. I see through him. But we're both trapped, the only people in both Tenebra and the Real World who can help each other.

It's not pretty, but desperation never is.

"I want to see Galilei." I want proof of what I'm fighting for. For all I know, Luc could be lying about his dad.

"He's not coherent."

I look at him. "I thought people couldn't be unconscious in the Nightmare."

"He's conscious but not lucid."

Meaning Galilei won't be able to tell me anything about the cure. "I have one more Sleep. If your old man doesn't share his information now, I'll never be able to bring the cure to the Real World."

"We'll find a way to wake up," Luc says, and I think of the device he used to try to save my life. It stopped my heart instead. Is that where his hope is?

"I have one chance to get your dad's LifeSuPod out of that high-rise. I don't want to take the wrong body. I need to know what he looks like." I mainly want to know he's real.

Luc relents. "All right. Crixus will take you there. But keep your distance." He eyes my hands as though I'm going to create a nightbeast. But what good would that do me? As though coming to the same conclusion, he waves his own hand, and the wheels of his chair spin of their own accord, leaving a trail of nightmist in their wake. He exits the prison area, and I'm not sure the wheels ever fully touch the ground.

I'm struck that even as sick as he is, he can do things like that.

Crixus waits by the cell but doesn't open the gate. He keeps his distance.

"I'm not going to infect you," I tell him. "I don't even have one of those weird Spore swords. I'm not contaminated." I actually don't know, but I might as well keep up the farce with Luc's lackey.

He snorts. "That much is clear. I know a Spore when I see one." Is he contradicting Luc's conclusion about me?

"Where are they?" I try to sound casual. But I wonder if

Stranna still blames me for leading Luc's tirones to their base. Is she alive? I try not to imagine her dead like Erik–stabbed without a moment's thought.

Crixus opens the cell door. "Come on." He gives no other response to my question. I don't ask again, and as we ascend crudely carved stone stairs, he remains silent. It's a filled silence like he wants to say something. He even opens his mouth a couple times, then closes it.

"Just spit it out," I encourage, somewhat amused at his discomfort.

"You're helping the Emperor's father."

Well, that depends on how successful Stranna's plan was to get our bodies somewhere safe. But I won't know until I wake up. "Yes."

Crixus eyes me. "The high-rise his father's in is quite large."

"I can't fix the power. I'm not an electrician, Crixus."

"I wasn't going to ask you to."

"Then what–"

His pace slows. "Hex Galilei's isn't the only LifeSuPod in there." There's something about the way Crixus's words come out that tells me he feels like he's betraying Luc by offering them.

"Are you suggesting I go in to find an empty one for myself and leave Galilei to die?"

"Don't be stupid. There's no power. A dead LifeSuPod won't do you any good." He yanks open a thick door like you'd find inside an old castle, and suddenly we're past two tirones and out on the street.

It's bright here under Luc's fire tower, especially compared to the dark of wherever I was. Dungeon? Prison? I'm sure there's some Roman word for it. I blink once and my eyes are adjusted. That's all it takes. Another reminder of how much I miss sunlight.

"I'm only saying there are more people in there than just Luc's father."

Is Crixus still talking? I raise an eyebrow. "Is there someone you're concerned about, Crixus? In the high-rise?" A young lady perhaps?

He glowers at me. "Life, Cain. It's as simple as that. You're either for life or you're against it. I happen to be for it, and you have a chance to *save* it."

"Ironic when you literally train noxiors to kill."

"I train them to survive."

"Ah, right. Because that's what I did in the Arena with the Spore girl."

"I never told you to kill her." He actually sounds sad about it. Little does he know that she came back to life in some mysterious way.

I shove my free hand in my pocket to keep from throttling him and fist the wheat kernels that have tucked themselves into the fabric creases and corners. Strangely, I'm glad those weren't taken from me.

"Look," I say. "I'm at my final Awake. As soon as the nightmist comes for me, I'll be back in the Real World for the last time." Two hours. That's all I'll have. Two hours. "I'm going to do what I can, but I'm also going to do what I have to."

In other words, I come first. And Galilei. I guess it's a tie.

In truth, I really hope there isn't somebody in the high-rise that Crixus cares about. I don't like the idea of entering a building filled with dying LifeSuPod people—even if they *are* rich. Up until now I'd thought only about Galilei, but I'm sure Crixus is right: there must be other people in there. Why wouldn't there be?

If so, Luc has never said a thing about them.

Crixus gives a sharp nod and turns back toward the Emperor's fire tower. "Got it." I'm irked that he accepts my response that easily. It makes me feel dirty. Heartless. It's as if the centurion who runs the gladiator games has more heart than I do—the guy who tried to find a cure for the world.

"I'll do what I can," I say. And I will. But at this point I don't even have a truck. For all I know, I'm still dying in that landfill.

"Sure." His tone is crisp. He doesn't believe me.

Well, that's his problem. I pull him to a stop. "Don't bother escorting me, centurion. I'm a citizen now. I know where to go."

"You're a prisoner until we deem you safe." He grips my arm again. "And you don't know anything."

I assumed we were going to Luc's atrium, but we bypass the fire tower. We're almost at the base when he leads me around it to the back where there is a white building with a stretch of long stairs leading to a door guarded by four tirones. Crixus knocks on the door to what I can only assume is an infirmary of some sort.

It opens, and a child stands on the other side. The boy gives a little head bow to Crixus and steps aside. It still weirds me out to see children acting as servants.

"So where are that kid's parents?" I ask Crixus when we're out of earshot down a marble entrance.

"Gone. Luc employs the orphans until they come of age."

"You mean until they stop being able to jump into the Real World?"

He nods.

"And then what?" I probe, despite already knowing what Stranna and Everett have told me.

"He waits to see if they become Spores or not." That's all he has to say. I believe him. I saw Stranna's sister in the Arena. Luc sent her there. "That's why it's so important we rescue the kids as soon as we can from the Spores. The longer they spend with them, the more likely they are to become Spores themselves once they come of age."

"Right. Rescue them faster so you can kill them when they don't meet your needs," I comment wryly.

He gives me a side-eye but says nothing. He knocks on another door. This time Luc opens it, still in his wheelchair. "One minute. That's all you get."

I nod and move to enter, but a child comes running up. "Emperor." The girl bows. "The Cole parents are here." She seems nervous, not meeting Luc's eyes.

"Tell them to wait."

The girl visibly trembles from head to foot. She stares at Luc now and opens her mouth, gaping like a noodled catfish.

"What is it?" Luc demands.

"It's urgent," the girl whispers. She takes a step back.

Luc runs a hand down his face, then turns to Crixus. "See that Cain is contained again before his final visit to the Old World."

"I'll see it done."

Luc rolls his chair after the skittering girl. I expect if he were still able to walk, he'd be stomping. The girl keeps a healthy distance ahead of him. They disappear down the next corridor. The door to Galilei's room has closed again, and I look to Crixus, waiting for him to open it, but then spy a map drawn on light calfskin stretched across the wall next to the door.

A map of Tenebra.

I step closer, feeling Crixus's eyes on me. There are hand-drawn depictions of the Tunnels, the coliseum, Luc's fire tower, and even the ghost town surrounding us. Then my gaze lands on the catacombs. They're not that far, and they're about half the size of the coliseum—quite large. I scan the edge of the map until I see the golden fields. There's a single wheat stalk to mark them, but nothing else significant. No depiction of the light or warmth or the safety of it being the holding place for children who get infected.

Other places on the map pique my interest. *Training Fields, Temples of Agon, Baths of Night, Ampitheatre, Circus Flaminus.*

"What are all these other places?" I gesture to the map. "I've only seen people living in the coliseum, but there's a whole *city* out there."

"That was part of the original Tenebra," Crixus informs me. "But the Spores have made them unsafe for citizens."

I look back at the map, trying to imagine Stranna and the handful of other Spores causing so much havoc that an entire culture is trapped in the coliseum because of them. Not possible.

"There used to be more Spores," Crixus continues. "We're making progress."

Progress meaning slaughter. Eradication.

"Come on." He opens the door to where Galilei is. "Let's get this over with."

I tear my eyes from the map and the vision of a Draftsman designing the whole thing only to watch it fall into disrepair from disuse. Luc's father.

I walk through the door into a sterile, white room with a single bed. An old man lies with his eyes closed, breathing labored. Weathered and wrinkled with veins and spots across his skin. His head is shaved, which makes him look rather fearsome. Most old men with a lot of money probably are. He looks more like Luc's grandfather than his father. Must have married someone pretty young to have a twenty-year-old son.

"You've seen what you need to see," Crixus says. "Let's go."

I don't move. Luc was right–Galilei is in no state to hold conversation or even comprehend any words I might say to him. But I can't bring myself to leave yet. The old man lying here is Luc's motivation for everything. He cares about his father so much he's willing to offer me a LifeSuPod, train me in nightmist, kill me if he has to. For a moment my thoughts travel somewhere darker.

I can use this. Somehow. Just like Luc has held the LifeSuPod over my head as a carrot, I could use his father to get anything else I want. Free the kids, let the Spores go. But, I remind myself, I'm already using it to get my LifeSuPod.

The biggest problem is that we both have the same piece of blackmail. If I don't save his father, I don't get the LifeSuPod or a cure. If he doesn't give me the LifeSuPod, I don't save his father.

It's infuriating, but brilliant.

He must have a great amount of love for his father to go to such lengths to save an old man who looks ready to die anyway. Does Galilei even want to live? Luc is deteriorating as well, and I can't help but wonder if this is his last good deed before his end. Maybe leukemia or a genetic disorder or something is causing him to decline in a way that his LifeSuPod can't help him.

How will this old man feel to be handed back his life only to watch his son lose his?

Will anyone tell him the lengths Luc went to, to save him?

Nightmist curls around my feet. I think, for a moment, it's from my emotions, but then I realize it's because I'm on the verge of waking up.

Behind me, Crixus curses.

This is my last shot: my last opportunity to save Luc's father and thus save myself. The Nightmare world fades around me. Everything will change after this final Sleep. I'm so close to securing my LifeSuPod.

The only question is: What life will I be living once I do?

29

I'M NOT IN THE LANDFILL. I'M NOT IN the Jeep. Above my head is standard, white-painted drywall with a ceiling fan that rotates slowly from a breeze coming in through an open window. It's dark outside–4:00 a.m. to be exact–but not the pressing darkness in Tenebra.

Here, there's a moon. And stars.

The very sight sends an ease through my muscles . . . until I sense the ache through my body. The fire and pain from my wounds.

I'm in the Real World, and I was right–Tenebra mutes the pain. Up here, my breathing is labored and agonizing. I need to adjust. I need more air. I barely manage to sit up, and my hands sink into something soft.

My body screams so loud against the movement I'd hold my head if it didn't hurt to lift my arms that high. I take a breath. Another. The pain from my wounds is definitely more potent up here.

It takes me a minute or two to adjust to the new position. My head stops spinning, and I blink to clear my vision. I'm situated on a twin-bed mattress. The room has three other empty beds in it. Everything feels out of place–normal, like before the virus. Like the old life I miss so much.

I'm in a house. In a *bed*. Alive.

Someone found us in the landfill. The Spores–Adelphoi. Stranna must have done this. She must have gotten the message to her people up here somehow. Either that or we were coincidentally found by some good Samaritans, which only ever happens in movies.

The empty beds around me bring a sharp realization. Stranna's not here. A bolt of panic shears through my chest. Did she die? Did Luc's tirones kill her in the catacombs? Did her people leave her body behind in that scorching Jeep?

A glass of water sits on an end table beside me. I chug it while my memories catch up–both Real World and Tenebra.

I was followed to the catacombs like an ignorant idiot, and I got Stranna and the others–the kids–taken. Imprisoned, most likely soon to be slaughtered. Plenty of those catacomb kids were sparking while they played with the basketball. They're Adelphoi.

And I've learned a lot more about what Luc does with Adelphoi kids.

I don't want to be responsible for any Adelphoi's death. They have had the only answers that seem solid. The explanations I've received from Luc have never seem quite right. That's either because he's lying or he's not sure of the answers himself.

Or because I'm infected.

But being infected by the Adelphoi only really works in the Nightmare, right? Stranna didn't stab me with a magic sword in real life. I am in control of my thoughts up here, and they're telling me I'm more drawn to the Adelphoi and their words. I work with Luc solely for the LifeSuPod.

I stand up, and my bare feet cause a creak on the wood floor beneath them. The room spins for a moment, but I force myself forward. I glance around for some sort of weapon. The relief and hope I'd felt initially at being rescued is muted by the fact Stranna isn't with me. Why would they rescue me and not her?

Something's wrong.

A set of crutches is propped up in the corner behind the door. They're the metal kind the hospital gives you–like when Nole shattered his knee attempting to longboard for the first time. I pull the bottom part of the crutch out and use it as a baton. It's light, so it'll take a firm swing to do any real damage, but I have a good grip with the little rubber stub on the end.

I ease my door open and peek into a carpeted hallway with a railing across from me. On the other side of the railing, down a level, is a living room with zigzagging stairs leading up to this balcony. What looks like 20 or 30 cushions and blankets are spread across the living room floor.

A dim light source out of my view illuminates the area with a warm glow. It flickers. Candle? Torch? My brain is still stuck in Tenebra. Do people use torches in the Real World? It's sad I even have to run that question through my head. Of course they don't. But there's likely no electricity here, so maybe they do.

Low voices come from below. I ease onto the landing. My room is at the end of the landing against a wall, so I go the only way I can–left to the other closed doors.

The first one is a shelved closet packed with identical white T-shirts and jeans marked with yellow Post-it notes showing the sizes of each. Either a lot of people live here or a lot of people come and go . . . needing new clothes. The majority of them are child sizes.

The next door opens to a bathroom. It's small and standard, but clean, with one of those fake-smelling candles from the mall on the counter. The wick isn't burned yet, and the cabinet might have some sort of medical supplies or pain relievers.

A lot of homes were broken into for that sole reason when

the Nightmare Virus first spread across the world. Whether from addiction or fear or a simple desire to use them for bartering or bribing, everyone went after Ibuprofen and simple pain-management meds that used to be so easy to snag at the store.

Not so once the pharmaceutical companies shut down.

I glance in the cabinet above the sink. Toothbrushes and one half-used tube of toothpaste. Nothing more. I sigh and limp out. I move to the next door but hear movement from downstairs. Am I being too loud?

I'm torn between peeking to see if it's possibly Stranna or concealing myself in case it's not. I opt for the latter. A door closes, a dish clinks, and then footsteps move from somewhere out of sight and come my way. I hurry to the next door and slip inside, easing it to a crack so I can peer out.

A *hiss* comes from the darkness behind me. I jerk around, crutch foot at the ready. The room is dark, and I immediately picture the snakes from the alleyways forming to latch on to my ankles, my neck, my eyes. The hiss comes again, and my heart thunders, but my eyes adjust to reveal two twin beds and two bunk beds–six sleeping spaces in total all shoved together in the small room. And all six beds are occupied.

The hiss comes a third time as a man's chest rises and falls from the bed to my right. I almost laugh out my relief. He's snoring. No snakes. No threat. I lower the crutch foot limply.

I'm about to turn back to peer through the crack in the door, but my eyes stop on the bed closest to me. A figure lays under the covers, tucked in like a small child, her brown hair splayed across the pillow.

Stranna.

She looks so different lying in peace as though napping rather than hiding under a hooded cloak in a blackened alleyway, surrounded by dead snakes. I cross the room in three strides and pull back the covers to see a nice thick bandage around the bullet wound in her leg and a cushion beneath the injury on her back. It's bandaged, but thinly, and I see the bulge of stitches.

Thank heavens. Only now do I realize my own shoulder is stitched up, though not bandaged. These Adelphoi people work fast.

I gently cover Stranna back up. My risks in Tenebra were worth it. Finally. I saved *someone.* Even though the attempt resulted in her capture along with about thirty innocent kids and the true death of Erik.

I slump. Can I do nothing right? Do all my attempts for life only end in death?

I think of Luc's father . . . waiting on me to rescue him. Will that somehow end in more death too?

I know life and death are a set of scales, balancing each other and always affecting each other, but all the stories I read as a boy and the sayings from Samwise Gamgee and Gandalf and Dumbledore promised me that life wins. Love conquers. Light is brighter.

All this time I've been surrounded by darkness, stripped of those who love me, and quickly dying. Yet hungry . . . so hungry for light and goodness. Why is it denied me?

My balance wavers, and I grip the bedpost, then lower myself onto the edge of the mattress. Imbalanced. That seems to be the theme of my life. Neither standing nor sitting, just wavering.

Undecided.

In the middle.

All the comparisons and analogies Nole loved to share stream into my mind. Is the reason I'm always causing death because I haven't chosen? I'm one foot in Tenebra and one foot in the Real World. One foot with Luc and one foot with the Adelphoi. One foot in wanting to cure the Nightmare but also one foot in wanting a LifeSuPod so I can live in the Nightmare.

I took Heidi to the Adelphoi instead of the coliseum, but that wasn't choosing a side. I've been leaving the back door of my mind open for an alternative. For a backup plan. Not willing to sacrifice one or the other. Not willing to choose.

Just like I did–and am still doing–with God. Using Him when I want, denying Him when I want.

Nole used to say Mom would be proud of me. Would be. Not was. For the first time I don't trust his words. I think she'd be ashamed of my inconsistency.

Stranna's eyes flit back and forth beneath her lids. Dreaming. Or Nightmaring. Her breath speeds up, and the muscles in her neck tense.

"Stranna."

Her breathing increases. Hitches. Gasps. I take her hand.

"Stranna!" Can my voice make it into Tenebra from here? Bring her some comfort? Maybe I'm trying to calm myself because I've seen this before with Nole right before he died.

Stranna's breaths grow faster and faster. Muscles tighter and tighter. The man across from her keeps snoring with his hissing breath, unbothered by the scene of growing panic unfolding mere feet from him.

Veins stand out like sharp cords beneath the thin skin of Stranna's temple. I grip her hand tighter and give her a shake.

"Stranna. *Stranna!*"

Someone rushes into the room from the landing, candlelight dancing.

"Get away from her!" A woman's voice.

If anything, I hold her even tighter. "Something's wrong!"

"I said to leave her alone!" My good shoulder is grabbed. I look up and startle. She's the woman from the Macella Quarter "counselor" booth with platinum hair shaved on one side and spiked in a half pixie down the other side of her face.

Here, instead of a toga wrap, she wears baggy gray sweatpants, a black tank top, and a whole bangle of bracelets that goes halfway up her forearm.

She was there when Stranna was mobbed. She's a Adelphoi too. I try to reconcile this with what I know. She's here–awake. Is this Adelphoi magic? If she's here, she must know how to help Stranna.

I release Stranna's hand and move aside. The woman shoves me as she comes up to Stranna's side. "You can't be in here. Get out!"

I don't move.

"Erik!" the woman shouts.

With a sharp gasp, Stranna goes limp. Quiet.

"No!" I launch myself at her and grab her shoulders. The Adelphoi woman doesn't bother to yank at me anymore. Instead, she pales and reaches a shaking hand toward Stranna.

The moment her fingers touch Stranna, Stranna bolts upright with an agonized scream. Then she dissolves into rough coughing and sputters as though emerging from being held underwater. The Adelphoi woman pounds her on the back.

I'm so relieved to see her alive that I wrap my arms around her and pull her tight to my chest. I know I'm the cause of the majority of her misery, but I hold her with no plans of letting go.

In this moment I know what side I'm on.

I don't have to have all the answers, but Stranna is life. She is hope to me. She's shown me again and again that life conquers. Whatever number of days I have left I want to spend them being a part of whatever she's a part of.

Somehow she feels more solid here in my arms–here in the Real World. Not a figment of my memory of physical touch and human interaction. We're actually both here. Breathing. Awake. Alive.

She coughs one last time, and I let her go, bracing myself for the moment she recognizes me. I don't meet her eyes, though I feel hers on me. I can practically taste her confusion, and I think to apologize.

"Cain," she breathes. Her tone is not angry. Not relieved. Not . . . anything, really. Which means there's also no fear.

The Adelphoi woman lets out a long breath. "You worried me this time, girl. Now tell us what's going on."

Us. I notice two more forms standing in the room, but the light from the hallways shadows their faces. I focus instead on Stranna.

She curls in on herself, resting her head in her hands. "They have us in the noxior quarters, and they're delivering us one by one to the Arena. Even the children! Jules, they're killing us one at a time." Her eyes, filled with accusation, slide to meet mine. "I put up a fight and . . . they slit my throat."

The woman, Jules, flinches.

"I can't go back," Stranna whispers. "I can't keep doing this." Her hand holds her neck like she still feels the blade splitting the skin.

A noxior slit her throat in the Arena, and the mob probably cheered. Yet here she is, alive. Since somehow the death that happens to her in the Nightmare doesn't carry over to real life. I already suspected as much from when I killed her, but it's different witnessing it from this side.

Jules hurries to the other beds and checks the pulse of each occupant. Someone behind me steps forward, and I catch his face.

"Erik?" I probably shouldn't be surprised anymore, but the last time I saw him, a tiro stabbed him in the chest. I watched him cough his way into the grave.

He grins, but it's pained. "That was my second time."

"Don't tell him anything," Jules snaps at Erik. "This was all his fault."

I wince.

"Don't." Stranna seems to be catching her breath. "Don't pin all the blame on Cain. He's only searching. I don't think he's the enemy."

Jules sniffs. "I'll need the names of the kids who are captured."

"Some are ours. Some are Jeremy's. It all happened so fast . . . I'll write them down. But, Erik, I have Heidi's information. She's close. You need to . . ." Stranna's eyes go to me, and she changes the course of her words. "Jules, I can't think. I need food."

"Yes. Of course." Jules flits from one end of the room to the other, flustered, then finally ends up in the doorway. "I'll set some out. Take your time. You know how it always is–you'll feel better in about an hour."

Almost as an afterthought, she grabs a book from a shelf next to the door and hands it to Stranna. "Come down when you're ready. We'll talk. Meanwhile, I'll prepare a message for Erik to take to Jeremy."

Jules looks like she wants to say more. The panic of slipping time hangs heavy in the room. Every minute spent awake is five minutes in Tenebra. They're losing ground. The kids are being sent to the Arena as we speak.

I have a feeling the kids don't wake the same way the Adelphoi adults do.

Stranna was wrong. This *is* my fault.

Jules leaves, and Stranna and I are left in a tense silence. I can almost predict what's coming next, and I'm not wrong.

"Cain, what did you do?" Stranna clutches the book to her stomach. She looks about to cry, the moment of embrace we recently shared is a thing of the past. "Did you betray us so quickly?" Her voice breaks.

I drop my head. "They followed me. I was a fool."

"You couldn't tell that an entire *army* was following you?"

"Neither could you from up on that phoenix," I retort, though I regret it immediately because her face falls.

"You're right."

I don't expect her to trust me. Not now, not ever. And she'd be right not to. I've been playing both sides since we met all because of Luc's offer of a LifeSuPod. But the Adelphoi seem to have *life* that would keep my spirit alive.

This betrayal–all but handing Luc the Adelphois' location–feels like I killed Stranna all over again. This time with a noxior's hands instead of my own.

"He's going to kill them all." Stranna flumps back against her pillow and closes her eyes. "You shouldn't be in here, Cain."

"Why not?"

"Because already you're learning names. Faces. You'll compromise the rest of us. Maybe even try to kill us."

"I'm not going to betray any of you." Again. "I want to help."

"How can you?" She looks at me. "This is your last Awake."

The reminder jolts me. I don't have a watch anymore, but I can already tell that ten minutes at least have passed. Yet something grounds me to Stranna's bedside. Not roots from my soles, but a desire to stay.

"Are you okay?" I need to leave, but I want to hear her tell me *yes* before I do.

"It's . . . a lot on the emotions."

"Dying?" I try to joke.

She manages a wobbly smile. "Not much fun, but at least it's fast."

"What does it matter if the Emperor captures you or kills you? You all just wake up here, it seems."

"If you were one of us, you'd understand."

I gaze at her for a moment, then whisper, "I want to be." *Tell me how.*

She gives me a sad smile, like she feels bad for me but knows I can never be a part of them. Something inside me crumbles as another hope for home and life is denied me. They dragged Erik into their ranks. At first I pitied him. Now I envy him. Why won't they drag me too?

Stranna throws back the covers. "I'm hungry. Have you eaten?"

"No." I offer my hand to help her up. To my surprise, she takes it. It's comical, really, as we both wobble, but then Stranna lets go and keeps her feet. She wears blue-jean overalls and a white T-shirt similar to those I saw in the closet. I'm glad someone changed her out of her bloodied and torn clothes. I'm equally glad no one tried to do that with me.

"How did you get a message to Jules when she's Above and you were in Tenebra?"

"Jules was dying in the Nightmare—she'd been stabbed trying to stop the Tunnel cart. I told her what you told me about the landfill and coordinates. When she woke up here, she was able to send help."

"So if you're a Spore, you just wake up in the Real World when you die?"

She shrugs. "Sometimes we don't. Sometimes it's our time to go."

"So every time you die, it's like Russian roulette. You don't know which death will be your last?"

"Basically."

"That's sick."

"That's grace."

I give her a side-eye and choke on another question. Grace? To never know which death will be your last? It's a twisted game, that's what it is.

"I don't expect you to understand."

There are too many questions to keep swallowing, especially right now when Stranna seems willing to give me answers. "Nole was like you, all . . . faithful. But he died in the Nightmare and didn't wake up."

"It might have just been his time," she whispers.

I don't like that answer. I shouldn't have brought him up, so I shift gears. "How do you go back into the Nightmare?"

"It happens the next time we go to sleep." Stranna rubs her eyes. "I'm so tired. But if I nap or fall asleep, then it's back into the Nightmare."

"So Jules has been keeping herself awake since she . . . died?" This is the weirdest conversation I've ever had.

"Yes. She'll start fading in another few hours, I'd guess. We each stay awake as long as we can. We have to, otherwise the garden wouldn't be tended, and there'd be no one here to feed those of us who are sleeping. If able, we also gather children lost in the Real World. Bring them here. But now that Luc has us captured, all this might look different."

We reach the stairs, and she grips the railing with white knuckles, moving down one cautious step at a time.

"Why does everyone in Tenebra want to kill you?" I ask.

"It's the smell–or the Spore dust as people seem to label it. It marks us as an enemy and triggers the anger emotion in those who aren't like us. So they attack, just like you did. Now if you'd please move and let me go *eat*."

I've stepped in front of her at the bottom of the living room steps. I move aside, and as she goes by, I realize the cushions and blanket lumps scattered across the living room floor are people.

Kids.

I tiptoe around them, nightmist hovering ever so subtly around their bodies, swirling with a hunger as I pass. They're all in the Nightmare. I spot Everett tucked up against the feet of a sofa, one elbow propping his head. Stranna takes a moment to stretch his limbs and readjust him. Then she squats next to a little girl at the edge of the carpet, checks her pulse, and rises after a relieved nod.

I recognize the hair. It's her sister, Olivia.

These are the older kids—the ones who can no longer wake up at will. Where are the little ones who still have the waking power?

"I bought your useless cure for her, you know," Stranna remarks. "Not for myself."

My gut twists. "I'm sorry. I truly thought it was going to work."

"I did, too, after your video. Clearly it did work. For you. For a time. But I never should have purchased it in the first place."

"You couldn't have known it would fail." Not even I knew.

"I mean that I should have had faith." There's that word again. This time, instead of making me angry it makes me sad.

"So faith told you not to buy the cure?"

"No. But I've been looking for a human way out of this since the virus struck. I could never quite trust God fully with this new existence. I knew in my heart that buying that cure was my way to try to take care of Olivia. Not what God was asking. It was because I left to fetch it that Olivia got put in the Arena in the first place. In trying to save her, I almost got her killed."

She heads toward the kitchen, her shoulders sagging a bit more than when we first came down the stairs.

Playful shouting and laughter comes from beneath our feet. There must be a basement to this place. Jules stalks out of the kitchen with a plate piled high with peanut-butter-and-jelly sandwiches. The bread is thick and crumbly—homemade.

My stomach growls, and she glares at me. "Your food is on the counter. Though I'm not sure we should waste it on you." She swings open the door under the balcony to reveal a blast of noise and another flight of stairs. All younger kids, by the sound of it.

"Enjoy feeding the piranhas," I quip. I think I see the quirk of a smile before she slams the door behind her.

I continue after Stranna, scanning the walls for a clock. For anything to give me an idea of how much time I have left. This is my last time awake . . . I need to be doing things. But the sense of urgency has fled. It's almost like I want to soak in my final two hours in the Real World, knowing they'll be my last.

I think about the first time I saw Stranna in the Arena and how my rage was unmatchable and all-consuming. I've been the opposite of her in every way. I killed her in the Nightmare, and she saved me in the Real World. I was a citizen of the coliseum that hunted Adelphoi, yet she led me to her Adelphoi home and showed me life. Their lifestyle enticed me even while I knew they would always be hunted, hated, and forced to hide within a giant tomb labyrinth without the sun. Their cinnamon smell didn't hurt either.

I want better for them. I want to be one of them.

I've robbed them of their home—maybe even caused some of their deaths with my recklessness. Once I'm back in Tenebra, I know what side I'm on. I'm going to rescue the Adelphoi and all the kids in the Arena. I'm going to find them a new home—one with light instead of tombs.

I'm going to turn this around.

But not in my own power. There's a mystery in the Nightmare wrapped up in that wheat field of light. I may not have gotten my Draftsman license, but I'm going to find out why that place is light, life, and safety. Somehow I know that was a gift beyond the reach of whoever created the Nightmare. It's a clue to something good in such a place.

It's not my doing, not my creation. But I feel as though I've been given permission and eyes to see it as an opportunity.

Adelphoi versus Emperor. I finally know where I fit. I may not be accepted by the Adelphoi yet, but they're not going to be able to get rid of me.

In order to do any of this, I need that LifeSuPod.

I make it to the kitchen. French doors open from the tiled

floor into a large backyard that stretches up to train tracks. A full moon illuminates about an acre of land that looks like a mini farm barfed on it. A dozen kids are out among the bushes and plants—some working, some playing. Some are hanging candle lanterns to give them more light.

The whole thing is fenced in with chicken wire, and a dozen or so chickens peck around garden plots of young corn stalks and flowering tomato vines. A pen toward the back corner holds a milk cow, and across the garden at the base of the window a small calf is tied to a post.

I'm not a gardener, but I can tell they've beaten the grocery store.

The only thing I don't see is a PB&J plant. These people prepared for the virus—they must have been those crazy preppers who empty store shelves at the first sign of apocalypse. Except they don't seem crazy. They seem passionate. Discerning, even. They would have had to plant this garden months before the virus first started to spread.

Or maybe they were weird suburbanites who wanted to live off the land before anything even happened. Whatever the case, this means food, and I'm grateful.

I hope to express it as best I can before I ditch them to help their enemy, the Emperor, save his father. But I'm no longer doing it for Luc or even for Galilei. I remind myself that my whole reason for wanting a LifeSuPod—for wanting life—has changed.

Erik is in the yard giving a hose to one of the kids and pointing to a patch of strawberries. The boy obeys without question. He also sprays some of the other kids before committing to the chore.

Strawberries. What a luxury. I hope my meal includes some.

"Here you go." Stranna plops a plate in front of me. It has baked beans, a fat slice of sourdough bread, and a handful of blueberries.

"A meal has never looked so good. Thank you." I imagine what the small family guarding Luc's gasoline can would do for a meal like this. They shot me and Stranna over a box of pasta. They'd probably burn this house down to access the garden.

Stranna sits next to me at the kitchen island with her own food, which is identical to mine. She scribbles a list of names on a piece of paper. When Erik comes into the kitchen, she hands it to him without looking up.

"Tell Jeremy the kids are all fine. So far." She swallows. "I'll wait for your report. And please get Heidi."

"Be back soon." Erik gives me a nod of acknowledgment before heading out the front door. On a whim, I go after him.

"Erik."

He stops and turns. I know he's in a rush, but he takes the time. "Pretty wild ride, eh, Cain?"

"What happened to you?" Surely he must have thought about how it looked to see him dragged away by his ankles across the bloodied stone road our first day in Tenebra.

"The Adelphoi took me to the catacombs. Bound like a prisoner. I thought they were going to kill me. Especially when one of them–Stranna, actually–drew her weird sword, and it stabbed me right between the eyes."

"She did that to me too." So this is a normal thing with the Adelphoi? Last time I saw Erik in the Nightmare he had his own magical sword at his side. Has he stabbed anyone with it?

"She did?" This information seems to surprise him. "Interesting."

I don't have time to ask why that's interesting. Clearly even after all that, Erik was comfortable enough to join the Adelphoi. Passionate enough.

"They reunited me with my daughter."

Ah, there it is. I nod. "That's amazing."

"Look, I gotta go." He holds up the scrap of paper Stranna gave him.

"You're getting Heidi? The girl I brought?"

"Yeah. Her and her mom's bodies are near us. If we can get them here, they'll be safe. And useful."

I want to go with him. I want to fulfill my promise to Heidi, but I can't. I have to go to the high-rise. "Where exactly is 'here'?" I ask, taking in the cul-de-sac and the overgrown lawns that were once manicured enough to meet HOA regulations. The lawn of the Adelphoi house is also overgrown and shoddy–likely to keep up appearances.

"Just your standard abandoned neighborhood," he says.

"No, I want the address."

His eyes narrow. "Why?"

"I'm not going to give it to the Emperor if that's what you're thinking. Not that he could do much with it if I did. He has little to no power left up here."

Erik considers this, then tells me the address–street name, city, and all. "The freeway is that way." He points. "But there's nothing there for you except a long walk. And if I'm right, you're almost out of time."

"Thanks." I don't bother to elaborate. I return to the house and shut the door after me. As I pull the crumpled map from my back pocket there's a jingle of keys and *snick* of a lock from behind me. Erik locking the front door. It'll keep looters out for a time, but all they'd need to do is smash some of the larger living-room windows to get in.

Every little thing counts, I suppose.

I return to my map. I recognized the street name he mentioned. It takes me a while to locate it, but when I do I have to check it twice to make sure I'm right. We are mere miles from the high-rise. Probably the closest neighborhood we could be in.

This might actually be possible.

When I return to the kitchen, Jules is there too. "Name?" she asks the minute I sit down. "I can't keep calling you 'Stranna's killer.'"

So Stranna didn't tell them about my botched cure attempts. I try to catch her eye, but she avoids my gaze.

"I'm Cain." I wait to see if Jules will place the name.

"Like Cain and Abel?"

I glower. "That's the one." Named after a murderer.

"Wouldn't mind hearing your mom's reasoning behind that one."

"Well, she's dead, so . . ." Mom named me Cain because she believed everyone was redeemable. She thought I could represent that vision. Instead, the name seemed to be prophetic for me in that I'd become a murderer in a way, not only of Stranna but of countless others who turned to me with hope for a cure.

"That's rotten. I'm sorry." Jules sounds like she means it, but she's also very casual with whatever she says. "Virus?"

"Cancer."

Stranna pauses eating. Her look tells me a lot more than words.

"It's fine." I shovel beans into my mouth and change the subject. "These are the best beans I've ever eaten."

Jules grins for the first time. "Thanks. Homegrown last summer." She heads into the garden.

"Don't people ransack your garden when they see the food?" I ask Stranna through mouthfuls.

"People don't really come this way anymore. They've either all fallen asleep or died. This neighborhood is mostly abandoned. The few times we've found people in the garden we bring them in and feed them."

"Robin Hood, eh?"

"Except we're not stealing."

I'm alive. I'm eating. Adelphoi or not, Robin Hood or not,

I owe these people. What would it be like for the Adelphoi and the kids to have a home, a refuge, like this place, but in the Nightmare? That's what I want to give them. That's what I want to give myself.

I need to get that LifeSuPod so I can be stronger and more alive in the Nightmare. And I need to rescue Luc's dad so we can have a cure. Do Stranna and the others know that about him? Do they know they pulled the plug on the high-rise only to doom the world?

A little girl walks in with a basket full of chicken eggs. "There are two blue ones this time, Stranna!"

Stranna smiles. "How exciting. Put them in the lime, would you?"

"Okay!" The girl hauls a five-gallon bucket of some sort of liquid out from under the sink. It takes her a lot of work, but Stranna holds up a hand when I move to help her.

"Let her do it," she says quietly. "She's so proud to be able to do it on her own. And sometimes these kids are all we have when our sleep cycles get thrown off."

The girl's face practically glows as she carefully plops each egg in, taking particular care with the two blue ones. I peer over and see at least a hundred other eggs in the liquid before she puts the lid back on.

"How long will it take to get Heidi?" I ask Stranna as the girl heads back outside with the empty basket.

"The little girl you brought us?" Stranna shakes her head. "Hours. Maybe longer. I gave Erik all the information I could, but it's hardest with the littlest kids. They never pay attention to where they live, and even if they do, sometimes their directions or information isn't accurate. She's four–"

"Four and a half," I correct.

She gives a tight smile. "She did her best. We have Adelphoi scattered around the country, so once we get a state or the name of a city, we can usually start the process of getting her help. Thankfully she knew New York and had a street name for us."

I finish my last bite and try not to stare too hard at the empty plate. I have so many questions about their way of life, who owns this house, how they prepped so much food, and how they keep all these kids fed and watered.

But I'm out of time.

I reach over and snag two blueberries from Stranna's abandoned bowl.

"Are you going to be okay?" I ask her.

She looks up in surprise. "Are you going somewhere?"

"Is it that obvious?"

Stranna nibbles at the crust on her sourdough. "You know you can stay here, Cain. We'll take care of your body."

My throat constricts, and I barely manage to swallow the final blueberry. Why would they do that? It's kind of Stranna to offer, but I can't picture Erik or Jules picking up the mantle to feed me broth while I'm in an eternal coma. I won't wake like they do if I get killed. My life would depend on their deaths because they're only in this house once they've died in the Nightmare.

"I know all of this is crude, but it works." Her face flushes, and she fiddles with the bowl of blueberries, digging through them and picking off random tiny stems.

Does she want me to stay?

I want to stay. This place feels similar to what I experienced in the golden wheat field. Safe. Warm. But I can't count on them to keep me alive–I can't expect that of them. And I want the cure.

She'll understand someday.

She glances up at me. "Stay, Cain."

I almost cave. But my body's location won't make a difference. In less than two hours I will fall asleep for good. Whether in a LifeSuPod or here in the Adelphoi house, I'll forget all about the Real World until we enact the cure. To stay would strain the resources of Stranna and the other Adelphoi.

So I might as well be in a LifeSuPod.

But I can't risk Stranna following me or trying to stop me if she learns my real plan.

"Thank you, Stranna. That's more than I ever hoped."

Her face breaks into a full-out grin. "Good. Well, if you're going to stay–no matter how long you're awake–you need to pull your weight."

I play along. Maybe because I want to imagine I *am* staying, at least for a moment. "Command me, oh gardener."

"Do you know what weeds look like?"

It's such a simple question that a child should be able to answer. "Not really, but I know chickens. When's the last time someone cleaned the coop?"

"If you're volunteering for chicken-poop duty, you got it. Not that respectable, but fairly admirable." She grins again.

"A guy can try." *You're about to admire me a lot less.* I wash my plate and put it on the drying rack, fully aware of Stranna watching me.

"Stranna." Jules pops her head into the kitchen. "I need to talk to you."

"Okay, be right there." Stranna slides gingerly off her stool. She stops, one hand on the doorframe. "There's a shovel in the shed and we should have some leftover straw for their nesting boxes. But first, overalls and T-shirts are in a closet upstairs. Unisex. Find your size."

"Overalls?" I glance down at my clothes. The hem is torn and flopping with every step, blood soaks through different sections of the denim, and a few gashes in the material make me look like I'm trying *way* too hard to be cool and edgy. I'm lucky these clothes are still hanging on to my body.

But overalls? I don't think I've ever worn overalls in my life.

"Baggy, sturdy, and way easier for different body types to

fit into." She hooks her thumbs in her own overall straps and whistles a short bit of "Old MacDonald Had a Farm" as she leaves the kitchen.

I smile, but my heart isn't fully in it.

Jules is already deep into the garden, the vigor with which she gathers fallen sticks from the trees surrounding the backyard reveals her tension. Stranna lays a hand on her shoulder and Jules relaxes, then straightens with a deep breath.

Then their conversation begins.

"I'm sorry," I whisper to the glass door.

I head upstairs. It took mere minutes to get enraptured with the Adelphoi life of gardening and clean clothes and a full belly. Do I really think I can save Galilei and get my LifeSuPod with the time I have left? Might it not be better to give up on that and stay here, where an enticing life is being offered and is tangible?

But it would mean giving up on the cure. And I've already sacrificed so much to get this LifeSuPod. I can't stop now.

Still, something in me tells me to let it go. To stay here in the Adelphoi house. Is this how Stranna felt when she left to get Olivia a cure? Did she feel a prompting or nudge and then ignore it?

I come to a full stop on the stairs, as if moving another foot will make the decision for me before I give my head a chance. I want to shovel chicken poop. I don't want to go save the old, dying father of the Emperor-boy who's about to murder Stranna's friends.

But the LifeSuPod. The cure. I take in a breath. I'm not going to follow some subtle faith-nudge that Stranna mentioned. God can't possibly want me to give up now. That would mean He's allowing this Nightmare to win. And no matter how tenuous my relationship is with Him, I can't believe that to be true.

Besides, the Adelphoi aren't loyal to me. Only Stranna

seems interested in helping me. Jules saved us from the desert because Stranna was with me. I doubt they'd have come for me if I'd been alone.

My hand grips the banister so tightly I'm surprised the wood doesn't crack. I *have* to go. I have to leave Stranna and her chickens. Maybe I can explain it to her inside Tenebra. At the very least I'll be able to do more to help her and the other Adelphoi.

So why does this feel like I'm betraying her?

The Adelphoi are the ones who cut power to Galilei's high-rise. They tried to kill him. I'm about to save him. That's why.

I'm undoing their work. But their work held the intent of murder.

I take the steps two at a time and trip on the torn hem of my jeans. On the balcony, I yank open the closet door and get what I need. I change quickly and then head back downstairs. I peek out a window to make sure Stranna is still working the garden. She and Jules are talking close and intense, but moving through the garden as they speak. Stranna sets a shovel and straw along the outside of the shed for me and gives a brief glance toward the house. I turn away quickly and don't look again.

I explore as quietly as I can and perk up at a hanger of keys on the wall behind the door near the base of the stairs. Before touching any of them, I peek through the door into a garage.

A small pickup truck, a rickety SUV, and the smell of gasoline. The best perfume I could have encountered. I grab the lone Ford key from the wall, slip into the garage, and give the key a half turn in the ignition of the pickup.

The gas gauge bounces upward until it points toward Full.

I can't believe they'd leave it full. That they'd leave the key right here. I suppose it makes sense, that way any of them can access it if needed. They're too trusting.

I head back inside and tuck the key to the SUV inside one

of the shoes by the door. They'll find it eventually, but that search will buy me enough time to get away without being followed. I don't want to leave them stranded. On a whim I snag the candle from the bathroom. After rummaging through the drawers, I find a plastic lighter and go back to the garage.

I punch the garage door button.

Nothing happens. Of course not, there isn't electricity. It takes a minute or two before I find the lock on the garage door, then I haul it open. It creaks and groans, screaming my betrayal to the silent cul-de-sac.

I jump into the pickup truck, turn the key, and back out. It's an automatic. My right hand misses the tangibility of a stick. But without The Fire Swamp on the back, I feel like I'm flying backward out of the garage and down the driveway.

As I crank the wheel to turn around, I see her. Stranna stands in the open door of the garage. Not running after me, not hollering, just standing. With crossed arms and a furious look.

"Sorry," I mouth.

Then I drive away.

THE HIGH-RISE IS AS DARK AS THE inky sky above it. It takes only twelve minutes to get there. It almost feels like God is making this easy for me.

I park the truck right outside the doors. This entire section of town looks ghostly without a single light. How many were affected when the town lost electricity? I think of all those families trying to bunker down in their homes during their last hours.

Did the Adelphoi even think about that when they cut the power?

I add it to the list of questions I still want to ask Stranna. If she'll ever give me straightforward answers or talk to me again. I may not see her in the Real World again, but I hope to see plenty of her back in Tenebra and to make everything right.

The glass double doors of the high-rise lie shattered on the sidewalk, probably from whoever ransacked this place, either with the Adelphoi or after them. Or even before. There is no placing a timeline on the human reflex to fight for survival. I step over the glass, thankful I'm not in those ridiculous Roman sandals.

The lobby of the high-rise is littered with more glass, trash, cigarettes, and burned furniture from where some squatters probably tried to light a fire. I skirt around it all, recalling the numbers and instructions from when I was in Luc's atrium. Dull moonlight gives some illumination to the lobby, but once I head toward the stairwell, blackness fills the space like it does in Tenebra. Except I don't feel the weight of it. The shadows do not press or threaten . . . or hiss. That's a relief.

I'm forced to slow my pace so I don't trip and fall on my face, but my heart thunders with urgency. I light the bathroom candle from the Adelphoi house. It smells like artificial apple and cinnamon and burns tall. Cupping it in the palm of my left hand, I tuck the lighter back into my pocket to keep my right hand free for defense. Not that I have a weapon. Or nightmist. I'll keep an eye out for something I could use if needed, but it might not be necessary since the silence of the building tells me I'm alone.

Except for Luc's father who lies dying in a zero-battery LifeSuPod somewhere in this behemoth building.

I take the stairs quietly all the same. At the third floor, I follow a maze of carpeted halls and doors, through giant-windowed office spaces until I reach a wing that starts to look medical. Cream-tiled floors reflect my candlelight, making my path brighter but the shadows darker. The wing is separated from the offices by what would have been a wall of glass, except it's smashed too.

My heart does a flip. What if someone got to Galilei before me? What if he's already dead? Stolen by someone to use his LifeSuPod for themself? But if the Adelphoi couldn't get to him, a looter likely couldn't either.

I wander through the hospital-like setting. Much of it is either glass or steel, and looks like it was built in a hurry. Not because it's cheap, but because it has one purpose: housing LifeSuPods. There's no nurse's station or closet filled with medical supplies or a check-in desk.

But a lot of glass. If this place was renovated after the virus, why so much glass? If Galilei wanted a safe place to live in his LifeSuPod, then why not make everything of secure steel? Why not have more security? He clearly had the money to do it. Maybe he didn't have the time.

I pass three empty rooms and don't even need to open their doors because half their walls are made of glass, and the blinds are left open. No people. No LifeSuPods. But in contrast, this glass isn't smashed. I've entered a different part of the ward.

The fourth room has the blinds shut except for a small crack between the end of the window and the curtain. This should be the one. I hold up the candle, but I see only its reflection. I press my face to the glass and squint, holding the candle back.

I make out a LifeSuPod with a clear curved case. There's a form inside it. I catch a glimmer of a bald head. No lights, no beeping, no sound of the Pod working. This has to be him.

I turn to the closed metal door, and that's when I notice the dents on its face. Deep and shallow, like from a sledgehammer. Another section near the handle has scratches and burn marks as though someone tried to laser through it with a welding tool. An abandoned crowbar lies a few feet from me. This is definitely the room.

The glass, too, holds marks. Parts of it are cracked, but that's all. It's triple-paned and bulletproof. Glancing down the hall at the other rooms, I see they are likely the same but empty of occupants.

Above the door handle rests a keypad and lock system. It's smashed. I try pressing some of the buttons, but nothing beeps or shows that the pressing makes any difference. I shake my head at myself. There is no power to this whole building, why would a programmed door code work?

Enter Plan B.

I pick up the crowbar. This was probably someone's

weapon of choice in trying to break through the bulletproof glass. Bummer for them, but a treasure for me.

I carefully pry at the keypad, getting under the edge and pushing until something gives way with a crack. I pry at another corner. My arms shake from the strain on my bullet wound.

Crack. Some of the keypad gives. I move to another corner. *Crack.* Then I start knocking the pieces off until the whole device finally succumbs and falls to the ground.

Beneath it sits a puzzle of gears, buttons, and sliding pieces, each made of metal and expertly fitted so the pieces are too small to tear off or crush. Interesting, but not surprising.

I don't need to destroy it.

I only need to solve it.

31

I UNWRAP MY FINAL STICK OF ORANGE gum and pop it in my mouth.

The lock mechanism is a slide puzzle that looks like a gray artistic globe. But it's already solved. The globe forms a perfect mini replica of North and South America and parts of Europe. I slide some of the pieces around. They must form another picture of some sort–the globe can't be the conclusion. It's the start.

I fiddle with them, moving and sliding and feeling like I'm in a heist movie or competitive reality show. Sweat lines my forehead as the seconds melt away . . . calling for my end. My death.

My hands move faster, but not more efficiently. What am I looking for? What picture am I supposed to be making?

Then I think of Luc.

He has always called this world the Old World. Our globe is not his home, and it wasn't his father's home. His true home is . . .

The coliseum.

I slide the pieces faster, rearranging them to the vision I've grabbed hold of until they finally form a hollowed oval. An Arena. I slide the last piece into place.

Something clicks in a way that sounds like completion.

I try the handle. It resists enough that when I press down, something *thunks* within the door. I push, and it opens. I breathe fully for the first time and check my watch.

One hour until I enter Tenebra. One hour already used.

I enter the room, propping the door open with the crowbar. The candle illuminates the space enough for me to see the old man beneath the glass. He's identical to the man I saw in Tenebra and just as sickly. He faces the wall of the LifeSuPod, almost as though looking for a visitor or someone to sit at his bedside. Maybe even looking for Luc.

"You'll see him soon," I whisper.

A small circular porthole is open above his face—probably a safety feature once the battery died to make sure the occupant could still breathe. I find the sturdy latches that keep the LifeSuPod sealed and pop them open. The coffin-like lid lifts without a sound and stays open with hydraulic hinges.

Even though he's alive, I feel uncomfortably like I'm about to search a dead body. In one of his suit pockets is the folded handkerchief Luc told me about.

Nothing is within. No address, no note.

A chill sweeps my skin. I check around his shoulders, gently lifting his head from the foam support insert to see if the paper got dislodged and fell underneath. Nothing out of the ordinary except a huge diamond stud of an earring. Like he's a rich pirate or something.

Luc has a diamond tooth. His dad has a diamond earring. To each his own, I suppose.

Then I see a corner of white poking from beneath his left palm. I fish it out and unfold it. There's a scribbled address above a cutout of a map with a blue circle marking the place where my LifeSuPod should be.

"Road 813 Northwest." I read the address aloud, knowing vocalizing it will make it stick in my mind should I lose the paper. "Where's that?" I consult the map in my pocket and find the spot off an old rickety freeway that's not in regular use anymore.

It's a fifteen-minute drive.

I don't have much time.

I could leave now and get the LifeSuPod for myself, abandoning Galilei, but then what? Luc would watch his father die in the Nightmare, and then he'd take out his wrath on me *and* the Adelphoi.

And no one would have the cure.

I'll have to race the clock. I stuff the paper into my pocket with the map and set my mind to figuring out how to disconnect and then move this huge thing.

I inspect the plugs, which are all still secured to the outlets and wall. An enormous battery pack connects at the head, but even it is dead. This guy is living on whatever sustenance was last pumped into his body, which was most likely days ago.

I locate a stamp of a cup, plate, and vitamin pill on the side of the LifeSuPod next to an oval button. I press the button and out of the bottom pops a chamber like a long drawer the size of a piano keyboard. I pull on it, and it slides out even farther, revealing bags sucked clean of their contents–about a half dozen of them. Forty or so more remain with unbroken plastic tops. The machine must rotate through these to get the nutrients Galilei's body needs to survive. I pull out one bag. *Ten-day supply.*

Wow. He's been in this thing for sixty days? That's almost a full year in Tenebra. The remaining food packs will sustain his body for another two hundred days in real life, which is almost three years in the Nightmare.

It's only then that I notice a secondary tray beneath this first one. I push the top one back in, pull out the other, and see several more lines of sealed food bags. If this LifeSuPod gets plugged back in, Galilei will live in Tenebra for well over a decade.

Will my LifeSuPod be stocked like this? It's supposedly sitting in the new location, waiting for me. Is it stocked at all? I wonder if I'm supposed to locate food packs for myself. Why didn't I think to ask more specific details? Like how the thing works. How do I plug myself in? Galilei has tubes all around his head and one snaking down into a vein in his arm. I've never put an earring into my skin let alone an IV. And where does all the waste go?

I look under the LifeSuPod to see a solid gray tube curve away into a space in the wall. Does this guy have a catheter? Will I need a catheter? I'm not about to install one on myself, thank you very much. I shudder at the thought.

My candle flickers and burns below the tin rim, dimming the room a bit. The Nightmare is coming. It's hungry. I'm so close. I can't fail now. *Focus and get going, Cain.*

The underside of the LifeSuPod has tracks like an army tank. I double-check to make sure everything is unplugged, then give it a small shove.

It moves surprisingly easily. I slide items out of the way to clear a path toward the door.

A scraping sound from the hallway jolts my nerves. I spin toward it.

A human silhouette crouches in the doorway, hood up and darkened by shadows . . . Before I have any time to react, the crowbar is yanked into the hall.

The door slams closed, snuffing out the candle and trapping me in darkness.

I RUN TO THE BULLETPROOF GLASS and try to peer through but can see nothing without light. I pound the glass.

"Hey!"

Whoever did this is gone.

Who followed me only to trap me in here? It has to be Stranna or one of the Adelphoi. The timing adds up, as well as the motivation.

But to trap me in here? That seems low. Stranna said they don't kill—they *die.* And yet they attacked Galilei—set to drain him of life. She lied to me. And now the Adelphoi are willing to kill *me.* Or, at the very least, doom me to a deteriorating death in Tenebra.

But the form I saw seemed taller and more built—not feminine. Erik? But he's searching for Heidi. Did Jules and Stranna send him after me?

I fish in my pocket for the lighter and reignite the little bathroom candle.

Then I try the door handle. It rotates easily—too easily. No resistance. It bypasses the latch altogether, and it's locked. What sort of door *is* this that doesn't allow an exit? Didn't Luc or Galilei think of that detail? Or has the mechanism been broken by the Adelphoi?

Since no one had been able to get into the room prior to my arrival, whoever locked me in here probably doesn't know how to do the puzzle and isn't going to let me out. So no one can.

I'm truly trapped.

I try the handle again, though I already know it's useless. The only other way out of this room is through the bulletproof glass, which already has gunshot cracks in it. Maybe it's weakened? But even I know–from movies, at least–that it takes a lot to get through bulletproof glass. Usually a dozen or more gunshots in the exact same spot. From a specific type of gun with specific types of bullets.

Which I don't have.

I don't even have my crowbar. I have a lighter and just over a half hour until the Nightmare takes me.

I glance at Galilei, who looks more like a corpse with every passing minute.

"Any ideas?" I mutter wryly.

I survey the room for something strong enough to batter the glass with. My eyes spy flimsy, thin metal poles holding empty IV bags or black-screen monitors. Nothing sturdy that would stand up to more than one strike against the many layers of glass.

I look in the bathroom. The support handle for getting up from the toilet might work if there was a way to get it off the wall. Which there isn't. And none of the pipes from the sink are accessible–they all lead directly into the wall.

In frustration I return to the main room, searching for anything I've missed.

Then I spot red.

A fire extinguisher in the corner behind the door. I pull it out of its slot, and the weight of it boosts my hope. This could work. I heave it over my head but stop before swinging it. I don't want the thing to explode. It's pressurized, after all.

I pull the pin, slip the nozzle through the cracked door, and release its contents into the bathroom. It takes several minutes to empty. Every tick of passing seconds grates on my impatient nerves. It sputters, and I pull it back into the hospital room.

That should do it.

I return to the pane of bulletproof glass, lift the metal canister, and slam it into the nearest bullet-hole mark.

The extinguisher practically rebounds right out of my hands. My shoulder is pierced with pain, and a stitch tears.

No change in the glass.

I strike again. A minuscule chip. I hit a third time with all my force, growing lightheaded from the agony in my shoulder. Another tiny chip.

This isn't going to work. My shoulder *and* the extinguisher will give out before the glass does. I need something heavier. Sharper.

No, wait. I force myself to slow down and think beyond the panic of my dwindling time and precarious situation.

I don't need a bigger weapon. I need something that will deliver a more direct impact. A nail or something, though that won't stand up to a strike from a fire extinguisher. What's stronger than metal? Stronger than bulletproof glass?

My breath catches. I lift the candle over the LifeSuPod, illuminating Galilei's face. I open the porthole and reach in until I feel the diamond stud in his right ear. Sweet victory.

I remove the backing and slide the earring off. It's not like he'll miss it. I can make him a replacement from nightmist in Tenebra. It takes me several minutes to pry the diamond from the prongs. It has a sharp point on the underside. Perfect.

I stick the point up against the cracked portion of glass, but there's no way to hold it in place and strike it without smashing my finger. Could I dip it in the candle wax? Would that dry firm enough to hold it in place?

An idea strikes me, and I almost laugh. I pull my wad of gum from my mouth and press it over the diamond. It sticks.

Please let this work. I may have only one shot.

With careful aim, I slam the butt of the fire extinguisher into the wad.

Crack.

The first layer breaks into pieces but stays suspended.

I re-situate the gum diamond, then strike it again. *Crack.*

And again. *Crack.*

And again. *Shatter.*

I make a hole through the layers of glass as fast as I can with the extinguisher. It takes some finagling, but I finally break pieces big enough that I can knock them away like swinging bits of sticky paper. I get an arm through enough to bend it to work at the door handle from the other side. The puzzle is one slide away from the solved status. I move the piece from memory and *click*, the door unlocks.

I open it, prop it with my foot . . . and am free.

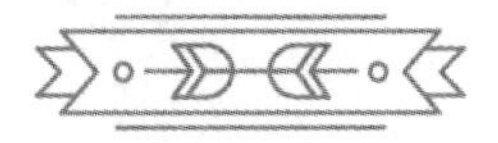

The LifeSuPod moves on its treads smoothly, but it still takes effort and sweat. It has a hover capability, but with the dead battery that's no use to me. Thankfully, the LifeSuPod seems to have shocks of some sort to keep it from jostling the occupant too much.

I heave it out of the room and then undertake the awkward process of getting it down three flights of concrete emergency stairs. I could be more gentle, but the threat of someone waiting to kill me speeds up my movements.

I'm also short on time. My nerves are on constant alert, particularly when I get out into the parking garage. I fully expect the truck to be gone, but it still sits in the shadows by the bushes. I put the key in and give it a half turn. The gas gauge is where I left it.

I'm relieved but question why the Adelphoi didn't take their truck back. Wouldn't whoever ambushed me have at least siphoned the gas?

Unless the attack came from another source. Though I can't imagine who. It was too intentional to be random. It wasn't for goods or even for revenge. This attack was to keep me from retrieving Galilei, and the only ones I know of who want him dead–or even know where he is–are the Adelphoi.

I load the Pod into the back of the truck using a makeshift ramp from a door knocked off its hinges. I run back up to the room to get my candle and grab the extra box of food bags for the LifeSuPod.

I check the clock on the truck dash. Twenty-eight minutes until I enter Tenebra again. With fifteen minutes to get to the new LifeSuPod location, that doesn't leave much time to get Galilei plugged in and get myself connected to the other LifeSuPod.

I throw the truck into gear and haul myself out of that parking lot and onto the freeway, driving well over 90 miles per hour.

I follow the path in my mind's eye, pulling up memories and navigating exits. Once I exit the city, I seem to enter the woods almost instantly. There are fewer cars on this road, many of which are pulled off to one side.

I gun it. One hundred miles per hour. The truck bucks, but the weight of the LifeSuPod in the back keeps it from getting airborne on every bump. Each gust of wind sends my grip tightening on the steering wheel, but I don't slow.

I'm so close to my own LifeSuPod and living my own life.

I check my rearview mirror every few minutes to make sure I'm not being followed by whoever locked me in that medical room, but there's nothing. Whoever it was probably went away, thinking their job was done.

I can't picture Stranna coming after me to kill me or even letting one of her Adelphoi friends do the job. Then again, if they'd been willing to cut the power to an entire building to kill Galilei, then it isn't that much of a stretch to imagine them coming after me.

If it was an Adelphoi, then I've ruined my chances of gaining their trust and joining them. They already know I took their truck. It'll be a hard sell to convince them to let me help after saving Galilei. I'll just have to prove myself on the other side, in Tenebra.

But if it wasn't an Adelphoi, who else knows I'm trying to help Luc? They'd have to have time left in the Real World, and I can't think of anyone with hours remaining. I frown. I don't like having a mystery enemy.

The clock jumps to another number. Fourteen minutes left. I check the mile marker. I am so close.

The correct marker looms from the darkness. I screech to the side of the road, slamming the brakes to make the turn. There is no street sign, no exit sign. Just a gravel road that I almost miss.

One mile, then right.

A deer springs across the road, and I clip its back hoof. My heart thunders as we bounce over the gravel, leaving a cloud of dust rising into the early morning air behind us.

The mile seems to take forever.

Twelve minutes left.

Right turn.

Eleven minutes.

Cabin.

Slatted-wood roof with missing shingles and pine cones littering the dirt driveway. I don't know what I expected, but Luc—with his diamond tooth and his promise of a

LifeSuPod–gave me the impression that his version of a cabin was my version of a luxury-retreat facility.

But nope. From the outside it looks to be one room. I zoom past the front door and around the side of the house then slide to a gravel-smoking stop until the truck is parked at the back. There's another car beside a pile of discarded furniture and rubbish, but not the Adelphoi's SUV. It's a little blue VW bug with dust coating it. Likely a backup vehicle.

Through the trees I catch sight of a clearing with three dozen solar panels laid out neatly in rows. So that's how this little cabin is powered. Luc seems to think that will be enough for a LifeSuPod–2 LifeSuPods.

Nine minutes.

I don't have time to unload Galilei's LifeSuPod and get into my own. What a mess. I leap from the truck and scan the outside of the cabin.

There. A small off-white rectangle. An outlet. I back the truck as close as I can, give the LifeSuPod a quick search, and pull a cord from the battery pack. There is plenty more that needs to be plugged in to make the whole thing work, but this will have to be enough.

I plug it into the outlet, and a tiny red light illuminates on the top of the backup battery. Thank heavens it's charging. Or doing something or other.

Seven minutes.

The door to the cabin is unsurprisingly locked. If I had more time, I'd search for a key. Today my foot will have to be the key. I kick the door near the latch, and it shudders, but not as badly as my battered body. I almost collapse from the slam of pain.

I grab a piece of firewood from the stack beside the door and chuck it through a window. The thing shatters easily. I knock away the leftover shards and then haul myself through.

The interior of the cabin is a bit more tidy than its outside, albeit dusty. Two armchairs, upholstered with maroon velvet and accented by wood arms and legs, sit by an empty fireplace. A rug. A nice bed with a writing desk behind it. It seems the type of place one would reserve for a couple celebrating their anniversary or something . . . all except for the enormous LifeSuPod in the center of the room.

My LifeSuPod.

That's what I'm here for. It looks like an older model than the one Galilei is in, but everything is plugged in and whirring with strong beeping lights, all calling to me. A beam on the top of the battery glows green. Fully charged. I have four minutes to get myself inside and connected.

Hoses and plugs attach to proper outlets in the wall. Next to it is another space and set-up, likely for Galilei's LifeSuPod.

Luc really did give me a new life.

I hurry to the LifeSuPod, ditching my boots and jacket as I walk. But when I reach the transparent coffin lid, I stop and my heart stops.

The LifeSuPod is not empty.

Someone is already in it.

Someone I know.

CRIXUS.

Crixus is in my LifeSuPod. He's been here this whole time, knowing I was working my tail off to get this. He never said anything while in Tenebra. Instead, he let me risk my neck and any semblance of a decent citizen life serving Luc.

With a yell I slam my fist on top of the LifeSuPod lid. It doesn't crack. It hardly even shudders.

Outburst expelled, I stand there. Numb. Staring.

Crixus's connections are much cruder than Galilei's—like he administered them himself. Half the wires and hoses aren't connected, and those that are seem crooked. There's a pool of blood near his arm where it looks like he inserted his own IV. I wouldn't have been able to do that in four minutes.

What do I do now? I have nothing. My stomach is mostly empty, the LifeSuPod filled, and I've taken myself too far from the Adelphoi house for saving. I sacrificed my life for Galilei, sacrificed my chance to be with the Adelphoi, and got nothing in return.

I have a sudden urge to unplug Crixus's LifeSuPod—show him what it's like to watch life fade and be helpless to do anything about it. Instead, I turn away.

Anger pulses through my muscles and if I don't get out of here I'm going to smash something. Or someone. I stalk outside and use my dwindling minutes bringing Galilei's LifeSuPod into the cabin. I hardly pay attention to my actions as my thoughts swirl, but I maneuver it next to Crixus and get the thing plugged in. The battery is charging. That will have to be enough.

With whatever minutes or seconds that remain, I go to the small kitchenette and rummage quickly through the cupboards. One glass jar of coffee grounds, a few cans of baked beans, and an unopened bag of pancake mix.

Two minutes left.

Too late for pancakes. No can opener for beans. What can I do to maximize my last seconds awake? Panic? Eat?

Pray?

I try the tap. Brown water comes out first, but after a few spurts there's clear water. I chug as much as I can until my stomach feels about ready to burst.

One minute.

I sense the nightmist before I see it and keep drinking until I sense the fog enter my mind. Then I stop. I don't want to fall asleep with a mouth full of water and choke.

I don't want to fall asleep at all.

Final Sleep.

I don't want this life in Tenebra. A life of darkness with people who cheer at bloody gladiator games and create nightbeasts with unbridled emotions. When Luc first gave me the offer of eternal life in Tenebra, it had been enticing. I was afraid to die.

I still don't want to die, but I've learned to value life differently, not living merely for the sake of breathing. I want to *live* for the sake of making a difference. To not waste the little time I have.

Tick. Tock. Tick. Tock.

It looks like that time is far less than I originally expected.

The nightmist billows in. I stumble to the small bed in the far corner of the room. Then I let the nightmist take me . . . for the last time.

34

I RISE TO A CIRCLE OF MISTBLADE gladii pointed at my heart. I'm back in Tenebra–forever, this time–and still in the white room where Galilei was kept. The bed is now empty.

The room, however, is not.

Tirones surround me–I recognize some faces from the attack on the catacombs. But one face stands out like a beacon. The one with the steadiest sword. Their leader.

"Crixus." The name comes out in a growl.

"Welcome back, Cain." He smiles like he knows. He knows I found his body in my LifeSuPod. He knows he's denied me life.

My emotions surge, but something splashes my face and startles me out of them. Icy water. A tiro lowers an empty wooden bucket and lifts his sword again. It trembles a little, as it should. There's no telling what I'll create, and I'm not about to stop it.

"When are you going to start controlling those emotions, Cain?"

"You mean silence them?" Bottle them up until they fester and drive me mad. He'd like that, wouldn't he?

"I mean dismiss the destructive impulses and nurture the proper responses."

What was he, a therapist in real life? "Maybe I would have done that if my time wasn't cut short."

He nods to a tiro nearest the door. "Fetch the Emperor."

I've done the math. In a worst-case scenario, a body can survive three days without water. Three days in the Real World is about two weeks in Tenebra. But since my body will be deteriorating, I probably have five days of good energy.

Five days until I lose what strength I have. At first thought, five days seems like a lot, but when I think about it as the end of my life . . . it's only a single workweek. A fading workweek. A workweek with no recovery weekend.

I'm not about to waste them.

"Why am I being treated like this, Crixus?" I ask in a sarcastic tone while the tiro scuttles from the room. "I completed the Emperor's greatest wish. I should be crowned and honored."

"You're no less of a threat than when you fell asleep the last time you were here."

"I'm no threat." At least not in this moment surrounded by swords. "But maybe I should tell Luc about his right-hand man? Reveal some secrets you've been keeping from him. I can't help thinking Luc doesn't know you're in my LifeSuPod."

Crixus startles. Actually fumbles his sword. That's new.

Have I surprised him? Interesting. He's known the location of his body this entire time, and he's also known I've been trying to get to that same LifeSuPod since entering Tenebra. Yet he never said anything. What did he *think* would happen when I got Luc's father to the cabin?

Unless he thought I'd never succeed.

"Enough of this." He sheaths his gladius. "He's right. He has served the Emperor at great cost. I'll take him to the Emperor myself."

The tirones don't immediately lower their weapons.

"Are you sure, sir?" one asks. "You've seen what he can create."

"Do you think I can't handle it, Marcus?" Crixus strides into the center of the circle of swords. The tirones hurriedly sheathe their weapons.

"Of course not, sir," Marcus mumbles, lowering his eyes in deference.

"Back to your regular posts," Crixus commands. Then he takes my arm, and we're out of the strange white building before I can blink.

We head toward the training area, not Luc's fire tower or the dungeons. Crixus isn't taking me to the Emperor: he'd be a fool to do so. I just threatened to reveal his secrets and betray him.

He's desperate. He's scared. And desperate, scared people do desperate, scared things: like murder their problems.

I'm Crixus's problem.

His grip on my arm grows tighter with each stalking step.

"How did you get out of that medical ward?" He grinds out the question like shoving it through a mouthful of rocks.

My body stops moving of its own accord. Crixus gives a tug, then stops.

"*You* locked me in the high-rise with Luc's father?" This doesn't make sense. Crixus is in Tenebra. He's been trapped here for likely months. How could he wake up in the Real World?

"You clearly got out." He doesn't sound pleased that I saved his precious Emperor's father. This means Crixus knew I was in the high-rise and somehow managed to travel to the cabin and connected himself to *my* LifeSuPod within the span of an hour. He expected me to die. He tried to keep me out of that LifeSuPod so he could steal it.

I yank my kris dagger from my belt as furious emotions build like a swirling hurricane. Crixus looks almost bored as he pulls out his own gladius.

"Really, Cain?"

A dagger against a gladius is like a spoon versus a carving knife. But it takes a mere second of reliving how I felt when I found Crixus in my LifeSuPod to ignite my rage. I let the memory crash over me. Crash out of me.

Nightmist spills from my fingers like a tipped cauldron and pools on the dirt, taking form.

Crixus pays no attention, only asks, "So you saved him then? Galilei?"

"Obviously." It's too much. Crixus has been at Luc's side this whole time. It's so cliché, the right-hand man betraying his leader. Crixus probably wants the throne or something equally predictable. "You're clearly not loyal to him, yet you do his bidding."

He levels me with a direct stare. "The Emperor can't know."

"That you're in my LifeSuPod? That I saved his dad? That you can wake up?" My eyes widen. "You're a Spore."

Of course. I was working for Luc, which means I was Crixus's enemy.

"You know nothing."

My nightmist solidifies into a lumbering troll, club and loincloth and all. There is no color to its form: it's black with swirling shadows and sections of its body are still transparent. I grin, equally surprised and pleased by my unintentional creation. My nerd self is coming out. It's about time.

"You can't blame me for ignorance when you and everyone else continue to keep knowledge from me." Ironically, the only person who's consistently given me answers since I arrived in Tenebra is Luc.

Sensing my irritation, the troll looks dumbly around for a moment, then stomps toward Crixus in an attack. I cringe as the oaf tries to locate Crixus beneath his huge, awkward body. Maybe my nerd should have stayed hidden. Crixus actually has time to roll his eyes before he thrusts his mistblade gladius upward beneath the troll's ribs and into his heart.

A single groan and the creature is felled like a tree, shaking the earth beneath our feet upon impact.

So much for that.

"You're really going to fight me, Cain?"

"'Fight for yourself, first and foremost,'" I say, quoting him. "Someone told me that's the only way to stay alive."

"You took it to the extreme." This time he doesn't wait for me to create a nightmist creature. He leaps at me, gladius raised. I throw up my dagger but dodge at the last moment. I don't want to try to stop a strike like that with a dagger. I'm likely to lose a hand.

Nightmist bursts out of me in desperation, putting a broadsword in my hand and forming a giant Minotaur with an axe. The Minotaur towers several feet above both of us and looks far more aware and fierce than my troll. It turns its eyes on Crixus and snorts, scuffing its hooves in the dirt.

But I don't want to kill Crixus. Not yet.

No, I tell myself, *not at all*. I want enough of a breather to get answers. If he is an Adelphoi, shouldn't we be on the same side?

The Minotaur doesn't seem to understand the complexity of my desires. It lunges with a decapitating swipe at Crixus's head.

"Slow down!" I holler. It doesn't listen—doesn't even seem to hear me.

Crixus quickly drops and rolls around the Minotaur's feet, coming up at its back, but the Minotaur spins and punches him in the face. *Crack.* A broken nose.

Crixus falls to the dirt, but that doesn't keep him down. He's back on his feet, wiping blood away from his eyes and lifting his gladius to meet a strike from the Minotaur's axe.

"I'm not your enemy, Crixus." Poor timing on my part for such a statement as Crixus takes another hit from the Minotaur. This guy's like Boromir with two arrows in him. The third is about to strike.

The Minotaur lifts his axe above his head, and while I do believe Crixus might be able to block or dodge or something, I leap between them with my own broadsword and knock the axe out of the Minotaur's hands.

"Stand down," I order the creature.

It doesn't look happy about the command, but it drops its arms and steps aside. Crixus is already back on his feet, responding to my previous statement.

"You want me to trust you, Cain?" He laughs. "One moment you're saving the Emperor's father, the next you're running off to the Spore base."

"I was trying to save Stranna."

"Who?"

"Stranna." I'm thrown by the fact that he doesn't recognize her name. "Someone I know." Someone I want to know better. Someone Crixus, if he really were an Adelphoi, should know.

"You claim to want to save Spore children and this person you know, but you left a high-rise filled with dying people."

"Is that what this is about?" Me ignoring his request to locate other people in the high-rise? "Look, I'm sorry that whoever you care about is stuck in that high-rise, but since you can apparently return to the Real World, you could have saved them yourself."

"It was *me*!" Crixus bursts out and swings his gladius. I meet it with a clang from my broadsword. The Minotaur snorts, waiting for permission to join the fight, but Crixus doesn't attack again. "*I* was in the high-rise, fading away in a dead LifeSuPod."

He's breathing hard. For the first time I see his emotions flare.

"I've been Luc's man since the beginning of all of this. He set me up in that LifeSuPod, yet when power was cut to the high-rise he didn't once talk about rescuing me. Instead he offered the one remaining LifeSuPod to you–a stranger. A nobody who happened to have a lot more Sleeps lefts than the rest of us."

His story explains a lot. Why he wanted me to consider other people in the high-rise. Why he tried to get Luc to change his mind about powering up the high-rise.

I put distance between us. "Why go through all of that when you could wake up and save yourself?"

"It's not that easy."

"So everyone keeps telling me," I say drily. "You have to die first."

"Yes, but I'd never died here before. I'd only ever heard stories. There's always the doubt: What if I'm not enough of a Spore?"

He admitted it. He's a Spore. Except . . . "Don't you mean Adelphoi?"

He looks at me blankly. "What?"

I relax a little even though I have the sneaking suspicion he's still going to kill me. *"We don't kill, Cain. We die."* But Crixus doesn't seem to know Stranna, and he doesn't recognize the name they call themselves. This doesn't make sense.

They said the Adelphoi cut power to the high-rise. If Crixus is an Adelphoi, why would he cut power to his own life source? He would have asked the Adelphoi to help move his body before they did that.

"It was clear you weren't going to help me. I could feel myself dying, so I did what I had to do." He doesn't refer to the Adelphoi as a group. He only talks about himself. On his own.

"You're a Spore, but you're alone, aren't you?" I hazard. He doesn't answer, but the grim press of his mouth gives him away. "So then how did you wake up in the Real World? Who killed you?"

He shrugs and then pats his own gladius.

I feel sick. He did it to himself. Something about that feels more wrong than all the things Stranna has told me.

"You're lucky it worked," I mutter.

He nods grimly. "I'll never do it again. I learned that much."

"If you're one of them then why don't you smell like tar? Or cinnamon? Or whatever?"

"Blood and sweat are enough stench for me. And I'm not one of them."

So he's been capitalizing on his gladiator stench to hide it this whole time. Haven't I always sensed something underneath all that? "Doesn't sound like you run in the Spore circles."

"It doesn't matter what circles I run in, you're not in them." He lifts his sword again and the Minotaur gives a throaty laugh, swaying his axe back and forth.

"We going to fight this out?"

He shrugs, and all it takes is a nod from me to send the Minotaur attacking. I'm not sticking around to fight Crixus until his tirones arrive for backup. Or worse, Luc. I can see the boost of energy Crixus has from the new LifeSuPod. He's only going to get stronger.

I watch the Minotaur leap like a video-game character, wielding his axe high over his head, and bring it crashing down into the ground beside Crixus who dodged at the last second. Crixus counters, and while he's locked in a battle of strength with the Minotaur, I dart forward and yank the cord of keys around his neck. It pulls him out of the fight and to the dust for a minute, but the cord snaps.

I blitz toward the training grounds, not caring to look back to see if the Minotaur took advantage of Crixus's downed position.

I have the keys. I know where I'm going.

And that's as far as my plan goes.

I bolt through the Macella Quarter, which is eerily empty. That tells me one thing: the Games are on. Citizens are watching noxiors get bloodied and annihilated in the Arena. My heart pumps faster, fueling the energy in my legs, and I increase my speed. My shoulder burns from the scuffle with Crixus, but I don't care. A lot of discomfort is about to come my way over the next few hours and days as my body deteriorates. No use letting that bother me now.

I reach the tiro entrance to the training grounds. The thing about the training grounds is that they always let people *in*. You have to earn your citizenship to get *out*.

"Hey, it's Icarus!" one of the guards remarks as I arrive. He must not know that Crixus and the other tirones were trying to kill me mere minutes ago.

I put on a grin. "I'm craving a fight today. Let me in?"

One guard laughs. "The crowd will freak out. You're going to obliterate those Spores." He unlocks the gate and I dart inside, a chill settling in my gut at his words.

I pop my head into the barracks since they're the first thing I pass, but, as I expected, they're empty. All except two noxiors sleeping. A few others train in the sparring area, but I blast by. The closer I get to the Arena corridor, the louder the cheering.

Then I hear a child's scream.

I veer that way and crash against the double gates, frantically peering through to the fire-lit sand.

There they are—all the Adelphoi children, huddled in a circle near the center of the Arena. Erik and Stranna guard the perimeter of the circle as best they can. They went to sleep in the Real World, and now they're here, fighting. Likely about to die again. I finally see the beasts they're up against.

Three coal-black lions with thick chains for manes instead of hair. One lunges and Erik swipes at it with a mistblade. The blade gets tangled in the chains. The lion bares its teeth—double rows like a shark's—and clamps down on Erik's arm. It tugs him forward, and he falls to the sand, still swiping at the creature despite his yells of pain.

One child disappears. Then another. Waking up in the Real World as an attempt to escape this attack. But only two. Several others blink hard, but to no avail. They're too old. Unless they're Adelphoi, if they're killed here . . .

I shake the bars, hollering for a tiro to let me in. But there isn't a tiro since they usually let the noxiors through and then go back to their own business. There's no reason to stick around unless they want to watch the massacre.

No one in their right mind should want to watch this.

The crowd cheers. The same crowd that shows up, desperately hoping their child's name will be called and they can have a sweet teary reunion on the sand. They don't mind watching other people's children die.

Luc allowed this. He most likely called for this. Instead of reuniting these kids with their parents, he's deemed them enemies because they can no longer wake up and serve him in the Real World. They're useless to him.

It's never been about saving kids–it's only ever been about using them. A low I didn't think he'd stoop to. But I also see the sick brilliance in his leadership–he created fear of the Adelphoi in the citizens, while also pacifying citizens by returning their "lost" children. He leads with fear *and* love. And the concoction somehow creates loyalty.

All this slaughter because the Adelphoi tried to kill his father.

This retaliation of his . . . it's not justice. It's vengeance. And vengeance is an ugly thing.

I shove key after key into the padlock holding the gates together. One of them has to fit. These are Crixus's keys, and he's the big guy in charge. But maybe he has another key ring somewhere–on his belt or something.

A lion gets one of the kids by the leg. She screams and swats at it. Stranna leaps on the lion's back and thrusts her sword in between its lips, trying to pry its jaw open. It releases the little girl and spins to snap at Stranna.

"Let me through!" I shout, hoping someone–anyone–will hear. I start over on the keys.

"You'll only get yourself killed," someone yells from behind me. I turn briefly and see nothing but a few green noxiors, cowering and watching. Then a figure enters the corridor at the far end.

Crixus. He defeated the Minotaur already.

Time's up.

I turn back to the gates and abandon the keys. Fists versus metal will lose every time. Though I've already created a troll and a Minotaur, I feel as though my nightmist well is full. Overflowing.

I close my eyes and focus my emotions into a creature, pouring everything out in a feral yell. A storm of mist bursts from me, growling and roaring. The gates burst to pieces, and I break away from the mist to cover my face as metal pieces pelt me. Then I see my creation.

A dragon.

It fills the entry tunnel, trapped halfway in the Arena and partway in the training area. Its tail thrashes, and screams rise from behind me. I leap over a sweep of its tail as it tries to wiggle through the tight hole. Stones break. Dust falls. I barrel forward and try shoving the beast from the rear. It roars. I pray it's not trying to eat the children.

But a dragon was what I'd pictured–not a flesh-hungry monster like Smaug but more the Norbert type with a little more obedience. I shove again, and the dragon claws at the ground, sending clods of dirt and sand spraying back into my face.

Finally it bursts through the tunnel with a crumble of stone. I snag its tail on its way through, and it pulls me free of the rubble.

And then we're in the Arena. The crowd screams, first from terror, but now they spot me.

"Icarus!" The screeches turn frenzied–obsessed–like fans at a rock concert. They're not bothered at all by this sickening display of entertainment.

The three coal-black lions back away from the dragon,

swatting at him like house cats. He snaps at them. Children run to huddle behind Stranna and a wounded Erik. The dragon swivels its head toward them.

Don't attack, I mentally command, a little helplessly, since I have no control over the beast. It comes down to when it was formed, not a command afterward. I hope I gave it enough thought before setting it loose from my mind.

It sticks its tongue out at the kids but doesn't try to eat them. It would have been comical if everything wasn't so dire.

"Get on!" I yell at them, gesturing and stumbling through the sand.

Stranna spots me and her eyes widen. "Cain?"

Tirones enter the Arena behind me, Crixus at the head.

"Get them on the dragon!" I bellow.

"And then what?" she hollers back but ushers the children toward the dragon nonetheless. A couple of the boys run forward, excited. The little girls hang back.

"Then you won't die!" I grab a little girl and carefully place her on the dragon's back. I want to tell her it's going to be okay, but I don't know that. The dragon snorts, and I don't quite let her go yet.

The boys clamber on top of the dragon, pulling at its spine for leverage and using its joints and spikes as stepping stones, hardly even thinking the creature might turn around and eat them.

Erik lifts a few children onto the dragon's back. Stranna moves to climb up but then shouts over the noise, "This dragon is too flimsy!"

A lion lunges at her, but the dragon snaps it up in its jaws and eats the beast with a single swallow.

"Flimsy?" I ask incredulously, indicating its head. "Did you see that?"

"It's made from nightmist! It's not reliable." She hauls herself up all the same.

Crixus shouts, and a spear flies my way. I duck, but the dual- mistblade spear sticks in the dragon's wing. The creature roars and rears up. The children all scream, grasping spines and spikes to stay seated. One little girl tumbles backward, but Stranna catches her and pulls her onto her lap.

The dragon knocks a guard down with its tail, then spreads its wings and surges forward. I barely manage to grab a spike and hoist myself onto its back in front of Stranna. Then we're on a roller coaster with no seat belts.

The dragon smashes its way through one of the Arena walls, spectators screaming and diving out of the way. Then it's flapping fiercely, and the gush of wind and shrieks of riders are the only things that fill my ears. I pray no one is falling off.

Come on, dragon. Get us airborne.

We're up. Climbing. But the dragon's body is almost vertical, and we all cling to it like a rising ladder instead of a flying carpet. My own grip slips with each flap.

"Cain!" Stranna yells my name in a desperate tone.

I nudge the dragon with my knee, which is absurd because there are fifteen other bodies on its back, but maybe it recognizes me as its creator because it relieves some of the incline and switches to a glide. We're hardly over the coliseum buildings, but at least we're in the air.

That's enough for now.

I breathe for what feels like the first time in forever and glance down at the ground. I don't see any injured kids or fallen bodies. *Thank you.*

We're flying. On a dragon I made. I laugh.

"This isn't over yet," Stranna shouts in my ear.

"It's working, Stranna. Be happy about that." I got them out of the Arena. We're free. For now.

"You made the dragon from nightmist."

"So what? I did the same thing for the saber-toothed tiger we rode out of the Macella Quarter."

"Light destroys nightmist and we're Adelphoi."

I think of when she dropped a match among the snakes and they all shriveled up. I think of how Erik sparked like a faulty lighter. The field of wheat–how nightbeasts couldn't enter it. The flashes from the children when they disappeared.

A hollow cold chills my chest.

Maybe she senses that she got through to me because she gives my arm a squeeze. "Thank you for saving us. But we need to land. And soon."

"We're almost there," I say.

"Where?"

I direct the dragon with a thought, and it miraculously obeys, adjusting its course. Then an electric shock snaps past my ear–a black lightning bolt. It plants itself in the dragon's shoulder. Startled, I jerk my head to glance behind us.

Luc is chasing us atop the back of his stingray. He's no longer the weak, frail Emperor I last saw.

The dragon roars. Luc throws another bolt. It sticks, and the dragon's wing starts to deteriorate. Stranna was right–this dragon is flimsy. A real dragon would have thick enough scales to deflect such an attack. Not mine. And Luc knows it.

A third bolt hits the dragon in the neck.

And we drop from the sky.

35

THE DRAGON SPIRALS THROUGH THE air, and my body lifts from its back in a free fall. The wind is so loud I can hear nothing else, but I see the children's mouths open in muted screams. Some lose their grip on the dragon's back. We are like a tossed handful of confetti, waiting to land in the darkness below.

I clamber up the dragon's back to try to gain some control. I wrench its head one way and actually slap its neck as best I can from behind. It tucks its wings to its side, and we fall faster, but then it spreads them out wide, and the deceleration is so extreme I smack into its back and lose my breath. Wheat kernels burst from my pockets and fall like golden rain.

Several children thwack into the beast's wings and then tumble down into the air.

"No!" I reach out to them, and this time what comes out of my fingers is not nightmist. It's not created from emotions but from desperation mixed with an inexplicable hope.

Bright red cardinals burst into existence–as big as SUVs. Three. Four. Five. They stream after the falling children and snap them from the air with their claws.

I'm so stunned by this new creation I hardly realize the dragon is still flying. Though it's wounded and teetering, it has gained control again. Several children are still holding on to its back.

The cardinals turn and follow us, each child safe. I set aside my awe and focus on directing the dragon, but my connection with it seems to have been lost. No thought changes its course or actions. It glides in whatever direction it had recovered itself in the air.

I scan the ground below us and then see my destination: the wheat field. It glows like a patch of gold to the right. Then I look behind us again to see Luc still in pursuit.

"Faster!" I yell to the cardinals. "To the field!" They speed past and the dragon, now acting like a true beast, adjust its course with a snap of its jaws.

Food.

"Stop that!" I smack the dragon on the head, but it only growls. This does no good if it's going to eat the children right out of the claws of the cardinals.

But the dragon has adjusted its course, and that's what I needed. It gives a flap to gain speed, but falters from its injury, and the cardinals barely stay ahead of him.

Faster. Faster, please, I pray.

The first cardinal swoops low over the field and drops the little boy into the wheat.

I hope this works.

Cardinal after cardinal makes it to the destination. As they descend, so does the dragon. It's right on the tail of the final cardinal.

"Get ready!" I holler to the kids behind me. We fly parallel to the ground by mere feet. I don't trust the dragon to stop or land gracefully. Or to leave us alone if it does land. "We'll need to jump!"

Only a few yards from the field do I see the nightbeasts surrounding its three accessible edges. Growling and snapping at the children already in the wheat. We pass over them, and

I fill my lungs to tell the kids when to jump, but right as its nose enters the air above the wheat field the dragon is thrown backward by an invisible source and we all fly forward into the wheat field as if by a bike whose brakes suddenly lock. I tuck my head and manage a roll, but the bangs and bruises send a flash of white-hot pain through my mind.

I tumble to a stop and give myself a few seconds before gaining–and keeping–my feet.

The dragon collapses to the ground on the edge of the wheat field. I berate myself. Of course it can't fly over the field. It's a nightbeast. Unlike Stranna's phoenix or my cardinals, which are made from color or whatever.

Nightbeasts attack the dragon, frenzied over its blood and the smell of us still on its back. The dragon fights back, but there are too many. Like ants swarming an injured bird.

The kids find their feet, and Stranna darts from one to the next, checking on them. A few hold their arms or heads. One has a bloody nose. Erik is the last to get up, and he's pale and bleeding from the arm the lion attacked. He still does a head count of the kids, then catches my eye and gives me a thumbs-up.

He's okay. We're all okay. For now.

Many of the children switch from pained whimpering to excited babbling over the dragon ride.

"Did you see me fall off the dragon when it went upside down? But then I grabbed its spike again . . . *while I was falling*!"

"Well I was carried by a *bird*!"

It doesn't take long for the traumatic experience to turn into the greatest adventure of all time. Stranna makes her way over to me, her face expressionless. My heart leaps as she approaches until I remember our last interaction in the Real World. How I abandoned her, stole her truck, and never came back.

"Why did you bring us here?" she asks when she reaches me. Her tone is not accusing, but there's warning in it.

I brush a hand over the tall sun-warmed wheat stalks, soaking in the light.

"It's the only place that felt . . . good." Right.

"We're not safe, Cain."

I survey the three sides of the wheat field that keep the nightbeasts back. "But they can't get through."

"They can't. But people can." Her eyes lift to the sky.

It's empty, but I catch her meaning. "Luc. He'll come back."

"With soldiers. And now we're trapped. The nightbeasts can't get in, but neither can we get out."

She's right. I hadn't noticed until now that the nightbeasts have doubled–tripled–in number now that the wheat field is filled with fresh meat. A dozen kids and three adults. There'll be no way to fight our way through them.

"Got any matches?" I joke.

She frowns, confused. "Matches?"

"What can we do?" Erik asks in a low voice, joining us.

Stranna slowly shakes her head. "It's going to be a massacre. There's nothing we *can* do except pray that we all wake up in the Real World again."

"That's not enough," I grind out. I knew this wouldn't be a permanent safe harbor, but I viewed it as a bit of a thinking place. I couldn't have led the dragon back to the catacombs. This, at least, bought us some time. But not as much as I'd thought.

She looks at me. "Prayer is always enough if you're willing to stop seeing it as a last resort."

"No, I mean . . ." What did I mean? I wasn't trying to knock prayer. If anything, I'm starting to believe more in it. And in God's involvement in my life. But I felt led to this field. Something about it feels like it's mine. Alive. I brought us here for a reason, not just to be fish in a barrel.

But what is it?

I go up to the translucent wall from which I first saw Heidi. The Nightmare's edge. A golden rift had let her through. How did that happen? Is there a way for us to get through from this side? The wasteland of rubble beyond doesn't look welcoming, but if we could get through, I have a feeling Luc wouldn't be able to follow.

A child cries out and I swivel, thinking a nightbeast must have breached the edge of the field. But the little girl points to the sky.

The stingray is here with Luc on its back, shoulder quiver filled with crackling black-lightning shards as well as a crossbow. With him are a half dozen tirones flying nightbeast crows and armed with javelins, spears, and crossbows.

Seven grown men with weapons against a dozen unarmed children and three weak adults.

"Gather together!" Erik hollers to the kids.

"No!" Stranna shouts. "Spread out and drop low in the grass. Make yourself as small as possible!" The sword at her side unsheathes itself as she spins toward the oncoming attack, not watching to see if the kids obey.

But they do. A couple of them still group together, driven more by fear than survival instincts. I know what it's like to not want to die alone. But she's right–if they spread out, they'll be harder to hit.

I pull out my kris dagger. It's not going to accomplish anything. I can't even deflect a spear with it. So I channel my focus inward, willing up emotions, trying to convince them to overwhelm me. But I'm strangely collected. Calm. In an eerie way. I've accepted that I'll deteriorate and die within the next couple days, and there's a freedom in having chosen which side I'm on.

The nightmist doesn't come. I can't even sense it. If nightbeasts can't enter here, then I certainly can't create one in here. How did I make those cardinals? They were a complete accident, but they were also different, solid.

I don't have time to find out.

The first tiro spear flies our way. It lands within two feet of a little boy. He stares at it with wide eyes but doesn't make a peep. There's no telling if the tiro knew this boy was there or not. But that's too close.

The kids need to get to safety. I've brought them to a graveyard.

More spears fly and stick in the ground. Some children hold their place, while others jump up and run in circles. Nowhere to go. I spin, scanning for something–anything. And then I see the flash of red. Another. First I think they're arrows, but then I see wings. They're my cardinals.

And they're flittering and flying on the *other* side of the mysterious veil.

I sprint to the border of the Nightmare. The Draftsman in me tells me it's no use. A dreamscape has its boundaries, and no one can change them except through programming in the Real World. But if there's anything I've learned about this place, it's that it defies all the rules I originally understood about dreamscapes.

If the cardinals were able to get through, that means there's a way. Heidi entered Tenebra through this transparent wall. Maybe all the kids did. They must be able to go through it too.

I press a hand against the wall, but it's as firm as glass. I knock the hilt of the kris dagger against it to see if it shatters. It wavers a bit, now acting like a thick plastic. One of the children hunkers down in the wheat a few yards or so from me. It's Heidi. I give her a smile, and she relaxes a little bit.

"Come put your hand on this," I whisper. "Can you push through it?"

She lifts her palm and presses it against the barrier.

Nothing changes. It remains firm and impassable. She looks back at me, as if to check that she did it right. I nod.

"Thanks, Heidi." She manages a smile.

My heart thunders.

The cries and shouts increase. Arrows have joined the spears coming from above. No lightning bolt yet. No one fights back. Stranna and Erik stare limply at the onslaught. It riles me, not because of their inaction, but because I understand their inaction. What can we do?

"Kids!" I holler. "Get over here!"

Surprisingly, they jump up and run my way. Trusting me. Trusting that I have some sort of answer. An arrow strikes a boy in the calf. He screams and tumbles to the ground, but Erik swoops him up. The tirones circle the border of the wheat field now, dropping lower and lower. They'll dismount any moment.

Luc keeps his distance and watches.

"Everyone, push on this wall at the same time," I instruct, desperation building in my chest.

Arrows ping off the translucent barrier. Any moment now I expect one in my back or in the back of a child. "Get in front of us adults!"

The children scramble to pile in front of me, Stranna, and Erik. They don't all fit, but I feel a little better about being a shield.

"Push as hard as you can!"

They all diligently press their palms, shoulders, and bodies against the barriers and push, straining. Stranna exclaims as an arrow skims her ear, leaving a streak of blood. But she stays at the wall. Not questioning me.

She thinks I know something. I don't correct her. Let her hope.

Tirones drop to the ground from their nightbeast mounts

and run for the wheat field. A nightbeast snaps the ankle of one tiro midair and drags him to the ground for a meal.

Those who make it into the field waste no time. They sprint toward us.

"Cain!" Stranna shouts. "Whatever you're doing, do it!"

Nothing. I'm doing nothing. I feel a sudden burn behind my eyes as the finality of the realization hits me. We're going to be cut down. All of us. All these children.

All because I brought us here with no escape.

Stranna must read the despair on my face because her own expression turns grim, and she nods. "It's okay."

She turns toward the tirones. Beside her, Erik does the same.

The kids keep pushing on the barrier, and I let them. Best to keep them distracted before their deaths. I pound the barrier with my fist to a hollow echo. I slam my kris dagger against it, and the dagger shatters, falling to the earth in pieces of smoke that disappear.

Even my weapon doesn't work for another purpose in this place.

Here I thought we were coming to a place of safety. Reprieve. But it's a trap—everything in this Nightmare is.

A tiro nears me and lifts his gladius. Weaponless, I grab Stranna's magical sword from the air with one hand and throw it up to block the tiro's blow.

"No, Cain! It's not for that!" Stranna manages to cry as she wrestles with another tiro since she has no other weapon.

The words are barely out of her mouth when my hand starts to burn. The hilt turns to fire. I move to release it, but it doesn't fall from my grasp. It stays, holding my fingers to it. Burning them.

I yell.

The tiro in front of me startles and backs away, turning his focus on the kids who still push on the wall. He lunges after the nearest one. Heidi.

I shove myself at him, and shoulder him into the grass. Then I lift Stranna's sword, but instead of stabbing the tiro, I strike at the wall.

The burning blade cuts through the barrier like a razor through plastic wrap. A burst of light comes through, clinging to the outline of the split curtain flapping before us. The sword falls from my scalded hand, taking pieces of flesh with it.

The children need no urging. They bolt through the flapping curtain into the dim shadow world. Those who trip are helped by older kids.

Stranna and Erik haul me up and toss me through. Then they're through too.

As though knowing the mission was accomplished, the barrier seals itself back up, leaving Luc and his tirones dumbfounded on the other side.

Leaving us trapped on this side.

For once, I don't mind being caged.

36

"WE'RE BACK IN THE GRAY SOUP!" A kid chirps, plopping himself on a rock.

It looks that way. Rubble and rocks, broken concrete, and everything gray and colorless. No form, no reason to the place. It's like the junkyard where Tenebra's Draftsman threw all the waste and excess. The only difference is that this place is cold, like the beginning whispers of winter. Not cold enough to freeze, but enough to warrant jackets.

The coliseum and surrounding areas were always the same temperature, something neutral and tolerable. Why is it different here?

I thought in passing through the barrier we'd wake up. Another rule broken.

"Who's injured?" Stranna asks, completely tuning out the shouts and bangs from the tirones on the other side of the barrier. Perhaps she concluded as well as I did that they can't get through. Not without one of the magical Adelphoi blades.

A few children amble her way for her to inspect their injuries. At least they're all walking.

I look back at the scene–it's like staring through a rippling waterfall on pause. Not quite as clear, but I see Luc gesturing from atop his stingray, and the tirones retreat. He's not going to give up.

"It's only a matter of time before they're back," Erik mutters to me. "With a plan, this time."

"He won't be able to get in," Stranna says with little conviction.

"His father created this place," I tell them. "He'll find a loophole."

"Hex Galilei has no more power here," Stranna says. She believes Galilei is dying in the high-rise.

"Because you killed him?" The question comes out before I can think through the wisdom or foolishness of asking it. I plunge on. "I thought Adelphoi didn't kill–you only *die.*"

"Not all of us hold to that conviction," Stranna says quietly. "Our friend, Jeremy, attacked the high-rise." She says this like an apology. "He hoped by killing Galilei the Nightmare world would collapse."

"I don't think it works that way," I say.

"We'll find out soon enough." She doesn't realize I've plugged Galilei's LifeSuPod back in. Undone all of Jeremy's work. Will it bother her or relieve her?

"Actually . . ." Stranna and Erik look at me. Waiting. I owe it to them to say what I'm about to say, no matter their reactions. "I saved him." Silence. "Hex Galilei. I got his physical body and LifeSuPod to a source of electricity."

Stranna looks a bit green. "That's why you stole our truck? To save the Emperor's father?" Her voice pitches. "You're still on his side?"

"Galilei has the cure." Coming from me, my defense falls flat.

"You think he'd give it to us? Tell us how to deconstruct the empire he built?" As apologetic as she sounded moments ago, she seems irritated that Jeremy's murder didn't pan out.

I can understand the internal conflict.

"We'll demand it." I spread my arms wide. "Unless you want to stay in this world of darkness."

"For having created a so-called cure, you're really not that much of a genius." She beckons to the boy who has an arrow in his calf. He limps over and sits at her feet. "Neither the Emperor nor his father will give us anything."

I don't bother telling her that Luc rescued Galilei from the Tunnel and he's regaining strength in the very coliseum we fled. "Nole created the cure attempt. I've never been the genius. I just figured out the final bits, which didn't work anyway."

The kids are silent under our heated discussion. Stranna seems to notice this and takes several calming breaths. "Okay, so Galilei is now getting stronger because you saved his body. We have to prepare for whatever attack he'll launch."

"You and Erik need to assemble a plan, because I may be dead by the time we figure out anything."

"Dead?" Stranna looks up from tending the boy the arrow pierced. He whimpers, but she already has it out and is bandaging his leg with a cut of cloth from her toga. I suppose that's an advantage of wearing Roman garb: trim off the hem and you have bandages without losing style.

"I have no more Sleeps, and I'm not an Adelphoi. I probably have five more Tenebra days at best." I don't meet her eyes. The reason I'm dying is because I betrayed them, stole her truck, and tried to save myself with a LifeSuPod. Had I stayed at the Adelphoi house, I might have had longer.

But they can't save me now. Not with what's happening here in the Nightmare. No one is going to wake up and use what's left of their gas to track me down and find my body in that forest.

And I'm done always trying to rescue myself.

It feels kind of nice existing for someone else now.

Stranna's voice is thick as she turns back to the boy. "If we go anywhere, Erik will give you a piggyback ride, okay?"

The boy nods.

"Sorry, Cain." Erik sounds truly bummed and claps a hand on my shoulder. "Thanks for helping us out."

Heidi sidles up to me. "I'm cold."

"We should find a place to bunker down," Erik says.

I inspect the expanse before us. Cold gray rubble, but as I limp around chunks of stone, I catch little threads and tiny blinks of light, like veins of ore. Whenever I look closer, they disappear, but instead of seeing empty destruction, something awakens inside me. It's the same feeling that drew me to the wheat field. The promise of more. Of something good.

This place isn't dead.

It's merely forgotten.

"We don't need a place to bunker down. We need a place to live."

"We'll find one," Stranna assures me, but her eyes settle on the horizon, like we'll be traveling for a long time until we do. I admit I'm curious what's beyond this rippling border wall we cut through, but somehow I know that's not where my final days need to take me.

"It's a wasteland." Erik follows my gaze to the rubble in front of us. "We can't build anything from this–certainly not in the state we're in."

"It's not a wasteland," I say. "It's a blank canvas." I walk up to the nearest chunk of stone and touch it with my burned and bleeding hand. Warmth fills my body just like it did when I was standing in the wheat field.

The stone shoots up from the ground, stretching and widening and growing like one of those nature videos on time lapse. Each stone multiplying and finding a shape, fitting together like a living puzzle. I stumble back, and the growth stops, but not before a perfectly formed castle turret stands before me with a toothy top for defense. It has windows partway up and is definitely not Roman. It's much more . . . Harry Potter.

Stranna gasps. "How did you do that?"

"There was light in the stone." That's all that makes sense. Well, maybe it doesn't make sense, but somehow I knew the light was waiting for direction. I'm merely surprised it listened to *me*.

"You should try it." I step forward and touch another stone, holding a mental picture as the warmth floods me again. This one grows like the other one but moves stones aside as it finds its proper place. I laugh in amazement.

It's absolutely pure creation.

The second tower settles, and in between the two turrets is a tall wooden drawbridge with copper chains. The kids shriek.

"He's making us a castle!"

They swarm the structure, running around the lone piece of wall and drawbridge, shouting suggestions.

"Keep going!"

"I want my own room!"

"We need a moat!"

"Can we have a pet dragon?"

"It needs a garden . . . and all the princesses need pretty dresses."

"*I* don't want a dress–I want a sword!"

I want to keep going. Keep creating. My mind grows tired, but my body doesn't. It's like I've worked a full day drafting a dreamscape–my creative well half empty, but the inspiration still going strong.

Stranna gapes at it all. "I don't understand. You can't use nightmist in here."

"It's not nightmist. It's . . . something else." The same thing that made those cardinals. "I think it's like your phoenix. How did you make her?"

"I didn't. She was in the wheat field when we found the children the first time."

That takes me aback. Questions rise, but now's not the

time. I walk around the drawbridge and find more stones with tiny light threads through them, building a scene in my mind before touching each piece. Walls form. More towers with conical roofs and snapping flags of red.

The children cheer, and Heidi runs to the base of a wall and scoops up a handful of stiff gray dirt. Yellow flowers bloom out of it. She squeals and plants them.

Somehow, this makes sense to me. Amid all the confusion of this Nightmare world, I understand this. It's creation. We've broken through Tenebra's boundaries and walls and found raw unprogrammed ImagiSerum. We're programming it and directing it from inside the dream . . . with our minds.

Except the power that allows us to do that is not a program. It's Light. It's Him. Just like that wheat field is Him.

My mind isn't the one connecting the dots, my soul is.

The children create an entire garden, complete with three fruit trees and a grape vine that climbs the newly made walls. The grapes are pastel pink and purple. A little girl touches a leaf, and a ladybug forms in the spot her finger touched.

Some of the boys create a small moat, though it's empty. They send a few turtles down its banks. Erik lowers the drawbridge, laughing the whole time. Stranna still stands dumbfounded.

"Come on, Stranna!" I call to her, running across the drawbridge into a courtyard in desperate need of grass.

She follows, but slowly. "I . . . I can't." She tucks her hands in the folds of her toga.

I stop celebrating and walk up to her. "If *I* can, so can you."

"How is this even happening?"

"You serve the Creator, right?" She nods but seems anxious. "So create with Him." It's like I've finally dropped my own walls—let my pride crumble—and accepted the God that Mom and Nole talked so often about.

The knowledge of Him is trickling from my head into my heart and . . . I'm not angry anymore.

Stranna shakes her head. "The Emperor will see all of this when he comes back. He's going to decimate us."

"Stop being afraid, Stranna. Fear not, and all that."

She stares at me. "How can you say that? You're going to die in a few days. Remember?"

"That's not in my control," I tell her. "It never was. So while I'm still alive, I'm going to live." I grin. "Just try it, okay?"

I take her hand and tug her arm gently toward the ground. I place her palm on the stones that are now cobbled and arranged in an attractive spiral. Nothing happens. She looks up at me.

I raise an eyebrow. "Hiding it under a bushel, are we?"

She huffs. "As if you should talk. Heathen." She turns her focus back to the ground and her brow furrows. Concentrating. Her body is still tense. I lean over and brush hair out of her face, and she takes a deep breath. She closes her eyes briefly and utters a barely audible prayer.

A tiny trickle of water comes from her fingers. She gasps and jerks her hand away, leaving a dark outline of her fingers and palm. Then, tentatively, she presses both hands against the ground and water gushes forth again, streams and streams of it. The stones beneath her touch shudder, and something shoots up around us, creating a circle of stone like a pool that fills.

She exclaims and quickly stands, but we're already in several inches of water. The water builds and grows and fills the stone circle. We clamber out as the stone stills itself into the shape of a small fountain, bubbling and spilling over fresh and clear.

"But how is this working?" she asks. "Fountains take underground infrastructure and drainage."

"You're not creating alone, Stranna. Someone else is filling in the gaps."

She looks at me, startled. "Are you sure you're not Adelphoi?"

I lift my arms. "No magical sword." The words pain me, but I try to stay lighthearted. "Besides, do I smell like cinnamon rolls?"

I see unshed tears as she replies. "No."

I yearn to be an Adelphoi. I know I've made the shift in my mind and heart, accepting God the way Nole and Mom did. I'm like the thief on the cross who waited until the last minute. Whatever level my faith is at, it's not enough to give me a magical sword or a weird stench to Tenebran citizens. It's not enough to give me that resurrection life they all seem to have.

I'm weak. I'm too new. When I die in a few days, I'll really die. But I'm not afraid. I'm willing to accept the things I don't understand.

From the other side of the drawbridge some of the boys shout. "The moat! There's water in the moat! Turtle race!"

"No, let's do alligators!"

Stranna makes a slight movement, but Erik beats her to it. "Uh, boys? Let's stick with turtles for now."

"Aw, man!"

After another half hour, our little fortress is built. It's made of rich multicolored stone, dark brown wood for the drawbridge, and decorated with flowers as though the girls got hold of a magical bedazzling wand.

We work on the rooms. I help form bunk beds while Stranna strains to make blankets and pillows. The blankets are stained, a few frayed, and some pillows have open seams that spill feathers all over the ground.

"Why is it so hard for me?" she complains as she stuffs feathers back into the pillow by the handful.

I don't have an answer. Erik waltzes in with a stack of

perfect pillows and tosses one onto each bunk bed before he notices the spilled feathers around Stranna.

"What happened here–"

"*Don't,*" she snaps.

He raises his eyebrows at me, and we both sidle out of the room. While we analyze the structure for defense and weaponry, the children dance and squeal in the courtyard, feeling safe and free with the drawbridge up. I make them another basketball. This time it has color like it should. But nothing is as bright as it should be. We're still trapped beneath the gray Tenebran sky. It's like playing and gardening at dusk–without the mosquitoes.

"What should we name our castle?" Erik hollers to the kids, setting up a game of four-square, but with doubles.

"Hogwarts!"

"Cair Paravel!"

"Hyrule!"

"Mordor!"

They shout out all the names that ignited passion in me for much of my life. The names of castles from favorite stories and places that made me want to be a Draftsman in the first place.

"What about you, Everett?" Erik asks. "You're the oldest, you should choose."

Everett sits on the edge of the fountain, swirling a finger in the water and playing with a scarlet beta fish. The kids stop their game and listen for his answer, revealing the respect and love they have for him, even though he's only a year or two their senior.

He looks up. "Home," he says simply. "Call it what you want, but its real name is Home."

I speak up. "Castle Ithebego." *In the beginning, God.* He created a home for us. It's like the name was waiting for this place ever since Nole and I scribbled it on that sticky note.

The children heartily approve, mainly on the merit that it sounds cool.

I mosey along a wall-walk, looking back toward the wavering barrier separating us from Tenebra. A young forest stretches out to meet it with a winding path from our drawbridge to the wheat field. I don't know who made the forest, but it fills our little castle home with life.

Even so, this won't keep. We haven't fortified our creation yet. We're all exhausted. Perhaps it was foolish to start with such beautiful things, but it gave the kids life. Hope.

"We need defenses," Erik says, coming up beside me.

"We shouldn't have to ask the kids to fight," I say. "They've seen enough battle firsthand."

"Luc is coming back, and he's going to bring soldiers. The barrier won't be enough."

"Where are all the other Adelphoi?" Surely he, Stranna, and Jules aren't the only ones. They've mentioned Jeremy several times, but where is he in Tenebra?

"Scattered. Not all want to work in unity. There used to be a bigger group, but I guess they argued about whether to hide, fight, or flee–and split."

Like Crixus: a loner. "Is there a way to get word to them?"

He ponders that a moment. "I'm sure Stranna has a way."

"What about the kids' parents? Since they're all trapped in the coliseum, do they even know their children exist out here? And that Luc is trying to kill them?"

Erik shakes his head. "Most of the parents have been trapped in the Nightmare too long. They're either dead or dying."

My whirling mind stops at this. Of course. These kids' parents are in the coliseum dying because they don't have LifeSuPods. Their kids are safe and taken care of, but that's not enough.

"Have the Adelphoi tried to reach them at all?"

He lifts a shoulder. "What can we do? We don't even know where their physical bodies are. We can't help them."

I gape at him. "Are you kidding me? You're an Adelphoi. A Spore."

He sobers and places a hand on his magical sword. "I'm still limited, Cain. This sword has a mind of its own."

"I'm not saying to fight, I mean . . ." I grip the tower wall. I'm growing angry too quickly. "You have the answer. Stranna has the answer! You all have the answer!"

Stranna emerges from the tower on my other side. "Hey, you're a little loud." She looks at me. "Are you mad, Cain?" She's seen what my anger can become.

"Erik says the Adelphoi have never even bothered to talk to the citizens in the coliseum," I say sharply.

She shrugs. "Why should we? They cheer on the nightbeasts in the Arena as they rip us to shreds."

"Because they're *dying*, Stranna!"

"Yes, I know," she says wryly. "Trust me, I know. I've watched more people die in the past couple months than I ever thought I'd have to see in my lifetime."

"No. You don't get it." I run a hand over my face. "You're both Adelphoi. You have faith and light and because of that you have life. When you're killed, you don't die." I take a deep breath and look at them both. "Don't you think everyone deserves a chance at that?"

Erik is listening, but Stranna nearly snorts. "You want to walk into the middle of the Arena and become a street preacher? That didn't even work in real life, Cain. When those people see a Spore, they want to kill it. Just like you did. You murdered me, remember?"

"So what?" My voice is so loud the kids stop their basketball game below and glance at us. I lower it. "I know it hurt. I know you hate it, but you still had life. It's because you were willing to die that I got a chance at life! Are we not willing to die for others and give them that same chance?"

She bristles. "You understand none of this, Cain. You think that just because you create some castle or cut through the barrier of the Nightmare world that now you know everything?"

"We don't even know how the resurrection part works," Erik adds, but he at least seems more thoughtful than Stranna.

"You don't know how it works?" I give a disbelieving laugh. "It's in the Bible! It's in the pulpits every Easter Sunday. My own brother and mother pounded it over my head again and again so much it drove me crazy. Believe in Him and have eternal life."

"That's for eternity," Stranna snaps. "Jesus wasn't talking about a Nightmare world."

"Then explain why you don't die here."

She clamps her lips shut. I'm not trying to anger her, but are they so blind?

"I get that I'm the heathen in this trio, but how are you not even thinking about this? You have the cure."

"That's what this is about?" Stranna throws her hands up and turns away. "Still. Cain, you just want to be the hero. Cure the world. Get the accolades."

"It has nothing to do with that–"

"You sent countless people to their graves!"

"At least I tried to offer life."

She's saying the same words that have rolled through my mind day after day, but it's different hearing them from her. I'd finally dared to hope I could move past the guilt, but she's been pocketing it this whole time . . . waiting to throw it at me.

She looks near tears, and I don't understand why. She has the security of waking up again. She has her special Adelphoi sword. She has community and purpose and answers.

I'm the one dying. I'm the one who joined the Adelphoi but

apparently haven't become one. I'm the one believing in their God more than they seemingly are. Perhaps I *am* being rash, but it's clear to me.

They have the answer. And even if it's too late for me to resurrect into the Real World, there are plenty of other people out there who deserve a chance.

Street preacher or not, if we don't share the true cure with people and give them the opportunity to accept it, then we're still guilty of murder. I've been down that road, and I'm not willing to walk it again.

A strange, lonely calm settles on me as I release the last threads of life and hope I cling to. "I think you're afraid, Stranna," I say.

"Just get away from me." She stalks away before I can say anymore.

Before I can say goodbye.

37

I'M GOING AFTER THE EMPEROR'S FATHER.

Luc's wrapped his little Roman world in the cloak of his power. He's given the people a life of lies, imaginary food, and temporary security. But he knows the Adelphoi come back to life after they've been killed. He's never shared that information with his citizens. He's kept it from them and made Adelphoi their enemy.

It's time to unravel his world.

If I can kidnap Galilei and get the cure information, the Adelphoi can use it in the Real World. When I die, they'll at least have something since they're apparently too cowardly to try to save the dying citizens.

And right now, Luc is distracted. He wants to destroy the Adelphoi crew–children and all–so badly that he'll leave Galilei vulnerable.

It takes a bit of searching to find a couple more rocks with threads of light in them. When I hold one, the warmth reaches through. It sends the same flare of excitement as a new dreamscape world idea used to. The desire to sit and create.

Though what I'm creating today is more out of necessity than passion. I send my thoughts into the stone and watch amazed as it morphs from stone to wood and stretches into sleek curves until it finally settles into a crossbow. It's the closest thing to a gun in this world, and I think I'll handle it okay.

Now for the arrows.

I want them made from nightmist so I can take out the nightbeasts surrounding the wheat field and Luc's stingray, but they won't form. No matter how much I direct my thoughts, the stone trembles in my hand but doesn't change. I think of the wheat field and my shattered kris dagger.

I can't create something with nightmist, not even to destroy nightbeasts. No nightmist is allowed here. The source of creation is different.

I'm asking it to war with itself, but it refuses.

So I form regular arrows, which means they'll work only on people. I don't want to shoot anyone, but if it's the difference between Luc murdering children . . .

I purse my lips. I must have faith—despite my history with that word—that God will redirect me.

I make a quick quiver and fill it, load one arrow into the crossbow but don't cock it, and take a deep breath before striding toward the drawbridge. The wood beneath my sandals is damp from morning dew, which feels achingly of the Real World. It makes it harder to leave this place, but to make sure Castle Ithebego and its residents survive, I need to abandon it.

A shadowed form emerges, having blended in with the drawbridge post on the edge of the moat. Erik. I swallow my disappointment over the flare of hope that it was Stranna.

"I'm coming with you," he says.

A knot forms in my throat. It's the first time I've felt something like brotherhood since losing Nole.

"Honestly, I'm not sure it will make a difference, Erik. It's a suicide mission in the end. The question is whether I survive one hour or several."

"I'm still coming." He won't actually die at the end of this. I think he'll come back, and he'll be able to keep helping Stranna and the kids. He and Stranna have been Adelphoi long enough that their resurrection power is secured. I'm the newbie who's out of time.

"You need to stay here and fortify the castle." I have to smile a little as those words pass my lips. Fortify the castle. I stand a little straighter, channeling my inner Aragorn. "Stranna can't do it here alone."

"She's stronger than you think," Erik states.

"She's more afraid than *you* think," I respond. "Luc's tirones are gathering and preparing an attack. He'd be an idiot not to. And–if I fail–he'll have the power of Galilei at his disposal, too. The kids need you. She'll need you."

That seems to get through. Erik sighs. "I understand what you were saying before, Cain. I get it."

That lightens my heaviness somewhat.

Erik draws his Adelphoi sword and holds it out to me. "I think you should take this."

I glance at my hands and look back up at him. "I can't. It burns me, remember?" I'm not worthy.

He reluctantly sheathes the sword. It bumps a little in the sheath of its own accord, like it's trying to move.

"What *can* I do?" he asks plaintively.

I take a breath. "I don't know if this is the answer, so I'm telling you alone because you'll think it through. Luc has built his empire here, and I think if power is taken from him, everyone can be freed."

"That's a pretty big *if*."

It's an *if* because of me. Because I wrecked the Adelphoi's attempts to stop Luc and Galilei. I look directly at Erik. "If his tirones attack the castle and kill you, you should know Luc's father is at Road 813 Northwest. He's in a LifeSuPod." I hesitate. "You could unplug it."

Erik hisses in a breath, and I feel dirty for even suggesting it.

But I'm not Adelphoi. I *do* kill. Maybe that's why I'm not one of them.

"It's not fully plugged in," I plow on, as if it's an excuse. "I don't think he knows that. Just the power cord. I ran out of time before I could arrange all the other tubes and things. I suspect he'll fade over time anyway. But you could use it as leverage."

Erik still hasn't really responded. I shove my thumbs in my belt and only then do I realize my citizenship scroll isn't there anymore. I must have lost it during one of the skirmishes.

"He's likely already gained a lot of strength. Once he and Luc start working together . . . no one can stop their power."

Erik nods.

I reach out my hand. "Thanks for everything. I mean that."

He grasps my hand and shakes it. "Be careful out there."

I laugh under my breath. "Right."

He smiles, too, like we both know how useless the suggestion is. He surprises me by saying a quick prayer, and then he claps me on the back. With a sharp nod, we turn away from each other–him back to the castle and me toward the barrier.

When I reach it, the wheat field becomes clearer, like a lens bringing things into focus. It's less rippled. I put a hand out to touch the barrier, and my fingers pass right through like going through a hologram. The only change I feel is a slight warmth from the wheat field that contrasts the coolness of this mystery land.

Thin threads of light spark around my wrist like they did around Heidi when she walked through that first time.

I take a breath and then a step. Nothing hinders me. The warmth of sunlight envelops my skin, and I resist the urge to sink down into the wheat and lie there with my eyes closed, pretending it's a summer day. But then the sounds come.

Loud sniffs. Yaps. I open my eyes. The nightbeasts on the edge have noticed my presence. They're thin and scattered. The skeleton of my dragon has become a haven for some sleeping nightbeasts, and their heads pop up and turn toward me as if I've made a noise.

I haven't.

They smell me.

They sense me. Nightbeasts now come from the shadows all around, gathering and growing in number like a swelling flood. If I'm going to get out of this field alive, I need to make a run for it before they get too thick. I rest my hand on the crossbow for reassurance, but then remember I have no nightmist arrows. It's useless against these creatures.

I break into a sprint. My heart pounds faster than my feet, and I try to match its rhythm with my pace, headed for the sparsest corner. My speed sends the nightbeasts baying and bounding toward my destination. On a whim, I yank some wheat stalks up by the roots.

Then I put on an extra burst and break through the field edge. I feint left then dart right all the while swinging the wheat stalks back and forth. A nightbeast lunges with teeth bared, but he ducks away from the *whoosh* of a wheat stalk. To my surprise, the other beasts seem hesitant, too, still chasing but not going in for the kill.

I keep running. They give chase. I'm losing energy and out of breath, but after several yards the nightbeasts must realize I'm not going to be a meal. Some slow. Some fall back. Then they suddenly start attacking each other and tearing one another's flesh.

They resort to cannibalism because, while I hold this wheat–for whatever reason–they cannot touch me.

I dare to slow my pace, but not my vigilance with the wheat. They eye me from a distance, but the change in my pace does nothing to encourage them. Most have turned back to the wheat field already.

I stop altogether, grounded by curiosity more than anything else. I tear off one of the heads of wheat and rub it gently between my palms until the kernels separate, the same way as when I first encountered the field. Each kernel remains golden and glistening. I pick up one between thumb and forefinger and toss it toward the nightbeasts. It's light, so it doesn't go far, but it lands a few feet away from the nearest nightbeast–a strange badger of sorts–which darts back as though I've thrown fire at it. The badger then hisses at the kernel, turns its back, and rapidly kicks dirt over it.

Even covered, the nightbeasts keep their distance.

All of that from a single kernel.

I remember now how, when the children fell off the nightbeast dragon, a few final wheat kernels had fallen from my pocket. And then the cardinals came and saved the children. Were those actually from the kernels? Was the thing Stranna dropped from the sky actually a kernel and not a lit match?

I tuck the rest of the wheat into what would have been my money pouch, had I made any money during my time here. I ponder while I travel. Are these kernels like the rocks with light threads in them? Can I create with them? Now that I'm away from Castle Ithebego I'm not sure *what* I can make. I don't want to use nightmist, even though it's easy here. But it makes the roots come from my soles, and all it ever does is make me want to create more out of it with emotions I can't control.

I liked my saber-toothed tiger and my hound dog. I was fond of them, and a little pang hits my chest at the feeling of betraying them by abandoning nightmist. But now that I've created with the strange light threads in the stone, I can't go back to the other way.

I set off toward my destination. It wasn't until I left the wheat field that I realized what that destination is. It's not the coliseum. Not yet. I need a way to get past its fire.

So I head toward the Tunnels.

THE TUNNELS ARE FAR OFF, AND ON foot the journey is slow and conspicuous, especially if Luc and his tirones fly overhead. But the Vetters at the Tunnel exits—like James from when I first arrived—have a key to one of the coliseum gates. And I need a way in.

I break into a light jog, causing my body to pound in pain from my Real World injuries. I keep glancing toward the sky, waiting for Luc to show up, but there are too many buildings and broken towers around to get much of a view beyond directly overhead.

I reach the catacombs and swallow irritation. I was heading too sharply along the edge of the Nightmare. I need to go more toward the bottom edge of the map. I can't make myself think of it as south because such cardinal directions imply there's a sun to read them by.

But here this no sun. There is no direction. Only death and confusion and darkness.

I use my arrival at the catacombs to my advantage and hike up the incline to where the phoenix's nest is. The phoenix isn't here. I grit my teeth. Flying would be faster. And safer. But from here I do have a view of the coliseum. It's distant, but close enough to reveal small specks circling the mammoth structure, like buzzards circling a kill, but none dive, and none seem to be carrying riders.

As I stare at the odd scene, there is a small puff of mist above. Three more buzzard creatures appear in the air.

They're being created. By Luc. Chills trickle down my skin. They're sky steeds, and there are enough for an army. The attack on Castle Ithebego is sooner than I expected.

I swivel my gaze to where the Tunnel exits should be, but they're cloaked in gray cloud, the same as when I first arrived. It's going to take hours to get there on foot. Where is the phoenix?

I search the skies to no avail. Did the buzzards get her?

I scan her nest for any threads of light or warmth or gold so I could possibly create something. Nothing but regular straw, colored the way it should be and not glowing the way the rocks do.

I reach into my pouch and pull out a wheat kernel. It still shines with the life of the wheat field bound in it. Surely this will work. I hold it tight in my fist, close my eyes, and let my imagination send a message. Not a command, but more of a dream.

The ground rumbles around me, and my eyes snap open and widen. The kernel is no longer in my hand.

Instead, before me, stands a giant rhino. Or maybe it's the size of a regular rhino–I wouldn't know. I've never been this close to one before.

Its skin is leathery and gray, and when it snorts, mucus lands on the ground. It bucks its head, and I hold back my reaction, not wanting to get gored. But when it meets my eyes, I see something I never witnessed in my nightbeasts: obedience. It's not tame, but it seems willing to submit. Why? Because I'm its creator?

I run my hand along its cheekbone, then shoulder, then back. It holds still. I mount with the help of a nearby boulder.

There's a small dip in its spine that gets the closest to imitating a saddle, but that doesn't mean the back of a rhino is comfortable.

"Let's go to the Tunnels," I prompt.

It swivels around. I lurch for a handhold, but there's nothing. No mane, no bridle, not even feathers like on the phoenix. I do the only thing I can: I drop low and hug its form like I would a horizontal tree trunk. It takes a while for me to meld with the rhythm of its lumbering gait. Once I think I'm stable, I dare to lift my head. We're in the midst of the abandoned houses, where the snakes attacked me and Larry. From what I can tell, we're making good time.

I'm thankful this creature seems to know where the Tunnels are. After half an hour we enter fog, and the rhinoceros slows but stays on target. I pat its side as it heaves and snorts.

"Slow down, big guy. Catch your breath." There'd be no sneaking up on the Tunnels with this loud mouth-breather.

I slide off his back. "You stay here for now, okay?"

He paws the ground and then flumps down on it with the impact of a level-4 earthquake.

I creep through the mist, not entirely sure how far I am from the Tunnels, but I must be close. Luc's map runs through my head as I navigate past rubble and houses and then . . . nothing. No trees, just sparse grass poking from dry rough ground. The same type of ground I landed on with my hands and knees the first moment I exited the Tunnels.

A few more gentle steps and the fog clears, revealing the crackling campfire of the Vetters. Beyond it are the four cages built around the exits to the Tunnels. The crooked, dying tree is still off to the side of the campfire, and the ring of keys gleams in the firelight. Two men and a woman huddle around the campfire, drinking their coffee.

Meanwhile, each Tunnel cave is filled with three or four to a cage. Most sit and cower—Fears. But there are two who stand

and shake the bars, pounding their fists against the wood. Occasionally shouting at the Vetters to explain, to let them out.

I remember that feeling.

Confusion. Entrapment. Anger. This cage only makes it worse for them. They need answers: they need freedom. How long have these dreamers been trapped here? While their physical bodies deteriorate in the Real World?

Some of them might have kids in Castle Ithebego. When I think of it that way, I lose focus of the keys altogether. I left the castle to stop Luc, but these people need help too.

"We've got enough for each of our quotas. Let's load 'em up." A Vetter tosses a final splash of coffee into the fire, and it hisses when the liquid hits the coals.

"Not while whatever's going on at the coliseum is still happening," the female Vetter says. Her face is turned away from me, but I recognize her voice. "I want no part in that battle. I'll take my chance here with the nightbeasts and dreamers."

It's Helene.

Helene is a Vetter? After all she's gone through to reunite with her daughter, now she's enabling the coliseum Games?

I pull up short as her head turns slightly. In the flicker of the campfire, I catch a glimpse of her face. I've seen that face, but younger. Same freckles, same narrow nose and wayward curl by her ear.

Helene is Heidi's mom.

One of the men speaks up. "We have a quota to fill, and I want to get paid. I chose Vetting for my conscription. They can't make me ride some skybeast in the Emperor's war."

"Barys . . ." Helene sounds weary. "Let's just finish our coffee."

The lead Vetter, Barys, rises with the other man. "Get working, Helene, or I'll report you." He crosses to a cage cart. Helene takes one final slow sip from her tin cup, then joins him.

I want to believe she's undercover, has some ulterior motive. But she checks the harnesses of two cougar nightbeasts hitched to the front of a much larger transport cart, like she's done it a hundred times.

I have information that could get her on my side. At least briefly.

I know where Heidi, her missing daughter, is. If I can only get her alone . . .

The Vetters lead the cougars and cart to the first Tunnel cage. The Fears who are trapped inside shy away. A brief light sparks.

"Did you see that flash?" the male Vetter, a short, tattooed man, exclaims. His hands jerk away from the cage lock.

"I didn't see anything," Helene says with a shake of her head, picking up where the tattooed Vetter left off with the lock. She's fibbing. The tension in her shoulders gives her away, but the other two Vetters don't seem to notice.

"I saw it," Barys says. "There's a Spore in here."

"Who was that?" the first Vetter demands from the Fears. "Who made that light?" The Fears keep silent, eyes wide. One woman whimpers.

"I'm not risking getting that close to a Spore," Tattoos mutters to Barys. "Quota or not. I'll take the penalty."

Barys stares him down. "Kill them. Dead Spores count toward our quota."

"Kill them?" Helene repeats, voice jumping an octave. "These are real people–not nightbeasts."

"Better safe than sorry. It's what the Emperor would do anyway if he saw the spark. We need to protect the citizens." Even I can tell Barys says this to assuage his own conscience, not because he cares about those in the coliseum.

He draws his sword. Tattoos does too. Helene stands numb.

The Fears move away from the edges of the cage. Some back all the way up to the Tunnel, but even then they don't retreat back inside. I don't blame them. When I first got out of the Tunnel, I was happy to die anywhere as long as I was free from that darkness.

They really are going to kill these people.

"This isn't going to work." Barys stridently sheathes his sword and goes to the cart. He removes the harness from one of the cougars. It snaps at him, but he prods it toward the Tunnel cage with his gladius. Tattoos unlocks the Tunnel cage door.

"Wait." Helene reaches out a hand. "This is wrong. We'll get sent back to the Arena for this!"

Her words make no difference. Barys nods to Tattoos, who swings open the gate to let the cougar in.

I abandon my cover and bolt from the mist. I grab the coliseum gate keys from the tree and stuff them in my belt, then shout, "Hey!"

The Vetters spin.

I throw a handful of glowing wheat kernels at them. The tiny seeds bounce off their chests as if I'd tossed canned lima beans, but the cougar leaps away. So these work only on the nightbeasts and not on Tenebran citizens who have sold their souls to the nightmist. Good to know.

"It's Icarus," Tattoos breathes. He fumbles for his sword and, in doing so, releases his hold on the cage door. The cougar leaps inside, making a beeline for the prisoners.

"Stop!" I run to the cage and throw another small handful of kernels inside. The cougar screams its banshee scream and dances around the tiny seeds, banging against the wood of the cage.

"Get out of there!" Helene shouts at the prisoners, hauling one out by the arm when there's a clear pathway. I'm glad to see she's not an enemy. Still not sure if she's an ally.

Barys advances on me with his sword. Tattoos reaches for the second cougar's harness. This is about to get ugly. I reach for my belt before I remember my kris dagger is gone. My hand finds the crossbow, but that won't stop the cougar.

All I truly have is this wheat.

Which is probably good. I don't want to kill people, but if it's a choice between the murderous Vetters and the trapped Fears, I know who I'll take down if I must. They know me as Icarus, and they're afraid of me. They don't know that I don't control nightmist anymore.

The second cougar tears away from its loosened harness and comes for me. I dive to the side. The cougar skids across the dirt and claws at me. I kick out my feet.

They connect with soft underbelly, and I catapult the giant cat over my head. Meanwhile, the other cougar in the Tunnel cage has managed to tiptoe its way around the scattered kernels toward its prey. Some of the Fears scramble for the stray kernels. Others go for the door, but Tattoos slams the door shut and clicks the padlock, even though Helene is inside.

"Hey!" Helene pounds her fist against the wood. "What are you doing?"

The first cougar jumps on her back, and she screams as she drops to the ground.

I'm on my feet and reach to create anything I can with a kernel of light. Instead, my focus spins away into the mist–almost like an emissary calling for help. It's outside my control, and I don't quite understand it until the ground pounds beneath us.

My rhinoceros bursts into view and lumbers for the Tunnel cage. It smashes its head and horn into the side, bursting the wood beams apart. Helene has managed to get a wheat kernel from the dirt and shoves it in the cougar's face. It leaps backward through the new hole in the narrow prison.

The rhinoceros stomps the cat to bloody smithereens until it's nothing more than a motionless pelt on the ground.

The prisoners scramble for freedom, seeming to have lost their fear. Every one of them has a couple wheat kernels in his or her hand. I swell with pride for a moment, though I have nothing to do with their courage. But there's something about seeing people step up despite fear to defend and protect what is good.

Helene runs to the other two Tunnel cages, banging at the padlock of the first with a rock. Barys goes after her with a sword. I throw a wheat kernel after him, this time channeling my thoughts into the kernel instead of expecting it to defend us with its light. It turns into a whip. The handle forms in my palm, and I grip it tight as the upper portion wraps around Barys's ankles.

I yank and he tumbles to the ground.

"Help her!" I yell to the rhinoceros who has been huffing and snorting after the second cougar. It obeys immediately and blasts through the second cage, almost trampling a couple people in its path, but miraculously no one gets squashed. Rhino does the same thing with the final cage.

The prisoners are free. There are about a dozen total. They go for Tattoos, and I holler after them, "His citizenship! I need his citizenship scroll!" But Tattoos bolts. The remaining cougar chases him into the mist, and all we hear is screaming.

I can't tell if it's him or the cougar.

Barys attacks with his gladius, slicing my whip from its handle. I chuck the handle at him and it *thunks* into his forehead. He growls, but it gives me enough time to put some space between us again. I bring up the crossbow but can't quite manage to pull the arrow back all the way.

I let the shaft rest in the weapon–he doesn't need to know it's not fully cocked. I go the intimidation route. "Your fellow Vetter is gone, and there are a dozen of us. You sure you want this fight?" I don't mention Helene. She stands with the prisoners, sword in hand and pointed toward Barys.

She's chosen her side.

Barys's glare is fierce. He was willing to kill the prisoners to avoid encountering an Adelphoi. Survival instinct is his god. Why would he fight alone when he has no loyalty to anyone but himself?

He glances over his shoulder then his lips curl. "I don't need to fight anymore, anyway." He turns and dashes into the mist, taking a different path than Tattoos and the cougar.

I scan the air beyond this hill for what may have given him the confident smirk.

Dark, distant shadows move, weaving through mist. Growing larger.

A stingray.

Luc is coming.

"Heidi!" I call out the girl's name intentionally. Helene's head jerks to me. I meet her eyes. "Heidi is safe."

She stills for a moment, then eyes me skeptically. "How do you know where she is? I've been monitoring these Tunnels day and night." So that's why she became a Vetter–to find Heidi, not to further Luc's kingdom.

"The younger kids don't arrive in the tunnels. They come through a wheat field. That's where she and the others are now." At least I hope Heidi is at Castle Ithebego. And I hope Helene believes me. "Follow the rhino. It'll take you to a castle beyond the edge of the Nightmare. I'll be right behind you. There are nightbeasts along the way, so keep the kernels in hand. The wheat field is protected from beasts, but not people. It's the gateway."

I pray this is making sense to her. I speak quickly because I need her out of here and to take the others with her. I need to keep Luc from following them. They should be safe at Castle

Ithebego . . . if they can get in. The veil let me out, but I don't have a magical Adelphoi sword to get back in.

I have to trust that the veil will know the new arrivals are not enemies.

I look at the sky again, but the shadows have disappeared in the mist. "You have to go *now.*"

She finally moves. She gives a sharp nod and removes her citizenship scroll out of her belt and tosses it to me. Then she heads after the rhino. The majority of the other Fears follow her, throwing furtive glances over their shoulders. A couple linger, eyeing the Tunnels, eyeing me.

"You're not safe here!" I thunder at them.

I scoop up Helene's citizenship and tuck it into my belt, then I dig in my pocket for the last of the wheat. This time I find a handful of broken stalks that I'd yet to strip into kernels. I stow one at the entrance of each Tunnel, hoping they'll protect anyone else who exits through them.

Two Fears haven't moved. My shouting probably frightened them more. If Stranna were here she'd know what to do.

"If any of you have children and want to find them, you need to follow Helene." I take my final wheat stalk and rub the wheat head between my palms, releasing the final collection of kernels. If I can help them feel safe, maybe they'll go.

"Take these." I pinch a little finger full and hold them out to the nearest man trembling from head to foot, gaze darting from the kernels to me to the shadows and back again. "These will protect you–"

A bolt of black lightning shoots from the sky and pins the man to the ground before he has a chance to move. His life fades from his terrified face in a split second. I whirl.

Luc.

The remaining Fear staggers away from the dead body. I dart in the opposite direction to draw Luc's attention.

He glides after me, directing the stingray with only his feet.

Another bolt flashes toward me, and I narrowly leap aside. It sticks in the ground with a burst of thunder right where I'd been about to plant my foot.

Despite having an awkward angle, I manage to properly load an arrow into the crossbow. I shoot, and it soars over his head, not even close enough to startle him.

For a moment I consider throwing a wheat kernel at him, but each one is so light and small it would never get the height.

Another bolt grazes my back. I utter a cry and arch away from the shock and burn and trip into the mist. My crossbow crunches beneath the fall of my body. Broken. Probably for the best, I can't even load it without a time-out.

Wheat kernels and arrows litter the ground. I scrabble for both despite the burning on my back.

"What do I do?" I mutter. "What do I do?" I don't want to create another weapon. When I form things using the power of the light threads it feels different–like life instead of death. Freedom instead of emotional overwhelm. I'm not opposed to grabbing one of Luc's bolts and hurling it back his way, but I don't trust that the weapon wouldn't turn on me first. Besides, the feeling of my kris dagger plunging into Stranna is still strong in my mind. Repulsing.

Am I afraid to fight? Am I weak?

"I don't want to go down killing," I whisper to God. "But I don't see any other way."

My fingers find kernels . . . not arrows. I wrap my fingers around them, and they grow warm within my palm. Hot. Forming something, though I haven't directed my thoughts any particular direction. I don't bother trying to insert my own control. I let the kernels do their own thing.

Suddenly I'm no longer holding on to little wheat grains, but instead feathers of red-and-gold fire.

Feathers.

They connect to one another, creating a huge tail, and I

lift my eyes. Before me sits the phoenix, regal and filled with vibrant color. No harness or saddle this time, but I know instinctively she's the same one.

She flaps her wings once, and the mist flees from around us. I clamber to my feet, and she braces herself, like our minds are one. I leap onto her back, and she shoots into the air. It's smooth and comfortable. The saddle was never needed. This is so much more natural. Somehow she's airborne by more than the power of her wings–like light is an air current, lifting her into the sky.

I spy Luc on his stingray, perfectly balanced in body but his face betrays surprise. For the first time I wonder if he's ever seen a creature made from something other than nightmist this close before. Has he even seen color like this? All the nightmist animals are shadows and grays and blacks.

He collects himself and reaches for a bolt.

I lean forward and the phoenix dives. Before he can hurl anything at me, I drop a wheat kernel above his stingray. It plops between the creature's eyes, and the ray spirals toward the ground–half falling, half fleeing from the strike of light.

Luc tumbles from its back.

Now I see how Stranna was able to obliterate the thousands of snakes with a single drop of fire.

As Luc falls, a second stingray forms from thin air directly beneath him. He catches himself on its back, steadies himself, and throws his lightning bolt at me.

The phoenix swerves, and I tear out several of her feathers trying to stay on her back. Luc is out of bolts–that, or it's taking more energy to create them. I ready another wheat kernel, but then he forms a handful of spears from nightmist and even from this distance I can tell they're split blades–half mistblade, half regular. They are meant to kill both me and my phoenix.

He gives a shrill whistle. Is he trying to command the stingray?

Hardly a dozen kernels are left in my hand. So far all I've succeeded in doing is distracting Luc and delaying him from attacking the people below or taking his army to Castle Ithebego. I'm not going to be able to take him down—either with the kernels or with the phoenix. My broken crossbow lies on the ground, pathetic after hardly even seeing battle.

Luc is so much stronger now. What happened to his wheelchair? He hides his weakness well. Hopefully that means he'll be easier to get past.

I steer the phoenix with my knees, and she bursts upward, leveling out with such suddenness I almost lose my seat. But I don't lose my chance. For a mere second we're directly above Luc and his stingray again. I scatter a buckshot of wheat kernels. They *ping* off his new stingray like popcorn, and the creature lets out a strange wail, holes appearing in its fins.

It evaporates from under Luc, who tries to create something else as he falls, but cascading wheat kernels obliterate any nightmist that tries to form.

He lands on the ground hard, dazed.

I don't wait to see if he recovers or what he creates when he does. I glance at the Tunnels. Abandoned. How far have the rhino and Helene and the Fears gotten? I pray they are all right.

My phoenix and I swoop down into the mist, and it separates as though it knows we're the enemy: revealing us and our path no matter which way I direct the phoenix.

So be it.

The great bird flaps carefully, then glides. Flap, glide. We break through the bottom of the strange mist and pass over the rooftops of the abandoned housing, and I head toward the coliseum.

Even with Luc on my tail and his army circling over the

coliseum, I have to try to get to his father. If I can pull Galilei onto the phoenix and get him to Castle Ithebego, we might have time to get the information we need.

I hear the high-pitched cry of what could be a bat, but louder. More ragged. Distant, but close. Then another. The sound multiplies, and I look through the opening of mist above us.

Pterodactyls.

Large enough to carry humans, several dozen pterodactyls are spread over the sky like a blanket. One breaks away from the formation and drops lower. A mounted tiro wears a domed helmet with hinged cheek pieces. His helmet bears a crest, marking him as a centurion. Several other tirones on their pterodactyl steeds drop and follow him. I glance to my other side and see another group of tirones doing the same.

Each one carries a long shield with darts strapped to the front. Better darts than crossbows, I tell myself.

I send the phoenix down into the maze of homes, but the airborne tirones follow like they've trained in sky battle. Did Crixus train them? Luc? Is this some sort of secret guard that's been preparing for a battle like this?

My phoenix glides easily through the corridors, and it's up to me to ease into her rhythm instead of trying to direct her. A dart lands in the dirt in front of her. She takes a sharp right turn. Another dart. We shoot upward, but these tirones create formations seemingly on every side, leaving only one direction for us to go.

I try to steer the phoenix to the left, but a dozen darts cut off her path, one striking her shoulder hinge. She lets out a mournful cry. I pluck it from her and throw it toward the mass of tirones on my right. Their pterodactyls swerve, and the dart falls through their ranks, useless.

Ahead is the coliseum and more pterodactyl tirones. Among them, riding another new stingray is Luc. How did he get there so fast?

He's replaced his short spears with a javelin set in a ballista–a giant crossbow catapult meant for one thing: total obliteration.

He takes aim. I send the phoenix down, but she careens back up of her own free will so as not to crunch into the wall of the coliseum.

"Look out!" I shout to her.

Luc fires.

I leap upward, creating a space between me and the phoenix for the bolt to pass through, but it hits her straight on. She explodes in a spray of fire and ash.

The bulk of her lifeless body crashes into the sandy Arena below.

I plummet through the air, surrounded by floating phoenix feathers. Things go eerily silent as I fall–silent enough for me to hear Luc's taunting voice.

"Fly, Icarus. Fly."

THE ARENA SAND IS JUST SOFT ENOUGH to keep me conscious, just hard enough to knock the wind out of me. Others land around me. At first I think it's pieces of my poor phoenix, but the only sign of her are floating feathers of fire, falling to the ground and turning to ash in defeat.

The bodies dropping around me are Luc's tirones, but they do it intentionally. An aerial dismount from their pterodactyls. The world spins in my vision, but I try to rise. I'm too sluggish. The tirones each grab a limb and stretch it out, so I'm spread-eagle in the center of the Arena.

"Hammer!" one calls.

A chill runs through my body. Are they going to crucify me or something? I picture metal going through my wrists. My feet. This *is* a Roman world.

I think of Jesus. *No. I'm not that brave.*

Another body arrives, and by now my vision is clear enough, despite the pain of fighting for breath, that I recognize him.

Crixus.

He holds a crude hammer and a handful of enormous metal spikes.

"Crixus," I croak. "Please. No."

He doesn't look at me. He passes two nails and the hammer to a tiro. Someone wraps something around my left ankle. I fight it, but too many hands hold me down, and my body is too broken to put up much resistance.

Clang. The hammer hits metal. A shock goes up my arm. I cringe, but there's no pain.

Clang. I try lifting my head, but it's too much strain on my abdomen and ribs. The same movements with hammer and nail repeat at my ankle and then my right hand. Once they reach my wrists, I'm able to see. A tiro wraps a thick piece of leather around my wrist and hammers it into the ground with the long spikes until I'm a bug on a display mat.

Disconcerting, but a bit more comforting than crucifixion.

Crixus does my left hand. While he hammers the nail deep, he doesn't double wrap the leather. There's enough wiggle room that, with time and stealth, I could possibly get my wrist out. An oversight?

I look at him, but he's already walking away.

He did this on purpose. He's too efficient of a centurion to blunder like that. Especially when I'm the Emperor's number-one enemy. But why would he do that when I left him to be killed by a Minotaur?

"Check his hands," Luc orders from somewhere around my head. "And pockets."

The tirones do so, emptying everything. One hisses and swiftly withdraws his hand. I barely make out the tiny kernel of wheat that rolls out. My last one.

Luc knocks it away with his foot, and it disappears into the mess of sand and phoenix ash.

"Prepare the Arena for this traitor. No food, no water. This won't take me long." He mounts his stingray and glides into the air, the airborne tirones following him.

I track their trajectory into the sky as much as I can, trying to gather my sense of direction. He flies away from the coliseum, opposite the Emperor's box.

Toward the wheat field. Toward Castle Ithebego.

No!

Then they're out of view. I think of Heidi's mom and the Fears. They're likely less than an hour from reaching the wheat field, and I won't be there. They'll be massacred.

"Crixus!" I manage to bellow.

No answer. A tiro mutters to another something about nightmist. He sounds wary, but cocky. Proud to have Icarus contained, but uncertain if I'm totally subdued.

I have no wheat kernels, and I've committed to the light too much to create out of darkness anymore. Nightmist no longer comes to my fingertips, even if I egg on my darker emotions. I don't think it's even in me anymore.

I'm truly helpless.

A few tirones move in and out of the stands, hauling big leather bags of something heavy. They set them up on the edge of the Arena, one filled bag every few yards. I've never seen these bags as part of the Games before. I recall Luc's words, *"Prepare the Arena for this traitor."*

The bags have something to do with me.

Though there's no sun, the heat of the fire tower beats down on me, accentuating my thirst. The thirst is more from real life than from the strain in Tenebra. I'll die from it in real life, but I'll be forced to endure the torture of it for hours and hours in here. How long until the next Games?

I tug a bit at the leather around my right wrist–the leather Crixus nailed. It's firmly nailed into the ground. There must be some sort of clay or stone beneath the sand to hold the spike so securely. I twist my hand a bit to test the looseness, but then a sandal presses against my fingers, crushing them so hard they're close to breaking.

A tiro stands above me. "Keep doing that and I'll cut off your hand."

"Noted," I retort.

He resumes his post, and I keep still, burning beneath the

heat and shriveling like a raisin from thirst. I try to tell myself it's all in my head and none of it is real, but that doesn't change the dread of lying here vulnerable while Luc and his airborne minions attack my friends.

For the first time I understand why Stranna doesn't want to risk her life to share the Adelphoi secret. Even though she knows she'll wake up in the Real World if killed, the fear involved is constant. And didn't Jesus do the same thing? When it was time for him to be captured, he kept praying that God would take the cup from him?

I suppose if Jesus could dread death, even knowing it would save the whole world and the pain would be temporary, it's okay for me to dread it too.

Except I don't know what's on the other side. Well, I know about eternity. Nole and Mom brought it up All. The. Time. Now I understand why–they had the answer. Despite my hard-headedness and stubborn heart.

But when it comes to Tenebra, I'm not an Adelphoi. When I die, I'll die.

I have the faith, but the nerves and anxiety still exist now that it's being tested.

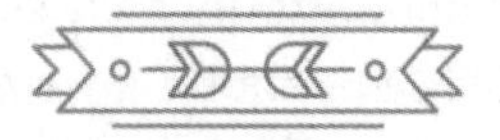

Hours pass before anything new happens. I lift my head a bit to see the stands through my spinning vision. People shuffle in early. Their curiosity is palpable. Many point and whisper. I hear the name Icarus a couple times as their tones get more excited. The Games are finally upon us.

What must it be like to look upon this as entertainment? Do they think they're coming to watch some sort of stage show with an escape artist? Do they think I put myself here solely to amuse them?

Then they spot the bags. The hush is heavy, reflecting surprise. Shock, even. One looks at me, then the bag, and whispers fiercely to a neighbor. The two plop themselves right in front of the bag. Others skirt the bags altogether and seat themselves far away from them, toward the highest seats of the Arena.

The muttering continues, but it's no longer casual chatter. There's a new awkwardness with my body splayed before them and something they understand about the bags that I don't.

Luc didn't kill me right away for a reason.

The only reason I can think of is that he wants my end to be public. But he's off attacking Castle Ithebego. Maybe he thinks it will be a quick victory and he plans to be back in time.

As more spectators take their seats, I realize my opportunity. I don't have a weapon or physical prowess, but I have a voice. And that has the power to fight these Games in a way Luc never anticipated.

"I know about a cure." The words feel cursed on my tongue, but I say them anyway because I remember the power they had in the Real World. My voice is a bit raspy, but the design of the Romanesque Arena sends it echoing up the stands.

The chatter stops. Faces turn toward me. I lick my lips. "There's a cure to death in Tenebra! It costs nothing. Nothing but faith."

Someone laughs. The muttering picks back up. Already I'm disregarded.

I try to raise my voice. "Listen to me!"

They do. I sound angry now, so perhaps that's why they give me attention, hoping to witness an explosion of nightmist.

"Your children understand the cure. They understand the faith, and they're waiting for you."

"Where are they?" a woman asks, timid, but loud enough to carry to my ears.

"They're with the Spores. They're protected for now. And aside from longing for their parents, for you–they're happy."

Hisses fill the air the moment I say *Spores*. Are they so set against the Adelphoi that they are willing to ignore the truth about their own children?

I speak up again. "Luc rescues only the youngest children who can return to the Old World and serve his purposes! Any of you who have been reunited with your kids have seen this. The reunion is here on this sand, but then your child is indentured to the Emperor, right?"

Complete silence. Tension fills the air, as I continue.

"Once they're too old to serve him, he makes them fight in the Arena for the right to live. At this very moment, the Emperor is attacking your children, intending to murder them. I was there yesterday. Luc and his tirones chased your kids, shooting arrows at them as they fled, trying to get away."

Gasps litter the crowd.

"Liar," someone shouts.

"Those of you with children, ask them," I challenge. "See what they'll tell you about life before the Emperor and his tirones captured them."

"You're a Spore!" comes the accusation.

"I'm not," I say, my heart sinking. "You know what Spores smell like. You see the sparks when they move. You've seen their Spore swords that have minds of their own. I have none of those things. But I share their beliefs." The grief of defeat in my voice is unavoidable. Never have I wanted to be an Adelphoi so badly. How long do I have to share their faith before I'm accepted and transformed into one of them?

I wish the spectators could smell me, whether as a stench or as cinnamon. I wish I sparked like Erik did in the cage. I wish the Adelphoi sword wouldn't burn me.

But I've done too much damage.

"We know who you are!" a woman yells from over my head somewhere. "Spore or not, you're the guy on the Outside who sold the fake cure. You lied to us and doomed us to life here!"

Will my past sins never leave me?

Voices rise in a cacophony. Most are angry. Some people are moving from the back rows of the Arena to the front. As close to the mysterious bags as they can get.

"I've only ever wanted to save lives!" My shouted plea is lost amid their rage. I close my eyes as it builds and am transported back to the Macella Quarter when the people attacked Stranna. I know once the anger takes root, it spreads and grows, and there's no stopping it.

The tirones around the edge of the Arena draw their swords, even though the crowd remains in the stands. For now. One tiro eyes the gate.

I'd flee too.

"This cure isn't like that," I say, though my voice is unheard. I have to say the words, even if no one will listen. No Adelphoi is willing to say them. And though they won't change the tide of the crowd, maybe one person–a tiro or a noxior or a parent missing their child–will take it to heart.

"It's warm," I blurt, thinking of the wheat field.

Some shush others, curiosity winning out, and the voices die down a little.

"It feels like the sun. No injection, no ImagiSerum, no LifeSuPod, no pills. The disease is in our minds . . . but the cure is there too. God has not left us without a way out." It's like Mom's and Nole's words are coming out of my mouth. "He is the way–"

Something strikes my cheek with such impact my vision goes black. When it returns, I see a man leaning over the wall to my right, a rock the size of a baseball in his hand. He reaches his other hand into the bag on the edge of the Arena and pulls out another rock. A few others come to his side and do the same.

The bags are filled with . . . rocks?

That's not what I expected. A chill sweeps over my body.

Now I understand. The bags. Luc's words about a traitor. The crowd's curious whispering. My body laid out in full vulnerability.

They're going to stone me.

THE CROWD PRESSES AGAINST THE edge of the Arena's seating barrier gathering their stones. This is going to get ugly fast. Those who don't join the rush do nothing to help me. They sit mute, watching. Resigned.

A form drops from the sky like a plummeting meteorite. Luc is here. He lands in the sand and straightens in an all-black Roman toga. No weapon at his side. No blood on his hands. Unafraid and in power. He's never looked so strong or commanding.

Most of the standing crowd stops cheering. I search for those who seem to remain silent, keeping away from the bags. Anyone who might still hear me.

"You started without me?" Luc says amiably.

There is laughter, like murder is nothing more than an inconsequential game of Uno. He creates a long straight sword from nightmist. It's not tapered like a gladius but is instead the type a Roman leader might wear. A spatha.

He paces around me in a circle, dragging the sword in the sand, sliding stones aside as he goes. "So tell me. What is his crime?"

"He's a Spore!"

"He lied about cures!"

"He wants to kill our Emperor!"

After a full circle, Luc surveys the ground. Then starts again, a yard farther than the first circle. He's making a bull's-eye. And I'm in the middle.

"All of those are correct." He completes the second circle. "I've just come from the stronghold of the Spores, where they are holding your children. We were unable to breach it."

Hisses from the audience.

"Those Spores could be doing anything to your children," he declares. "They are the worst kind of people, and he"–Luc points his spatha at me–"supports them. What kind of person wants to keep children hostage?"

He's stoking the fire, and anger rages. Nightmist roils off the crowd like a waterfall, cascading down to the sand and sending all manner of unformed venom toward me.

"Let's remove this poison from our city. And once we've done that, let's take up arms together and get our children back!" He thrusts the spatha into the air to the eruption of cheers and stomping.

A stone flies my way, followed by ten more. I can see which ones will hit their mark as they arc through the air. One strikes my hip. Another my midsection, and for a moment I can't breathe. Luc steps back and watches, spatha sheathed and arms crossed.

I struggle against my bonds. I twist my right wrist in the looser leather strap. It hardly gives, but it's the only one that will allow me any hope of escape.

A stone smashes the knuckles on my other hand. I roar, tugging harder. Twisting, yanking. Thinking of the martyr Nole so admired. Stephen or something. I don't want to be Stephen.

I'm not brave enough.

Finally, my right hand slips out of the leather. I swing my body over and hunch as best I can to protect my core, while picking at the bond on my left hand. I have a bit of leverage now. Stones pelt my body from every angle. Spine, knee, shoulder, head.

My consciousness slips for a moment.

I suppose that wouldn't be too bad–to be knocked out and miss the death part. But I can't die. Once the crowd is finished with me, Luc is taking them to the wheat field. To Castle Ithebego. The children will let their parents through, drawn in by the desire to be reunited. But when those parents enter, Luc and his tirones will too.

I force myself to sit up and yank my right hand against the spike in the ground. It gives a little, and that's all I need for adrenaline to kick in. If it's able to give at all, it's able to give the rest of the way. I pull, ignoring the flying stones, except for when I need to duck one.

Finally my arms are free.

Luc still watches me with an amused expression. He holds up a single hand. It takes a few seconds, but the crowd gets the message and stops throwing.

Warmth trickles down my body in so many areas I'm not sure if it's blood or torn muscles or if my body will still obey me once I get my feet free. I'm nearly numb from pain.

If I get my feet free.

Luc shakes his head. "This is what I liked about you, Cain. I liked the fight in you. How you never give up. You could have been such an asset to our city."

"I don't want to be an asset to just one city, Luc." My words are slurred with pain, and I have to deliberately form each syllable through the swelling of my face. "Not when it's a prison. There's a whole world out there that you're keeping from your citizens, all in the name of fearing and hunting Spores."

He stabs his spatha into the sand. "You've been infected. Every word you speak is a deception." He lifts his hands to the sky, and the gray blanket above swirls in obedience, sending down a black lightning bolt that crackles with promised pain.

He grips it in the middle. The hairs on my arms straighten.

I get a foot free and force myself upright, pivoting around my anchored foot. Searching my belt for a weapon. I've never fought a lightning bolt before.

Luc surveys me and seems genuinely sad. "No roots. No nightmist. We don't even recognize our Icarus anymore."

"Good," I retort with effort. "That was the problem from the beginning."

He looks past me at the tirones. Gives a small nod. They leave their posts against the walls and approach me. I try to dodge them, but that's hard to do when I'm chained at the ankle like a dog. They grab my arms and tunic and hold me in place.

"Really, Luc?" I croak. "You're not even going to fight me man-to-man?"

"Why endanger myself in the name of pride?"

A tiro grips me from behind, yanking my head back. The crowd hoots its approval. I can see only the top of Luc's head. His lightning bolt raised to the gray lifeless sky.

I hear the swoosh and static of the weapon. It pierces my gut. I make a sound of agony foreign to my ears. Jolts of electricity pound my body like waves.

The tiro releases me. Luc yanks out the lightning bolt. Warmth spreads across my middle. He lifts the weapon again.

This time, in the last moments before he lunges, my body relaxes of its own accord. Submission. Fear flees. When he splits my chest open, all I can think is, *I'm going home.* To light. To Nole.

41

HEAVEN SMELLS LIKE DUST AND grandmother quilts.

My eyes hurt like a headache has been pounding behind them for days. I try to open them, but it's too bright. I'm gasping for breath. My body hurts. But my chest and stomach are still intact. I manage to reach up and rub my sternum, expecting blood. Burns. Shocks of electric nightmare.

Everything feels too real. Too physical.

I'm not in heaven–I know this before I manage to keep my eyes open. I force myself into a sitting position.

I'm in the cabin with the two LifeSuPods. Galilei's body and Crixus's body. I'm awake.

With a jolt I realize what this means.

I'm a Spore. An Adelphoi.

I leap to my feet, but my body reminds me what it's been through. I lurch sideways and brace myself on the bed. I suppose I rolled off in the Real World at some point during Luc's attack in Tenebra.

The strange feeling of spiked fear and resigned peace still thrums in my veins. I still feel the cut of the lightning bolt and the severing of my consciousness. As I feel it, I notice all my swelling and inner pain is healed. So when an Adelphoi dies, the wounds from the Nightmare disappear.

Amazing.

I get my balance and take a few steps, but the greatest need that hits me is a parched throat. Water. I need water. Food.

My muscles quiver as I toddle toward the sink and turn the tap. I guzzle as much as my belly will hold before I stop. Afterward I grab the bag of pancake mix from the cabinet. Feeling weirdly normal, I slap a pan on the stove and combine the pancake powder with water and get one giant pancake browning on low heat in the skillet. I'm tempted to eat a mouthful of raw batter, but I refrain.

I watch in a tangle of wonder and disbelief. Here I am, alive. Gutted mere moments ago, and now cooking pancakes while my murderer's father lies helpless in a LifeSuPod a few feet away.

At that thought, my hand on the pan stills, and my surroundings seem to fade, leaving only the LifeSuPod directly across from me.

Galilei. I cross the space and look down at the weathered face with the bald head.

He's not as pasty as when I saw him last. In fact, he looks ready to rise out of his LifeSuPod like a vampire waking to feed.

Because I rejuvenated him by saving his LifeSuPod and plugging it in.

I sigh and turn away, feeling like I'm letting down the Adelphoi. The children. I'm not defending or protecting them like I promised.

But can I betray my own soul to do it?

They are more important to me than Luc or Galilei. They're more important to me than me, but they're not more important to me than God. Somehow I know neither Luc's life nor Galilei's is mine to take in hand. Maybe He'll give them to someone else, but it's not me.

I have to trust.

I take a breath and flip the pancake.

When it's done I transfer it to a paper towel on top of the counter and get another one cooking. I tear off a bite of the cooked one and stuff it in my mouth.

So what now?

I flip the second pancake as a thud comes from behind me. I whirl so quickly the pan flies off the stove, clattering to the ground. My eyes are fixed on Galilei's LifeSuPod.

The thud comes again, with a cry this time, and the heavy lid of the second LifeSuPod pops open.

Crixus sits up so suddenly the IV is pulled out of his arm. He growls and grabs his arm to clamp the small spurt of blood. Serves him right for stealing my LifeSuPod.

Apparently he got killed in Tenebra too. Does that mean he turned on Luc?

He looks over at Galilei's LifeSuPod, then at me. Neither of us says anything for a moment. Actually, I'm not sure what to say.

I pick up the dropped pan and hold it out to Crixus. "Pancake?"

"So you were a Spore this whole time," he says.

I shrug. "I only just found out." I wave a hand toward his body. "How did you get here? Well, I guess, how did you die there?"

"Tried to stab Luc in the back when he decimated you."

I lift my eyebrows. "My great defender." I pour the last of the batter into the pan.

"It wasn't about you." He detangles himself from the cords of his LifeSuPod and steps out. Joints crack as he stretches his arms over his head.

"Not an ideal time to reveal your duplicity." I tear a pancake in half and wad the entire thing in my mouth. "So you missed, then?" I say in a muffled voice.

"Got his shoulder before he got my heart."

Stabbed heart versus a thorough gutting. Not fun for either

of us. "Why now? Why in the Arena surrounded by other tirones?" Was it possible Crixus attacked Luc solely to stop him from going after the Adelphoi?

He walks over and takes a corner of one of my pancakes, despite the fact that his body has been living off the LifeSuPod. Well, I did offer him one. "I did it for the people."

"That's a bit vague."

"I am the noxior trainer," Crixus states. "Almost everyone in that Arena is alive because of *me.* I trained and taught them and got them their citizenship."

"They trust you."

"For the most part. At the very least, they see me as a leader they're used to following. If they saw *me* turn against the Emperor, perhaps they'd ask themselves why I did it."

"You really thought that through," I comment.

"Well, it didn't work."

"Maybe it did. You're gone right now, you don't know." I flip the next pancake too early, and batter splatters the counter. This guy-buddies-on-a-camping-trip conversation feels itchy and refreshing at the same time. It's surreal. Like if there were no virus or apocalypse we'd be friends who actually grilled over an open fire together or something.

"Why have you never joined the other Adel–Spores?" I ask. "They could have been a great support for you and you for them. All this time they've seen you as an enemy."

He huffs. "What can they offer me?"

My reply is instant. "Friendship, for one."

He turns an annoyed gaze to me. "Do I look like I need friendship?"

"Grinches and Scrooges need friends most of all." I finish the pancakes and turn off the stove.

He shakes his head and moves to the window. "Look, you found a girl you like and that's great. You're new to the whole

Spore scene—equally great. But even before the Nightmare Virus, I kept to myself.

"I went to church for almost thirteen years. Volunteered, attended regularly, and got lunch after service with various families. But when my daughter died, the pastor didn't even know her name. I got one Sunday of 'I'm so sorry for your loss,' and that was it. They held the funeral, but then they went about their lives. It was like I'd never been a part of them."

Crixus had a daughter? How different was he before his daughter's death? Grief changes people—I know that firsthand.

Crixus has been so stuck in his Old World experience of church that he's missed out on being part of the new one.

"I'm going back to the Spores," I say. "They need me, and I need them. That's where life is, Crixus." I look at him. "Come with me."

"No thanks." He tugs at the tube weaving from his LifeSuPod into the wall, checking its connection.

"C'mon. Give them another chance."

He moves to the IV to get a new needle for reattaching it. "There are no second chances."

"That's not what I understand."

He stills but doesn't give. This is Crixus's opportunity, but he needs to choose it for himself. And I need to get to the Adelphoi house, check on the kids, and get back into Tenebra.

"I'll be in the truck. I'm going to the Spore base. You get one minute." I walk outside, not sure if I should have offered what I did. Who in their right mind would leave behind a perfectly good LifeSuPod to trust strangers to keep him alive?

Maybe I'm not in my right mind. But part of me hopes Crixus isn't either.

The moment my foot lands on dust, a strange mixture of emotions hits me. Relief and something else. Something invigorating. I stand still for a moment before I place it.

Sunlight.

I'm in the sun. I almost drop to a knee beneath the glorious heat I've longed for. It's a dim sun and near to setting, but it's bright and life and warm.

With a literally lightened heart, I get in the truck and start it up. I count to 60. Then I do it again. Then, determinedly, I turn on the engine, ready to be rid of this place. I glance at the cabin door one final time, wondering if this is going to be one of those movie scenes where Crixus walks out just as I start to drive away.

I inch forward. Surely he's heard the truck engine by now. But he's still not here.

Disappointment settles in my gut. I pull away from the house. It's like he *wants* to stay behind, on his own. He thinks he's playing both sides, but he's not *involved* in the Adelphoi side at all. He's an Adelphoi, yes–even if he doesn't know the title–but no one besides me knows who he is. How is that serving anyone?

He turned on Luc. And yet he's stuck. What does he plan to go back to?

The road curves and the trees sway. I drive at a crawl, roll down my window and breathe in the fresh air, relishing the fact it's real. Not simulated air. The sky–

Crack. Something smacks the back window of the truck. I hit the brakes, sliding along the gravel. Through the dust behind me comes another rock. This one slams into the metal bed of the truck.

I shove my head out the window. "Hey! I stopped, okay? And this isn't even my truck!"

Crixus saunters into view through the clouds of dust. It would be a cool moment except one second later he coughs violently until his eyes start watering.

"How else was I supposed to get you to stop?"

"You could have acted like a *sane* person and come out of the cabin before I left. I gave you a one-minute warning!"

"I didn't think you'd stick to it." He hauls open the passenger-side door and climbs in. "And I was right. You waited at least three. First rule of parenting: stick to what you say."

"Every second counts," I mutter, rolling up the window now that the dust is billowing into the cab.

"We could have brought the LifeSuPods with us, you know."

"There's not enough electricity at the Adelphoi house. If the Adelphoi want it, they can come back." We merge onto the highway, and I navigate by memory.

"You used that word before–Adelphoi."

"It's what they call themselves."

He glances in the side mirror. "It's Greek. Means *brothers.* Or more broadly . . . *family.*" He seems to ponder it a moment.

"Definitely sounds more inviting than *Spore.*" We ride in silence, and something niggles at the back of my mind from earlier..

It's only after several miles that I realize what it is. It's not about the Adelphoi, it's about what he said before that. He said *LifeSuPods*. Plural. Implying we could have brought them both with us.

I glance in my rearview mirror–habit, maybe. Or instinct.

A billow of black smoke rises in the sunset sky several miles behind us. Where the cabin should be. I look sharply at Crixus. He stares fixedly out the windshield.

That's when I see the blood still drying on his hands. My own goes cold.

"Crixus, what did you do?"

42

I SCREECH TO A HALT AND WHIP THE truck around.

"What are you doing?" Crixus grabs the dash to keep himself from slamming against the passenger window. "It's too late to go back for the LifeSuPods!"

"I'm not going back for a LifeSuPod," I growl. "I'm going back for a life."

"Galilei?" He barks a short laugh.

My hands tighten on the steering wheel. I don't expect him to understand because I don't really understand. Part of me hopes I'm too late, hopes whatever Crixus did has already done its job. Luc betrayed me—surely his father is going to wreak his own havoc. The Adelphoi knew how dangerous he was. He likely deserves to die.

But Galilei has the cure. Supposedly.

"Is that his blood?" I ask, referring to Crixus's hands.

"It's from his LifeSuPod. I broke the glass." He leans back against the seat and folds his arms like he's settling in for a good movie. I suppose this is what comes from having watched noxiors die day after day in the Arena—a numbness toward life.

There's a lot of smoke. Surely the fire has consumed the cabin and LifeSuPods by now. I take the turn to the gravel road a bit too hard, and the back tires screech on the asphalt until hitting the gravel and sliding over the edge of the road into the brush. I accelerate to give us momentum out of the ditch and then overcorrect and almost hit a tree.

Crixus's popcorn-eating nonchalance disappears, and he grips whatever his hands find. "Easy, Cain."

It's hard to hear him over the roar of the gravel, but I slow because we're approaching the smoke. I smell it through the truck grill, and it brings back immediate memories of almost burning to death in The Fire Swamp.

"Why are you even trying to save him?"

"Because I'm tired of killing."

"So am I!" Crixus shouts. "But isn't this worth it? Luc's a killer. Galilei raised him. He's probably a killer too. You, me, Spores, those kids!"

"We're still alive, aren't we?"

"That doesn't change his heart."

"But maybe it changes ours."

We reach the cabin, and the heat of the flames breaches the truck cab. I think of Stranna, and the irony in the full circle of this is not lost on me.

"It's too late, Cain."

"I have to try."

"There's no way in–" Crixus abruptly cuts off as I gun it.

The truck smashes through the main cabin wall, and I reverse as burning timber falls on us. It smothers part of the flames. I leap from the cab and rush forward while I have a short window.

The heat sucks my breath out of my lungs in seconds. I pull my shirt over my mouth and shield my eyes as best I can.

I duck under a hanging beam half on fire and try to wave away the smoke. Then I see Galilei's LifeSuPod.

The cover is broken. But it's also open.

One step closer, and I see something that brings a chill to my body in complete contrast to the surrounding flames.

Galilei's body is no longer in the LifeSuPod.

A gunshot comes from outside.

I stand frozen for a heartbeat, then I abandon the cabin, heart thundering. How could Galilei possibly be awake? He can't be an Adelphoi. There's no way.

I emerge from the flames and smoke in time to see Crixus heading for the forest opposite us. He runs with a broken gait and holds his side with both hands, a trail of blood following him from the truck to the woods. I hunch down and scan the area until I see him.

Galilei.

He's awake, alive, and hurrying toward our truck, gun in hand. Much different from the nearly comatose man I observed in Tenebra not long ago. Did Luc use his strange device on Galilei? But why?

I crawl into the cab of the truck through Crixus's open door. I rapidly shut and lock the doors, then rev the engine, popping my head just barely over the dash to see how close he is.

He ducks behind an old mattress propped up against the trash heap.

I don't have a weapon, unless I drive the truck over the mattress. He seems to register this possibility and races the opposite direction, hurtling around the corner of the burning cabin.

I steer the truck after Crixus, honking the horn. I roll down the window and yell, "Crixus, get over here!"

He emerges from behind a tree several yards in, a giant rock in each hand. When he sees it's me, he hobbles my way, blood streaming from his side.

He's only a few trees away when a light blue streak of metal flies past me and slams into him.

It's the VW bug that I assumed was out of gas. Galilei has Crixus pinned between the grill and the tree.

"No!"

With a quick reverse, Galilei barrels his vehicle into mine. I duck as the windshield shatters over my head. When I straighten, he's peeling away from the cabin in a cloud of dust.

I jump out of the cab and hurry to Crixus. It doesn't take much of a glance to tell me he's broken beyond repair. Portions of his body bend in all manner of unnatural angles.

"No, Crixus. Oh man . . ." I drop to my knees beside him on the forest floor, reaching out but not sure what to touch.

His hand, slick with blood, finds my wrist. His breathing is labored. My chest is punched with the fist of reality–he's dying. Really dying.

"Do you . . ." he licks his lips. "I'm not . . . not a Judas, am I?"

That's what's going through his mind right now?

"Of course not," I choke. "Look at me, Crixus." He does. "It's about your heart now. At this moment."

He nods, but even that seems labored. He's fading.

"I'm sorry you've been alone," I whisper, remembering how hard it was to be by myself in The Fire Swamp and then in Tenebra.

"I'm not alone . . . now." He gives my wrist a faint squeeze.

Then he's gone.

43

THE ADELPHOI HOUSE IS A SCENE straight out of the Lost Boys' secret hideaway. Kids sliding down the banister, a messy feast of vegetables strewn on the table and kitchen floor, a blanket-and-pillow fort out in the garden.

While my initial response is that they're destroying their own food supply, I'm grateful they've been able to find joy and be carefree after what happened in Tenebra.

Most of these children are awake because they fled the battle scene in the wheat field or the Arena. Fled for their lives.

And now they're here just being kids.

"It's Cain!" one of them yells. Like one giant creature, they swarm my knees and waist–even those who don't really know me. "Cain's back! Cain's back!" It's such a different response than I've received, well, *ever.*

Heidi wiggles in between the mass of limbs and hugs me the tightest before looking up. "Did you defeat the bad guys?"

"Heidi!" My heart leaps. "You're here!" Erik got her to safety. He did what I couldn't. Her eyes are so hopeful. I want to say that yes, we defeated them. I want to tell her I saw her mom in Tenebra. But I can't. I don't know if her mom is still alive.

"We're putting up a fight, kid. That's actually why I'm here."

I look around the house and assess what needs to be done. My eyes flit to the second-story landing, hoping Stranna will emerge from her room. I need her advice. But there's no movement. There doesn't seem to be an adult awake in this house.

So responsibility for these kids is up to me. Instead of focusing on the Tenebran battle, it's up to me to do what Stranna and the other Adelphoi have been doing since they first got infected: caring for others.

Mom would get to cleaning and organizing right away, but I'd like to save the garden from the kids' shenanigans.

It's been almost three hours since I met death in Tenebra, and that was fifteen hours in Tenebran time. By now, Luc might have already attacked. But what was going on with his dad? Why–*how*–had Galilei woken up? Did someone kill him? Was he part of a battle?

My heart fails for a moment, and I peel the children's arms off me.

"I'll be right back." I run up the stairs and into the room that hosts Stranna's body. She lays in bed, completely still and unusually pale. I press two fingers against the side of her throat. My head pounds so hard I don't feel anything for a long moment. But then I feel a pulse.

She's still alive.

I check Erik and Jules, too, and I exhale a relieved breath. James is in a bunkbed and breathing fine. Someone new lies in the bottom bunk–Helene. And she's still breathing. The extra pillow beside her head tells me Heidi's been sleeping with her. I can't help but smile a little.

I check the sleeping children downstairs who are still scattered around on the carpet. Everett first. He has a pulse. Most of the others do, too, and their pulses are quickening. Their breathing picks up too.

Something is happening in the Nightmare.

"Kids!" I shout to the young ones who are awake. They stampede into the room. "Nap time!"

"No!" Several flee the room.

That probably wasn't my best move. I need to get to Tenebra, but I can't leave the kids going wild like this. Then again, do I really want to haul them back to the Nightmare?

There's no telling how long all of us adults will be in Tenebra. It could be days. I have to do what I have to do.

I take a deep breath and force myself to go about this a different way. I go to the back yard and milk the cow. Afterward, I let her calf back into her pen to nurse and give the dairy cow relief. That way if we don't return for several days, the mother won't be in pain.

I frown. I hope that's how that works.

I warm the milk on the stove, then find apples wrapped in old paper inside the fridge. I slice up half a dozen, then spread peanut butter on them. I check the freezers and fridge for hot dogs but discover a pile of frozen cooked turkey breasts next to several frozen loafs of sourdough bread instead. Even better. Everyone knows Thanksgiving food puts people to sleep.

I pull a turkey breast out of the freezer and pop it in the microwave, but it doesn't work. I could run it under hot water. Well, not the bread, of course.

I sigh.

I'm not a parent. I'm a loner. I've never even babysat. I try to think of what my mom would do, what she did do when our electricity was cut off because of late payments. I turn the gas oven on low and pop both bread and meat in to thaw.

Then I go to the basement. It's a pigsty. Blankets, pillows, toys, old crusts of bread. I tidy it up quickly, creating a dozen individual sleeping areas–each one with a pillow and nicely folded blanket. I manage to find a stuffed animal to go with each pillow. Even I know that whether the kids are tired or not, a neat space is more desirable to hang out in.

And they need to stay in here until they fall asleep.

All the awake kids are playing tag outside when I go back upstairs, but their energy is fading. They've been awake for hours, and even now, I see a few of them lolling in what remains of the evening sun.

Perfect.

I lower the blinds so the lighting inside the house is more conducive to sleep. Then I slice enough turkey off the cooked breast and call the kids inside.

They hold to their Lost Boys temperaments and swarm the kitchen at the mention of food.

"Everyone, sit at the table!" I order.

They climb on chairs, on the table, and wiggle themselves up on the barstools until finally I raise my hands and shout. "Everyone, quiet or you get no food!"

That silences them, even though I wouldn't really follow through on that threat. But they don't know that.

I hand out paper plates with turkey, a slice of bread, and peanut-butter apples as fast as I can. A few say thanks. A few protest, "I don't want peanut butter on the apple!" I ignore them and pass out cups of warm milk. One boy dips his turkey in it.

For one blessed moment there's nothing but silence.

I use that time to take what's left of the warm milk and trickle it into the mouths of the sleeping kids. I lift Everett up so he won't choke and pour the tiniest dribble in his mouth. On reflex, he swallows so I give him more. His reflexes seem to take over, and he swallows several big gulps, all while staying asleep.

I do the same to the several other sleeping children as well as adults, then change the plastic sheets that rest under the kids. All but one are soiled. I find the washing machine before I remember that it won't work. There's no electricity.

So I wash them with dish soap in the kitchen sink. Stranna

and Jules probably have a different system, but I don't care. I lay the sheets out on the lawn to dry them. I find clean ones folded and stacked in a closet and set them up for each sleeping child.

By now, the kids have finished eating. "Downstairs," I tell them quietly. "You too, Heidi."

They file down the stairs while the turkey meat and warm milk does its job. The girls squeal when they see the sleeping arrangements. But as they whisper to one another, the boys rush to claim their own beds, making some of the girls scream in protest because they wanted a certain stuffed animal. It takes me another 20 minutes to get them calm and tucked in. I promise them that if they stay in their beds and fall asleep I'll give them a big treat when they wake up.

Not sure how to follow through with that, but I'll do my best.

I turn off the light and head up the stairs. I set up my own bed at the door at the top of the stairs. I leave the door open so I can hear them but also so they can step over me if they need to. I'm about to lie down when Heidi peeks over the top of the stairs and whispers, "I want to sleep with Mommy."

I'm about to tell her I need to keep an eye on her here when I realize how absurd that is. I'm going to sleep, too. And why deny a girl the safe space of her mother's arms?

"Come on." I take her hand and lead her upstairs to Helene's bunk. Heidi nestles in close and I tuck her in.

I'm about to leave when she says in a small voice, "I don't want to go back."

I kneel beside her. "You have to sleep eventually, Heidi. Wouldn't you rather go back surrounded by friends?"

"Will you be with me?"

I want to say yes. I want to comfort her. But children can handle more than I can imagine. I've seen that firsthand in Tenebra. "I don't quite know where I'll wake up, but you won't be alone. Okay, Heidi?"

"Mommy says Jesus is always with us." She pulls her covers up to her chin. "But I'm still scared. Even when I pray."

I take her hand, wishing Mom or Nole were here to respond. "I am, too, Heidi. But I can promise you this: He wins in the end."

"He does?"

"Yes."

"I hope he doesn't wait too long to do it."

I have to laugh. "Me too."

She rolls over and tucks herself against Helene's body. I return downstairs and lay in my own spot, willing myself to fall asleep to rejoin them. Now that I'm actually resting, my brain spins faster instead of slowing down to sleep. I think of the kids mere yards away from me, drifting off at this very moment. Wondering where they're going to wake up in Tenebra.

Luc once told me they'd wake up wherever they called home. But these children have never had a home. Until now. Have they lived in Castle Ithebego long enough to call it home?

I will myself to think only of the Arena. That is where I want to wake. It's been 24 hours since my Tenebran death, which means the Arena will be filled and in the middle of some new Games. Everyone will be confronted with the truth. I'm alive. And they saw me stoned and then sliced open with a lightning shard.

Now they'll see me resurrected. The surest proof that what I told them is true. There is a cure. And all it takes is a shift of heart, a choice of mind.

There's a momentary passing of sleep. A transition of sorts. The Adelphoi house fades. Darkness silences all thought and sound.

Then my eyes open again in the Nightmare.

My heart stutters. I'm not in the Arena.

I stand tall on the outer wall of Castle Ithebego like I've

just finished a conversation with Erik. All is silent, but not in peace. It is a silence of dread. Death, even. Time is paused as my mind takes in the scene.

Across the expanse of moat and forest, the veil separating Tenebra and Castle Ithebego hangs in shreds–a translucent curtain abused and destroyed.

Black flames consume the wheat field. Not a single grain of light remains.

Waiting on the other side to charge are Luc and his army.

44

WE HAVE MERE MINUTES BEFORE LUC and his army swarm through the blackened wheat field and onto our turf. I feel like Theoden King atop Helm's Deep, helpless to stop the battle that will force children to wield swords and hearts to fail.

Any confidence I hold in waking to Real Life quails beneath the threat before me. Knowing death is not my master brings a deep peace, but it doesn't calm the present dread. Even when Jesus knew His death on the cross would result in salvation for the world, He still prayed so desperately for relief that He sweat drops of blood.

A happy ending doesn't free one from the pain of the process it takes to get there.

"Cain?" Stranna's soft voice from beside me yanks me from my spiral. I tear my eyes from Luc and his army of tirones and see her. She wears Roman armor, and for the first time since I met her, fear doesn't linger behind her eyes.

A shift happens in this moment.

I dread the battle coming, yes, but determination wins out. I've felt life. I've lived love. I've seen the power of light. Even if darkness seems to be victorious today, it is a farce. Luc may have the power to cause pain and loss, but he has no power for victory. And because of that he—and darkness—will always lose.

"It's going to be okay, Stranna." I don't say we're going to live or we're going to win the battle. I say only what I know to be true.

She rests her hand on the edge of the wall. It trembles. "Erik told me you were killed."

"I was. At least, my Nightmare form was. My body is at the Adelphoi house now." I want to tell her the kids are tucked in, the cow is okay, the laundry is done–anything, even trivial, to set her mind at ease.

She grips the stone with pale fingers. "You just . . . left."

"I know. I'm sorr–"

Stranna leans over and kisses my cheek. "You smell like cinnamon rolls."

"Ha!" I bark a laugh, but then process what she said. "Do I really?" Any other life and it would be a bit weird hearing these words. But here, next to her, facing battle . . . it's the most inspiring thing she could have said.

She winks. "With extra frosting."

With that, the mysterious night flames burn low, and Luc's army charges.

My hand searches my belt and pockets for any sort of weapon. Nothing. I turn around and see the courtyard filled with kids from the Adelphoi house. They don't seem afraid. In fact, they seem to be bracing themselves. Only now do I see that the gates to Castle Ithebego are blocked from the inside with beams and stones. The moat is filled with alligators and even schools of piranha.

I can see the kids' touch on all the preparations–like a castle instead of a fortress prepared for a battle of blood and death.

Maybe it's better this way.

But Luc's army is airborne. The moat and the braced door aren't going to do much to stop them.

Small wooden catapults dot the corners of the castle wall

with piles of stones next to them. My eyes widen. These are manned by Erik and Jules. Children stand in groups of three or four next to huge crates strapped closed with leather or cages of falcons, hawks, eagles, and even a horned owl–all irregular sizes compared to the real thing.

Adults I don't recognize stand with each group of children. They wear Adelphoi swords at their sides or hold javelins. This must be Jeremy and his crew. The longer I look, the more unfamiliar children I see. Although I do recognize the father and his two daughters from my first fight in the Arena.

Why aren't there more useful weapons? Modern or magical ones? Are we still limited by the Roman setting created by Galilei? I don't see him with the army–with his son.

"We used everything we could." Stranna seems to read my mind. "Every strand of light we could find in the rocks."

"Wheat kernels work too–*worked*." I am dismayed and yet encouraged to see that none of the children hold swords or bows and arrows. They shouldn't have to kill, but they also shouldn't have to fear being killed. They need defenders.

"Luc got to the field before we could."

"Is there any light left?" I ask almost desperately. "For me to use?"

Her cringe says it all. "We thought you were dead, Cain. I'm sorry. Like I said, we used everything we could find."

Maybe there's another hope. "Did any adults come from the coliseum? With a rhinoceros?"

She shakes her head.

I try not to show my distress. Heidi's mother and the other Tunnel escapees must have been caught. Killed on sight or dragged back to the Arena. How will I break the news to Heidi? I scan the courtyard below, but she's not there.

At that moment, Erik yells, "Fire!" and releases a giant stone from the catapult. It strikes one of the pterodactyls from the sky. Jules takes down a second. Both tirones crash to the ground but regain their feet. Before they can return to their army, a third pterodactyl breaks formation and dives toward the two grounded tirones.

It pierces one through the chest with its beak.

Mouth open in shock, the man collapses. The pterodactyl lands and sets to eating its victim. The riding tiro leaps off the savage pterodactyl's back and slices its head off to try to save his comrade. I look behind me, glad the children cannot see what's happening.

That is the difference between nightmist and creating something from light. The nightmist will serve you until it wants to devour you.

The full swarm of pterodactyl riders streams overhead. I watch helplessly, wanting a gun, a sword, a grain of light . . . something. All I had was my phoenix and she was killed, or rather, she burst into flame.

Luc's tirones are upon us, and they swing down toward the courtyard, bringing their pterodactyls with them. The children throw open three of their cages, releasing the birds of prey as a pterodactyl goes after Everett.

I time a jump from the wall and land on the beast with a hard jar to my bones. The pterodactyl swivels its head toward me, its long neck twisting like a length of rope. It snaps, revealing sharp pointed teeth within its beak. I lurch back, then grab it around the beak and twist. It overcompensates to spare its neck and topples over.

"Cain!" Everett calls out and tosses me a javelin. I release the pterodactyl's mouth to catch the weapon midair, then ram it through the creature's wing and into the earth between the cobblestones. The beast roars but can't pull free.

A light falcon screeches and attacks the pterodactyl, clawing at its eyes and throat. I leave them to their fight, trusting light will win. The pterodactyl seems only able to get a few snaps in before it has to shrink away from the more colorful creature.

"Everett!" I shout. "What else do you have?"

"Slingshots!" He tosses me one.

I catch it with one hand. Better than nothing, though I can't account much for my aim. Small leather buckets of rocks sit every few yards along the inside of the wall. I grab a handful, giving them a quick glance to see if any hold light threads in their crevices. No, just regular rocks.

And yet . . . they were enough for David against Goliath.

The difference is, he had practiced with his weapon. I can't do much harm without a bullet or trigger.

I run back up to the wall where Stranna is reloading a spear bolt into the catapult device. All the pterodactyls have attacked and engaged in battle inside the castle with the light beasts while the dismounted tirones go after the children. The small group of Adelphoi adults fights them off, but this is only a distraction.

We're outnumbered.

But that's not enough for Luc. He hovers in the air atop his enormous stingray, and an army of foot tirones comes to the wall, led by a herd of nightbeast bison.

They have one purpose. At Luc's cry, the bison outside charge the gate of Castle Ithebego. The first wave tumbles into the moat in mindless obedience, but the ones behind trample right over their downed bison brothers until they've created a bridge of flesh.

They slam their heads into the gate. Again and again and ag–

Crack.

The children scream from inside.

"Get up on the walls!" I holler. "Retreat to the inner courtyard!"

Miraculously, they obey. Every Adelphoi passes the command along until everyone is running for one of the two locations. I shoot a stone at a tiro running after the kids. It hits the back of his head, and he falls. The children make it through the courtyard door and slam it behind them.

The bison keep pounding on the gate, but Luc spreads out his hands, and new nightbeasts form behind the bison herd.

Some of the light creatures have trapped–but not killed–Luc's tirones. They can keep that up for only so long. It's evident that any creature made from light won't destroy a human. It will take down a nightbeast, but that's where the killing stops.

Interesting that there are rules and limitations written into their lifeblood.

The tirones don't put up too much of a fight once their steeds are down. They may have been noxiors at one point, but I imagine most people still have a problem with killing young children. They relied on their nightbeasts.

And more are coming.

The gate splinters to pieces. Bison charge in, followed by the flood of leopards, gorillas, all other destructive beasts Luc thought up. They'll be through the second gate in mere moments. We're out of light beasts. We're out of weapons.

Then I hear a thunderous call from the other side–a battle cry of a hundred voices as people charge through the veil behind the nightbeasts and Luc's tirones.

Citizens of Tenebra. Each one armed with weapons from the coliseum. Scattered among them are noxiors. But at their head is a woman with a little girl in her arms, riding a rhinoceros with swirling gold fog puffing from its nostrils.

Helene. And in her arms sits Heidi. I piece it together instantly. When Heidi fell asleep in House Adelphoi she woke up in her mama's arms. That is her home, and her heart sent her there. They finally found one another.

Helene didn't come to Castle Ithebego when I sent her with the rhino. Instead, she took it to the coliseum. She rescued her family and didn't stop there. She brought the other parents.

And now they're here to fight for their children.

EVERYTHING IS DIFFERENT WITH THE parents in the fray. They know how to fight. They were all noxiors once. Crixus trained them to survive the Nightmare, and now they're using their skills to destroy it.

They charge into the castle, hacking at the pterodactyls and bison as they go. The nightbeasts are feral and give a good fight, leaping for throats, clawing at exposed stomachs. But the parents aren't to be stopped. They hack and stab and tackle. Their efforts grow more fierce when the children begin to cry out for their parents.

Luc's tirones flee, and the fighting parents give chase. The children continue to cheer them on and come out from their hiding spots.

I don't cheer.

A hand slips into mine as I watch the tirones retreat through the broken gate.

"This isn't over," Stranna says, speaking my thoughts.

I tighten my fingers around her hand. "I know." If that was Level 1 and we maxed out our arsenal . . .

Luc raises his hands in the air. Most of his retreating tirones stop to watch. The parents in the courtyard and on the walls around us still.

Mist pours from Luc's hands, forming in the air as it falls to the ground. Chimera, griffin, three-headed dogs, Minotaurs, basilisks . . . all the Roman mythical creatures rise up from the ground by the hundreds, armed and sniffing for blood.

How does Luc have the energy and emotions to keep creating so much?

His tirones turn back toward Castle Ithebego, victorious smugness on their faces, energy renewed. They know they'll win now. But Luc isn't done.

Black shrubbery bursts from the ground sending vines flying toward Castle Ithebego. The vines pull at the stones and the forest we created, tearing out chunks like a many-toothed monster. One turret wobbles. Trees crack and tumble, splintered into firewood.

A storm swirls overhead with shards of black lightning growing like inverted icebergs. Preparing to fall upon us. Waves of tar seep up from the ground, rolling through the cracks and crevices of our keep, filling the courtyard with the sticky Tunnel darkness that we all fought so hard to escape when first infected.

We brace ourselves. Not for the fight, but for the death that is coming. That is here.

The nightbeasts charge. The tirones charge.

I take aim with my slingshot, but not at the army. At Luc. He's far away, but I release stone after stone. They all fall short.

Stranna runs for the ballista and loads one last broken spear from the ground. She aims at Luc's stingray, but he sees it before she releases, and the stingray swoops beneath the bolt. That movement brings him a few yards closer, so I shoot again. I have five stones left in my pocket.

C'mon, I tell myself. *He's just another Goliath.*

Tar suffocates Stranna's fountain. The left turret of Castle Ithebego crumbles and Stranna screams, almost tumbling with it. Our forest is flattened.

I know you win in the end, God, but . . . can't we skip the battle?

One of my stones hits Luc's wrist. I would have preferred his forehead, but I'll take any small win at this point. He shakes off the pain, then picks up the creative stream once again. It's another chimera, and this one breathes fire. It bounds toward the corner of Castle Ithebego, its sights on Stranna who has only just regained her footing.

A Minotaur cuts down a parent. The three-headed dog corners several children. Our light creatures flap and flail against the dar now sticking to their feathers. Someone screams, and I glance over my shoulder and see parents and children circled up, surrounded by advancing nightbeasts–a bull's-eye of death.

The nightbeasts howl or thump the ground, smelling victory. Smelling blood. The chimera clambers up the wall like a gecko and drags Stranna off her ballista. I shoot at it with my slingshot, frantically searching for nightmist inside me despite knowing it won't serve me. Won't obey. And I really don't want to create something that may turn and attack Stranna. Or me. Or the children.

A screech breaks the air. I whirl.

My phoenix streaks across the sky, a stream of fire and gold trailing behind it.

Hope blossoms. She's here. She's alive! I can get in the air and go after Luc and chase him off. Or even better, she'll take him down.

But she passes him. I raise my arms so she'll see me. She veers downward. Luc releases lightning shards from the sky like rin blades. They slice through her wings, her tail, her body. Again and again.

"No!" I yell.

She screeches and tucks her wings tight against her body, a bullet headed straight toward me. With a mighty flap that sprays phoenix blood through the air, she slows long enough to drop something at my feet. Then she whines, crackles like a wet log in fire, and bursts into flame, falling like a meteorite into the sticky sea of tar. Nearby nightbeasts scatter from her impact, but there's nothing but a pile of dying coals.

I am too stunned to react.

A Minotaur stomps through the tar and crushes the phoenix coals beneath its hooves. The tirones shout their approval. Then they turn as one to Luc, awaiting his command just like the Roman gladiators awaited the emperor's thumbs-up or thumbs-down in the games.

And Luc does hold out a thumb, parallel to the ground, then drops it. "Kill them all!"

They don't need to be told twice.

Parents swoop in front of their children–vulnerable shields against the advancing death blows.

I scan the ground for the item the phoenix brought me. It's a single grain of glowing wheat, still covered in ash–the one Luc kicked away in the Arena. He thought it had burned. Thought he'd destroyed it.

Yet here it is in my hands. Waiting for my command.

The fate of this battle rests in the palm of my imagination. The circle of a hundred nightbeasts closes in on the parents and children. What sort of creature can I create that would destroy so many nightbeasts? What weapon?

Luc commanded and created these animals–will they disappear if he is killed?

Time doesn't stop for contemplation. The circled group is seconds away from death.

I send my thoughts far beyond this moment–to the end goal. Jesus thought beyond the cross. I need to do the same.

And then I know. I know what to make, but the only question is if it's possible. I close my eyes and grip the kernel tight in my fist.

It grows warm. Then hot. Before it can scald my hand, I

launch back my arm and hurl the kernel into the air like a major league pitcher. Despite its small size, the grain shoots into the sky, propelled by something other than the force of my throw.

It grows and grows, brighter and stronger, but farther away.

Even farther.

Not flying, but floating. Rising on some magical helium. Then it explodes in blinding light.

I tear my eyes away. Roaring fills my ears. My skin blisters under the instant heat, but then the heat levels out.

I blink away momentary blindness. A blanket of silence fills the castle. The tar shrinks back and sizzles into nothingness when it crosses the water of the moat. The black forest withers like overcooked asparagus and every last nightbeast lies dead.

Stranna shoves the carcass of the chimera off her. Luc's stingray lies on the ground like a discarded blanket. Every child and parent stands, shielding their eyes and looking up at something that has been denied us all since the very beginning of this virus. Something that not even nightmares could quench.

Sunlight.

In the sky, bright and golden and with the warmth of summer, shines a perfect golden sun.

46

LUC BOLTS. THROUGH THE VEIL OF THE Nightmare's edge, across the wheat field, back toward the coliseum.

"Oh no you don't."

I sprint down the stairs of the castle wall and leap from the fifth stair onto the back of my rhino. He stands there like he was waiting for this moment. With nothing more than a nudge, he lumbers through the broken gate, over the pile of dead bison, and after Luc.

"Cain, no!" Stranna yells from the wall. "Leave him be!"

I don't know what I plan to do, but I can't just let him run back to his place of power–even if the sun did obliterate his nightbeasts. He'll recover somehow. And then he'll be back.

I gain on him. He glances over his shoulder, spots me, and pivots to a stop, drawing his gladius.

"You really want to do this, Cain?" he shouts. "Against me?"

Good question.

He's in the blackened wheat field, but it's clear that this is his territory. Though he has to try twice, he manages to call up enough nightmist to cover himself in Roman armor and line his belt with fresh weapons.

He throws a single dagger, and it plants itself in the head of my charging rhinoceros. The rhino's front knees buckle, and I go flying into the blackened stalks of wheat.

Luc darts forward. I gain my feet in time to dodge his first strike. With that single move, I know I'm beat. He's as good at swordplay and noxior fighting as he is at creating from nightmist. Go figure.

"You think you can defeat me in my own world?" he growls.

"Seems like we did just that," I return, using snark as my weapon even though that will only incense him. "Not all of it is your father's creation. God has the last say. You can't keep Him out."

"God is a figment of imagination."

I contradict him. "God is the *source* of imagination." I gesture to the wheat field. "Who do you think put this here?"

He grinds his boot into the earth, sending up little puffs of ash. "It doesn't matter who made it. What matters is who has the power to destroy it." He lunges. I brace myself, then duck and tackle. I miss, sprawling on the ashy ground.

"Cain!" Stranna's voice is unexpected and fairly close.

"No!" I want to shout. She followed me, and now she'll get herself killed.

I flip to my back just as Luc plunges the blade. It pierces the dirt, but he redirects within seconds, swiping at my neck. I throw up my arm, and the blade glances off my forearm with a sharp cut. Blood spills from the wound, but numbed by survival instinct, I hardly feel it.

I scramble for my feet, feeling the threat of his blade at my back and the gaping weakness of being unarmed. Why did I follow him? Did I think we'd stop and have some sort of heart-to-heart?

I manage to stand, but Luc gives me no ground.

Advance. Cut. Advance. Swipe.

Stranna calls my name again, and I vaguely register that she's not alone. Erik and many of the parents from Ithebego came with her. I pray I can dodge Luc long enough for one of them to cut him down.

But when they reach the veil between Castle Ithebego and the wheat field, it has reformed enough under the sunlight that it doesn't open to let them pass through. It seals itself, despite the shreds and tears from Luc's attack.

Stranna pounds against it like glass. I can hear her, but she can't come through. None of them can.

Something tells me I can't get back through to them either.

I stop my retreat, tired and gasping for breath. My arm bleeding and stinging more by the minute. Luc's grin touches on the maniacal. He knows this was a foolish battle, and he's determined to claim at least one victory.

"This time, you'll stay dead." He lifts his sword, and for the first time I see three colors in the blade instead of just metal and nightmist. There's light in the blade too. Light from the wheat field.

And somehow I know that *this* blade will truly kill me. There will be no waking up in the Real World.

He swings down and I tense for impact.

Clang. Metal on metal.

An Adelphoi sword. I spin expecting to find Stranna behind me, but she's still trapped on the other side of the veil. What I do see is a mysterious new sheath at my belt.

This Adelphoi sword is *mine.* And it blocked the blow.

Luc snorts. "Look at you. Spore to the core."

I reach for the pommel of my sword, but it evades me, driving Luc back. He swings at it, it parries. He cuts, it blocks. This hardly seems like a fair fight. I'm not even in it.

Then I realize my sword is driving Luc around and toward me. He stumbles a few steps back, getting closer. Closer. I search my belt for a dagger or something to end this, but there's nothing. I'm relieved. I don't want to stab anyone in the back.

But the magical Adelphoi sword is making it easy for me.

I waver briefly. If it's driving Luc right into my grasp, is that a sign? Some sort of divine permission to take his life?

Luc angles his body, trying to distance himself from me, but the Adelphoi sword is too efficient. Two more steps, and Luc's life will be in my hands.

He draws another dagger from his belt and swipes it at me. The Adelphoi sword knocks it from his fingers, and there it sits, at my feet.

I bend to pick it up, but the airborne Adelphoi sword swoops down and places its own hilt in my outstretched hand. This time, it doesn't burn.

I grip it tight and Luc steadies, ready to fight me. In this moment understanding pierces my mind–like the sword has its own thoughts, its own instructions, and I know them implicitly.

Pierce to bone and marrow. To spirit and soul.

I lunge. Luc throws his blade up to block, but he's not fast enough. My blade impales his skull. There is no resistance. It's like cutting into butter. He crumples to the ground, and I wrench the blade free.

There is no blood. In the place where a wound should be is a slit of light and darkness, writhing like two snakes.

I hear shouts from people with Stranna, but Luc's not dead. I didn't kill him. I did whatever the sword told me to do, and now . . . I watch.

His skin withers.

At first I think he's disintegrating, but then his skull morphs, and for a wild moment I think he's turning into a rhinoceros like mine.

Instead, his wiggling and morphing body goes still, and when I take a step back I take in the full sight.

Luc is gone.

And in his place is Hex Galilei.

Except now, with a shock, I realize it was never his father.

This old bald man with the diamond-stud earring whom I saved was Luc himself. My Adelphoi sword cut through the farce and the fog and revealed truth. And the truth is that Luc was never young.

Luc created this Nightmare world.

In doing so, Luc gave himself a new body. A new life.

Luc drew me in with his story about his father, and all that time I was risking my life to save *him*. To give him more power to run this world.

I should have seen it–should have connected the dots of his weakening body with his "father's" dead LifeSuPod. But I was still blocked by my limited knowledge of dreamscapes and Draftmanship. No one had ever created or changed their own avatar. Of course Luc would be the one to do it.

He must have used his device to come into the Real World to defend his body. To kill Crixus . . . and me.

Luc groans and gingerly pushes himself onto all fours.

My sword returns to my side.

Luc gets shakily to his feet. He totters a moment and reaches a frail hand out to me to steady himself before he realizes what he's doing and quickly withdraws it. As he does this, he glimpses his own skin. Wrinkled and spotted and weak.

Horror crosses his face. "What have you done?"

"Nothing more than reveal the truth."

"*I* write the truth here, not you!" he screeches. It strikes me that his suit and tie look absurdly out of place in the Roman world.

"Clearly there's a power beyond you–even in your own created world." My words come out sad. This man before me desired a new life and new power so badly that he entrapped the world to get it.

"You can't out-create the Creator," I say.

No matter how much Luc creates in this place, God is going

to interfere and add His own creations. And His will always be unmatched. He's not bound by science or ImagiSerum.

"Get away from me," Luc growls, feral. But he's the one who staggers in the opposite direction–headed back toward the coliseum. Toward his tower. He waves a weak hand in the air. Nightmist forms the stingray, but the nightbeast shies away like it doesn't recognize him.

"No one in your kingdom knows you anymore, Luc. Not even your own creation."

He climbs on the stingray's back, but it bucks him off. He stabs the thing through the head with one of his daggers, then strides off as if he doesn't even care whether he's attacked from behind or not.

I let him go, wondering if he'll make it to the coliseum. There are plenty of nightbeasts out there to attack him. But even if he gets back to his atrium, he has no Crixus to vouch for him. The people won't know him. They know only the mirage-Luc. The young face of confidence and control. This Luc created a Roman world where the citizens eat their own, trying to survive.

And they will devour him. This frail old man claiming to be their leader.

His time is over.

I turn toward our wounded Castle Ithebego and walk through the veil. It parts to let me through, and Stranna comes up to me. I take her hand. We look at each other but say nothing. In this moment our silence speaks more than words. I'm not sure what it's saying . . . only that it's comforting.

It's just us out here. The parents and children tend to wounds or haul the carcasses of dead nightbeasts out of the castle.

"You defeated him," she declares. "You defeated the Draftsman." Not Luc. Not the Emperor. The Draftsman. The creator who wanted to think of himself as the Creator.

"The sword defeated him, not me."

"You had the choice of whether or not to wield it," she replies, "whether or not to obey."

I didn't think of it that way, but now that she says it, I know she's right. I start to tug her toward the castle, but she doesn't move.

"Do you think it's over? Will this world fade? Will we all go back home?"

I shake my head, wishing I could give her a different answer. "This virus is here to stay. Luc was right about that. This *is* our new world. Even the death of Luc wouldn't have changed that."

"So what now?"

I lift a shoulder. "Another Emperor will rise. Or maybe we'll call him president or king or whatever. But we have the power to make a new life for ourselves–to build things of life and light."

We have a sun and a wheat field to plant. A fortress to mend and forest to nurture. I lead Stranna toward Castle Ithebego, walking in sweet stillness, hand in hand. The castle is a silhouette against a beaming horizon that I expect we'll explore some day–the bits of the dreamscape that no man made, the new landscape that God laid out in this intricate, imagined new world.

Who can predict what we'll find when we dare such an adventure?

"We have a home, Stranna." For the first time, I see this place as truly beautiful. Coated in potential and adventure.

"We have something even more than that," Stranna comments quietly as the new sun sets for the first time in our new world. We both take it in–the warmth, the beams, the miracle. "We have the *eternal* cure."

The night is far gone; the day is at hand.
So then let us cast off the works of darkness
and put on the armor of light.
ROMANS 13:12 ESV

ACKNOWLEDGEMENTS

Always first is my Creator. You gave me this story almost a decade ago and have helped (and sometimes dragged) me every step of the way. You've had special plans for this story from the beginning. Thank You for bringing it together, for entrusting it to me, and for helping me write it.

Daylen, my incredible husband and constant enabler. I've never seen you so excited for a story. More than any other book, this feels like our book. It took so much teamwork to make it come together. Thank you for loving me and–even more–thank you for loving Jesus. To my four children who were so patient as Mommy struggled and learned to juggle deadlines and homemaking. Thank you for letting me grow. I love you more than all the stories in the world and in my imagination.

To my brother Reuben . . . you've waited over a decade for this story. I hope it makes you laugh and is everything your brilliant imagination expected.

Sara Ella, as always you were an encourager, cheerleader, and truly ran next to me through the finish line for this story. I never want to write a book without you as my bestie! And I'm glad I'll never have to. Ashley Townsend–you'll never not be the person who hears my most haphazard story concepts and reads the roughest drafts. You always see the good in the stories I write, and that is a rare gift and an endless encouragement.

To my agent and editor, Steve Laube–I'll never forget when I first tried to tell you about this story and it all came out wrong, yet somehow you saw the potential in it and gave it a publishing home. Thank you always for being in my corner and for your endless patience and biblical encouragement as I wrote this book during one of the hardest seasons of my life.

Emilie Haney . . . you know what you did for this cover. You brought my hopes and vision to life, you prayed over it, and it's clear that you value the author and their story. I think readers' jaws are *still* on the floor after seeing this beauty. Thank you, thank you, thank you friend. You are incredibly humble and far more talented than you give yourself credit for. Every author who has the privilege of working with you doesn't realize how blessed they are.

To my incredible editorial team: Lisa Laube, you set all my fears to rest with your sharp and brilliant eye that was the first ever to read this story (in its worst form!). Thank you for not only settling my heart, but for calming it and lifting it up. Thank you, Sarah Grimm, for a delightful copyedit that had me laughing through your comments, even as I stayed up way too late finishing edits. Thank you, Jodi Hughes, for going above and beyond as my proofreader! You always read and give feedback at a depth that truly helps the story shine.

Thank you also to Trissina Kear for being such a champion for this book and all your authors. I don't think anyone truly understands how very much you do for us. And of course thank you Jamie Foley and Lindsay Franklin as well as the entire Oasis team for treating this book with such love and care.

Thank you to my street team for your enthusiasm and commitment to getting this book in front of other readers. To my ever-faithful ninjas, see Chapter 11. ;-)

Lastly, to my patient readers who waited two years for this story even when it wasn't the one you thought I was going to write. I hope you love it. I hope it inspires you. Most of all, I hope it shows you the Light in the darkness. Light always–*always*–wins. You need only to invite it in.

About the Author

Nadine Brandes has been known to do wild things (like ride a sleeper train across Russia) in the name of book research. She's the four-time Carol Award-winning author of seven young adult books and has been a professional fiction editor for over a decade. She is passionate about Jesus, motherhood, and creating with the Creator. When she's not busy inventing worlds and magic systems, she's adventuring through Middle Earth with her Auror husband and their four Halfling children.